# DARK AT HEART

# DARK AT HEART

— Edited By —

## KAREN and JOE R. LANSDALE

— All New Tales of Dark Suspense From —

JOE R. LANSDALE
F. PAUL WILSON
NEAL BARRETT, JR.
ANDREW VACHSS
LEWIS SHINER
RONALD KELLY
NORMAN PARTRIDGE
BILL CRIDER
STEVE RASNIC TEM
ROBERT PETITT
STEPHEN GALLAGHER
DAVID J. SCHOW
ED GORMAN
DAN LOWRY
CHET WILLIAMSON
ARDATH MAYHAR
WILLIAM F. NOLAN
JOHN KEEFAUVER
THOMAS SULLIVAN
DAVID MORRELL

Arlington Hts., Illinois · 1992

ISBN 0-913165-64-6



Manufactured in the United States of America

**FIRST EDITION**

Dark Harvest / P.O. Box 941 / Arlington Heights, IL / 60006

This book is dedicated to Phyllis and Harlie Morton,
Reta Lansdale Cronn, and Keith and Kasey Lansdale.

The publishers would like to express their gratitude to the following people. Thank you: Ann Cameron Mikol, Kathy Jo Camacho, Stan and Phyllis Mikol, Dr. Stan Gurnick PhD, Greg MacIntyre, Randy Williams, Raymond, Teresa and Mark Stadalsky, Tom Pas, Chris Kadow, and Peter Scanlan.

And, of course, special thanks go to Karen and Joe Lansdale, and to all the writers who contributed their time and effort to this project.

# Table of Contents

# INTRODUCTION

## Karen and Joe R. Lansdale

Dark Crime. Dark Suspense.

Stories of that nature will be for the nineties what horror was for the eighties. Except they'll be scarier, and less restrictive.

Dark Crime and Dark Suspense are broader terms. They can incorporate horror, mystery, detective, hardboiled, you name it.

Hopefully these labels won't carry the stigma that horror, and its sub-branches, splatterpunk for example, have carried. They should invite a lot of new readers in. Readers who might not pick up a book with a horror moniker on it, wouldn't touch one spattered with the Splatterpunk logo, would shy away from mysteries because their idea of a mystery is a puzzle, no characters, and writing that's only marginally above a Dick and Jane reader.

What we have here is an anthology that should satisfy most. We've attempted to put together a varied blend. All types of dark suspense and dark crime are represented here. Stories by well known writers, up and comers, as well as relatively new writers. There are short-shorts, average length stories, and two novellas. Some are as grim as a rape and murder trial, as realistic as today's headlines. At least one is frivilous, and another is something of an old fashioned thriller. Well, almost.

A couple are as short and shocking as an ice-pick in the eye. One is quiet, very quiet—the way cancer is quiet.

But no matter what suit of clothes they wear, they're all the same in one way. Under their literary flesh, each deals with the dark side of human nature. Touches on that fine line between the good citizen and the mass murderer.

## DARK AT HEART

Explores the underbelly of everyday life. Shows us that beneath many "Leave It To Beaver" facades there are grimmer forces at work. And in some cases, there are no facades whatsoever. There is only the darkness. Raw as a wound. Nasty as a bloated, fly-infested corpse.

All of these stories have as their back beat, the rhythmic thumping of a very dark heart.

Dark indeed. Most are so well grounded in reality, leaving the lights on won't help one bit. Theirs is a darkness that no light can illuminate.

But we've said enough.

The stories will speak for themselves.

Read them. And listen for the heart beat.

Joe R. Lansdale is the author of many short stories and nine novels. He is the editor or co-editor of four anthologies. DARK AT HEART being one of them, of course. The following story is somewhat in the gleeful, dark suspense vein of Alfred Hitchcock.

# THE EVENTS CONCERNING A NUDE FOLD-OUT FOUND IN A HARLEQUIN ROMANCE

## Joe R. Lansdale

Looking back on it, I wouldn't have thought something as strange as all this, full of the real coincidence of life, would have begun with a bad circus, but that's how it started, at least for me.

My luck had gone from bad to worse, then over the lip of worse, and into whatever lower level it can descend into. My job at the aluminum chair plant had played out and no rich relatives had died and left me any money. Fact was, I don't think the Cooks, least any that are kin to me, have any money, outside of a few quarters to put in a juke box come Saturday night, maybe a few bucks to waste on something like pretzels and beer.

Me, I didn't even have money for beer or juke boxes. I was collecting a little money on unemployment, and I was out beating the bushes for a job, but there didn't seem to be much in the way of work in Mud Creek. I couldn't even get on at the feed store carrying out bags of fertilizer and seed. All the sixteen year olds had that job.

It looked like I was going to have to move out of Mud Creek to find work, and though the idea of that didn't hurt my feelings any, there was Jasmine, my teenage daughter, and she still had a year of high school to finish before she went off to Nacogdoches to start her degree in anthropology at Stephen F. Austin State University, and I planned to follow her over there and find a place of my own where we could be near, and improve our relationship, which overall was all right to begin with. I just wanted more time with her.

Right then Jasmine lived with her mother, and her mother doesn't care a damn for me. She wanted to marry a guy that was going to be a high roller, and believe me, I wanted to be a high roller, but what she got was a guy who each time at the mark throws craps. No matter what I do, it turns to shit. Last break I felt I'd had in life was when I was ten and fell down and cracked my ankle. Well, maybe there was one good break after all. One that wasn't a bone. Jasmine. She's smart and pretty and ambitious and the love of my life.

But my marital problems and life's woes are not what this is about. I was saying about the circus.

It was mid-June, and I'd tried a couple places, looking for work, and hadn't gotten any, and I'd gone over to the employment office to talk to the people there and embarrass myself about not finding any work yet. They told me they didn't have anything for me either, but they didn't look embarrassed at all. When it's you and the employment office, better known as the unemployment office, feeling embarrassed is a one way street and you're the one driving on it. They seem almost proud to tell you how many unemployment checks you got left, so it can kind of hang over your head like an anvil or something.

So, I thanked them like I meant it and went home, and believe me, that's no treat.

Home is a little apartment about the size of a wash room at a Fina Station, only not as nice and without the air-conditioning. The window looks out over Main Street, and when a car drives by the window shakes, which is one of the reasons I leave it open most of the time. That and the fact I can hope for some sort of breeze to stir the dead, hot air around. The place is over a used book store called MARTHA'S BOOKS, and Martha is an all right lady if you like them mean. She's grumpy, about five hundred years old, weighs two-fifty when she's at her wrestling weight, wears men's clothing and has a bad leg and a faint black mustache to match the black wool ski cap she wears summer or winter, on account of her head is as bald as a river stone. I figure the cap is a funny sort of vanity, considering she doesn't do anything to get rid of that mustache. Still, she always does her nails in pink polish and she smokes those long feminine cigarettes that some women like, maybe thinking if the weeds look elegant enough they won't give them cancer.

Another thing about Martha, is with that bad leg she has a limp, and she helps that along with a golf putter she uses as a cane, putter side up for a handle. See her coming down the street, which isn't often, you got to think there's not much you could add to make her any more gaudy, unless it's an assful of bright tail feathers and maybe some guys to follow her playing percussion instruments.

I liked to go down to Martha's from time to time and browse the books, and if I had a little spare change, I'd try to actually buy something now and then, or get something for Jasmine. I was especially fond of detective books, and Jasmine, bless her little heart, liked Harlequin Romances. She'd read them four or five a weekend when she wasn't dating boys, and since she was dating quite regularly now, she'd cut back mostly to one or two Harlequins a weekend. Still, that was too many. I kept hoping she'd outgrow it. The romance novels and the dates. I was scared to death she'd fall in love with some cowboy with a cheek full of snuff and end up ironing Western shirts and wiping baby asses before she was old enough to vote.

Anyway, after I didn't find any jobs and nobody died and left me any money, I went home and brooded, then went downstairs to Martha's to look for a book.

Jasmine had made out a list of the titles she was looking to collect, and I took the list with me just in case I came across something she needed. I thought if I did, I might buy it and get her a detective book too, or something like that, give it to her with the romance and maybe she'd read it. I'd done that several times, and so far, to the best of my knowledge, she hadn't read any of the non-Romance novels. The others might as well have been used to level a vibrating refrigerator, but I kept on trying.

The stairs went down from my place and out into the street, and at the bottom, to the left of them, was Martha's. The store was in front and she lived in back. During business hours in the summer the door was always open since Martha wouldn't have put air-conditioning in there if half the store had been a meat locker hung with prize beef. She was too cheap for that. She liked her mustache sweat-beaded, her bald head pink beneath her cap. The place smelled of books and faintly of boiled cabbage, or maybe that was some soured clothing somewhere. The two smells have always seemed a lot alike to me. It's the only place I know hotter and filthier than my apartment, but it does have the books. Lots of them.

I went in, and there on the wall was a flyer for a circus at three o'clock that day. Martha had this old post board just inside the door, and she'd let people pin up flyers if they wanted, and sometimes she'd leave them there a whole day before she tore them down and wrote out the day's receipts on the back of them with a stubby, tongue-licked pencil. I think that's the only reason she had the post board and let people put up flyers, so she'd have scratch paper.

The flyer was for a circus called THE JIM DANDY THREE RING CIRCUS, and that should have clued me, but it didn't. Truth is, I've never liked circuses. They depress me. Something about the animals and the people who work there strike me as desperate, as if they're living on the edge of a cliff and the cliff is about to break off. But I saw this flyer and I thought of Jasmine.

When she was little she loved circuses. Her mother and I used to take her, and I remembered the whole thing rather fondly. Jasmine would laugh so hard at the clowns you had to tell her to shut up, and she'd put her hands over her eyes and peek through her fingers at the wild animal acts.

Back then, things were pretty good, and I think her mother even liked me, and truth to tell, I thought I was a pretty good guy myself. I thought I had the world by the tail. It took me a few years to realize the closest I was to having the world by the tail was being a dingle berry on one of its ass hairs. These days, I felt like the most worthless sonofabitch that had ever squatted to shit over a pair of shoes. I guess it isn't hip or politically correct, but to me, a man without a job is like a man without balls.

Thinking about my problems also added to me wanting to go to the circus. Not only would I get a chance to be with Jasmine, it would help me get my mind off my troubles.

I got out my wallet and opened it and saw a few sad bills in there, but it looked to me that I had enough for the circus, and maybe I could even spring for dinner afterwards, if Jasmine was in the mood for a hot dog and a soda pop. She wanted anything more than that, she had to buy me dinner, and I'd let her, since the money came from her mother, my darling ex-wife, Connie—may she grow like an onion with her head in the ground.

Mommy Dearest didn't seem to be shy of the bucks these days on account of she was letting old Gerald the Oil Man drop his drill down her oil shaft on a nightly basis.

Not that I'm bitter about it or anything. Him banging my ex-wife and being built like Tarzan and not losing any of his hair at the age of forty didn't bother me a bit.

I put my wallet away and turned and saw Martha behind the counter looking at me. She twisted on the stool and said, "Got a job yet?"

I just love a small town. You fart and everyone looks in your direction and starts fanning.

"No, not yet," I said.

"You looking for some kind of a career?"

"I'm looking for work."

"Any kind of work?"

"Right now, yes. You got something for me?"

"Naw. Can't pay my rent as it is."

"You're just curious, then?"

"Yeah. You want to go to that circus?"

"I don't know. Maybe. Is this a trick question too?"

"Guy put up the flyer gave me a couple tickets for letting him have the space on the board there. I'd give them to you for stacking some books.

I don't really want to do it."

"Stack the books or give me the tickets?"

"Neither one. But you stack them Harlequins for me, I'll give you the tickets."

I looked at my wrist where my watch used to be before I pawned it. "You got the time?"

She looked at her watch. "Two o'clock."

"I like the deal," I said, "but the circus starts at three and I wanted to take my daughter."

Martha shook out one of her delicate little cigarettes and lit it, studied me. It made me feel funny. Like I was a shit smear on a laboratory slide. Most I'd ever talked to her before was when I asked where the new detective novels were and she grumped around and finally told me, as if it was a secret she'd rather have kept.

"Tell you what," Martha said, "I'll give you the tickets now, and you come back tomorrow morning and put up the books for me."

"That's nice of you," I said.

"Not really. I know where you live, and you don't come put up my romance novels tomorrow, I'll hunt you down and kill you."

I looked for a smile, but I didn't see any.

"That's one way to do business," I said.

"The only way. Here." She opened a drawer and pulled out the tickets and I went over and took them. "By the way, what's your name, boy? See you in here all the time, but don't know your name."

Boy? Was she talking to me?

"Plebin Cook," I said. "And I've always assumed you're Martha."

"Martha ain't much of a name, but it beats Plebin. Plebin's awful. I was named that I'd get it changed. Call yourself most anything and it'd be better than Plebin."

"I'll tell my poor, old, grey-haired mother what you said."

"You must have been an accident and that's why she named you that. You got an older brother or sister?"

"A brother."

"How much older?"

Earning these tickets was getting to be painful. "Sixteen years."

"What's his name?"

"Jim."

"There you are. You were an accident. Jim's a normal name. Her naming you Plebin is unconscious revenge. I read about stuff like that in one of those psychology books came in. Called KNOW WHY THINGS HAPPEN TO YOU. You ought to read it. Thing it'd tell you is to get your named changed to something normal. Right name will give you a whole nuther outlook about yourself."

I had a vision of shoving those circus tickets down her throat, but I restrained myself for Jasmine's sake. "No joke? Well, I'll see you tomorrow."

"Eight o'clock sharp. Go stacking 'em after nine, gets so hot in here you'll faint. A Yankee visiting some relatives came in here and did just that. Found him about closing time over there by the historicals and the Gothic Romances. Had to call an ambulance to come get him. Got out of here with one of my Gothics clutched in his hand. Didn't pay me a cent for it."

"And people think a job like this is pretty easy."

"They just don't know," Martha said.

I said thanks and good-bye and started to turn away.

"Hey," Martha said. "You decide to get your name changed, they'll do stuff like that for you over at the court house."

"I'll keep that in mind," I said.

I didn't want any more of Martha, so I went over to the drug store and used the pay phone there and called Jasmine. Her mother answered.

"Hi, Connie," I said.

"Get a job yet?"

"No," I said. "But I'm closing in on some prospects."

"Bet you are. What do you want?"

"Jasmine in?"

"You want to talk to her?"

No, I thought. Just ask for the hell of it. But I said, "If I may."

The phone clattered on something hard, a little more violently than necessary, I thought. A moment later Jasmine came on the line. "Daddy."

"Hi, Baby Darling. Want to go to the circus?"

"The circus?"

"The Jim Dandy Circus is in town, and I've got tickets."

"Yeah. Really." She sounded as if I'd asked her if she wanted to have her teeth cleaned.

"You used to like the circuses."

"When I was ten."

"That was just seven years ago."

"That's a long time."

"Only when you're seventeen. Want to go or not? I'll even spring for a hot dog."

"You know what they make hot dogs out of?"

"I try not to think about it. I figure I get some chili on it, whatever's in the dog dies."

"Guess you want me to come by and get you?"

"That would be nice. Circus starts at three. That's less than an hour away."

"All right, but Daddy?"

"Yeah."

Don't call me Baby Darling in public. Someone could hear."

"We can't have that."

"Really, Daddy. I'm getting to be a woman now. It's . . . I don't know . . . kind of . . ."

"Hokey?"

"That's it."

"Gottcha."

The circus was not under the big top, but was inside the Mud Creek Exhibition center, which Mud Creek needs about as much as I need a second dick. I don't use the first one as it is. Oh, I pee out of it, but you know what I mean.

The circus was weak from the start, but Jasmine seemed to have a pretty good time, even if the performing bears were so goddamned old I thought we were going to have to go down there and help them out of their cages. The Tiger act was scary, because it looked as if the tigers were definitely in control, but the overweight Ringmaster got out alive, and the elephants came on, so old and wrinkled they looked like drunks in baggy pants. That was the best of it. After that, the dog act, conducted by Waldo the Great, got out of hand, and his performing poodles went X-rated, and the real doo-doo hit the fan.

Idiot trainer had apparently put one of the bitches to work while she was in heat, and in response, the male dogs jumped her and started poking, the biggest male finally winning the honors and the other five running about as if their brains had rolled out of their ears.

Waldo the Great went a little nuts and started kicking the fornicating dogs, but they wouldn't let up. The male dog kept his goober in the slot even when Waldo's kicks made his hind legs leave the ground. He didn't even yip.

I heard a kid behind us say, "Mommy, what are the puppies doing?"

And Mommy, not missing a beat, said, "They're doing a trick, dear."

Children were screaming. Waldo began kicking at the remaining dogs indiscriminately, and they darted for cover. Members of the circus rushed Waldo the Great. There were disappointed and injured dogs hunching and yipping all over the place. Waldo went back to the horny male and tried once more to discourage him. He really put the boot to him, but the ole boy really hung in there. I was kind of proud of him. One of the other dogs, innocent, except for confusion, and a gyrating ass and a dick like a rolled back lipstick tube, made an error in geography and humped air past Waldo and got a kick in the ass for it.

He sailed way up and into the bleachers, went so high his fleas should have served cocktails and dinner on him. Came down like a bomb, hit between a crack in the bleachers with a yip. I didn't see him come out from under there. He didn't yip again.

The little boy behind me, said, "Is that a trick too?"

"Yes," Mommy said. "It doesn't hurt him. He knows how to land."

I certainly hoped so.

Not everyone took it as casually as Mommy. Some dog lovers came out of the bleachers and there was a fight. Couple of cowboys started trying to do to Waldo what he had done to the poodles.

Meanwhile, back at the ranch, so to speak, the two amorous mutts were still at it, the male laying pipe like there was no tomorrow.

Yes sir, a pleasant afternoon trip to the circus with my daughter. Another debacle. It was merely typical of the luck I had been experiencing. Even a free ticket to the circus could turn to shit.

Jasmine and I left while a cowboy down from the bleachers was using Waldo the Great as a punching bag. One of the ungrateful poodles was biting the cowboy on the boot.

Me and Jasmine didn't have hot dogs. We ended up at a Mexican place, and Jasmine paid for it. Halfway through the meal Jasmine looked up at me and frowned.

"Daddy, I can always count on you for a good time."

"Hey," I said, "what were you expecting for free tickets? Goddamn Ringling Brothers?"

"Really, Daddy. I enjoyed it. Weirdness follows you around. At Mom's there isn't anything to do but watch television, and Mom and Gerald always go to bed about nine o'clock, so they're no fun."

"I guess not," I said, thinking nine o'clock was awful early to be sleepy. I hoped the sonofabitch gave her the clap.

After dinner, Jasmine dropped me off and next morning I went down to Martha's and she grunted at me and showed me the Harlequins and where they needed to go, in alphabetical order, so I started in placing them. After about an hour of that, it got hot and I had to stop and talk Martha into letting me go over to the drug store and buy a Coke.

When I came back with it, there was a guy in there with a box of

Harlequin romances. He was tall and lean and not bad looking, except that he had one of those little pencil line mustaches that look as if he'd missed a spot shaving or had a stain line from sipping chocolate milk. Except for a black eye, his face was oddly unlined, as if little that happened to him in life found representation there. I thought he looked familiar. A moment later, it came to me. He was the guy at the circus with the performing dogs. I hadn't recognized him without his gold lamé tights. I could picture him clearly now, his foot up in the air, a poodle being launched from it. Waldo the Great.

He had a box of books on the desk in front of Martha. All Harlequin Romances. He reached out and ran his fingers over the spines. "I really hate to get rid of these," he was saying to Martha, and his voice was as sweet as a cooing turtle dove. "Really hate it, but see, I'm currently unemployed and extra finances, even of a small nature, are needed, and considering all the books I read, well, they're outgrowing my trailer. I tell you, it hurts me to dispense with these. Just seeing them on my shelves cheers me . . . Oh, I take these books so to heart. If life could be like these, oh what a life that would be. But somebody always messes it up." He touched the books. "True love. Romance. Happy endings. Oh, it should be that way, you know. We live such a miserable existence. We—"

"Hey," Martha said. "Actually, I don't give a shit why you want to get rid of them. And if life was like a Harlequin Romance, I'd put a gun in my mouth. You want to sell this crap, or not?"

Martha always tries to endear herself to her customers. I reckon she's got a trust fund somewhere and her mission on earth is to make as many people miserable as possible. Still, that seemed blunt even for her.

"Well, now," Waldo said. "I was merely expressing a heart felt opinion. Nothing more. I could take my trade elsewhere."

"No skin off my rosy red ass," Martha said. "You want, that man over there will help you carry this shit back out to the car."

He looked at me. I blushed, nodded, drank more of my Coke.

He looked back at Martha. "Very well. I'll sell them to you, but only because I'm pressed to rid myself of them. Otherwise, I wouldn't take twice what you want to give for them."

"For you, Mister Asshole," Martha said, "just for you, I'll give you half of what I normally offer. Take it or leave it."

Waldo, Mr. Asshole, paused for a moment, studying Martha. I could see the side of his face, and just below his blackened eye there was a twitch, just once, then his face was smooth again.

"All right, let's conduct our business and get it over with," he said.

Martha counted the books, opened the cash register and gave Waldo a handful of bills. "Against my better judgement, there's the whole price."

"What in the world did I ever do to you?" Waldo The Great, alias, Mr.

Asshole, said. He almost looked really hurt. It was hard to tell. I'd never seen a face like that. So smooth. So expressionless. It was disconcerting.

"You breathe," Martha said, "that's enough of an offense." With that, Waldo, Mr. Asshole, went out of the store, head up, back straight.

"Friend of yours?" I asked.

"Yeah," Martha said. "Me and him are fuckin'."

"I thought the two of you were pretty warm."

"I don't know. I really can't believe it happened like that."

"You weren't as sweet as usual."

"Can't explain it. One of those things. Ever had that happen? Meet someone right off, and you just don't like them, and you don't know why."

"I always just shoot them. Saves a lot of breath."

She ignored me. "Like it's chemistry or something. That guy came in here, it was like someone drove by and tossed a rattlesnake through the door. I didn't like him on sight. Sometimes I think that there's certain people that are predators, and the rest of us, we pick up on it, even if it isn't obvious through their actions, and we react to it. And maybe I'm an asshole."

"That's a possibility," I said. "You being an asshole, I mean. But I got to tell you, I don't like him much either. Kind of makes my skin crawl, that unlined face and all."

I told her about the circus and the dogs.

"That doesn't surprise me any," Martha said. "I mean, anyone can lose their cool. I've kicked a dog in my time—"

"I find that hard to believe."

"—but I tell you, that guy hasn't got all the corn on his cob. I can sense it. Here, put these up. Earn your goddamn circus tickets."

I finished off the Coke, got the box of Harlequins Waldo had brought in, took them over to the romance section and put them on the floor.

I pulled one out to look at the author's name, and something fell out of the book. It was a folded piece of paper. I picked it up and unfolded it. It was a magazine fold-out of a naked woman, sort you see in the cheaper tits and ass magazines. She had breasts just a little smaller than watermelons and she was grabbing her ankles, holding her legs in a spread eagle position, as if waiting for some unsuspecting traveler to fall in. There were thick black paint lines slashed at the neck, torso, elbows, wrist, waist, knees and ankles. The eyes had been blackened with the marker so that they looked like nothing more than enormous skull sockets. A circle had been drawn around her vagina and there was a big black dot dead center of it, like a bulls eye. I turned it over. On the back over the printing there was written in black with a firm hand: Nothing really hooks together. Life lacks romance.

Looking at the photograph and those lines made me feel peculiar. I refolded the fold-out and started to replace it inside the book, then I thought maybe I'd throw it in the trash, but finally decided to keep it out of curiosity.

I shoved it into my back pocket and finished putting up the books, then got ready to leave. As I was going, Martha said, "you want a job here putting up books I'll take you on half a day five days a week. Monday through Friday. Saves some wear on my bad leg. I can pay you a little. Won't be much, but I don't figure you're worth much to me."

"That's a sweet offer, Martha, but I don't know."

"You say you want work."

"I do, but half a day isn't enough."

"More than you're working now, and I'll pay in cash. No taxes, no bullshit with the employment office."

"All right," I said. "You got a deal."

"Start tomorrow."

I was lying naked on the bed with just the night light on reading a hard-boiled mystery novel. The window was open as always and there was actually a pretty nice breeze blowing in. I felt like I used to when I was twelve and staying up late and reading with a flashlight under the covers and a cool spring wind was blowing in through the window screen, and Mom and Dad were in the next room and I was loved and protected and was going to live forever. Pleasant.

There was a knock at the door.

That figured.

I got up and pulled on my pajama bottoms and put on a robe and went to the door. It was Jasmine. She had her long, dark hair tied back in a pony tail and she was wearing jeans and a shirt buttoned up wrong. She had a suitcase in her hand.

"Connie again?"

"Her and that man," Jasmine said as she came inside. "I hate them."

"You don't hate your mother. She's an asshole, but you don't hate her."

"You hate her."

"That's different."

"Can I stay here for awhile?"

"Sure. There's almost enough room for me, so I'm sure you'll find it cozy."

"You're not glad to see me?"

"I'm glad to see you. I'm always glad to see you. But this won't work out. Look how small this place is. Besides, you've done this before. Couple times. You come here, eat all my cereal, start missing your comforts, and then you go home."

"Not this time."

"All right. Not this time. Hungry?"

"I really don't want any cereal."

"I actually have some lunch meat this time. It's not quite green."

"Sounds yummy."

I made a couple of sandwiches and poured us some slightly tainted milk and we talked a moment, then Jasmine saw the fold-out on the dresser and picked it up. I had pulled it from my pocket when I got home and tossed it there.

She opened it up and looked at it, then smiled at me. It was the same smile her mother used when she was turning on the charm, or was about to make me feel small enough to wear doll clothes.

"Daddy, dear!"

"I found it."

"Say you did?"

"Cut it out. It was in one of the books I was putting up today. I thought it was weird and I stuck it in my back pocket. I should have thrown it away."

Jasmine smiled at me, examined the fold-out closely. "Daddy, do men like women like this? That big, I mean?"

"Some do. Yes."

"Do you?"

"Of course not."

"What are these lines?"

"I don't know exactly, but that's what I thought was weird. It got my mind working overtime."

"You mean like the 'What If' game?"

The "What If" game was something Jasmine and I had made up when she was little, and had never really quit playing, though our opportunities to play it had decreased sharply over the last couple of years. It grew out of my thinking I was going to be a writer. I'd see something and I'd extrapolate. An example was an old car I saw once where someone had finger written in the dust on the trunk lid: THERE'S A BODY IN THE TRUNK.

Well, I thought about that and tried to make a story of it. Say there was a body in the trunk. How did it get there? Is the woman driving the car aware it's there? Did she commit the murder? That sort of thing. Then I'd try to write a story. After fifty or so stories, and three times that many rejects, I gave up writing them, and Jasmine and I started kicking ideas like that back and forth, for fun. That way I could still feed my imagination, but I could quit kidding myself that I could write. Also, Jasmine got a kick out of it.

"Let's play, daddy?"

"All right. I'll start. I saw those slashes on that fold-out, and I got to thinking, why are these lines drawn?"

"Because they look like cuts," Jasmine said. "You know, like a chart for how to butcher meat."

"That's what I thought. Then I thought, it's just a picture, and it could have been marked up without any real motive. Absent minded doodling. Or it could have been done by someone who didn't like women, and this was sort of an imaginary revenge. Turning women into meat in his mind. Dehumanizing them."

"Or it could be representative of what he's actually done or plans to do. Wow! Maybe we've got a real mystery here."

"My last real mystery was what finished your mom and I off."

That was the body in the trunk business. I didn't tell it all before. I got so into that scenario I called a friend of mine. Sam, down at the cop shop and got him geared up about there being a body in the trunk of a car. I told it good, with details I'd made up and didn't even know I'd made up. I really get into this stuff. The real and the unreal get a little hard for me to tell apart. Or it used to be that way. Not anymore.

Bottom line is Sam pursued the matter, and the only thing in the trunk was a spare tire. Sam was a little unhappy with me. The cop shop was a little unhappy with him. My wife, finally tired of my make believe, kicked me out and went for the oil man. He didn't make up stories. He made money and had all his hair and was probably hung like a water buffalo.

"But say we knew the guy who marked this picture, Daddy. And say we started watching him, just to see—"

"We do know him. Kind of."

I told her about Waldo the Great and his books and Martha's reaction.

"That's even weirder," Jasmine said. "This bookstore lady—"

"Martha."

"—does she seem like a good judge of character?"

"She hates just about everybody, I think."

"Well, for 'What If's' sake, say she is a good judge of character. And this guy really is nuts. And he's done this kind of thing to a fold-out because . . . say . . . say . . ."

"He wants life to be like a Harlequin Romance. Only it isn't. Women don't always fit his image of what they should be—like the women in the books he reads."

"Oh, that's good, Daddy. Really. He's gone nuts, not because of violent films and movies, but because of a misguided view about romance. I love it."

"Makes as much sense as a guy saying he axed a family because he saw a horror movie or read a horror novel. There's got to be more to it than that, of course. Rotten childhood, genetic makeup. Most people who see or read horror novels, romance novels, whatever, get their thrills vicariously. It's a catharsis. But in the same way a horror movie or book might set someone off who's already messed up, someone wound up and ready to spring, the Harlequins do it for our man. He has so little idea what real life is like, he expects it to be like the Harlequins, or desperately wants it to be that way, and when it isn't, his frustrations build, and—"

"He kills women, cuts them up, disposes of their bodies. It's delicious. Really delicious."

"It's silly. There's a sleeping bag in the closet. Get it out when you get sleepy. Me, I'm going to go to bed. I got a part time job downstairs at Martha's, and I start tomorrow?"

"That's great, Daddy. Mom said you'd never find a job."

On that note, I went to bed.

Next morning I went down to Martha's and started to work. She had a store room full of books. Some of them were stuck together with age, and some were full of worms. Being a fanatic book lover, it hurt me, but I got rid of the bad ones in the dumpster out back, then loaded some boxes of good condition books on a hand truck and wheeled them out and began putting them up in alphabetical order in their proper sections.

About nine that morning, Jasmine came down and I heard her say something to Martha, then she came around the corner of the detective section and smiled at me. She looked so much like her mother it hurt me. She had her hair pulled back and tied at her neck and she was starting to sweat. She wore white shorts, cut a little too short if you ask me, and a loose red tee shirt and sandals. She was carrying a yellow pad with a pencil.

"What you doing?" I asked.

"Figuring out what Waldo the Great's up to. I been working on it ever since I got up. I got lots of notes here."

"What'd you have for breakfast?"

"Same as you, I bet. A Coke."

"Right. It's important we pay attention to nutrition, Baby Darling."

"You want to hear about Waldo or not?"

"Yeah, tell me, what's he up to?"

"He's looking for a job."

"Because he got fired for the dog kicking business?"

"Yeah. So, he's staying in the trailer park here, and he's looking for a job. Or maybe he's got some savings and he's just hanging out for a while before he moves on. Let's just say all that for 'What If's' sake."

"All right, now what?"

"Just for fun, to play the game all the way, let's go out to the trailer park and see if he's living there. If he is, we ought to be able to find him. He's got all these dogs, so there should be some signs of them, don't you think?"

"Wait a minute. You're not planning on checking?"

"Just for the 'What If' game."

"Like I said, he could have moved on."

"That's what we'll find out. Later, we can go over to the trailer park and look around, play detective."

"That's carrying it too far."

"Why? It's just a game. We don't have to bother him."

"I don't know. I don't think so."

"Why not?" It was Martha. She came around the corner of the bookshelves leaning on her golf putter. "It's just a game."

"Aren't you supposed to be counting your money, or something?" I said to Martha. "Kill some of those roaches in your store room. That club would be just the tool for it."

"I couldn't help but overhear you because I was leaning against the other side of the bookshelf listening," Martha said.

"That'll do it," I said, and shelved a Mickey Spillane.

"We've spoke, but I don't think we've actually met," Jasmine said to Martha. "I'm his daughter."

"Tough to admit, I'm sure," Martha said.

Jasmine and Martha smiled at each other and shook hands.

"Why don't we go over there tonight?" Martha said. "I need something to do."

"To the trailer park?" I asked.

"Of course," Martha said.

"Not likely," I said. "I've had it with the detective business, imaginary or otherwise. It'll be a cold day in hell when I have anything else to do with it, in any manner, shape or form. And you can take that to the bank."

That night, presumably an example of a cold day in hell, around nine thirty, we drove over to the only trailer park in Mud Creek and looked around.

Waldo hadn't moved on. Being astute detectives, we found his trailer right away. It was bright blue and there was red lettering on the side that read: WALDO THE GREAT AND HIS MAGNIFICENT CANINES. The trailer was next to a big pickup with a trailer hitch and there were lights on in the trailer.

We were in Martha's old Dodge van, and we drove by Waldo's and around the loop in the park and out of there. Martha went a short distance, turned down a hard clay road that wound along the side of the creek and through a patch of woods and ended up at the rear of the trailer park, about even with Waldo's trailer. It was a bit of distance away, but you could see his trailer through the branches of the trees that surrounded the park. Martha parked to the side of the road and spoke to Jasmine. "Honey, hand me them binoculars out of the glove box."

Jasmine did just that.

"These suckers are infra-red," Martha said. "You can see a mole on a gnat's ass with one of these dead of night during a blizzard."

"And why in the world would you have a pair?" I asked.

"I used to do a little surveillance for a private investigation agency in Houston. I sort of borrowed these when I left. You know, boss I had hadn't been such a dick, I'd have stayed with that job. I was born to it."

"Sounds exciting," Jasmine said.

"It beat smelling book dust, I'll tell you that." Martha rolled down her window and put the glasses to her face and pointed them at Waldo's trailer.

"He's at the window," she said.

"This has gone far enough," I said. "We're not supposed to be doing this. It's an invasion of privacy."

"Settle down. He ain't got his pecker out or nothing," Martha said. "Wish he did, though. He's an asshole, but he ain't bad looking. I wonder what kind of rod he's got on him?"

I looked at Jasmine. She looked a little stunned. "Listen here," I said. "My daughter's here."

"No shit," Martha said. "Listen, you stuffy old fart. She's grown up enough to know a man's got a hooter on him and what it looks like."

Jasmine's face was split by a weak smile. "Well, I know what they are, of course."

"All right, we're all versed in biology," I said. "Let's go. I've got a good book waiting at home."

"Hold the goddamn phone," Martha said. "He's coming out of the trailer."

I looked, and I could see Waldo's shape framed in the trailer's doorway. One of the poodles ran up behind him and he back kicked it inside without even looking, went down the metal steps and closed and locked the trailer, got in his pickup and drove away.

"He's off," Martha said.

"Yeah. Probably to a fried chicken place," I said.

Martha lowered the binoculars and looked over her seat at me. "Would you quit fucking up the game? 'What If' is going on here."

"Yeah, Daddy," Jasmine said. "We're playing 'What If.'"

Martha cranked the van and followed the clay road as it curved around the park and out into the street. She went right. A moment later, we saw the back of Waldo's pickup. He had an arm hanging out the window and a cigarette was between his fingers and sparks were flaring off of it and flickering into the night.

"Smokey Bear'd come down on his ass like a ton of bricks, he seen that," Martha said.

We followed him to the end of the street and out onto the main drag, such as it is in Mud Creek. He pulled into a fried chicken joint.

"See," I said.

"Even murderers have to eat," Martha said, and she drove on by.

My plan was to end the business there, but it didn't work that way. I pulled out of it and let them stay with it. All that week Martha and Jasmine played 'What If.' They pinned up the foldout in my apartment and they wrote out scenarios for who Waldo was and what he'd done, and so on. They drove out to his place at night and discovered he kept weird hours, went out at all times of the night. They discovered he let the poodles out for bathroom breaks twice a night and that there was one less than there had been during the circus act. I guess Mommy had been wrong when she told her kid the poodle knew how to land.

It was kind of odd seeing Jasmine and Martha become friends like that. Martha had struck me as having all the imagination of a fence post, but under that rough exterior and that loud mouth was a rough exterior and a loud mouth with an imagination.

I also suspicioned that she had lied about not being able to pay her rent. The store didn't make that much, but she always seemed to have money. As far as the store went, it got so I was running it by myself, full-time, not only putting up books, but waiting on customers and closing up at night. Martha paid me well enough for it, however, so I didn't complain, but when she and Jasmine would come down from my place talking about their "killer", etc., I felt a little jealous. Jasmine had moved in with me, and now that I had my daughter back, she spent all her time with a bald-headed, mustached lady who was her father's boss.

Worse, Connie had been on my case about Jasmine and how my only daughter was living in a shit hole and being exposed to bad elements. The worst being me, of course. She came by the apartment a couple of times to tell me about it and to try and get Jasmine to go home.

I told her Jasmine was free to go home anytime she chose, and Jasmine explained that she had no intention of going home. She liked her sleeping bag and Daddy let her have Coke for breakfast. I sort of wish she hadn't mentioned the Coke part. She'd only had that for breakfast one morning, but she knew it'd get her mother's goat, and it had. Only thing was, now Connie could hang another sword over my head. Failure to provide proper nutrition for my only child.

Anyway, I was working in the store one day—well, working on reading a detective novel—when Martha and Jasmine came in.

"Get your goddamn feet off my desk," Martha said.

"Glad to see you," I said, lowering my feet and putting a marker in the book.

"Get off my stool," Martha said. "Quit reading that damn book and put some up."

I got off the stool. "You two have a pleasant day, Massah Martha?"

"Eat shit, Plebin," Martha said, leaning her golf club against the counter and mounting her stool.

"Daddy, Martha and I have been snooping. Listen what we got. Martha had this idea to go over to the newspaper office in LaBorde and look at back issues—"

"LaBorde?" I said.

"Bigger town. Bigger paper," Martha said, sticking one of her dainty cigarettes into her mouth and lighting it.

"We went through some older papers," Jasmine said, "and since LaBorde covers a lot of the small towns around here, we found ads for the Jim Dandy Circus in several of them, and we were able to pin point on a map the route of the circus up to Mud Creek, and the latest paper showed Marvel Creek to be the next stop, and—"

"Slow down," I said. "What's the circus got to do with your so called investigation?"

"You look at the papers and read about the towns where the circus showed up," Martha said, "and there's in everyone of them something about a missing woman, or young girl. In a couple cases, bodies have been found. Sometimes they were found a week or so after the circus came to town, but most of the news articles indicate the missing women disappeared at the time of the circus."

"Of course, we determined this, not the papers," Jasmine said. "We made the connection between the circus and the bodies."

"In the case of the bodies, both were found after the circus passed through," Martha said, "but from the estimated times of death the papers gave, we've been able to figure they were killed about the time the circus was in town. And my guess is those missing women are dead too, and by the same hand."

"Waldo's?" I said.

"That's right," Martha said.

I considered all that.

Jasmine said, "Pretty coincidental, don't you think?"

"Well, yeah," I said, "but that doesn't mean—"

"And the two bodies had been mutilated," Martha said. She leaned against the counter and reached into her shirt pocket and pulled out the fold-out I had found. She smoothed it out on the counter top. "Body parts were missing. And I bet they were cut up, just like this fold-out is marked.

As for the missing body parts, eyes and pussies, I figure. Those are the parts he has circled and blacked out."

"Watch your language," I said to Martha.

No one seemed to take much note of me.

"The bodies were found in the town's local dump," Jasmine said.

"It's curious," I admitted, "but still, to accuse a man of murder on the basis of circumstantial evidence."

"One more thing," Martha said. "Both bodies had traces of black paint on them. Like it had been used to mark the areas the killer wanted to cut, and I presume, did cut. That's certainly a lot of goddamn circumstantial evidence, isn't it?"

"Enough that we're going to keep an eye on Waldo," Jasmine said.

I must admit right now that I didn't think even then, after what I had been told, there was anything to this Waldo the Great as murderer. It struck me that murders and disappearances happen all the time, and that if one were to look through the LaBorde paper carefully, it would be possible to discover there had been many of both, especially disappearances, before and after the arrival of the circus. I mean that paper covered a lot of small towns and communities, and LaBorde was a fairly large town itself. A small city actually. Most of the disappearances would turn out to be nothing more than someone leaving on a trip for a few days without telling anyone, and most of the murders would be committed by a friend or relative of the victim and would have nothing to do with the circus or marked up fold-outs.

Of course, the fact that the two discovered bodies had been mutilated gave me pause, but not enough to go to the law about it. That was just the sort of half-baked idea that had gotten my ass in a crack earlier.

Still, that night, I went with Martha and Jasmine out to the trailer park.

It was cloudy that night and jags of lightning made occasional cuts through the cloud cover and thunder rumbled and light drops of rain fell on the windshield of Martha's van.

We drove out to the road behind the park about dark, peeked out the windows and through the gaps in the trees. The handful of pole lights in the park were gauzy in the wet night and sad as dying fireflies. Their poor, damp rays fell against some of the trees—their branches waving in the wind like the fluttering hands of distressed lunatics—and forced the beads of rain on the branches to give up tiny rainbows. The rainbows rose up, misted outward a small distance, then once beyond the small circumference of light, their beauty was consumed by the night.

Martha got out her binoculars and Jasmine sat on the front passenger side with a note pad and pen, ready to record anything Martha told her to. They felt that the more documentation they had, the easier it would be to convince the police that Waldo was a murderer.

I was in the seat behind theirs, my legs stretched out and my back against the van, looking away from the trailer most of the time, wondering how I had let myself in on this. About midnight I began to feel both sleepy and silly. I unwrapped a candy bar and ate it.

"Would you quit that goddamn smacking back there," Martha said. "It makes me nervous."

"Pardon me all to hell," I said, and wadded up the wrapper noisily and tossed it on the floorboard.

"Daddy, would you quit?" Jasmine said.

"Now we got something," Martha said.

I sat up and turned around. There were no lights on in the trailers in the park except for Waldo's trailer; a dirty, orange glow shone behind one of his windows, like a fresh slice of smoked cheese. Other than that, there was only the pole lights, and they didn't offer much. Just those little rainbows made of bad light and rain. Without the binoculars there was little to observe in detail, because it was a pretty good distance from where we were to Waldo's trailer, but I could see him coming out of the door, holding it open, the whole pack of poodles following after.

Waldo bent down by the trailer and pulled a small shovel out from beneath it. The poodles wandered around and started doing their bathroom business. Waldo cupped his hands over a cigarette and lit it with a lighter and smoked while he noted the dog's delivery spots. After a while he went about scooping up their messes with his shovel and making several trips to the dumpster to get rid of it.

Finished, he pushed the shovel beneath the trailer and smoked another cigarette and ground it hard beneath his heel and opened the trailer door and called to the dogs. They bounded up the steps and into the trailer like it was one of their circus tricks. No poodle tried to fuck another poodle. Waldo didn't kick anybody. He went inside, and a moment later came out again, this time minus the poodles. He was carrying something. A box. He looked about carefully, then placed the box in the back of his pickup. He went back inside the trailer.

"Goddamn," Martha said. "There's a woman's leg in that box."

"Let me see," I said.

"You can't see it now," she said. "It's down in the bed of the truck."

She gave me the binoculars anyway, and I looked. She was right. I couldn't see what was in the bed of the truck. "He wouldn't just put a woman's leg in the back of his pickup," I said.

"Well, he did," Martha said.

"Oh God," Jasmine said, and she flicked on her pen light and glanced at her watch and started writing on her note pad, talking aloud as she did. "Twelve-o-five, Waldo put woman's leg in the bed of his truck. Oh, shit, who do you think it could be?"

"One could hope it's that goddamn bitch down at the county clerk's office," Martha said. "I been waiting for something to happen to her."

"Martha!" Jasmine said.

"Just kidding," Martha said. "Kinda."

I had the binoculars tight against my face as the trailer door opened again. I could see very well with the infra-red business. Waldo came out with another box. As he came down the steps, the box tilted slightly. It was open at the top and I could see very clearly what was in it.

"A woman's head," I said. My voice sounded small and childish.

"Jesus Christ," Martha said. "I didn't really, really, believe he was a murderer."

Waldo was back inside the trailer. A moment later he reappeared. Smaller boxes under each arm.

"Let me see," Jasmine said.

"No," I said. "You don't need to."

"But . . ." Jasmine began.

"Listen to your father," Martha said.

I handed the binoculars back to Martha. She didn't look through them. We didn't need to try and see what was in the other boxes. We knew. The rest of Waldo's victim.

Waldo unfolded a tarp in the back of his pickup and stretched it across the truck bed and fastened it at all corners, then got inside the cab and cranked the engine.

"Do we go to the police now?" Jasmine said.

"After we find out where he's taking the body," Martha said.

"You're right," I said. "Otherwise, if he's disposed of all the evidence, we've got nothing." I was thinking too of my record at the police station. Meaning, of course, more than my word would be needed to start an investigation.

Martha cranked the van and put on the park lights and began to ease along, giving Waldo the time he needed to get out of the trailer park and ahead of us.

"I've got a pretty good idea where he's going," Martha said. "Bet he scoped the place out first day he got to town."

"The dump," Jasmine said. "Place they found those other bodies."

We got to the street and saw Waldo was headed in the direction of the dump. Martha turned on the van's headlights after the pickup was down the road a bit, then eased out in pursuit. We laid back and let him get way ahead, and when we got out of town and he took the turn off to the dump, we passed on by and turned down a farm to market road and parked as close as we could to a barbed wire fence. We got out and climbed the fence and crossed a pasture and came to a rise and went up that and poked our heads over carefully and looked down on the dump.

There was smoke rising up in spots, where sounds of burning refuse had been covered at some point, and it filled the air with stink. The dump had been like that forever. As a little boy, my father would bring me out to the dump to toss our family garbage, and even in broad daylight, I thought the place spooky, a sort of poor boy, blue collar hell. My dad said there were fires out here that had never been put out, not by the weight of garbage and dirt, or by winter ice or spring's rain storms. Said no matter what was done to those fires, they still burned. Methane maybe. All the stuff in the dump heating up like compost, creating some kind of combustible chemical reaction.

Within the dump, bordered off by a wide layer of scraped earth, were two great oil derricks. They were working derricks too, and the great rocking horse pumps dipped down and rose up constantly, night or day, and it always struck me that this was a foolish place for a dump full of never dying fires to exist, next to two working oil wells. But the dump still stood and the derricks still worked oil. The city council had tried to have the old dump shut down, moved, but so far nothing had happened. They couldn't get those fires out completely for one thing. I felt time was against the dump and the wells. Eventually, the piper, or in this case, the pipeline, had to be paid. Some day the fires in the dump would get out of hand and set the oil wells on fire and the explosion that would occur would sent Mud Creek and its surrounding rivers and woodlands to some place north of Pluto.

At night, the place was even more eerie. Flames licking out from under the debris like tongues, the rain seeping to its source, making it hiss white smoke like dragon breath. The two old derricks stood tall against the night and lightning wove a flickering crown of light around one of them and went away. In that instant, the electrified top of the derrick looked like Martian machinery. Inside the derricks, the still working well pumps throbbed and kerchunked and dipped their dark, metal, hammer heads then lifted them again. Down and up. Down and up. Taking with them on the drop and the rise, rain wet shadows and flickers of garbage fire.

Waldo's truck was parked beside the road, next to a mound of garbage the height of a first story roof. He had peeled off the tarp and put it away and was unloading his boxes from the truck, carrying them to a spot near one of the oil derricks, arranging them neatly, as if he were being graded on his work. When the boxes were all out, Waldo stood with his back to us and watched one of the derrick's pumps nod for a long time, as if the action of it amazed or offended him.

After a time, he turned suddenly and kicked at one of the boxes. The head in it popped up like a Mexican jumping bean and fell back down inside. Waldo took a deep breath, as if he were preparing to run a race, then got in his truck, turned it around, and drove away.

"He didn't even bother to bury the pieces," Jasmine said, and even in the bad light, I could see she was as white as Frosty the Snowman.

"Probably wants it to be found," Martha said. "We know where the corpse is now. We have evidence, and we saw him dispose of the body ourselves. I think we can go to the law now."

We drove back to town and called Sam from Martha's book store. He answered the phone on the fifth ring. He sounded like he had a sock in his mouth.

"What?"

"Plebin, Sam. I need your help."

"You in a ditch? Call a wrecker, man. I'm bushed."

"Not exactly. It's about murder."

"Ah, shit, Plebin. You some kind of fool, or what? We been through this. Call some nuthouse doctor or something. I need sleep. Day I put in today was bad enough, but I don't need you now and some story about murder. Lack of sleep gives me domestic problems."

"This one's different. I've got two witnesses. A body out at the dump. We saw it disposed of. A woman cut up in pieces, I kid you not. Guy named Waldo did it. He used to be with the circus. Directed a dog act."

"The circus?"

"That's right."

"And he has a dog act."

"Had. He cut up a woman and took her to the dump?"

"Plebin?"

"Yes."

"I go out there, and there's no dead body, I could change that, supply one, mood I'm in. Understand?"

"Just meet us at the dump."

"Who's us?"

I told him, gave him some background on Waldo, explained what Martha and Jasmine found in the LaBorde newspapers, hung up, and me and my fellow sleuths drove back to the dump.

* * *

We waited outside the dump in Martha's van until Sam showed in his blue Ford. We waved at him and started the van and led him into the dump. We drove up to the spot near the derrick and got out. None of us went over to the boxes for a look. We didn't speak. We listened to the pumps doing their work inside the derricks. Kerchunk, kerchunk, kerchunk.

Sam pulled up behind us and got out. He was wearing blue jeans and tennis shoes and his pajama top. He looked at me and Jasmine and Martha. Fact is, he looked at Martha quite a while.

"You want maybe I should send you a picture, or something?" Martha said.

Sam didn't say anything. He looked away from Martha and said to me, "All right. Where's the body?"

"It's kind of here and there," I said, and pointed. "In those boxes. Start with the little one, there. That's her head."

Sam looked in the box, and I saw him jump a little. Then he went still, bent forward and pulled the woman's head out by the hair, held it up in front of him and looked at it. He spun and tossed it to me. Reflexively, I caught it, then dropped it. By the time it hit the ground I felt like a number one horse's ass.

It wasn't a human head. It was a mannequin head with a black paint mark covering the stump of the neck, which had been neatly sawed in two.

"Here, Jasmine," Sam said. "You take a leg," and he hoisted a mannequin leg out of another box and tossed it at her. She shrieked and dodged and it landed on the ground. "And you that's gonna send me a picture. You take an arm." He pulled a mannequin arm out of another box and tossed it at Martha, who swatted it out of the air with her putter cane.

He turned and kicked another of the boxes and sent a leg and an arm sailing into a heap of brush and old paint cans.

"Goddamn it, Plebin," he said. "You've done it again." He came over and stood in front of me. "Man, you're nuts. Absolutely nuts."

"Wasn't just Plebin," Martha said. "We all thought it. The guy brought this stuff out here is a weirdo. We've been watching him."

"You have?" Sam said. "Playing detective, huh? That's sweet. That's real sweet. Plebin, come here, will you?"

I went over and stood by him. He put an arm around my shoulders and walked me off from Jasmine and Martha. He whispered to me.

"Plebin. You're not learning, man. Not a bit. Not only are you fucking up your life, you're fucking up mine. Listen here. Me and the old lady, we're not doing so good, see."

"I'm sorry to hear it. Toni has always been so great."

"Yeah, well, you see, she's jealous. You know that."

"Oh yeah. Always has been."

"There you are. She's gotten worse too. And you see, I spend a lot of time away from the home. Out of the bed. Bad hours. You getting what I'm saying here?"

"Yeah."

He pulled me closer and patted my chest with his other hand. "Good. Not only is that bad, me spending those hours away from home and out of the bed at bed time, but hey, I'm so bushed these days, I get ready to lay a little pipe, well, I got no lead in the pencil. Like a goddamn spaghetti, that's how it is. Know what I'm saying?"

"Least when you do get it hard, you get to lay pipe," I said.

"But I'm not laying it enough. It's because I don't get rest. But Toni, you know what she thinks? She thinks it's because I'm having a little extra-curricular activity. You know what I mean? Thinks I'm out banging hole like there's no tomorrow."

"Hey, I'm sorry, Sam, but . . ."

"So now I've got the rest problem again. I'm tired right now. I don't recover like I used to. I don't get eight hours of sack time, hey, I can't get it up. I have a bad day, which I do when I'm tired, I can't get it up. My shit comes out different, I can't get it up. I've gotten sensitive in my old age. Everything goes straight to my dick. Toni, she gets ready for me to do my duty, guess what?"

"You're too tired. You can't get it up."

"Bingo. The ole Johnson is like an empty sock. And when I can't get it up, what does Toni think?"

"You're fucking around?"

"That's right. And it's not bad enough I gotta be tired for legitimate reasons, but now I got to be tired because you and your daughter and Ma Frankenstein over there are seeing heads in boxes. Trailing some innocent bystander and trying to tie him in with murder when there's nobody been murdered. Know what I'm saying?"

"Sam, the guy looks the part. Acts it. There's been murders everywhere the circus goes . . ."

"Plebin, ole buddy. Hush your mouth, okay? Listen up tight. I'm going home now. I'm going back to bed. You wake me up again, I'll run over you with a truck. I don't have a truck, but I'll borrow one for the purpose. Got me?"

"Yeah."

"All right. Good night." He took his arm off my shoulders, walked back to his car and opened the door. He started to get inside, then straightened. He looked over the roof at me. "Come by and have dinner next week. Toni still makes a good chicken fried steak. Been a while since she's seen you."

"I'll keep it in mind. Give her my love."

"Yeah. And Plebin, don't call with anymore murders, all right? You got a good imagination, but as a detective, you're the worst." He looked at

Jasmine. "Jasmine, you stick with your mother." He got in his car, backed around and drove away.

I went over and stood with my fellow sleuths and looked down at the mannequin head. I picked it up by the hair and looked at it. "I think I'll have this mounted," I said. "Just to remind me what a jackass I am."

Back at the apartment I sat on the bed with the window open, the mannequin head on the pillow beside me. Jasmine sat in the dresser chair and Martha had one of my rickity kitchen chairs turned around backwards and she sat with her arms crossed on the back of it, sweat running out from under her wool cap, collecting in her mustache.

"I still think something funny is going on there," Jasmine said.

"Oh, shut up," I said.

"We know something funny is going on," Martha said.

"We means you two," I said. "Don't include me. I don't know anything except I've made a fool out of myself and Sam is having trouble with his sex life, or maybe what he told me was some kind of parable."

"Sex life," Jasmine said. "What did he tell you?"

"Forget," I said.

"That Sam is some sorry cop," Martha said. "He should have at least investigated Waldo. Guy who paints and cuts up mannequins isn't your everyday fella, I'd think. I bet he's painting and sawing them up because he hasn't picked a victim yet. It's his way of appeasing himself until he's chosen someone. Akin to masturbation instead of real sex."

"If we could see inside his trailer," Jasmine said, "I bet we'd find evidence of something more than mannequins. Evidence of past crimes maybe."

"I've had enough," I said. "And Jasmine, so have you. And Martha, if you're smart, so have you."

Martha got out one of her little cigarettes.

"Don't light that in here," I said.

She got out a small box of kitchen matches.

"I can't stand smoke," I said.

She pulled a match from the box and struck it on her pants leg and lit up, puffed, studied the ceiling.

"Put it out, Martha. This is my place."

She blew smoke at the ceiling. "I think Jasmine's right," she said. "If we could divert him. Get him out of the trailer so we could have a look inside, find some evidence, then maybe that small town idiot cop friend of yours would even be convinced."

"Waldo's not going to keep a human head in there," I said.

"He might," Martha said. "It's been known to happen. Or maybe something a victim owned. Guys like that keep souvenirs of their murders. That way they can fantasize, relive it all."

"We could watch his place tomorrow," Jasmine said, "then if he goes out, we could slip in and look around. We find something incriminating, something definite, there's a way to cue the police in on it, even one as stubborn and stupid as Sam."

"I'm sure Waldo locks his doors," I said.

"That's no trouble," Martha said. "I can pick the lock on Heaven's door."

"You're just a basket of fine skills," I said.

"I used to work for a repo company, years back," Martha said. "I learned to use lock jocks and keys and picks on car doors and garage doors. You name it, I can get in it, and in a matter of moments."

"Listen, you two," I said. "leave it be. We don't know this guy's done anything, and if he is a murderer, you damn sure don't need to be snooping around there, or you may end up on the victim list. Let's get on with our lives."

"Such as yours and mine is," Martha said. "What have I got to look forward to? Selling a few books? Meeting the right man? Me, a gargoyle with a golf club?"

"Martha, don't say that," Jasmine said.

"No, let's call a spade a spade here," Martha said. She snatched off her wool cap and showed us her bald head. I had seen a glimpse of it a time or two before I went to work there, when she was taking off and adjusting her cap or scratching her head, but this was the first time I'd seen it in all its sweaty, pink glory for more than a few moments. "What's gonna pull a mate in for me? My glorious head of hair. I started losing it when I was in my twenties. No man would look twice at me. Besides that, I'm ugly and have a mustache."

"A mate isn't everything," I said.

"It's something," Martha said. "And I think about it. I won't kid you. But I know it isn't possible. I've been around, seen some things, had some interesting jobs. But I haven't really made any life for myself. Not so it feels like one. And you know what? After all these years, Jasmine and you are my only real friends, and in your case, Plebin, I don't know that amounts to much."

"Thanks," I said.

"You could get a wig," Jasmine said.

"I could have these whiskers removed," Martha said. "But I'd still be a blimp with a bum leg. No. There's nothing for me in the looks department. Not unless I could change bodies with some blond bimbo. Since that isn't going to happen, all I got is what I make out of life. Like this mystery. A real mystery, I think. And if Waldo is a murderer, do we let him go on to the next town and find a victim? Or for that matter, a victim here, before he leaves?

"We catch this guy. Prove he's responsible for murders, then we've actually done something important with our lives. There's more to my life than the book store. More to yours Plebin than a bad name and unemployment checks. And . . . well, in your case Jasmine, there is more to your life. You're beautiful, smart, and you're going places. But for all of us, wouldn't it be worthwhile to catch a killer?"

"If he is a killer," I said. "Maybe he just hates mannequins because they look better in their clothes than he does."

"Women's clothes?" Jasmine said.

"Maybe it's women's clothes he likes to wear," I said. "Thing is, we could end up making fools of ourselves, spend some time in jail, even."

"I'll chance it," Jasmine said.

"No you won't," I said. "It's over for you, Jasmine. Martha can do what she wants. But you and me, we're out of it."

Martha left.

Jasmine got out her sleeping bag and unrolled it, went to the bathroom to brush her teeth. I tried to stay awake and await my turn in there, but couldn't. Too tired. I lay down on the bed, noted vaguely that rain had stopped pounding on the apartment roof, and I fell immediately asleep.

I awoke later that night, early morning really, to the smell of more on-coming rain, and when I rolled over I could see flashes of lightning in the west.

The west. The direction of the dump. It was as if a storm was originating there, moving toward the town.

Melodrama. I loved it.

I rolled over and turned my head to the end-table beside the bed, and when the lightning flashed I could see the mannequin head setting there, its face turned toward me, its strange, false eyes alight with the fire of the western lightning. The paint around the manikin's neck appeared very damp in that light, like blood.

I threw my legs from beneath the covers and took hold of the head. The paint on its neck was wet in my hands. The humidity had caused it to run. I sat the head on the floor where I wouldn't have to look at it, got up to go to the bathroom and wash my hands.

Jasmine's sleeping bag was on the floor, but Jasmine wasn't in it. I went on to the bathroom, but she wasn't in there either. I turned on the light and washed my hands and felt a little weak. There was no place else to be in the apartment. I looked to see if she had taken her stuff and gone home, but she hadn't. The door that led out to the stairway was closed, but unlocked.

No question now. She had gone out.

I had an idea where, and the thought of it gave me a chill. I got dressed and went downstairs and beat on the book store, pressed my face against the windows, but there was no light or movement. I went around to the rear of the building to beat on the back door, to try and wake Martha up in her living quarters, but when I got there I didn't bother. I saw that Martha's van was gone from the carport and Jasmine's car was still in place.

I went back to my apartment and found Jasmine's car keys on the dresser and thought about calling the police, then thought better of it. Their memory of my body in the trunk stunt was a long one, and they might delay. Blow off the whole thing, in fact, mark it up to another aggravation from the boy who cried wolf. If I called Sam it wouldn't be any better. Twice in one night he'd be more likely to kill me than to help me. He was more worried about his pecker than a would-be killer, and he might not do anything at all.

Then I remined myself it was a game of "What If" and that there wasn't anything to do, nothing to fear. I told myself the worst that could happen would be that Jasmine and Martha would annoy Waldo and make fools of themselves, and then it would all be over for good.

But those thoughts didn't help much, no matter how hard I tried to be convinced. I realized then that it hadn't been just the rain and the humidity that had awakened me. I had been thinking about what Martha said. About Waldo picking a victim later on if we didn't stop him. About the mannequins being a sort of warm up for what he really wanted to do and would do.

It wasn't just a game anymore. Though I had no real evidence for it, I believed then what Jasmine and Martha believed.

Waldo the Great was a murderer.

I drove Jasmine's car out to the trailer park and pulled around where we had parked before, and sure enough, there was Martha's van. I pulled in behind it and parked.

I got out, mad as hell, went over to the van and pulled the driver's door open. There wasn't anyone inside. I turned then and looked through the bushes toward the trailer park. Lightning moved to the west and flicked and flared as if it were fireworks on a vibrating string. It lit up the trailer park, made what was obvious momentarily bright and harsh.

Waldo's truck and trailer were gone. There was nothing in its spot but tire tracks.

I tore through the bushes, fought back some blackberry vines, and made the long run over to the spot where Waldo's trailer had been.

I walked around in circles like an idiot. I tried to think, tried to figure what had happened.

I made up a possible scenario: Martha and Jasmine had come out here to spy on Waldo, and maybe Waldo, who kept weird hours, had gone out, and Jasmine and Martha had seen their chance and gone in.

Perhaps Waldo turned around and came back suddenly. Realized he'd forgotten his cigarettes, his money, something like that, and he found Jasmine and Martha snooping.

And if he was a murderer, and he found them, and they had discovered incriminating evidence . . .

Then what?

What would he have done with them?

It struck me then.

The dump. To dispose of the bodies.

God, the bodies.

My stomach soured and my knees shook. I raced back through the tangled growth, back to Jasmine's car. I pulled around the van and made the circle and whipped onto the road in front of the trailer park and headed for the dump at high speed. If a cop saw me, good. Let him chase me, on out to the dump.

Drops of rain had begun to fall as I turned on the road to the dump. Lightning was criscrossing more rapidly and more heatedly than before. Thunder rumbled.

I killed the lights and eased into the dump, using the lightning flashes as my guide, and there, stretched across the dump road, blocking passage, was Waldo's trailer. The truck the trailer was fastened to was off the road and slightly turned in my direction, ready to leave the dump. I didn't see any movement. The only sounds were from the throbbing thunder and the hissing lightning. Raindrops were falling faster.

I jerked the car into park in front of the trailer and got out and ran over there, then hesitated. I looked around and spotted a hunk of wood lying in some garbage. I yanked it out and ran back to the trailer and jerked open the door. The smell of dogs was thick in the air.

Lightning flashed in the open doorway and through the thin curtains at the windows. I saw Martha lying on the floor, face down, a meat cleaver in the small of her back. I saw that the bookshelves on the wall were filled with Harlequin romances, and below them nailed onto the shelves, were strange hunks of what in the lightning flashes looked like hairy leather.

Darkness.

A beat.

Lighting flash.

I looked around, didn't see Waldo hiding in the shadows with another meat cleaver.

Darkness again.

I went over to Martha and knelt beside her, touched her shoulder. She raised her head, tried to jerk around and grab me, but was too weak. "Sonofabitch," she said.

"It's me," I said.

"Plebin," she said. "Waldo . . . nailed me a few times . . . Thinks I'm dead . . . He's got Jasmine. Tried to stop him . . . Couldn't . . . You got to. They're out . . . there."

I took hold of the cleaver and jerked it out of her back and tossed it on the floor.

"Goddamn," Martha said, and almost did a push up, but lay back down. "Could have gone all day without that . . . Jasmine. The nut's got her. Go on!"

Martha closed her eyes and lay still. I touched her neck. Still a pulse. But I couldn't do anything now. I had to find Jasmine. Had to hope the bastard hadn't done his work.

I went out of the trailer, around to the other side, looked out over the dump. The light wasn't good, but it was good enough that I could see them immediately. Jasmine, her back to me, upside down, nude, was tied to the inside of the nearest derrick, hung up like a goat for the slaughter. Waldo stood at an angle, facing her, holding something in his hand.

Lightning strobed, thunder rumbled. The poodles were running about, barking and leaping. Two of the dogs were fucking out next to the derrick, flopping tongues. The great, black, hammer head of the oil pump rose up and went down. Fires glowed from beneath debris and reflected on the metal bars of the derrick and the well pump, and when the rain hit the fires beneath the garbage they gave up white smoke and the smoke rolled in the wind like great balls of cotton, tumbled over Jasmine and Waldo and away.

Waldo swung what he had in his hand at Jasmine. Caught her across the neck with it. Her body twitched. I let out a yell that was absorbed by a sudden peal of thunder and a slash of lightning.

I started running, yelling as I went.

Waldo slashed at Jasmine again, and then he heard me yelling. He stepped to the side and stared at me, surprised. I ran up the little rise that led to the derrick before he could get it together, and as I ducked under a bar on the derrick, he dropped what he was holding.

A long paint brush.

It fell next to a can of dark paint. Rain plopped in the paint and black balls of paint flew up in response and fell down again. One of the dogs jumped the can of paint for no reason I could determine and ran off into the rain.

Jasmine made a noise like a smothered cough. Out of the corner of my eye I could see a strip of thick, grey tape across her mouth, and where Waldo had slashed her neck with the brush was a band of paint, dissolving in the rain, running down her neck, over her cheeks and into her eyes and finally her hair, like blood in a black and white movie.

Waldo reached behind his back and came back with a knife. The edge of the blade caught a flash of lightning and gave a wicked wink. Waldo's face was full of expression this time, as if he had saved all his passion for this moment.

"Come on, asshole," I said. "Come on. Cut me."

He leapt forward, very fast. The knife went out and caught me across the chest as I jumped back and hit my head on a metal runner of the derrick. I felt something warm on my chest. Shit. I hadn't really wanted him to cut me. He was a fast, little bastard.

I didn't invite him to do that again.

I cocked my piece of wood and let him get as close as I could allow without fear taking over, then I ducked under the metal runner and he ducked under it after me, poking straight out with the knife.

I swung at him, and the wood, rotten, possibly termite ridden, came apart close to my hand and went sailing and crumbling across the dump.

Waldo and I watched the chunk of wood until it hit the dirt by the derrick and exploded into a half dozen fragments.

Waldo turned his attention to me again, smiled, and came fast. I jumped backwards and my feet went out from under me and dogs yelped.

The lover mutts. I had backed over them while they were screwing. I looked up between my knees and saw the dogs turned butt to butt, hung up, and then I looked higher, and there was Waldo and his knife. I rolled and came up and grabbed a wet cardboard box of something and threw it. It struck Waldo in the chest and what was in the box flew out and spun along the wet ground. It was half a mannequin torso.

"You're ruining everything," Waldo said.

I glanced down and saw one of the mannequin legs Sam had pulled from a box and tossed. I grabbed the leg and cocked it on my shoulder like a baseball bat.

"Come on, asshole," I said. "Come on. Let's see if I can put one over the fence with you."

He went nuts then, dove for me. The knife jabbed out, fast and blurry.

I swatted. My swing hit his arm and his knife hand went wide and opened up and the knife flew into a pile of garbage and out of sight.

Waldo and I both looked at where it had disappeared.

We looked at one another. It was my turn to smile.

He staggered back and I followed, rotating the leg, trying to pick my shot.

He darted to his right, dipped, came up clutching one of the mannequin's arms. He held it by the wrist and smiled. He rotated it the way I had the bat.

We came together, leg and arm swinging. He swung at my head. I blocked with the leg and swung at his knees. He jumped the swing, kicked beautifully while airborne, hit me in the chin and knocked my head back, but I didn't go down.

Four of the poodles came out of nowhere, bouncing and barking beside us, and one of them got hold of my pants leg and started tugging. I hit at him. He yelped. Waldo hit me with the arm across the shoulder. I hit him back with the leg and kicked out and shook the poodle free.

Waldo laughed.

Another of the poodles got hold of his pants legs.

Waldo quit laughing. "Not me, you dumb ingrate!"

Waldo whacked the poodle hard with the arm. It let go, ran off a distance, whirled, took a defiant stance and barked.

I hit Waldo then. It was a good shot, clean and clear and sweet with the sound of the wind, but he got his shoulder up and blocked the blow and he only lost a bit of shirt sleeve, which popped open like a flower blossoming.

"Man, I just bought this shirt," he said.

I swung high to his head and let my body go completely around with the swing, twisting on the balls of my feet, and as I came back around, I lowered the blow and hit him in the ribs. He bellowed and tripped over something, went down and dropped his mannequin arm. Three poodles leapt on his chest and one grabbed at his ankle. Behind him, the other two were still hung up, tongues dangling happily. They were waiting for the seasons to change. The next ice age. It didn't matter. They were in no hurry.

I went after Waldo, closing for the kill. He wiped the poodles off his chest with a sweep of his arm and grabbed the mannequin arm beside him, took it by the thick end and stuck it at me as I was about to lower the boom on him. The tips of the manikin's fingers caught me in the family jewels and a moment later a pain went through me that wasn't quite as bad as being hit by a truck. But it didn't keep me from whacking him over the head with everything I had. The mannnequin leg fragmented in my hands and Waldo screamed and rolled and came up and charged me, his forehead streaked with blood, a poodle dangling from one pants leg by the teeth. The poodle stayed with him as he leaped and grabbed my legs at the knees and drove his head into my abdomen and knocked me back into a heap of smoking garbage. The smoke rose up around us and closed over us like a pod and with it came a stink that brought bile to my throat and I felt heat on my back and something sharp like glass and I yelled and rolled with Waldo and the growling poodle and out of the corner of my eye, in mid-roll, I saw another of the poodles had caught on fire in the garbage and was running about like a low flying comet. We tumbled over some more junk, and over again. Next thing I knew Waldo had rolled away and was up and over me, had hold of six-feet of two-by-four with a couple of nails hanging out of the end.

"Goodnight," Waldo said.

The board came around and the tips of the nails caught some light from the garbage fires, made them shine like animal eyes in the dark. The same light made Waldo look like the devil. Then the side of my neck exploded. The pain and shock were like things that had burrowed inside me to live. They owned me. I lay where I was, unable to move, the board hung up in my neck. Waldo tugged, but the board wouldn't come free. He put a foot on my chest and worked the board back and forth. The nails in my neck made a noise like someone trying to whistle through gapped teeth. I tried to lift a hand and grab at the board, but I was too weak. My hands fluttered at my sides as if I were petting the ground. My head wobbled back and forth with Waldo's efforts. I could see him through a blur. His teeth were clenched and spittle was foaming across his lips.

I found my eyes drifting to the top of the oil derrick, perhaps in search of a heavenly choir. Lightning flashed rose-red and sweat-stain yellow in the distance. My eyes fell back to Waldo. I watched him work. My body started trembling as if electrically charged.

Eventually Waldo worked the nails out of my neck. He stood back and took a breath. Getting that board loose was hard work. I noted in an absent kind of way that the poodle had finally let go of his ankle and had wandered off. I felt blood gushing out of my neck, maybe as much as the oil well was pumping. I thought sadly of what was going to happen to Jasmine.

My eyelids were heavy and I could hardly keep them open. A poodle came up and sniffed my face. Waldo finally got his breath. He straddled me and cocked the board and positioned his features for the strike; his face showed plenty of expression now. I wanted to kick up between his legs and hit him in the balls, but I might as well have wanted to be in Las Vegas.

"You're dog food," Waldo said, and just before he swung, my eyes started going out of focus like a movie camera on the fade, but I caught fuzzy movement behind him and there was a silver snake leaping through the air and the snake bit Waldo in the side of the head and he went away from me as if jerked aside by ropes.

My eyes focused again, slowly, and there was Martha, wobbling, holding the golf club properly, end of the swing position. She might have been posing for a photo. The striking end of the club was framed beautifully against the dark sky. I hadn't realized just how pretty her mustache was, all beaded up there in the fire light and the occasional bright throb of the storm.

Martha lowered the club and leaned on it. All of us were pretty tuckered out tonight.

Martha looked at Waldo who lay face down in the trash, not moving, his hand slowly letting loose of the two-by-four, like a dying octopus relaxing its grip on a sunken ship timber.

"Fore, motherfucker," she said, then she slid down the golf club to her knees. Blood ran out from beneath her wool cap. Things went fuzzy for me again. I closed my eyes as a red glow bloomed to my left, where Waldo's trailer was. It began to rain harder. A poodle licked my bleeding neck.

When I awoke in the hospital I felt very stiff, and I could feel that my shoulders were slightly burned. No flesh missing back there, though, just a feeling akin to mild sunburn. I weakly raised an arm to the bandage on my neck and put it down again. That nearly wore me out.

Jasmine and Martha and Sam came in shortly thereafter. Martha was on crutches and minus her wool cap. Her head was bandaged. Her mustache was clean and well groomed, as if with a toothbrush.

"How's the boy?" Sam said.

"You'd listened, could have been a lot better." I said.

"Yeah, well, the boy that cried wolf and all that," Sam said.

"Jasmine, baby," I said, "how are you?"

"I'm all right. No traumatic scars. Martha got us both out of there."

"I had to rest awhile," Martha said, "but all's well that ends well. You did nearly bleed to death."

"What about you?" I said. "You look pretty good after all that."

"Hey," Martha said, "I've got enough fat and muscle on me to take a few meat cleaver blows. He'd have done better to drive a truck over me. When he caught us sneaking around his trailer, he came up behind me and clubbed me in the head with a meat cleaver before I knew he was there, or I'd have kicked his ass into next Tuesday. After he hit me in the head he worked on me some more when I went down. He should have stuck to my head instead of pounding me in the back. That just tired me out for a while."

"Daddy, there were all kinds of horrid things in his trailer. Photographs, and . . . there were some pieces of women."

"Pussies," Martha said. "He'd tanned them. Had one on a belt. I figure he put it on and wore it now and then. One of those pervert types."

"What about old Waldo?" I asked.

"I made a hole in one on that sonofabitch," Martha said, "but looks like he'll recover. And though the trailer burned down, enough evidence survived to hang him. If we're lucky they'll give his ass the hot needle. Right, Sam?"

"That's right," Sam said.

"Whoa," I said. "How'd the trailer burn down?"

"One of the poodles caught on fire in the garbage," Jasmine said. "Poor thing. It ran back to the trailer and the door was open and it ran inside and jumped up in the bed, burned that end of the trailer up."

"Ruined a bunch of Harlequin Romances," Martha said. "Wish the little fuck had traded those in too. Might have made us a few dollars. Thing is, most of the photographs and the leather pussies survived, so we got the little shit by the balls."

I looked at Jasmine and smiled.

She smiled back, reached out and patted my shoulder. "Oh, yeah," she said, and opened her purse and took out an envelope. "This is for you. From Mama."

"Open it," I said.

Jasmine opened it and handed it to me. I took it. It was a get well card that had been sent to Connie at some time by one of her friends. She had blatantly marked out her name, and the senders name, had written under the canned sentiment printed there, "Get well, SLOWLY."

"I'm beginning to think me and your Mom aren't going to patch things us," I said.

"Afraid not," Jasmine said.

"Good reason to move then," Martha said. "I'm getting out of this one dog town. I'll level with you. I got a little inheritance I live off of. An uncle left it to me. Said in the will, since I was the ugliest one in the family, I'd need it."

"That's awful," Jasmine said. "Don't you believe that."

"The hell it's awful," Martha said. "I didn't have that money put back to live on, me and those damn books would be on the street. Ugly has its compensations. I've decided to start a book store in LaBorde, and I'm gonna open me a private investigations agency with it. Nice combo, huh? Read a little. Snoop a little. And you two, you want, can be my operatives. You full time, Plebin, and Jasmine, you can work part time while you go to college. What do you think?"

"Do we get a discount on paperbacks?" I asked.

Martha considered that. "I don't think so," she said.

"Air conditioning?"

"I don't think so."

"Let me consider it," I said.

Suddenly, I couldn't keep my eyes open.

Jasmine gently placed her hand on my arm. "Rest now," she said.

And I did.

(For Roman Ranieri)

F. Paul Wilson is best known for THE KEEP, which is a very fine horror/adventure novel that was made into one of the all time worst films ever. Not his fault. People who made it thought it would be best to film something that looked like a series of shampoo commercials strung back to back. Hollywood assholes. Go figure. May they grow like onions with their heads in the ground. Paul's a highly versatile writer who's written everything from Science Fiction to Horror to Fantasy to stage plays. And crime. Like this story.

# THE LONG WAY HOME

## F. Paul Wilson

Jack saw the whole thing. Another minute's delay in leaving for home and he'd have been a block away when it went down. And then a different man would have died on the pavement.

But Julio held him up, detailing his current bitch about all the yuppies chasing out his tavern's regular customers. He was especially irate about one who'd offered to buy the place.

"You believe that, Jack?" Julio was saying. "He wanna turn it into a bistro, man. A *bistro!*"

An incomprehensible stream of Puerto Rican followed. Which meant Julio was royally pissed. He was proud of his command of English and only under extreme provocation did he revert to his native tongue.

"He was only asking," Jack said. "What's wrong with that?"

"Because he offered me a lot of money, man. I mean a *lot* of money."

"How much?"

Julio whispered it in Jack's ear.

Right: A *lot* of money.

Jack said, "I repeat: What's wrong with that? You should be proud."

"Man, I was tempted to take it."

"No!" Jack said, genuinely shaken. "Don't say that, Julio. Don't even think it."

"I couldn't help thinking it. But I tol' him to get lost. I mean, I like money as much as the next guy, man, but I'll only risk so much for it." He jerked a thumb over his shoulder at the motley collection of scruffy locals leaning on the bar behind him. "You know what those guys would do to me if I sold out to a yuppie? I'd have to run for my life!"

"You may still have to if Maria finds out how much you turned down."

"Don't tell her. Don't breathe a word, man."

"Your secret's safe with me."

Jack left with his cold six-pack of Rolling Rock long necks and turned the corner onto Amsterdam Avenue, heading south. Quiet on the Upper West Side tonight. A lot of the restaurants were closed on Monday nights—a fair number had locked their doors for good in the past couple of years—and it was too cold for a casual stroll. Jack had the street pretty much to himself.

The area was changing again, but gradually. Nothing like the hurtling gentrification of the early eighties. He'd survived that, watching his ethnically and socioeconomically mixed neighborhood homogenize into an all-white, upper-income enclave, the mom-and-pop grocery stores and bodegas metamorphose into gourmet delis, the neighborhood taverns into brasseries and bistros, and his rent triple. Then the October 1987 crash. A lot of worried stock brokers, investment bankers, and junk-bond pushers on the Upper West Side. The bubble they'd created had burst. Gentrification stumbled, then lurched to a halt. Now there was retreat and retrenchment. Empty storefronts where sidewalk cafés and over-priced shoppes—always spelled with the extra "*-pe*"—and boutiques had flourished, but not a disaster area by any stretch. There was still lots of money being made by the survivors, and money to be made off them, but the euphoria of the go-go eighties was gone, existing only in wistful reminiscences around the tables of the latest local hot spot—like Julio's.

At the next corner Jack spotted a blue-and-white parked by the fire hydrant in front of Costin's. His first instinct was to turn and walk the other way, but that might be a little too obvious. So he stayed on course.

Waiting on the curb for a car to pass, he did a quick scan of the scene. Quiet. Only one cop in the unit, in the passenger seat, looking relaxed. His partner was atop the short run of stone steps that led up to the front door to Costin's. In the light that shone through the front window, Jack noticed how young the cop looked. Baby-faced. Probably heading for the teething biscuits.

Costin's had been there forever—a prototype of the convenience store. Now it was one of the last mom-and-pops this far south. Old Costin had to stay open all hours just to meet the rent. The locals left over from the old days remained loyal, and most of the cops from the 20th Precinct stopped in regularly to help keep them going.

Jack was halfway across the street when he heard a boom. He knew that sound. Shotgun. Instinctively he ducked behind the nearest parked car on the far side. The sound had been muffled. An indoor shot.

Shit. Costin's.

He set the six-pack down and peeked over the hood. The cop was out of the unit's passenger seat now and on the sidewalk, drawing his pistol. Just then the door to Costin's burst open and a giant of a man leapt onto the top step. He stood six-six at least and looked completely bald under the flat black leather cap squeezed onto the top of his head; the loose sweatsuit he wore only emphasized the massive, bulked-up frame within. He was snarling, his shiny black features contorted in rage. He held a sawed-off ten-gauge pump-action against his hip, aimed down at the cop.

In the clear air, lit by the mercury vapor lamps lining the block, the scene had an unreal look, like something out of a movie.

The cop raised his pistol, giving warning, going by the book.

"Drop it or I'll—"

He never got to finish the sentence. The big guy barely blinked as he pulled the trigger.

The left side of the cop's face and neck exploded red. His pistol flew from his hand as he was spun to his left and onto the hood of the unit. He left a wet, red smear as he slid across the hood on his chest. He rolled over the grille and landed on the asphalt in front of the bumper, flat on his back, twitching.

The big black guy's face changed as soon as the cop went down. The snarl melted into a smile, but the rage was still there, hiding in the teeth he showed. Casually laying the shotgun across his shoulder, he approached the cop like a gardener strolling toward a cabbage patch with his hoe.

"Well, Mr. Man In Blue," he said, standing over the moaning cop. "How's it feel to bleed?"

The cop couldn't speak. Even from down the street Jack could see the blood pumping from his neck. Another sixty seconds and he'd be history.

Jack found himself on the move before he knew it, his sneakers whispering along the pavement as he raced down the sidewalk in a crouch, watching the scene through the windows of the parked cars he kept between himself and the other side of the street.

A voice inside urged him the other way. Cops were the enemy, a threat to his own existence. *This isn't your fight—butt out.* But another, deeper part of him overruled the voice and made him pull the Semmerling from his ankle holster. Still in a crouch, he started across the street.

"You know," the big black was saying, "I could let you bleed some more and make a bigger puddle, and pretty soon you'd be just as dead as if I blowed your head off." He grinned as he worked the pump on the sawed-off. A red and brass cartridge arced into the street. "But somehow that wouldn't be the same."

He leveled the truncated barrel into the cop's face.

"Forget it," Jack said as he came up behind him. He had the Semmerling pointed at the back of the guy's head. "You've done enough for one night."

The guy glanced over his shoulder. When his eyes lit on the Semmerling, he smiled.

"Ain't never been threatened with a pop gun before."

"Just drop the hog and take off," Jack said.

"You mean you ain't gonna arrest me?"

Jack had acted on impulse without really thinking this out. At the moment, the best course seemed to be to get rid of the shooter and call an ambulance for the cop. Then disappear.

"One more time," Jack said. "Drop it and go."

"You kiddin' me, man?" the guy said, his voice jumping an octave. "I could take a couple of slugs from that pop gun and sit down for breakfast."

"It's a Semmerling L-4," Jack said. "World's smallest forty-five."

The gunman paused.

"Oh. Well, in that case—"

The guy ducked to his right as he made a hard swing with the shotgun, trying to bring it to bear on Jack. Jack corrected his aim and pulled the trigger. The Semmerling boomed and bucked in his hand. The gunman's right eye socket became a black hole and his leather cap spun away like a frisbee. His head was haloed in red mist as it jerked back with enough force to yank his feet off the pavement. The sawed-off tumbled from his hand and skittered along the sidewalk as he sprawled back on the pavement and flopped around until his body got the message that what litle remained of the brain was mush. Then he lay still.

Jack knelt beside the fallen cop. He looked like hell. The mercury light further blanched the deathly pallor of his face. Eyes glazing, going fast. Where the hell was old man Costin? Where was the cop's partner? Why wasn't anyone around to call an ambulance? Jack felt naked and exposed out here on the street, but he couldn't take off now.

He switched the Semmerling to his left hand, located the spot in the fallen cop's throat that was doing the most pumping, and jammed his thumb into it. The flesh was wet and hot and sticky. He'd read novel after novel that mentioned the coppery smell of blood. He didn't get it. He'd never known copper to have an odor worth mentioning, and if it did, it sure as hell didn't smell like this.

Jack was about to look around again for help when he heard footsteps behind him.

"All right! Hold it right there, you fucker!"

Jack turned his head and saw a uniformed cop crouched on his right, taking two-handed aim at his head with a .38. Another blue-and-white was blocking the street behind him.

Jack's gut looped into a knot and pulled tight.

"I'm holding it," he said.

"Drop the gun and put your hands up!"

Jack dropped the Semmerling and raised his left hand.

"C'mon!" the cop said. "Both of them!"

"This guy's already half dead," Jack said. "If I take my hand off this pumper, he'll go the rest of the way in no time."

"Christ!" the cop said, then shouted: "Jerry—you make the call?"

"Ambulance and back-up on the way," said a voice from the unit.

"All right. See who's down."

Another uniform dashed out of the darkness behind the first cop and stopped within half a dozen feet of Jack. He squinted at the ruined face above Jack's hand.

"Oh, Jeez, it's Carella!"

"Shit!" said the first cop. He spoke through clenched teeth as he glared at Jack. "You dirty—"

"Hey-hey!" Jack said. "Let's get something straight here. I didn't shoot your pal here."

"Just shut the fuck up! You think I'm stupid?"

Jack bit back an affirmative and jerked his head toward the guy on the sidewalk.

"He did it."

Apparently the cop hadn't seen the other body until now. He jumped to his feet.

"Oh, great. Just great."

The second cop, the one called Gerry, eased around to the sidewalk and checked out the body.

"This one's cooling," he said. "Head wound." He whistled. "Looks like a hot load."

"And I suppose you had nothing to do with that, either?" the first cop said.

"No. Him I did. But there was another cop. He went into Costin's. There was a shot, and then this guy—"

"Jeez!" Gerry said. "The kid was with Carella!"

"See if he's all right!" the first cop said.

Gerry dashed up the stairs and grabbed the door handle. As he pulled it open, a voice screamed from within.

"Stay back! I got your buddy and the owner in here! Stay back or I'll kill 'em both!"

Gerry scuttled back down the steps.

"We got a hostage situation here, Fred," he said.

"He's got the kid!" Fred said. "God *damn!* Call the hostage team. *Now!*"

As Gerry ran off, an emergency rig howled down the street and screeched to a halt. Jack explained to the EMTs what had happened and why he had his thumb sunk an inch into the wounded man's neck. One of the techs pulled on a rubber glove and substituted his finger for Jack's. He held it there as the wounded cop was lifted onto a stretcher.

Jack watched for a second, then began to edge backward, preparing to slide between two parked cars.

"No, you don't!" Fred the cop said, jerking his pistol up level with Jack's head. "You ain't goin' nowhere! Hands on the car and spread 'em!"

Desperation gnawed on Jack's spine as his eyes hunted for an escape route. There were uniforms all around now, and they all seemed to be watching him. Slowly he forced his lead-filled limbs to move, slapping his hands against the hood of the patrol car, spreading his feet. He held up okay during the frisk, but he almost lost it when his hands were yanked behind his back and the cuffs squeezed around his wrists.

Cops, arrest, cuffs, interrogation, investigation, fingerprinting, exposure, court, lawyers, judges, jail—a recurrent nightmare for most of his adult life.

Tonight it was real.

"You sure you don't want a lawyer?"

Jack looked up at the 20th Precinct's chief of detectives, Lieutenant Thomas Carruthers. Forty-ish, wearing a rumpled suit and no tie—a thrown-on set of clothes. Tall, dark, and handsome. Every woman's crystal-ball dream. Jack's nightmare.

"Yeah. I'm sure," Jack said.

"Say it again. I want to make sure I've got it on the tape."

Jack directed his voice toward the tape recorder nearby on the battered oak table between him and Carruthers.

"I'm sure I don't want a lawyer. At least not yet."

Jack did want a lawyer. Very badly. But he didn't know any, at least any he could trust. And the first thing a lawyer would tell him was to keep his mouth shut. He didn't want to do that. These cops thought he'd shot one of their own. Things could get nasty here at the precinct house if he clammed up completely.

A nightmare. Booked, photographed, and worst of all, fingerprinted. He'd wanted to throw an epileptic fit when they'd coated his fingers in ink and began rolling the tips on that white card. But what would that do other than delay the inevitable?

With or without a lawyer he was screwed. If they didn't get him for killing the cop, and if he was't prosecuted for killing the guy with the shotgun, he'd still be up for possession of an unregistered firearm. Plus his cover would be permanently blown. Years of hiding in the cracks, of forging an existence in the interstices of society would be wiped away. And then the IRS would get involved, wondering why this man had no Social Security number. They'd begin investigating every nook and cranny of his entire 1040-less life.

And then the shit would really hit the fan.

Jack knew he was facing time. Hard time, soft time, state time, Fed time, it didn't matter. He was going inside, no doubt for a long stretch.

Jack had sworn he'd never do time. And he wouldn't.

"Good," Carruthers said, spreading a selection of Jack's I-Ds on the table between them. "Maybe now you can tell me what's all this bullshit?"

Jack stared at the contents of his wallet and felt the walls of the interrogation room close in on him. He said nothing.

"So who the hell are you?"

"The name's Jack."

"I gathered that." He picked up the I-D cards and shuffled through them. "Jack Berger, Jack Callahan, Jack Menella, Jack Jones"—Carruthers glanced up at him on that one—"and Jack Schwartz. So yeah, I guess your first name is Jack. But what's the rest?"

"Jack will have to do, I'm afraid."

Carruthers shot forward, leaning over the table, eyes ablaze.

"It won't do at *all*, scumbag! One of our guys is in surgery fighting for his life and another's a hostage and you're up to your neck in it. So Jack ain't gonna cut it!"

Jack didn't flinch; gave back a glare of his own.

"If I hadn't come by, Mr. Detective, your guy in surgery never would've make it *to* surgery. You'd still be scraping his brains off the street. But maybe I should've kept walking. If I had I wouldn't be cuffed up here looking at you right now. Would you be happier if I'd done that? I know I would."

Carruthers stared at Jack. For an instant, he seemed unsure of himself. As he opened his mouth to reply, another detective, a sergeant named Evans who'd been through a couple of times before, popped into the room again.

Evans had brought Jack into the interrogation room, and had been none too gentle getting him seated. A big guy—his jacket sleeves were tight. Jack had no doubt that if it had been up to Evans, he'd take Jack out in the nearest alley and kick him to death. Slowly.

But the cold light was gone from Evans' eyes as he glanced Jack's way on entering.

Carruthers stiffened at the sight of him.

"What's up, Charlie? Any news?"

Evans shook his head. "Not really. Nothing bad, anyway. No more shots. The hostage team's made phone contact. They're trying to talk the guy down. Sounds really wired. Don't worry, Tom. They'll get him out."

Carruthers nodded absently. "Yeah. How's Carella?"

"Still in surgery as far as I know. Piacentino called from the Eighteenth. Says if there's anything you need—"

"Tell him we're okay, but thanks for asking." After a pause, Carruthers said, "That it?"

"Nope. Got an I-D on the dead guy. A prelim from the M.E. too."

"So who is he?"

"You mean who *was* he. Abdul Khambatta, born Harvey Andrews. Out of Attica two months after a stretch for armed robbery. His sheet's as long as my leg. One bad-news mother."

"What's the M.E. say?"

"No surprises. Single head shot. A pre-frag in the eye."

Carruthers winced. "Ouch."

"Yeah. M.E. said if the guy ever had a brain, you couldn't prove it by him. Matches up with the three rounds left in our mystery man's pop-gun."

Carruthers glanced at Jack. "Which isn't registered, of course."

"You got it."

"How do we know the Semmerling belongs to him?"

"His prints are the only ones on it."

"And the sawed-off?"

"Andrews'. 'Scuse me—Khambatta's. Thing's lousy with his prints." He jerked a thumb at Jack. "I think we owe this guy."

"Yeah? Maybe."

Jack watched for some sign of relaxation from Carruthers but saw nothing. The lieutenant stayed wound tight as ever.

Carruthers said, "You ever meet anybody with five I-Ds who was straight, Charlie? If he's not dirty on this he's dirty on something else."

"So?" Evans did not seem impressed.

"I want to know: Who *is* this guy?"

"Tell you one thing, Tom: His prints aren't on file anywhere. And I mean *anywhere.*"

"How come I'm not surprised?"

"I got a better question," Evans said. "How come you're here and not over at Costin's?"

Carruthers walked to the window and stared out at the night, saying nothing.

"I'll take over at this end," Evans said. "You should be there."

Carruthers shook his head, still staring out the window.

"I'll go nuts over there. The hostage team knows what to do. I'll just get in the way, maybe even screw things up."

"No you won't. Why don't—"

"Thanks, Charlie," he said, turning quickly and flashing him a tight smile. "I appreciate the thought, but let's drop it. Okay?"

Evans shrugged. "Okay. But if you change your mind . . ."

Carruthers nodded. "Yeah. I know."

When Evans was gone, Carruthers returned to the table and shifted through Jack's I-Ds again.

"Prefragmented rounds?" he said. "What's the matter? You got something against wounding a guy?"

Jack said nothing. Truth was, he'd been loaded for indoor work. And in general, he didn't like to have to shoot someone twice.

Suddenly Carruthers stiffened.

"I'll be damned!" He picked up the I-Ds and flipped through them again. "Christ! It all fits!"

As Carruthers stared down at him, eyes wide, Jack felt his chest tighten, wondering what he'd found.

"Jesus! I always thought you were make believe. For years I've been catching a word here and there about this guy who hires out for all sorts of jobs, anything from kinda shady to out and out, down and dirty illegal. But when I ask about it, I get blank stares, dumb grins, and shrugs. So I figure it's one of these New York City myths, like the giant alligators in the sewers. But shit! You're him! You're Repairman Jack!"

Jack's throat went dry, giving his voice a croaky sound.

"Who's he?"

"Don't play cute. You're him. Gotta be. Jesus, I don't believe this. I never thought you were real." He looked down at the pile of phony I-Ds in his hand. "And I guess you aren't. At least not officially, huh?"

"I don't know what you're talking about."

"Yeah. Right. You know, I'm thinking. If memory serves, some of the stuff I heard about you was pretty good, some of it wasn't. And what wasn't came from scumbags. But all of it sounded pretty rough. So I take it you're a rough character, Repairman Jack. One with a Robin Hood complex or something. A guy like that can be dangerous."

"And who are you?" Jack said. "The Sheriff of Nottingham?"

While Carruthers mulled that, Jack pulled inside himself and fought the sick dread growing in his gut. Identified as Repairman Jack: this nightmare was deteriorating into a hell ride. He had to get out of here.

Jack considered that. If he could get close enough to Carruthers, even handcuffed, he might be able to do something. Anything. A crazy thought, but he was as good as dead if he stayed in custody, so he didn't see how anything he tried could make matters worse.

"Yeah, well, whatever," Carruthers was saying. He had that worried, distracted look again. "What are we going to do with you, Repairman Jack?"

"How about letting me go?"

Carruthers offered him a small, pursed-lips smile. "Right."

"I did one of yours a favor, so now you do me a favor. Quid pro quo."

Jack knew his request was useless, but he wanted to keep Carruthers talking, get him relaxed, maybe a bit careless.

"Don't bullshit me, pal. The only one who says he helped Carella is you. How do I know you and Andrews and whoever's still holed up in Costin's weren't together on this job?"

"Forget it!" Jack said, genuinely insulted. "Boosting a mom-and-pop?"

"Why not? Maybe business is slow. You operate on their level, Mr. Repairman Jack. You're an unknown quantity. You're capable of anything as far as I'm concerned. So maybe Andrews did shoot Carella and maybe you two had a falling out over who was gonna get his service revolver, or who was going to finish him off. So you shot Andrews."

"Sure. And then I tried to finish off your friend by clamping down on that artery in his neck." Jack lifted his cuffed wrists and wiggled the fingers of his right hand. "Here. Take a look. I've still got his blood under my fingernails."

Carruthers stared at Jack's hand but didn't move.

"Come on," Jack said. *Get close . . . real close.* "See for yourself."

Carruthers shook his head. "Maybe you knew you were about to get caught and were just putting on a show."

Jack dropped his hands. "You're all heart."

"Hey," Carruthers said, scowling. "Even if I wanted to let you go—which I don't—it's out of the question."

"We're not just talking about me losing my *way* of life here," Jack said. "We're talking about my *life.* Put me in the spotlight and I'm a dead man. I've made a lot of enemies over the years. I can handle them fine by myself out on the street, but put me in the joint and every slimeball and two-bit wise guy with a grudge who's got a friend inside will be gunning for me. All for helping out a cop."

Evans barged in the door then, grinning.

"Carella's out of surgery! Gonna be okay!"

Carruthers leaned back and closed his eyes. "Thank God!"

"And you know what he says? Some citizen saved his life—blew away the guy who was gonna off him."

The big sergeant looked at Jack and winked.

After a protracted pause, Carruthers opened his eyes, rose from the chair, and went to the window to do his staring routine.

"Our suspect here thinks we should let him go and forget he was ever in custody."

"What suspect?" Evans said, looking around the room. "I don't see no suspect. I don't remember booking anybody tonight. Do you?"

Another long pause, with Jack holding his breath the whole time.

"Check the files," Carruthers said without turning. "See if there's any unaccounted-for paperwork or property out there, and bring it in."

"You got it."

Evans gave Jack a thumbs-up as he left the room.

Jack sat quietly, watching Carruthers' back. He said nothing, fearing to break the spell of unreality that had taken control of the room.

Evans was back in no time with a brown folder and a manila envelope.

"Here's all of it," he said as Carruthers joined him at the table. "Personal property, print cards, booking sheets, photos, and miscellaneous paperwork referring to some suspect I've never heard of."

"Unlock him."

As Evans keyed the cuffs open, Carruthers scooped up Jack's array of I-D and dropped it in the envelope. He slid the folder and envelope across the table to Jack.

"Sergeant Evans will take you out the back."

Jack's legs were rubbery as he stood. He could barely speak.

"I don't—"

"Damn right, you don't," Carruthers said, looking him in the eyes. "You don't know me and I don't know you. And you don't *owe* me and I don't owe you. This is it. We're even. I don't want to see or hear of you again. And if I do see you and you're so much as jaywalking, I'll pull you in. We clear on that?"

"Yeah. And thanks."

"No, thanks, dammit! Just evening up. You didn't have to do what you did but you did; I don't have to do what I'm doing, but I am. Like you said: Quid pro quo. This for that. Now get out of my sight."

Jack got. He followed Evans out to the bgack of the precinct house.

"Not easy for him to do this," Evans said along the way. "He's a real straight arrow."

"So I gather."

Jack understood what Carruthers was going through in overcoming a career's worth of conditioning, and he appreciated it. He stopped at the back door and faced Evans.

"He thinks we're even but we're not. I owe him. I'll give you a number. If there's ever anything I can do for him—"

"Too bad you can't get his kid brother out of Costin's."

The shock pushed Jack back a step into the alley.

"The hostage cop is Carruthers' brother?"

"Yeah. Patrolman Louis Carruthers. Twenty years old. Got any miracles in your pocket?"

Jack suddenly remembered something Julio had showed him in the basement of his tavern.

"You never know."

He turned and hurried toward the street.

Downstairs, ten feet below the bar, past the cases of booze and kegs of beer, an old hutch stood against the wall. The glass was long gone, and a thick layer of dust hid the scars in the warped mahogany veneer.

Jack coughed and grunted as he and Julio slid it away from the wall.

"See?" Julio said, pointing to the rectangular opening in the brick. "It's still there."

Costin's backed up against Julio's. Years ago Jack had asked Julio if there was an emergency escape route from the tavern. Julio had brought him down here and shown him the old airshaft that ran up from his basement.

"Refresh me on this. Where does it go?"

Julio handed him the flashlight and smiled.

"It goes up. After that, I don' know. Never wanted to find out. You're gonna be the first guy in there since I bought the place."

Jack poked his head and shoulders into the shaft and shone the flash upward. Crumbling brickwork, cobwebs, and an inky blackness that devoured the beam of light. The basement of Costin's was only a few feet away. Maybe the shaft could get him there.

"If this is an airshaft," Jack said, "how come I don't feel any airflow?"

"Because about fifty years ago, somebody who owned this end of the block covered all the buildings with a single roof. Probably a dead end. You're wasting your time, man. 'Sides, it's not like you to get involved in this kinda thing."

"I owe somebody a try."

Jack tied a string around the neck of the flashlight, looped the rest of the length around his neck, and let the light dangle over his sternum where the beam splashed up over his face. A miner's lamp hat would have been better but this would have to do. He pulled on a pair of heavy work gloves.

"Hang around, okay? In case I get stuck."

Julio seated himself on some cases of Budweiser.

"Don' worry. I'll be right here."

Jack took a deep breath, let it all out, and squeezed through the opening. He hated tight places. Especially *dark* tight places. He straightened up inside the rectangular shaft. The crumbling brick surface was rough and craggy. He braced his hands against the wall along the wide axis of the shaft, dug the side of one of his sneakers into one of the countless little crevices, and began to climb.

A long climb. A three-story struggle, with a long, maiming impact lurking below, hungering for a slip. And above—the very real possibility of finding the upper end of the shaft sealed.

But it wasn't. Jack reached the top and found a two-foot gap between the roof and the last of the bricks. Directly to his right, mated side by side to this one, was another shaft. Hopefully leading to Costin's.

Jack slid over the top of one and into the other. He had a bad moment when his sneakers began to slip, but he hung by his hands till his feet found purchase. Then he began the long descent, dragging his denimed butt against the brickwork as an extra brake. The trip down was quicker. He was glad he'd thought of the gloves. Without them his hands would have been raw meat by now.

When he reached bottom, he stood perfectly still and let his ears adjust.

Quiet.

He turned on the flashlight and checked out the base of the shaft. The opening was at knee level and blocked with a smooth brown surface. Jack nudged it with his foot and it gave easily. Cardboard. With the flashlight off again, he knelt and inched back the stack of cartons that formed the barrier. He peeked into the basement: empty, cavelike darkness. He listened again. Someone upstairs in the store was talking—shouting—in a high-pitched voice. Even through the floor Jack could feel the hysterical edge on that voice. Only one voice. Probably Khambatta's partner talking on the phone to the hostage team.

Jack squeezed through the opening and stood up. From this angle he could make out a faint sliver of light high up and off to his right. Had to be a doorway. He pulled the flashlight free of the string and flicked it on and off, just long enough to find a clear path. The basement was piled high with stock. Straight across the floor was a set of steps. Jack drew the Semmerling and slid through the dark.

As he neared the other end he flicked the flash off and on again. And froze.

Someone was on the stairs.

Jack waited, listening for movement, for breathing. Nothing. Just an occasional squeak of the floorboards above. And something else. Whoever was up there had stopped talking and was making another sound. Jack cocked an ear toward the ceiling. It sounded almost like . . . sobbing.

But who was on the stairs?

Jack turned on the flashlight and trained it straight ahead. A man was sprawled there, head down, one arm flung out, the other under him, legs splayed, eyes wide, staring. Very still. And wet. The front of his uniform glistened a deeper blue where a thick, dark fluid had soaked through it. His throat was a ruin and half of his lower jaw had been torn away. But deathly white and upside down though it was, enough of the face was left undamaged for Jack to catch the resemblance to Lieutenant Carruthers.

"The kid." Louis.

"Son of a bitch!" Jack said aloud.

Another throat shot. Same style as Khambatta's: aim high in case the cop was wearing a vest.

Jack slipped the Semmerling into his pocket and stretched a hand toward the Louis' forehead. No question that he was dead, but Jack needed to touch him. To be absolutely sure.

The skin felt dry and thick and cold. "The kid" was very dead.

Cold black anger surged up in him. Twenty years old, stopping by Costin's for a late-night snack, and getting blown away.

"Son of a *bitch!*"

Jack straightened and turned the flashlight off.

What next? He'd come here as a payback, to see if he could get Carruthers' brother out of this jam. But the kid was beyond help. So there was nothing left for him to do.

Except maybe settle a score on the lieutenant's behalf.

But old man Costin was upstairs somewhere. Jack had known Costin since moving to the city. He didn't like to think of the old guy held hostage, maybe face-down on the floor, shivering with terror. But he could back away from that. He didn't *owe* Costin—not enough to risk exposure by making a move on the remaining gunman. Better all around to leave old Costin's fate in the hands of the hostage team.

It was time to fade away.

Jack was turning toward the rear when the door above slammed open and a wide shaft of fluorescent light pinned him like a frog on a log. A high male voice began screeching at him.

"Hold it, muthafucka! Hold it or I'll blow you away just like I did him!"

Jack turned slowly and saw a wide silhouette in the doorway. He showed his flashlight and his empty right hand.

"I'm not armed."

Jack was glad he had only the tiny Semmerling. It lay flat in his pocket.

"Yeah, right. An' I'm Ice-T. You a cop, fucka. An' you was tryin' to sneak up on me."

"I'm no cop. And I was just leaving."

"The fuck you was. There ain't no door down here. I checked already."

"If you say so." Jack waved his empty hand. "Bye!"

Jack dove into the darkness to his right, rolled to his feet, and ducked behind a stack of canned goods. As a stream of curses erupted from the stairwell, he pulled out the Semmerling and crept toward the rear. Behind him he heard some fumbling against the wall, then a click and the cellar lights came on—a few dim, widely spaced naked incandescent bulbs set among the ceiling beams. Jack got his first look at the guy as he rushed down the steps, nearly tripping over his feet in his haste.

He had one of those tower haircuts—a four-inch stack rising above close-shaved sidewalls—and he was fat. No more than five-eight, but at least three-hundred pounds. Baby-faced with huge cheeks and tiny dark eyes barely visible above them. His black skin glistened with sweat. *Fat.* Not brawny fat, not hard fat. Jello fat that lurched and rolled around his middle as he moved. The sawed-off shotgun he carried looked like a toy in his pudgy fingers.

"Ain't no use in hiding, fucka. Ain't no way outta here."

*Then how'd I get in?* Jack thought, wondering when that notion would strike Fatso.

He stayed low, listening as the guy moved through the dimly lit cellar like a bull, knocking over stacks of cans, smashing cases of bottles. The odor of gherkins began to filter through the air. Jack wondered how long it would take Fatso to find the opening.

From the rear of the cellar: "Shee-*it!*"

He'd found it.

And then as Jack crouched and waited, he heard a frantic scratching, scrabbling sound, like Gregory Hines on speed doing a softshoe routine to Metallica. Coming from the airshaft entry. Jack crawled over to investigate.

Fatso was there. He had his head and one shoulder rammed into the airshaft opening and was trying to squeeze the rest of his body through. He grunted and groaned as his Reeboked feet scraped madly on the dusty floor in a desperate effort to force his way in. But it wasn't happening. He was a bowling ball trying to drop into a billiard pocket. No way.

Finally, he gave up. Panting, gasping, retching with the exertion, he pulled himself free and slumped to the floor where he cradled his sawed-off shotgun in his lap and began to cry.

Jack was standing over him by now, but for a moment or so he could only stare and listen to the guy sob. Pitiful. He'd wanted to pop the guy. But now . . .

"Okay, Fatso. Cut the blubbering and get up—*without* the shotgun."

Fatso started and looked up at Jack, at the Semmerling, and got to his feet. But the shotgun still hung from his hand.

"I said drop the sawed-off or you're dead."

"Go ahead," he said, sniffling but still clutching the stock grip. "I'm good as dead already."

"For blowing away a cop—yeah, I guess you are."

"Didn't kill no cop." He was sulky now.

"That's not what you told me a couple of minutes ago."

"That was Abdul. He did it. He didn't have to shoot. He had the drop on the guy, but he just pulled the trigger and liked to took his head off."

That jibed with Jack's take on young Carruthers' neck wound. He tasted his saliva turning bitter.

"Swell. He was only twenty. A little younger than you, I figure."

"I didn't do it, man!"

"Doesn't matter who pulled the trigger. You're a part of a felony where a killing's gone down. Automatic murder-one for you."

"I knew you was a cop."

"I already told you—I'm not a cop. Don't have to be a cop to know you're heading for big time in the slammer."

His fat lips quivered. "Already done that."

He lifted the shotgun and Jack ducked to his right, his finger tightening on the Semmerling's trigger. But the sawed-off barrel kept on rising till the bore was snug against the underside of Fatso's chin. Jack cringed, waiting for the boom and brain-splatter.

It never came. A sob burst through Fatso's lips as he dropped the weapon back to his side and slumped to the floor again.

"I can't *do* it!" he screeched through clenched teeth.

Jack said nothing. He was speechless before this utterly miserable creature.

"I can't hack the joint again, man," Fatso moaned. "I *can't!*"

"What'd you go in for?"

"Dealing."

"Swell. How about old man Costin—the owner? He okay?"

Fatso nodded. "Locked him in the crapper."

"What's your name?"

"Henry. Henry Thompson. They call me Fat Henry."

*I wonder why?*

"The joint—is that where you met Khambatta?"

Fat Henry nodded again. "He was on the back end of three-to-five when I got in. We became . . . friends."

"You two don't seem to be each other's type."

"He protected me."

Jack nodded. Suddenly it was all clear.

"I see."

"No, man. You don't see," Fat Henry said, his voice rising. "You don't see *shit!* You don't know what it was like in there! I was *tail* meat! Guys'd be lined up in the shower to get at me! I wanted to *die!*"

"And Khambatta saved you."

Fat Henry let out a tremulous sigh. "Yeah. Sort of. He took me in. Protected me."

"Made you his property so he could have you all to himself."

"I ain't like that, man! I just did what I hadda to get through it! Don't you dump on me if you ain't been there!"

Jack only shook his head. He didn't know how many things were worth dying over, but he was pretty sure that was one of them. And he didn't know what to make of Fat Henry. He was one pathetic son of a bitch, but he wasn't a killer. He was going to be treated as one, though—a cop killer.

"So how come you're still with Khambatta?"

"I ain't. He ain't like that, either—least not outside. We got out about the same time and he call me last week about picking up some quick cash."

"Swell. What you picked up instead was another jolt in the joint."

"No way I'm goin' back inside! I'm getting outta here."

"How?"

"Gettin' a car from the cops."

"You sure about that? What've you told them about their dead pal?"

"Nothing. Told them he's safe and sound but that I'll shoot him dead if they make a move on me."

"You really think they're going to let you have a car without talking to their man, without making sure he's all right?"

"Yeah. Sure." Fat Henry's voice faltered. "They gotta. Don't they?"

Jack shook his head, slowly, deliberately. "Switch places: Would you let you have a car?"

"I ain't goin' back." Tears began to stream down his face. "I'll off myself first!"

"You already tried that."

Fat Henry glared at him. Again he lifted the shotgun. Jack thought he was going to put it under his jaw again; instead he offered it to Jack.

"Here. You do it."

Jack took the weapon and sniffed the bore. It hadn't been fired tonight. He was almost tempted to aim it at Fat Henry's face to see how serious he was about this, but decided against it. Instead, he worked the pump, sending red and brass cylinders tumbling through the gloom one after another until they were scattered on the floor like party favors. He tossed the empty shotgun back to Fat Henry. Hard.

"Do your own dirty work."

"You fucker!"

Thoroughly fed up, Jack stepped over him toward the airshaft opening.

"And I'm not hanging around listening to you blubber."

"I need help, man." He was whining now.

"No argument there. But there's only one person here who can help you and he's sitting on the floor whining."

"Fuck you!"

Jack had one leg through the opening. He turned and jabbed a finger at Fat Henry.

"You're the one who's fucked, Fatso. Look at your life! What've you ever done with it? You got busted selling crack—probably to kids, right? You let yourself be the shower room bimbo until some tough guy came along and made you his private tool. You went along on this armed robbery bullshit, and now somebody's dead and you're bawling 'cause it's time to pay the piper.

You make me sick!"

Another whine. "But what can I *do?*"

"First of all, you can get off your ass and on your feet."

Fat Henry rolled over and struggled to his feet.

"Good," Jack said. "That's a start. Now you've got to go upstairs and face the music."

He stepped back. "No."

"Either they take you up there, or they come down those stairs, step over the body of their buddy, and take you here."

"I told you. I can't go back to the joint!"

"You've got to stand up, Henry Thompson. For once in your life you've got to stand up."

"But I *can't!*"

Jack stared him down in the silence that followed.

"Then sit here all night and play with yourself until somebody else makes the choice for you. That seems to be the story of your life, Henry."

Fat Henry looked toward the steps up to the first floor. He stood like a statue, staring.

"I can choose," he said in a soft, far-away voice. "I can choose. I'll show you I can choose."

"Sure you can, Henry."

Jack left him like that.

A little while later Jack was out on the street, standing on the fringe of the crowd. He wanted to tell the vultures to go home, that it was going to be a *long* night. He was about to leave for home himself when Fat Henry came out.

Costin's front door slammed open and there he was, all three-hundred pounds of him, brandishing his shotgun and screaming like a wild man. He got off one blast that looked like it was aimed at the moon. All around Jack the crowd screamed and dove for cover, leaving him standing alone as the two-dozen cops out front opened up.

The fusillade slammed Fat Henry back against the door frame, his sawed-off went spinning, and then he was turning and falling and rolling down the steps. It was over in seconds. No Peckinpah slo-mo. No ballet-like turns. Quick, graceless, ugly, and red. He hit the sidewalk face first and never moved again.

Fat Henry Thompson had finally stood up. And he'd got his wish: He wouldn't be going back to Attica.

Jack turned and walked away, stepping over the prone onlookers as they peeked between their fingers and made horrified noises. As he headed home he tried to put his finger on the feelings massed in his chest like a softball-sized lump of putty—*cold* putty. Not sadness, certainly not glee or satisfaction. More of a bleakness. A dark despair for all the hardcore losers in this city, the ones it created and the others it attracted.

He passed a corner litter basket and gave it a hard kick, adding an especially deep dent to its already bruised flanks.

A waste. A damn stupid fruitless futile ass-brained waste.

When he got to his door he realized he didn't have his beer. The six-pack he'd gone out for earlier in the evening was long gone from where he'd left it sitting on the curb across the street from Costin's. He could really use a Rolling Rock about now. And he could probably find an all-night deli to where he could buy some.

*Nah.*

Jack stepped inside and locked the door behind him.

He couldn't risk it. The way things were going tonight, he might not make it home again.

Neal Barrett, Jr. is incredible. This guy is one of the best writers we have. He's original, whacky, and there's not a writer in any of the genres, category, mainstream, literary, that can hold a candle to him. This guy's the king. If you don't believe me, read his most recent novel THE HEREAFTER GANG. And until you do, warm up with the following story.

# HIT

## Neal Barrett, Jr.

Artie thinks the bar was a bad idea. The place has got a 40-watt bulb, it's got sawdust on the floor. The juke plays greaser hit tunes. Pig set up the meet with this guy Jimmy Sims and Pig picked the place out, which sounded okay at the time because the dump is on the Houston ship channel and no one anybody knew is going to drop in for a beer. A cop, a cop wouldn't come within a mile. There's nothing here a cop wants to see.

The music's too loud, and Artie don't care for greaser songs. All the fucking records sound alike. A nigger or a white guy, he'll do a lot of different songs. You're driving, you listen to the spic radio, it's all the same song.

He'd like to get another beer but if he does he'll have to pee. He doesn't want to pee in here. From the window, he can see the gas flares from the Exxon place across the bay. The flares burn all day and night. There's no one else in the bar except some sailors off a ship. Artie figures the guys are Swedes. The Swedes are in a booth by the bar, feeling up a Mexican whore. The girl is maybe twelve. She's got a Minnie Mouse shirt comes down about her ass and nothing else. The Swedes like this a lot. Jesus, Artie thinks, this ain't a decent place to be.

The guy comes in the door and looks around. Right away Artie knows the guy's a goof. He's wearing wingtip shoes, black and white shoes with little holes on top, shoes big as fucking boats. Artie didn't know they sold them anymore. Wingtip shoes and a seersucker suit. A fresh haircut a white shirt. Maybe the goof sells shoes, Artie thinks. He's got a face like a guy sells shoes.

The goof is just standing there, he can't see nothing in the dark. Artie stands halfway and waves him down. The goof comes over real quick. He doesn't sit. He stands there and sticks out his hand.

"You're Mr. Smith I bet, right?" The goof gives Artie a sly little wink which Artie doesn't care for at all. "Hey-hey, all right. *Funky* place, *something* else. I'm Bill *Jones*, okay?"

Artie ignores the hand. "You're Jimmy Sims," Artie says. "Sit the fuck down."

The guy sits. "Hey, I thought we didn't do names."

"I do names. You don't do names. You got something to give to me."

The goof grins. "Say, right down to it. My kind of man." He reaches in the pocket of his suit and comes up with a wad of bills, the wad's big as a cantaloupe.

"Jesus," Artie says, "put that shit away."

"Hey, what's wrong?" the goof wants to know.

"You ever hear of a envelope?" Artie says. "You want to give a guy something, you use a envelope. You can buy 'em at the store, you don't hand a guy nothing like that."

"Right, you got it. My mistake. What do I know? I think I'll get a beer."

"No you won't. You get through here you can go and get a beer. What you want to do is put it on the floor."

"Do what?"

"Put the fucking money on the floor. You put it down. I pick it up."

The goof puts the wad on the floor. Artie leans down and picks it up. He gets a look at the wingtip shoes.

"You want to do some business," Artie says. "I hear you got business you tell me what you got."

"Hey, that's what we're here for, right? Let's do 'er, let's go. Ceil, we're kinda separated now I mean we sort of live apart, okay? Christ, what a looker. Miss Universe? 1986? Hey, they could be sisters, all right? Listen, nothing happens to Ceil, okay? I mean Ceil can't help it. She drives guys nuts. We're talking your love goddess, man. I mean, *Ho*ly shit, what's a guy to do. You get a look at Ceil that's it."

"Hey." Artie holds up his hand. "I don't want to hear about the wife. Your wife ain't in this I don't want to know."

"Yo, that's it," says the goof. "You got it. Button up the lip. Loose talk." The goof stops. He looks over at the Swedes. The whore's stark naked. One of the guys is wearing the Minnie Mouse shirt, he's got it stuck around his head.

"Say, what's going on over there?" The goof looks alarmed. "We got trouble, I'd say. Doesn't look good to me, is that little girl okay?"

"No," Artie says. "So what kind of business you got with me?"

"How long you been doing what you do? Wow, I'm sittin' right here, what a kick. I'm in sales myself. RVs for every need."

Artie grabs the table and leans in on the goof. "I know what you are. You're an asshole with funny looking shoes. I don't give a shit. I don't want to hear what you do. You don't want to talk about me."

"Okay, no offense. I like people, I'm a people kind of guy. So this is where we're at. This guy's giving me a hassle with Ceil. She runs this electrolysis place, you know? Unwanted hair? Where'd she meet the guy, how you figure that? Anyway she's seeing this guy, she's over at his house every night. He works all day, he's a CPA. The guy's in a wheelchair, right? The guy went to Nam he's a vet. He can't do a thing without the chair."

"This guy's in a chair," Artie says. "The guy we're talking about, he's in a chair."

"You got it. Right on. Waist down, he can't feel a thing. So he can't do anything with Ceil, I mean in a sexual manner, nothing like that. So he's got this dog to do that. Like, she goes over to see the guy, the dog gets it on with Ceil."

"Jesus," Artie says.

"Right. Listen, I don't care for this at all. I'm saying to myself, this is bad news. This is not a normal thing to do. You shouldn't ought to do it with a dog. You off the guy you want to get the dog too. Be sure and get the dog."

"Forget it," Artie says. "No dogs."

"That's extra or what? Right, okay, I can live with that."

Artie feels tired. He wishes he was back in his condo where the air works fine and nothing smells. Maybe go out and get a lobster or a steak. Christ, what kind of people are we talking about here? We're talking fucking trash.

"How do you know she's doing it with the dog?" Artie says. "How you know that?"

"Hey, I saw her, that's how, what do you think?"

"You saw her doing this."

"I look in the window she's doing it with a dog. Say, I got the right. Who's the injured party here? I got a marriage on the rocks. I tell myself, hey, we can work this out."

Artie finishes off his beer. He don't want to mess with this goof but the money's okay. "Here's the way it goes," Artie says. "I need an address. I need the guy's name. You walk out of here you never saw me anywhere, that's it."

"So hey, when you think you'll do it. Real soon or what? I mean, hey, whatever you think, okay with me."

"Get the fuck out of here," Artie says.

"Right *on*. Read you loud and clear. You ever think about the RV life?"

"Get yourself a suit," Artie says. "Get some real shoes. That's what I think you ought to do."

At ten the next morning, Artie leaves his car at Pig's garage and gives the Pig a grand, which is Pig's ten percent. He tells Pig he ought to give *him* an extra grand for fucking with the goof. He tells Pig about the wingtip shoes, he doesn't tell him anything else. He takes the Honda and heads out north on 45. The Honda is registered to a wino in Nacogdoches, Texas, the wino don't know he owns a car.

Artie hates to drive. The guy lives up north of Conroe, maybe thirty, forty miles. It looks real nice when you get up where the pine trees start, but the traffic's real bad before that and the people drive like fucking maniacs.

Artie's thought about the vet and figures that's okay. Screw him, a guy in a wheelchair's a guy like anybody else, he's sitting down instead of standing up. He isn't sure about the dog, he hasn't ever hit a dog. This is a pervert dog, okay, but the dog don't know about that. He gets a chance to hump something, that's what he's going to do. He's going to say what? Hey, this broad ain't a dog. I shouldn't ought to do that. The dog don't know. He sees it up there, he figures fine, that's what I need to do.

So he'll think about the dog. The goof's real hot about the dog, but it isn't up to him. The goof don't tell him what to do.

The house is in a development that winds in off of 45. There's plenty of trees around, and no street lights except one at the end of every block. That's fine with Artie, he doesn't want a lot of light. He drives around in daylight to get real familiar with the streets. The neighborhood's a little run down, like everything went along fine for a while, then the people who were there when it was new moved away and the also-rans came and moved in. Some of the houses need paint and a lot of the lawns have gone to pot. Artie looks for rent-a-cop signs and he only sees two.

Three blocks from the vet he finds two empty houses in a row. All the other houses on the street are occuppied. If he parks in front of the empties, no one in the houses close by is pissed off. They don't wonder why he's there, they think he's seeing someone else.

* * *

Back on 45, Artie checks into the Cactus Bloom Inn, the first motel he passes on the right. He eats at a Burger King and goes back and watches TV. There's nothing on good, he watches a bunch of soaps. Everybody looks nice. The guys are all perfect, the women are flat knocked out. The broads are mostly screwing doctors or cops or architects. Sometimes they let you see a lot then they get right where they do it and they stop. You don't get to see anymore. This one girl's great. She's got nice tits and she don't have a rash anywhere. He thinks about Angie. Angie doesn't look that great but so what? He doesn't look like a doctor in a suit.

At six Artie's driving through the neighborhood again. He goes by the guy's house once, just checking things out. He's wearing dark gray sweats and running shoes. He's got a pound of steak and a Browning 380 automatic under the seat. The Browning's got a long leather loop around the butt. When he does his jogger act he puts the loop around his neck and tucks the Browning in his waist. If the Browning comes loose it doesn't fall down his pants and maybe out on the ground. Which is hard to explain, some jerkoff is raking up the lawn.

At 6:45, Artie pulls up three houses down across the street from the vet. He keeps the motor running and has a smoke. What he wants to know is what everybody does. Like who's home from work, who has a bunch of kids and who lives next door. He likes to know who's next door. He did a guy in Tulsa one time, a guy owes the wrong people a lot of dough. He goes in through a window and waits in the dark until the guy gets home, waits maybe two, three hours, just sitting in the dark. The guy comes in, goes to the bathroom to pee, Artie shoots him in the head. He goes out the way he came in. He takes a good look and nearly does it in his pants. There hadn't been a car in the street, now there's cars everywhere, maybe twenty, thirty cars. Lights are flashing on the cars and there's cops all over the place. Artie goes back in the dead guy's house and throws up. He stays in the house all night and it's on the TV the next day, how the mayor has a stroke and kicks off, and Artie don't have to ask where.

Artie sees the car in his mirror. It slows down and stops, stops right behind him maybe three feet away. He reaches for the Browning and holds it in his lap. A guy gets out, and Artie sees it's the goof. He can't fucking believe it, it's the goof. The goof just walks right up and gets in.

"Say-hey," says the goof, "is this *heavy* shit or what? It is *go*ing down, right? You're gonna *off* this dude, you're—"

Artie grabs the goof by his shirt and slams his head against the roof. "What the *fuck* are you doin' here? Huh? Huh? What the fuck!"

Artie rattles the guy good a couple of times and throws him hard against the door. "*Uh*-oh," says the goof, "ex*cuse* me." He holds up his hands like he's seen on TV. "You are really pissed, right? I'm saying to myself, this guy is *pissed* at *me*."

"I asked you a question, asshole. Why the fuck you following me around?"

The goof shakes his head. "Huh-unh, *no* way. I'm driving around, I'm in the neighborhood—"

"Bullshit." Artie grabs the guy again. "Get your ass out of here. Go. Don't fucking come near me again. Am I getting through to you or what?"

"Yo, I am *gone*. I am flying out today, I am hopping on the train. I am reading *you* loud and clear."

The goof jumps out. He gets in his car and whips by Artie fast. He waves all the way down the block.

Jesus. Artie can't believe the guy. Pulling up and getting right in. Artie's parked in front of the vet's, the guy jumps right in. He knows what the goof is doing. What he's doing is he's checking on his wife. He's trailing her around all day he isn't selling RVs. He's making sure she isn't fucking any dogs he doesn't know.

Artie drives off. He circles a couple of blocks to make sure the goof is gone. Back on 45 he stops off and gets a beer. It's a little after seven and he needs to kill some time. He drives up 45 for a while, turns around and comes back. When he reaches the neighborhood again it's getting dark. He passes the house and there's the van. Right behind it is a light blue Chevy so the goof's wife is in there too.

Artie keeps going. The goof's wife is early, this'll work out fine. He isn't about to do the vet until the broad is out of sight. They'll maybe find the guy the next day. Artie figures he can get back to Houston by ten. Maybe Angie's still up. He'll call her and they'll go and get a steak. They'll have a few laughs, he'll tell her about the wingtip shoes. Just the part about the shoes.

There's a dog dish in the backyard and half a tub of water by the tap. There's dog shit everywhere. Artie figures the dog is in the house, he's getting ready for his date. He won't tell Angie about the dog. Angie's kinky enough the way she is. A woman likes to dump Del Monte cling peaches in the tub, she don't need to hear about a dog.

The backyard is good and dark with all the trees, and the guy's got a high cedar fence. There's a concrete slab behind the house, a little built-in patio. The back of the living room has sliding glass doors you can walk out on the slab. The curtains are pulled but there's a two-inch gap. When he stands up close, Artie can see what they're doing inside.

What he sees makes him wonder what the fuck is going on. The goof's wife is there. But there isn't just one guy, there's two. The vet is in the wheelchair, a black dude is sitting on the couch. The black guy's wearing these Ray Charles wrap-around shades and he don't have any arms. All he's got are little stubs, that's all he's got. The broad's sitting by the black, she's feeding the guy a drink. Artie can't see her too well from where he is, he can only see her back. The stereo's turned up high. The black guy's flapping his stubs, he's stomping his feet on the floor. The broad feeds the guy too fast and there's booze running down the dude's front. The dude thinks this is a hoot. He laughs and waves his stubs. The goof's wife giggles on the couch. The vet says something and the broad gets up, stands up and turns around.

Artie nearly has a stroke. Christ, the goof's wife is ugly and a half. The broad's got a face would stop a train. A long pointy nose and little BB eyes. Buck teeth with nowhere to sit because her chin goes right down to her neck. She's got red high heels, a red dress, she's fucking skinny as a mop. With her hair pulled back, little kinky black wires, she looks to Artie like a rat. This is what she is. The goof's love goddess is a rat. The goof's too dumb, he don't know, he don't know he's got a rat.

The rat wobbles off to the kitchen for a drink, she can hardly stand up. The rat is fucking whacked. The heels don't work and she's walking on the sides of her shoes. Artie can't see the dog. Maybe the dog's off hiding somewhere, he don't want to do the rat.

In a minute, the rat comes out with a drink. She does a little dance and turns the music up high. She whirls around and nearly falls on her ass. She winks at the vet and plops down in his lap. She gives the guy a big kiss. He sticks his hand down the front of her dress. He don't find anything to grab but the rat thinks this is great. The rat knows what to do next. She stands up and kicks off her shoes and peels herself out of the dress. Big surprise, she's got nothing on under that. The vet yells and claps his hands. The black dude flaps his stubs. He don't know what the hell is going on but everybody's having fun.

Artie wants to leave and have a smoke but he can't take his eyes off the rat. He hasn't ever seen a broad looks worse naked but it's something more than that. The rat's got funny looking skin. Her skin's not right, it isn't pink it isn't white. She looks like she's maybe made of wax. Artie keeps looking and it comes to him at once. The rat doesn't have any hair. She don't have hair between her legs or anywhere. It isn't like she's shaved it all off it's not there. Nothing on her arms or her toes or anywhere. Artie knows what's happened, he remembers what she does. The rat's not busy all day, she's got nothing else to do. She sits down at the shop she figures, hey, I don't guess I'm ugly enough, I'll electrocute another coupla hairs. Miss fucking Universe.

Artie doesn't want to watch what happens next, he doesn't want to see this at all. The dog's somewhere in the house, he's maybe got the night off, and Artie's got bad news for the goof. The rat's on her knees and she's going at the vet and it's clear he doesn't need the dog at all. The vet's staring at the wall he's going nuts he's going *uh! uh! uh!* He's banging on the wheelchair with his fists.

Great, Artie thinks, that's it, let's get this fucking show on the road. Artie's tired, but the rat's not through, the rat's not ready to pack it in. She's crawling around the floor. She's looking for her drink. She squints her little BB eyes and tries to focus on her watch. She looks around like there's something she forgot. She spots the black dude on the couch. Right, that's it. There's still another guy in the room she forgot about that. She picks herself up and stumbles over to his lap. The black dude grins and does his Ray Charles act. He can't see shit but he can feel. He's got a naked girl in his lap he knows that, and he don't know how she looks. He whispers something in her ear. The rat laughs and wrinkles up her nose like she's found a piece of cheese. A minute after that they're gone. She's dragged the guy off somewhere, maybe another room.

Artie backs off and has a smoke. He looks at his watch but he can't see a thing in the dark. Okay. So the rat'll go home he knows that. The goof says she never spends the night. The black guy's something else. The vet had to bring him in the van, he isn't go nowhere by himself. Artie doesn't care for this at all. He's getting paid to do the guy and the dog. He isn't getting paid to do the black. He offs the black he'll have to do it free, the goof's not about to pay for that. Fuck it, Artie thinks. It's that or he's got to come back, he's got to make another trip, he's not about to do that.

He watches while the goof's wife stumbles to her car. She lays about thirty feet of rubber and she's gone. Artie feels a lot better now. He doesn't mind work, he doesn't like to stand around and wait. The vet's in his wheelchair the black dude's on the couch. Artie thinks about a bedroom window, but he doesn't want to run into the dog. He tries the sliding door real easy. Great. The fucker isn't even locked. He leaves the Browning where it is. There's a broken barbecue on the porch, a pile of bricks and a rusted rake.

Artie feels around, and finds a length of two-inch pipe. He picks up the pipe. He slides back the door and he's in the room fast. The vet looks at him real surprised and Artie hits him once between the eyes. He goes to the black dude on the couch. The guy knows someone's in the room but that's fine. He grins and says "What's happening, man?" and that's that.

Artie works fast. He gets the two guys' wallets and takes the cash. He drops the wallets on the floor. There's a big TV and he can't take that. He takes the VCR. There's a portable TV in the kitchen, he decides to take that. He can't carry anything else. It's enough to let the cops know a burglar's been around. He opens all the drawers and dumps stuff out on the floor. He knows he ought to mess the other rooms, but he doesn't know which one holds the dog. He doesn't want to fuck with the dog. The goof wants to do the dog, he can hit him with a truck.

He leaves the house quickly, stops in the shadows to check the street. It's nearly nine. No one's anywhere about. He runs across the street. The VCR's heavy, and the TV's banging against his leg. He cuts across a lawn. Lights hit the street and he ducks behind a tree. A van turns in the vet's drive, right behind the van that's there. The lights go off. The side door opens and a big dog jumps out in the yard. A ramp slides out of the van. A guy in a wheelchair appears, and the ramp takes him down to the ground. The guy pets the dog. The dog runs around like crazy, finds a good spot and takes a dump. Another light brightens up the street. A blue Chevy pulls up to the curb. The goof's wife gets out. She runs up the driveway and gives the guy a hug. The dog sees the broad and goes nuts. He wags his tail and puts his paws up on her chest. He licks her face and starts humping on her leg.

Artie looks at the dog. He looks at the guy in the chair. What the fuck is this? Artie thinks. What the fuck is going on? He can't hang around to find out. He starts jogging for the car. In about eight minutes, the place'll be crawling with cops, and he doesn't want to wait around for that.

Artie drives six or eight miles down 45. He finds a dirt road that goes off into the trees. He finds a bridge and a dried up creek where everybody stops to throw their junk. He tosses out the TV and the VCR. He hightails it back to the Cactus Bloom Inn and packs his stuff. He's trying to get a picture in his head. His head's not working right at all. There's two guys in the house. There's the guy outside and there's a dog, we got a couple of extra guys. We got the rat driving off and coming back. It don't add up. Something's wrong here, but Artie can't figure what it is. Jesus, what a fucking mess.

Artie thinks about the goof, but not much. So what's the guy going to do, call the cops, he's going to sue? There's no way he can get back to Artie, there's no way he can get back to the Pig. A guy looks for Pig, he's not there. So the goof, he's going to have to write it off.

Artie checks the room. He checks the closet and the bathroom and under the bed. He hasn't left a thing. He picks up his overnight bag and flips the lights and someone's knocking on the door. Artie stands perfectly still. He pulls the Browning from his belt and racks the slide, he goes flat against the wall beside the door. Maybe it's a maid, she wants to leave some towels. No way, it's nearly ten o'clock at night.

"Like hey, are you in there, man?" Another little knock. "Yo, let's talk, we gotta rap, okay?"

This ain't happening, Artie thinks. The goof's not out there knocking on the door. It's somebody sounds like the goof, he's not there. Artie pulls the door open fast, grabs a handful of shirt, turns the goof around, and throws him on the bed. He snaps on the lights and aims the Browning right at the goof's head.

"Say, *whoa* there," says the goof, "cool the small arms, take it easy, okay?"

"How the fuck did you find me, jerk?" Artie steps closer to the goof. "You want to find an answer real quick."

The goof grins. The guy's too stupid to worry about the gun. "Matches," says the goof. "Hey, that's all, okay? *No* problem, no big deal."

"What you mean, matches?"

"Like *matches*, man. You got matches in your car. I'm sitting in your car, you're kinda knocking me *around*, I'm saying to myself, hey-hey, matches on the dash. Cactus Bloom Inn. I'm saying, yo, everybody's gotta have a place to *stay*, that's cool. You're in the RV biz, you gotta know where everybody's at, you gotta touch 'em where they live. Mention a guy's hometown. Say something nice about his tie—"

"Shut the fuck up," Artie says. "Just shut the fuck up." Artie sits down in a chair. He looks at the goof. "Don't say nothing. Just listen. You're here, okay, I'm going to put it to you straight. Something went wrong at the house. I don't give a shit what. It ain't my problem anymore. You don't like it, okay. You keep your fucking mouth shut."

"Hey, yo, you don't have to tell *me*." The goof grabs his heart like he's going to have a stroke. "Like, I'm hearing sirens and shit, I'm thinking, whoa, *what* is going down, what is—"

"You fucking jerk." Artie sits up straight. "You're driving around. I said stay away, you're out in your fucking car."

"Say, no *way*." The goof holds up his hands. "Hey, I got the message loud and clear. What I am doing is I'm watching TV. I'm sitting there, I'm looking at the tube."

Artie frowns. "You're watching TV. You're watching TV where?"

"Like I'm in my house, man. I'm two doors down, I can hear all the racket going on, I'm thinking, hey, something is happening out there."

Artie is on his feet. He goes to the bed and slams the goof down hard and puts the Browning in his ear. "Listen, asshole," Artie says. "You are going to start making sense. I am going to count to maybe three. This guy with the dog, the dog's making out with your wife, you're living down the street."

"Okay. So it's not where I *live*. I mean it's where I kinda stay. I gotta lease, right? I got a cot, I got a TV."

"You're checking on your wife."

"Yo, I am *concerned*, okay? I got a right. You haven't seen her, man. Ceil's got the power of love. What's a guy gonna do?"

"Fuck that," Artie says. "You hear the sirens, you what?"

"I am up and *gone*, man. I am running up the street and there's Ceil, she is totally berserko, right? I take her in my arms, like wow, what a sweetie and a half. I'm saying, babe, like I want to be with *you*. She's bawling like a kid, she's saying, honey, that's where I gotta *be*."

"Jesus," Artie says.

"I'm holding on to Ceil, I'm hearing what's going down inside the house, I'm thinking, *Holy shit*, have we got a screwup here or what? I'm talking to Rick, he's the guy in the chair—listen, I meet the guy he's okay. Rick's saying, boy, like it's lucky he and Ceil weren't around. Like he's sorry but he's glad it's not them. He doesn't hardly know these guys, okay? He knew 'em at the VA hospital, right? They come through town they look him up. Rick says fine, so you guys go on to the house, I'll get there when I can. He calls Ceil, he says he won't be there until nine, he's gotta finish something up. He says there'll be a couple guys at the house, they'll have a drink, the guys'll go. He says come around nine, maybe ten, it's okay."

Right, Artie thinks. He can see the way it goes from here. The rat's got nothing to do, she's maybe whacked, she's maybe tired of doing hairs. She thinks okay, she'll maybe drop by, she'll maybe have some fun. She does her act, she leaves and drives around. She waits for the guy to get home. She hops out of the car and says, hi there, hon, here I am, how's the dog? Jesus, what a bunch of jerks.

"Get up," Artie says to the goof. "Get up off the bed."

"What for?" says the goof.

Artie grabs the goof and jerks him to his feet. He holds the goof up close and shoves the Browning in his mouth. The goof gets the picture pretty quick.

"Listen good," Artie says. "This is how it's going to be. You walk out of here, you go home. You hump Miss Universe, you watch the TV. I don't give a shit what you do. You walk out of here you don't remember me at all. You never seen me in your life. You do that, we're okay. You don't, we got a problem, you know what I mean?"

"Uhuh, wight." The goof tries to talk around the gun. Artie figures he's made a point and lets him go.

"Hey, *no* problem," says the goof. "I can see what's on your mind, okay? You're thinking, *uh*-oh, this guy maybe wants his money back, he is *not* a happy customer, right? Listen, everything is cool. Ceil and me are straight. Off into the sunset, Violin City, okay? Hey, I'm glad we got together, it's really been a kick. I mean that, right?"

"Get out of here," Artie says. "Get the fuck out of my life."

Artie thinks how he'll stop and have a steak and then call and see if Angie's still up. He doesn't want to think about the goof. He doesn't want to think about the rat and how she don't have any hair. What he wants to do is get the fuck back on the road and out of town.

The only thing is, he knows there's things he's got to finish up. He knows what the goof is going to do. He knows the goof has got to tell the rat. Artie knows he's got to do that. He tells her what he did, how he did it just for her. That's what the goof is going to do. He'll tell her fucking anything to keep the rat at home, and Artie knows he can't put up with that.

It's two, maybe three, and the neighborhood's dark except for one house on the block, someone's still watching TV. There's the goof's car and the rat's blue Chevy, two doors down from the vet. It's late, and Artie doesn't want to park on the street. He turns off his lights, and pulls into an alley behind the house, where everybody leaves their garbage cans.

The house the goof's leased is built a lot like the vet's. He doesn't have a fence around the place but there's plenty of trees and shrubs. Artie stands in the back in the dark for a while, then walks up to the house. It's a two bedroom house. One on the left side, the other on the right. Artie wonders who gets the cot. You can't sleep two on a cot, there isn't any way to do that. So maybe they're sacked out on the floor.

The goof's got a patio too, and Artie figures he'll try the sliding door. He's got a small crowbar from the trunk, he can snap the lock with that. He's walking toward the house, keeping real close to the trees. He's walking toward the house when something big moves off the patio and comes at him fast across the lawn. Artie nearly pees in his pants. The thing's black as night and it doesn't make a sound. It slams paws the size of dinner plates on Artie's chest and starts humping on his leg.

"Jesus," Artie says. He tries to push the dog away. He tries to get the Browning which he's stuck inside his pants. The dog won't let him go. He's pressed in close to Artie's chest and he can't get to the gun.

"Ace don't like everyone. He don't like you, he won't come near you at all."

Artie doesn't have to ask who it is. He can see the guy now past the dog. He's sitting in a wheelchair in the dark, he's on the patio.

"You got a real nice dog," Artie says. "I been thinking about a dog. Only you got to have a yard."

"You ought to have a yard," the guy says. "You got a little dog you can keep it in the house. A big dog ought to have a yard. You and him had some business, Jimmy says."

"Jimmy said that."

"Jimmy and Ceil are okay. They ought to have a chance for romance."

"Great. I'm for that. You want to call the dog?" The dog is humping Artie's leg. Artie tries to get him off he wants to get the Browning out, but the dog doesn't want to go away.

"I might get a RV," the guy says. "Jimmy says they're great for summer fun."

"Hey, that's what you ought to do. You and the dog could take a trip." The dog starts to shake, the dog is shaking like a leaf.

"Where I'd like to maybe go is Yellowstone. You got a RV, you can camp out anywhere you like. You and me are okay, then, with Jimmy and Ceil?"

"Right. You and me are fine. You want to call the dog?"

"I'm just trying to do the right thing, you understand. That's all it is with me."

"Listen, I'm with you." The dog makes a funny little sound. "You get the dog and I'm gone, I'm out of here, I'm on my—oh, *shit!*" Something hot and wet hits Artie's leg. He hits the dog as hard as he can across the jaw. The dog yelps and drops at Artie's feet. Artie jerks the Browning from his belt, drops his arm just right and shoots the vet. The guy doesn't move. He knows he hit the guy but maybe not. Maybe the guy can't feel it, he never thought of that. All this takes a second and a half, he's squeezing off another shot. Then the guy's got something in his lap it's going *blrr-r-r-t! blrr-r-rt! blrr-r-rt!* like in fucking *Platoon, blrr-r-rt! blrr-r-rt! blrr-r-rt!* the guy's wheelchair is jerking like he's plugged it in the wall, he's knocking over shit he's going backwards everywhere. Artie's got to laugh, it's the funniest thing Artie's ever seen, this is funnier than the rat with no hair or the wingtip shoes only something's going wrong something isn't working right it isn't how it ought to be, and it doesn't seem all that fucking funny anymore . . .

Andrew Vachss writes excellent novels that are unlike any other writer. Same with his short fiction. His prose is razor sharp. He doesn't waste words. He kicks ass. He's also unique in that his stories are not only brief, with kicker endings, they're actually about something. Not easy to do in such a short space, but Mr. Vachss does it, and the rest of us who write just have to envy his technique and wonder how he does it.

# TREATMENT

## Andrew Vachss

### I

The prosecutor was a youngish man, better dressed than his government salary would warrant, ambition shining on his clean-shaven face. He held a sheaf of papers in his hand, waving them for emphasis as though the jury were still in the courtroom.

"Doctor, are you trying to tell this court that it should leave a convicted child molester free in the community? Is that what you're saying?"

I took a shallow breath through my nose, centering myself, reaching for calm. "No, Mr. Montgomery, that is what *you* are saying. The defendant suffers from pedophilia. That is, he is subject to intense, recurrent sexual urges and sexually arousing fantasies involving sexual activity with prepubescent children."

"Fancy words, doctor, but they all come down to the same thing, don't they? The defendant is a homosexual who preys on little boys . . . isn't that right?"

"No, it is *not* right. In fact, your statement is rather typical of the ignorance of the law enforcement community when it comes to any of the paraphilias. A homosexual is an individual whose sexual preference is for those of his or her own gender. Such a preference is not a disorder, unless such feelings are dystonic to the individual . . . and that is relatively rare. You would not call a man who engaged in sexual activity with young girls a *heterosexual* offender, would you? Of course not. The root of much of the hostility against pedophiles is, actually, nothing more than thinly-veiled homophobia."

The prosecutor's face flushed angrily. "Are you saying the State has prosecuted this offender because of *homophobia*, doctor?"

"It is surely a factor in the equation. Isn't it true that you personally believe homosexuals are 'sick,' sir?"

"They are! I . . . I'll ask the questions here, if you don't mind."

"I don't mind. I was trying to answer your questions more fully, to give the court a better understanding of the phenomena involved. If you check the Diagnostic and Statistical Manual of the American Psychiatric Association, you will see that homosexuality is not listed as a disorder. Pedophilia is. The specific code, for your information, is 302.20. Homosexuality is present at birth. Hard-wired, if you will. Sexual activity with children is, on the other hand, volitional conduct."

"And they're not born that way?"

"No. There is no bio-genetic code for pedophilia. The essential etiology is an early sexual experience—those you would call perpetrators began as those you would call victims. Once infected, the victim learns to wear a mask. They are capable of the most complex planning, often with great patience."

"So every child who is molested becomes a molester?"

"Certainly not. Some do, some don't. As I explained, it essentially comes down to a matter of choice. No matter what a person's circumstances, he always owns his own behavior."

"So, then . . . what does this manual of yours say about recidivism, doctor?"

"That's a good question. The course of the disorder is usually chronic, especially among pedophiles fixated upon the same sex. Recidivism, however, fluctuates with psychosocial stress—the more intense the stress, the more likely there will be a recurrence."

"So you admit offenders like Mr. Wilson here are more likely to commit new crimes?"

"All things being equal, yes. However, we don't treat such individuals with conventional psychotherapy. We understand the chronicity of their behavior, and it is the goal of treatment to interdict that behavior. To control their conduct, not their thoughts. I am completing my research for a journal entry now, but all the preliminary data indicate an extremely high rate of success. That is, with proper treatment."

"This 'treatment' of yours, doctor . . . it doesn't include prison, does it?"

"No, it does not. Incarceration is counter-indicated for pedophiles. The sentences, as you know, are relatively short. And the degree of psychosocial stress in prison for such individuals is incalculable. In fact, studies show the recidivism rate for previously-incarcerated pedophiles is extraordinarily high."

"But he wouldn't be molesting children in prison, would he?"

"I understand your question to be rhetorical, sir, but the real issue is long-term protection of the community, not temporary incapacitation. Even when therapy is offered in prison, and it rarely is, it is an axiom of our profession that coercive therapy is doomed to failure. No treatment is perfect, but we know this: the patient must be a participant in treatment, not a mere recipient of it."

The judge leaned down from the bench. With his thick mane of white hair and rimless glasses, he looked like Central Casting for the part.

"Doctor, so what you're saying is that motivation is the key?"

"Yes I am, your honor. And Mr. Wilson has displayed a high level of such motivation. In fact, he consulted our program before he was ever arrested, much less convicted."

The prosecutor slapped the table in front of him. "Sure! But he knew he was about to be indicted, didn't he, doctor?"

"I have no way of knowing what was in his mind," I replied mildly. "And the source of the motivation is far less significant that its presence."

"So what's this 'cure,' doctor? What's this wonderful 'treatment' of yours?"

"The treatment is multi-modality. Not all pedophiles respond to the same inputs. We use groupwork, confrontation, aversive therapy, insight-orientation, conditioning, even libido-reducing drugs when indicated."

"How much were you paid for your testimony today, doctor?"

The defense attorney leaped to his feet. "Objection! That isn't relevant."

"Oh, I think I'll allow it," the judge said. "You may answer the question, doctor."

"I was paid nothing for my testimony today, sir. I evaluated Mr. Wilson, provided a report to his attorney, a copy of which has been furnished to you. I charge my time at seventy-five dollars an hour. I haven't sent in a bill yet, but I imagine the total will come to around fifteen hundred dollars."

"No further questions," the prosecutor snarled.

## II

"You're as good as they say you are," the defense attorney told me, shaking my hand in his paneled office. "Nobody knows those people like you do."

I nodded, waiting patiently.

"It's just amazing . . . the way you predicted everything the prosecution would do. Hell, I thought we were dead in the water on this one. Told Wilson he could expect to do about five years in the pen. And here the judge hands him probation on a platter."

"Psychiatric probation," I reminded him.

"Yeah, I know. He has to stay in treatment with you for the full term or he goes inside. But so what? It's a better deal than he would have gotten in the joint."

"I kept my word?" watching him carefully.

"You surely did, my friend. And don't think I've forgotten about our arrangement, either. Here you are, just like I promised."

The check was drawn on his escrow account. Fifteen hundred dollars. I put it in my attaché case along with the ten thousand in cash lying next to it on his teakwood desk. As agreed.

## III

Wilson sat across from me in my private office, his face a study in eager anticipation.

"This won't be easy," I told him. "We have to remake you, start from the beginning. And we begin with honesty, all right?"

"Yes, that's what I want. Honesty. I didn't see much of it during my trial."

"Tell me about that."

"Well, the boys lied. I don't mean about . . . what we did. But about how they felt about it. You know what I'm saying? I didn't force them . . . *any* of them. It was love. A special love. All I wanted to do was be something special to them. A loving, special friend. That D.A., he turned it into something ugly. The jury never heard my side of it."

"How did it start?"

"With that boy Wesley . . . the first one to testify. When I first met him, he was eight years old. And you never met a more seductive little boy, always wanting to be cuddled. He doesn't have a father, you know. I mean, it's natural for a boy to seek love."

"I know."

"And I loved him. Why should that be a crime? I never used force, never hurt him even once."

"How do you feel . . . about being prosecuted?"

"I feel like *I'm* the victim. I did nothing wrong—it's the laws that are wrong. And, someday, you'll see, the laws will change. I mean, kids have rights too, don't they? What good is the right to say 'no' if they don't have the right to say 'yes'?"

"The law says they're too young to consent to sex."

"That's a lot of crap. Kids know what they want. You know how willful they can get, how demanding. I've been around kids all my life. That's the way they are."

"Okay, look. Your problem is a simple one, isn't it?"

"What do you mean?"

"You got caught."

"But . . ."

"That's your problem, Mr. Wilson. You got caught. And our treatment here, it's to guarantee it doesn't happen again."

Suspicion glazed his eyes. "How could you do that?"

"First of all, we set the stage. You'll get therapy for a while, learn how to talk the talk. Then, eventually, you'll be relocated. You'll never be able to live around here after what happened. Never get a job working around kids. But, after a while, you'll be able to move to a new town. And start over."

"Is this a trick?"

"No trick. I know my business. And I'm smart enough to know it's all a matter of packaging. This is America. Whatever we *call* things, that's what they become. And what they're going to call you is 'cured,' understand?"

He nodded, dry-washing his hands, still apprehensive. "You said something in court . . . about drugs . . ."

"Don't worry about it. Sometimes a court insists on depo-provera . . . so-called 'chemical castration.' But that's not a problem here. And even if it were, we could give you one of the androgen group, reverse it almost instantly."

"My lawyer said it would be real expensive."

"Oh yes. We're the only clinic in the country that provides this range of services, but look what you're getting for your money . . . no victim confrontation, no shock treatments, no encounter groups, no drugs. Just preparation for how you're going to . . . successfully . . . live the rest of your life. And you don't spend a day in jail. Pretty good, isn't it?"

"How did you . . .?"

"Get into this? It's easy enough to understand. While I was still in medical school, I realized that pedophile treatment is the growth industry of the 90's. The money's great, the malpractice premiums are low, and there are other benefits too."

"Like being paid in cash," he said, smiling the sociopath's smile.

"Like that," I said, holding out my hand for the money.

## IV

"Okay, Mr. Wilson, you're about ready for discharge. Our records will show you've completed intensive individual psychotherapy, participated in group, undergone aversive conditioning. All satisfactory. I can truthfully say you're ready to live without probation supervision. Have you made plans?"

"I sure have. In fact, I've been corresponding with a few boys in an orphanage in Florida. You know, counseling them about their problems. I've been offered a job down there, and I'll be leaving as soon as my lawyer gets me released from probation."

"Good. There's just one more thing. You've never really apologized to the boys, and most therapists think that's a key element in treatment."

"I don't want to . . ."

"No, of course you won't have to see them. What would really help persuade the court is a letter from you to the boys . . . just telling them you understand what you did, how you take full responsibility. Like we taught you, remember? Urge them to go on with their lives, and promise they'll never see you again, okay?"

"You think it'll work?"

"I'm sure it will work. I know these people. Write me out a couple of drafts, and I'll stop by tonight when I'm done with the last group and look them over. Then we'll pick the best one."

"Thanks, doc. You saved my life again."

# V

Wilson lived in a modern highrise right near the city line. I rang his bell around 11:30. He buzzed me in. The lobby was deserted—the place is mostly a retirement community. I insisted he move from his old address to a place where there were few children around. To reduce the temptation.

I took the steps to the 26th floor, not even breathing hard. I don't get to work out at the dojo anymore, but I like to stay in shape.

Wilson had a half-dozen samples ready for me, all in his educated handwriting on personalized light blue stationary. He stepped out onto the balcony to smoke a cigarette while I read them through. Finally, I found one that was suitable.

> I'm sorry for everything I did. I know now that no excuse, no rationalization will ever make things right. I've been learning about myself, and now I know the truth. You are the victims, not me. I know why I did what I did, and I'm sorry for all the pain I caused. It's better this way. You will never see me again. I hope you grow up to be good citizens, and always stay true to yourselves. Goodbye.

His signature was strong, self-assured. I left the letter I selected on his desk. Then I went outside to join him on the balcony.

The night was warm, velvety dark. City lights winked below, quiet and peaceful.

"Was that what you wanted, doc?" he asked.

"Perfect," I said, patting him gently on the back. "Look out there, Mr. Wilson . . . see your future."

He leaned over the balcony. I knife-edged my right hand, swept it into a perfect power-arc to the back of his neck, followed through with the blow, spinning on my right foot and sweeping him over the side with my left hand.

He didn't scream on the way down.

I stepped back inside, dialed 911, told them he had jumped. While I waited, I tore the other letters into small bits and flushed them down the toilet.

Treatment works.

Lewis Shiner is best known for his science fiction work, but that's changing. His novels DESERTED CITIES OF THE HEART and SLAM both received mainstream attention, and he seems to be moving in new and exciting directions. The following story is nastier than he often is, and I'm glad of it. Fine prose, fine characters, by a major writer.

# DIRTY WORK

## Lewis Shiner

The office smelled like money. Clean filtered air, new carpeting, somebody's expensive perfume still hanging around. The chairs in the waiting room are leather and the copy machine has a million attachments and there's pictures on the wall that I don't know what they're supposed to be. Made me ashamed of the shirt I was wearing, the cuffs all frayed and some of the buttons don't match.

The secretary is a knockout and I figure Dennis has got to be getting in her pants. Red hair and freckles and shiny skin that looks like she just got out of the shower. A smile like she really means it. My name was in the book and she showed me right on in.

Dennis shook my hand and put me in a chair that was all slings and tube steel. The calendar next to his desk had a ski scene on it. Behind him was a solid wall of books, law books all in the same binding, also some biographies and political stuff.

"Too bad you couldn't make the reunion," Dennis said. "It was a hoot."

"I just felt weird about it," I said. I still did. It looked like he wanted me to go on, so I said, "I knew there'd be a bunch of y'all there that had really made good, and I guess I . . . I don't know. Didn't want to have to make excuses."

"Hard to believe it's been twenty years. You look good. I still wouldn't want to run into you in a dark alley, but you look fit. In shape."

"I got weights in the garage, I try to work out. When you're my size you can go to hell pretty quick. You look like you're doing pretty good yourself." Charlene is always pointing to people on TV and talking about the way they dress. With Dennis I could see for the first time what she's talking about. The gray suit he had on looked like part of him, like it was alive. When I think about him in a track suit back at Thomas Jefferson High School, sweaty and trying to run laps, it doesn't seem like the same guy.

"Can't complain."

"Is that your Mercedes downstairs? What do they call those, SLs?"

"My pride and joy. Can't afford it, of course, but that's what bankers are for, right? You were what, doing something in oil?"

"Rig foreman. You know what that means. 'I'm not saying business is bad, but they're telling jokes about it in Ethiopia.'"

Dennis showed me this smile that's all teeth and no eyes. "Like I told you on the phone. I can't offer you much. The technical name for what you'll be is a paralegal. Usually that means research and that kind of thing, but in your case it'll be legwork."

Beggars can't be choosers. What Dennis paid for his haircut would feed Charlene and the kids for close to a week. I must look ten years older than him. All those years in the sun put the lines in your face and the ache in your bones. He was eighteen when we graduated, I was only seventeen, now I'm the one that's middle aged. He was tennis, I was football. Even in high school he was putting it to girls that looked like that secretary of his. Whereas me and Charlene went steady from sophomore year, got married two weeks after graduation. I guess I've been to a couple of topless bars, but I've never been with anybody else, not that way.

It was hard to call Dennis up. What it was, when I got the invitation for the class reunion, they had addresses for the other people in the class. Seemed like fate or something, him being right here in Austin and doing so good. I knew he'd remember me. Junior year a couple of guys on the team were waiting for him in the parking lot to hand him his ass, and I talked them out of it. That was over a girl too, now that I think about it.

Dennis said, "I got a case right now I could use some help with." He slid a file over from the corner of the desk and opened it up. "It's a rape case. You don't have a problem with that, do you?"

"What do you mean?"

Dennis sat back, kind of studying me, playing with the gold band on his watch. "I mean my client is the defendant. The thing is—and I'm not saying it's this way all the time or anything—but a lot of these cases aren't what you'd think. You got an underage girl, or married maybe, gets caught with the wrong jockey in her saddle, she hollers 'rape' and some guy goes to the slammer for nothing. Nothing you and I haven't ever done, anyway."

"So is this one of those cases?"

"It's a little fishy. The girl is at UT, blonde, good family, the guy is the wrong color for Mom and Dad. Maybe she wanted a little rough fun and then got cold feet. The point is, the guy gets a fair trial, no matter what he did." He took a form out of the file. "I'll get you a xerox of this. All I want is for you to follow this broad around for a couple of days, just kind of check her out."

"How do you mean?"

"Just get an idea of what kind of person she is. Is she some little ice princess, like she wants the DA to believe? Or is she showing her panties to anybody with a wallet and a dick?"

"Geez, Dennis, I really don't know . . ."

"There's nothing to it. This is absolutely standard procedure in a case like this. She knows she's going to have people watching her, it's just part of the legal bullshit game." When I didn't say anything he said, "It's ten bucks an hour, time-and-a-half if you go over forty hours a week, which I don't see this doing. We pay you cash, you're responsible for your own taxes and like that, and if you forget to declare it, that's your problem. Hint hint. If this works out we can probably find some other things for you."

Here's the carrot, and here's the stick. Good money, tax free, if you do it. Turn this case down because it sounds a little hinky and you're back on the street.

"What's this woman's name?"

"Some horrible yuppie name . . ." He looked at the file. "Lane, that's it. Lane Rochelle. Isn't that a hoot?"

I didn't like the way her name made me feel. Like I was standing outside the window of one of those big Highland Park mansions back in Dallas, wearing last week's clothes, watching guys in tuxedos and women in strapless dresses eat little sandwiches with the crusts cut off. I blamed her for it. "I don't know anything about this kind of work," I said. "I mean, if she sees me I'm liable to scare her off. I don't exactly blend into a crowd."

"Let her see you. It's not a problem."

I still wasn't sure. "When would you want me to start?"

He slapped me on the shoulder as he came around the desk. "There you go," he said. He walked out of the office and I heard the hum of his big new copy machine.

So I drove over to campus in my good corduroy jacket and my frayed cuffs and my black knit tie. I parked my pickup in the Dobie garage and walked down 21st Street to the Perry Casteneda Library, where Lane Rochelle works. The piece of paper Dennis gave me shows her address and her job history and her criminal record (NONE). Also a xerox of a photo of her from the society page of the *Statesman.*

She's older than Dennis let on, twenty-eight, working on her master's degree in History. She's paying her own way with her job at the library, not living off her rich parents back in Virginia, which makes me like her more too. The photo doesn't tell me much. Blonde hair, nice smile, wears her clothes the way Dennis wears his.

I went past the security guard and the turnstiles and looked around. I mean, I don't spend a lot of time in libraries. The place is big and there's this smell of old paper that makes me a little sick to my stomach. The Circulation desk is off to my left and across from it there are some shelves with new books and a yellow naugahyde couch. I found a book that looked interesting, a true-crime thing about this guy that kept a woman in a box. I sat down and every so often looked up and finally I caught sight of Lane moving around behind the counter.

She's not an ice princess, and she's not some kind of sexpot either. She's just a real person, maybe a little prettier than most. Right then she looked like somebody that didn't get a lot of sleep the night before and is having a tough day. The second time she caught me looking at her I saw it hit home—some big guy lurking around her job. I hated to see the look on her face, which was mostly fear.

A little before eleven o'clock she came out a door to one side of the counter with her purse and a bookbag. I let her get out the front door and then followed. It was nice out, warmer than February should have been. The trees were getting their first buds, which would all die if it froze again. There were even birds and everything. She headed up 21st Street and turned at the Littlefield fountain, the one with the horses, and climbed the steps toward the two rows of buildings on top of the hill. Once she looked back and I turned away, crouched down to pretend to tie my shoe, not fooling anybody.

I watched her go in the first building on the left, the one with the word MUSIC over the door. I followed her inside. The halls were full of students and I watched her push through them and go in one of the classrooms. Just before she went in she turned and gave me this look of pure hatred.

Made me feel pretty low. I stood there for ten minutes just the same, after the hall cleared and the bell rang, to make sure she stayed put. Then I went outside and walked around the side of the building. The classrooms all had full-length windows. The top halves were opened out to let in the warm air. I found Lane's room and sat in the grass, watching a woman teacher write on the board. She had heavy legs and glasses and dark hair in a pony tail. Charlene always talks about going back to college, but I can't imagine it. I had a semester of junior college, working construction all day and sleeping through class at night. They didn't have football scholarships and I wasn't good enough for the four-year colleges that did. So I went with what I knew and took a job on my daddy's drilling crew.

By eleven thirty I was starving to death. There was a Vietnamese woman with a pushcart down by the fountain selling eggrolls. I walked down there and got me a couple and a Coke and took them back up the hill to eat. It would have been okay, really, eating eggrolls outside on a pretty spring day and getting paid for it. Only Lane knew I was there watching and I could see what it was doing to her.

At noon we went back to the library. Lane sat off to herself in the shelves behind the counter. She had brought her lunch in her bookbag, a carton of yogurt and a Diet Coke. She didn't seem to be able to eat much. After a couple of bites she threw it away and went to the rest room.

She got off work at two in the afternoon. I watched her climb on a shuttlebus and then I drove out to her apartment and waited for her. She has a one-bedroom on 53rd Street near Airport, what they call a mixed neighborhood—black, white, Chicano, all low-income. This is where the rape happened. There's a swimming pool that doesn't look too clean and a couple of 70s muscle cars up on blocks. A lot like my neighborhood, over on the far side of Manor Road.

She walked right past me on her way to her apartment. I was sitting in my truck, watching the shuttlebus pull away. She went right past me. I could tell by the set of her shoulders that she knew I was there. She went in her apartment, toward the near end of the second floor, and I could hear the locks click shut from where I sat. She pulled the blinds and that was it.

I did what Dennis told me. I got out and made a log of all the cars parked along the street there, make and model and license number, and then I went on home.

I was in time to give the kids a ride back from the bus stop. Ricky is fifteen and going through this phase where he doesn't talk except to say yes or no to direct questions. Mostly he just shrugs and shakes his head in amazement at how stupid adults are. So naturally he didn't say anything about me wearing a tie. Judy, who is seventeen, wouldn't let it alone. "What's it for, Dad? You look way cool. You messing around? Got a girlfriend?" She doesn't mean anything by it, she's just kidding me.

I had TV dinners in the oven by the time Charlene got home. Salisbury steak, mashed potatoes, and that apple cobbler dessert she loves. Her new issue of *Vogue* was there and she took it into the bathroom with her for a while. When she came out she was showered and in her blue-gray bathrobe and fuzzy slippers, with her hair in a towel. She loves *Vogue* magazine. I guess it takes her to some other world, where she isn't pushing forty and she still weighs what she did in high school and she doesn't spend all her days answering phones for a heating and air conditioning company.

"How'd it go?" she said. We had *Wheel of Fortune* on, the kids on the floor with their dinners between us and the TV.

"I got four hours in today, ten bucks an hour. I should make at least that tomorrow."

"That wasn't what I asked."

One reason I never ran around on Charlene is I don't think I could fool her for a second. "I don't like it," I said. "I think he's using me to scare somebody, because I'm big and ugly."

Charlene grabbed the back of my neck and shook me like a cat. "You're big all right. But I always thought you was handsome." Then she leaned back and picked up her magazine again and she was gone.

Everybody was asleep by eleven. I went out quietly and drove over to Lane's apartment. There were a lot more cars out front this time and I wrote down all the new ones on my log sheet. The light was still on in her apartment. I was about to head home when the blinds moved and she looked out and saw my truck.

I wanted out of there bad enough that I squealed the tires doing it.

I would sleep awhile and then lie awake awhile and then it was morning. I had a lot of coffee and not much to eat and that made my stomach hurt.

I was already at the library when Lane came in. She saw me and went straight through the STAFF door and stayed out of sight. A few minutes later a campus cop knocked on the door and she stood in the doorway with him and pointed me out.

I felt like high school again, like I'd been caught with a *Playboy* in the toilet. The campus cop walked over and asked me if I had any ID. I showed him my driver's license.

"What you up to here?"

I gave him one of Dennis' cards, like Dennis said I should. "I'm doing research for a law office. Call this number, they'll back me up."

"Don't look like you're doing research to me. Maybe you should move along."

"Fine," I said. I put my book back on the shelf, which was too bad because it had gotten interesting. Only I couldn't check it out because I wasn't a student. I went outside and sat on a wall.

It was a nice day for something. Warm again, a few clouds, the birds getting ready for spring. College girls all around. I never saw so many good-looking girls in one place. Young and healthy, in tight jeans and running shoes, clean soft hair blowing around, sweet smells trailing along behind them. It hurts to see so much that you want, that you can never have, to be so close you could reach out and touch it.

About a half hour later Lane came out of the library and headed down Speedway, right through the middle of campus. I didn't think she saw me. I found myself noticing the way she walked, the way her young, firm ass strained against her jeans. Don't even think about it. I waited until she had a good lead on me before I started after her.

She turned left on 24th Street, by the Experimental Science building, and I lost sight of her. When I turned the corner she was gone. I hesitated for a second, kids shouldering by me on both sides and then I went up to the first door I came to and looked inside. Not there.

When I turned around she was right in front of me. "What do you want?" she said. She was shaking and her voice was too loud.

"I'm working for a lawyer—"

"That defense lawyer? That fuck? Did he hire you to follow me around? What the fuck does he want from me? Is this Gestapo bullshit supposed to make me drop the case?"

"I don't think he—"

"What kind of slimebag are you, anyhow? Haven't I had enough shit already? How can you stand to go around and humiliate people this way?" Crying now, people stopping to stare at us. "Do you know what happened this morning? My boss called me in and wanted to know why I was being followed. Like it was my fault! I had to tell him everything. Everything! Can you imagine how humiliating that was? No. Of course you can't. If you could imagine it you would go shoot yourself."

A boy walked up and put his hand on her arm. She shook it off and shouted at him, too. "Leave me the fuck *alone!*" She turned back to me, her mascara running all over her face, and spit on my left shoe. Then she shoved her way through the crowd and started running back down Speedway, back the way she came.

I started shaking myself as soon as I got in the truck. I shook all the way to Dennis' office.

He was with "one of his people" when I came in. After a few minutes his door opened and this good-looking Chicano came out. He was in his twenties, with longish hair and a mustache and an expensive black leather coat that hung down to his knees. He smiled at the red haired receptionist and pointed at her and said, "You be good, now."

"You too, Javier."

"No chance," he said, and rubbed his mustache and sniffed. The receptionist laughed. I couldn't help but think that Dennis was paying him more than ten bucks an hour for whatever it was he did.

Dennis was standing in the doorway of his office. "Come on in," he said.

I sat on the edge of the armchair. It wasn't really built for that and it made me feel off-balance. There was a dusty-looking mirror and a soda straw on his desk.

"You want a little toot?"

I shook my head. "It's about this case. This is really nasty. I don't know if I can go on with it."

"Okay," he said. He put the mirror and the straw in the top center drawer and then got a bank bag out of another one. It was one of those rubberized deals with the zipper and the little lock, except it wasn't zipped or locked. "How many hours did you have?"

I guess I expected him to argue with me at least, maybe even offer me something else. "Call it seven," I said. "And two parking receipts." I put my log sheet with the license numbers on it and the receipts on the corner of his desk. I felt small sitting there, just waiting for him to pay me.

"So what happened?" he said.

"She turned on me, started screaming. Said I was trying to scare her off."

"Gave you the old not-a-moment's-peace bit, right?" He counted out four twenties and put them in front of me. "Haven't got any singles, you can keep the change."

"Something like that, yeah."

"Well, I understand. If you can't hack it . . ."

"It's not that I can't hack it, I just don't see why I should want to."

Dennis sat back in his chair. Today he was wearing his casual outfit. I'd never seen a silk jacket before, but Charlene had showed me pictures and I was pretty sure that's what it was. The pants were khaki, the shirt was pale blue, the shoes had little tassels on them. "Let me explain something to you. This business isn't about who makes the most noise or who sheds the most tears. At least it's not supposed to be. It's about the *truth.* And the truth is not always what it seems. Ever have some asshole nearly run you off the road, and then he gives *you* the finger? A guilty conscience can make for a lot of righteous-sounding anger. This Rochelle bimbo has been going to one of those dyke counselling centers, and who knows what kind of crap they've been feeding her."

"But what if she's telling the truth?"

"If she is, my client goes to jail, probably does ten years of hard time. If she's lying, she could go up herself for perjury. These are not matchsticks we're playing for, here." He leaned forward again. Everytime he moved he did something different with his voice and I felt my emotions getting yanked around in another direction. "Look, I understand where you're coming from. It takes a while to build up your callouses. Just like working on an oil rig, right? You get a lot of blisters at first and it really hurts. Then you toughen up and you can really get the job done." He put the bank bag in the drawer. "Take the afternoon off, think it over. If you still want out, call me tonight, I'll put somebody else on the case. I'll be here in the office, I'm working late all week. Okay?"

"Okay," I said. I took the small stack of bills and folded it and put it in my front pants pocket. I wondered when was the last time Dennis got a blister on his hands.

As I got up he said, "Just one thing you want to keep in mind. Everybody's got something to hide."

I can't remember the last time I had that much cash in my pocket. It made me a little drunk. I drove to the Victoria's Secret store at Highland Mall and spent $58 on a crepe de chine sarong-wrap chemise in mango, size L. I took it home and hid it in the bedroom, and all through supper I was goofy as a little kid, just thinking about it.

I gave it to Charlene after we went to bed. She started crying. She said, "I'll get back on my diet tomorrow. It's so beautiful. I can't wear it the way I look now." She put it in the back of her drawer. She didn't even try it on.

She kissed me on the cheek and lay down with her back to me. I sat there, my hands all knotted up into fists. After a while she went to sleep.

I just sat there. I hadn't called Dennis. I was supposed to call him if I wasn't going back on the job. If I didn't do it he would just get somebody else. Somebody with all those callouses I don't have. Finally I got up and put my clothes back on and went out driving.

I guess I was supposed to be thinking things over, but what I did was drive to Lane Rochelle's apartment. It was a quarter to twelve. I wrote the time down on a new log sheet and walked around writing down all the cars and license numbers. Lane's window was dark. I got back in the truck and tried to find a comfortable way to sit. I wondered what she wore to bed. Maybe it was a crepe de chine sarong-wrap chemise in mango, size S. Maybe it was nothing at all.

A car door slammed and woke me up. The digital clock on my dash said one AM. I saw a guy walking away from a black Trans Am, two slots down on the right. It was the guy I saw in Dennis' office that afternoon. I slid a little lower in the seat.

What was he doing there? Did Dennis give him my job? He went through the gate by the pool, headed for the far set of stairs.

The apartments are kind of L-shaped, with the long part parallel to the street and the short part coming toward where I was. There was another set of stairs on the end of the building closest to me. I got out of the truck as quiet as I could and went up the stairs. I got to the corner just as the guy was knocking on Lane's door.

I could hear my heart. It sounded like it was in my neck. The guy knocked again, louder this time. I heard the door open and catch on its chain.

"Javier," Lane said. She sounded only a little surprised.

"I got your message," the guy, Javier, said.

"It's late. What time is it?"

"Not that late. You gonna let me in or what?"

"Not tonight. Come back tomorrow, okay?"

"Listen, I went to a lot of trouble to drive over here. How about a beer or something, anyway?"

"Fuck off." I wondered where she learned to talk like that. "Come back tomorrow night."

The door slammed and two or three locks turned. I didn't hear any footsteps. Javier was still standing there. Then he said, *"Chingase, puta!"* and walked away.

I moved away from the corner and pushed my back flat against the wall. I was in the shadows, I didn't think he could see me. He took one last look at Lane's apartment and then spit in the swimming pool and got in his Trans Am and drove away.

I was covered in sweat when I got home. I had to sponge myself off with a wet washcloth before I could get back into bed. Charlene was still asleep, snoring away.

I wondered if I should call Dennis. What if he already knew Javier was hanging around? What if it was his idea? I thought about the smooth way he handled me that afternoon in his office and decided it wasn't any of my business. If Dennis wanted to ask me a question I would answer it. Otherwise I was on my own.

Being on my own is okay. I've been that way most of my life. It makes some things a lot easier. Like taking Dennis' money.

* * *

I got to the library about ten o'clock and went right up to the circulation desk. Lane was there and when she saw me she turned and walked away. This older woman came over and asked if she could help me.

"I need to talk to Lane for a second."

"What is this in reference to?"

"It's in reference to I would like to apologize to her."

The old lady went to talk to Lane. They went back and forth a little and at one point the old lady put her arms around Lane and gave her a hug. It made me feel lonely to look at them like that. Then Lane came up to the counter. She took hold of the edge with both hands and waited for me to talk.

"Look," I said. "I'm sorry I scared you. I've been out of work for two years. This is just a job to me." She stared, no expression. "I thought about the things you said, and maybe I don't trust this lawyer very much either. What I'm trying to say is, you don't have anything to be afraid of from me. If you're . . . I mean, if things are the way you say they are, I would maybe like to help a little if I could."

She stared a while longer, and then she said, very quiet, "If you want to help, just go away. Just get the fuck away from me and stay out of my life."

"I can't do that right now," I said. "I have this job to do and it's the only thing I've got. All I want is to try to make the best of it."

Her eyes teared up. "Make the best of it. Oh God. What do you know about anything?"

She walked away and there was no use calling her back. I got my true crime book again and took it over by the card catalog, where I could see her if she left the building but she wouldn't have to watch me hanging around all day. At eleven I followed her to her class at the Music building and back again after. I had an eggroll lunch while I was waiting and if she noticed me she didn't let on.

It was another nice day. I sat outside until she left at two, watching the clouds move around in the sky. She got on her shuttlebus and I sat there a little longer, wishing things were different but not knowing what exactly I would change. Just a mood, I guess. Then I started the long uphill walk back to the Dobie Garage.

Dobie is the only place a non-student can park anywhere near the library. It's across from Dobie Mall, which is this combination shopping center and dormitory. Kids can eat, shop, sleep, go to movies, have sex, live and die there without ever going outside. The garage is always full so I had to park on the fourth level, one down from the roof. Homeless guys, what we used to call winos, what the kids call Drag worms, sleep in the stairwells, which smell of piss and vomit. I can't stand to see those guys, I want to knock them down to get away from them. If it wasn't for Charlene that could be me. No work, no future.

I got up to level four and even from the end of the row I could tell something was wrong. The truck was not sitting right. I felt sick. It goes back to my days on the rigs. Your wheels are your livelihood. If you can't get around, you can't work, if you can't work you can't feed yourself, if you can't do that you're not a man anymore.

I wanted to run over and see what was wrong and at the same time I wanted it not to be happening and the two things were pulling me in opposite directions. By the time I got to the truck my heart was pounding and my eyes were blurry.

It was all four tires flat. They weren't cut, not that I could see. The valve stem covers were off and they'd let the air out with a Bic pen or something. In addition they had taken their car keys or something and put long, ugly scratches down both sides of the body. I walked all the way around and then I started kicking one of the tires, which was stupid. It wasn't the tire that had done it.

It wasn't Lane that had done it either. She wasn't out of my sight all morning.

There was a note under the windshield wiper. It was in block capitals on lined yellow legal paper. It said GO AWAY.

I called Triple A and they sent a truck. The driver said something about those fucking college kids and I nodded along. While he was doing the tires I looked under the frame and inside the hood to make sure there wasn't a bomb or anything. Then I had the guy wait to make sure it started, which it did.

I stopped off at Airport Auto Supply and got some white primer and sprayed it on the scratches and it didn't look quite so bad. Then I went home. I wasn't shaking this time, not outside. It was all inside. It's like the constant vibration from the rotary table out on the drilling platform. It goes right through you. The kids were already there so I went out in the back yard and looked at the dead yellow grass. There were patches of green coming through and every one was a weed.

Call Dennis. He can get the note fingerprinted.

Sure. Students use legal pads, but so do lawyers. Maybe it was his cocaine buddy Javier did my tires. I can handle him one on one, but I know he's the kind of guy who carries a gun.

The house needs a paint job, the lawn needs a gardener. The kids are nearly old enough for college and I got no money to send them. I wish I had a Mercedes SL instead of a Pinto wagon and a Ford pickup truck. I need a drink but I don't dare start. When was the last time I thought about who I am, instead of what I have? When did it start being the same thing?

In the bedroom, on the bottom of my undershirt drawer, was my daddy's gun. A colt Woodsman .22 target pistol, loaded, because my daddy taught me an unloaded gun is worse than no gun at all. I went in the bedroom and locked the door and got it out. It smelled of oil and a little bit like cedar from the drawer. It felt great in my hand. I made sure the safety was on and stuck it in my pants. No, that was stupid. It would fall out or I would shoot myself in the foot. I folded it up in an old Dallas Cowboys nylon jacket.

Charlene was home. I heard her try the bedroom door, then knock quietly. I opened it. "I need to use the wagon," I said.

We never ask each other a lot of questions. It's like we don't really have the words for it. I could see her trying to make up her mind if she wanted to ask now. She must have decided not because she gave me the keys and got out of my way.

Judy said, "I need the wagon tonight, Dad, I got choir."

"Take the truck."

"I hate the truck. I don't like that stick shift."

"Just take the truck, all right?"

Now Judy was ready to start crying. I put the truck keys on the little table by the door and went out.

I was starving to death. I hadn't eaten anything since those two eggrolls before noon. I bought a hamburger and fries and a chocolate shake at Gaylord's there on Airport and ate them in the car. Then I got worried about Lane recognizing me, even in a different car. I looked around and found a bandanna in the back seat. I took off my tie and rolled up my shirt sleeves and put on my sunglasses. Then I tied the bandanna over my head, pirate style, the way I'd seen some biker guys do. Looked stupid as hell in the rear view mirror, but at least it didn't look much like me.

I made a pass all the way around the apartments and then parked out of sight of Lane's window. No sign of the Trans Am. The lights had been on behind her mini-blinds when I drove by. It was seven-thirty and full dark. A little after eight my bladder started to kill me. I got out and peed against the windowless back of the apartments. From the smell there I wasn't the first.

A little after nine it started to rain.

By ten I thought maybe I'd made a mistake. That old Pinto wagon is too small for me and the springs in the seats are shot. I hurt like hell after ten minutes, let alone two and a half hours. I could have been in bed asleep. Worse yet, Javier could have showed up without me seeing him, or in another car.

I got out and walked up and down the parking lot. No Trans Ams. Lights still on in Lane's apartment. The rain soaked my bandanna and got in my shoes. Half an hour, I thought. Then I either go home or I go upstairs for a look. I was about to get back in the wagon when a black Trans Am pulled into the lot.

I ducked down and listened. The engine revved, then stopped. I could hear the hot metal ticking and the softer ticking of the rain. The door opened, the springs groaned, feet rasped against the asphalt. The door shut again. Silence. What if he can see me? My gun was still inside the Pinto.

I heard his footsteps move away. I could see his black leather coat as he went in the gate, Javier for sure, headed for the stairs. I waited until he was blocked by the corner of the apartment and then I crawled in the wagon head first. I stuck the little Colt in the back of my pants and jogged over to the other set of stairs, putting the jacket on as I ran.

By the time I got to the corner of the building, Lane had her door open. I heard her say, "There you are."

"You look nervous." Javier's voice. "Something wrong?"

"What do you think, you fucking prick? I'm going to welcome you with open arms?" I couldn't get used to the language she used. It just didn't fit with the way she looked.

"It's like raining out here, okay? Are you going to let me in, or what?"

"Yeah, I'm going to let you in."

A second later I heard the door close. The locks went again and then there was a crash and a muffled shout and then silence.

I couldn't just stand there. Even if it was none of my business, even if I was carrying a gun I had no permit for, even if somebody in that apartment had trashed my truck and left me threatening notes.

I turned the corner and tried to see through the blinds. Nothing. I heard voices but I couldn't tell male or female, let alone what they were saying.

Shit, Christ Jesus. It's happening right now, and I can't let it go on.

I knocked on the door. It went so quiet in there I could hear the raindrops ping on the railing behind me. I stepped back and kept my hands away from my sides, away from the gun stuck down the back of my pants. I don't know how long I waited but it felt like at least a minute.

Something moved behind the peephole and the door opened on the chain. It was Lane, fully dressed, not a mark on her. I suddenly realized I was still wearing the bandanna and sunglasses. She laughed and it sounded more nervous than anything. I wadded up the glasses and bandanna in my left hand.

"Just go away," she said. "Don't pull any knight-in-shining-armor numbers, don't give me any shit, just go away. Tell your lawyer friend it's over. I'm dropping the charges. The law sucks, you can tell him that too.

Happy now? Go fuck yourself and stay away."

She started to close the door. I stuck my foot in, I don't know why. I couldn't let it end that way.

"Look," I said, "I just want to say—"

"I don't want to hear it." She leaned on the door, and it hurt.

To hell with it. "Let me get my foot out and I'm gone," I said.

She eased off on the door and right then something crashed in the back of the apartment and I heard Javier's voice, muffled, yelling.

"Oh shit," Lane said. She took a step back.

A woman's voice from off to the side said, "Bring him in."

All of a sudden Lane's apartment didn't seem like such a good idea. The door slammed and I heard the chain come off and I turned around and ran for the stairs. Something hit me in the back of the knees and I skidded into the railing at the edge of the walkway. Then something metal poked me in the ear and a woman's voice said, "Get up and go inside."

My knees hurt where I'd slid. I got up real slow and the woman got behind me where I still couldn't see her. I walked back to the apartment. I was so scared that everything looked tilted and the light hurt my eyes. Then I was inside and she pushed me and I went down on my knees again, next to the far wall of the living room.

"Put your hands on your head," the woman said, "and turn around and sit against the wall." I did what she said. There was the gun still stuck down the back of my pants. All I wanted was out of there. If I could get the gun out without getting shot in the process, maybe I could walk away.

Lane was there, and two women I didn't know. The one with the gun was close to six feet tall, heavy, with crewcut blonde hair. She wore jeans and a plain white sweatshirt and a green flannel shirt over that. The sleeves of the flannel shirt were rolled up to show the sweatshirt underneath. The gun was a revolver and there was a silencer screwed on to the end of the barrel. That was when I realized for the first time that I was probably going to die.

The other woman was closer to my age. She had on jeans and a bulky orange sweater. Most of her hair had gone white. She had a pair of pliers and she was taking apart a plain wire coat hanger. I could see a wad of paper on the breakfast bar that she'd torn off the hanger.

Against the wall across from me, behind the door, was Javier. They'd done something to his hair, cut a lot of it off the front, and it gave him a startled look. His hands were behind his back. One of his shoes was off and the sock was gone. His mouth was taped shut with silver duct tape. It looked like there was something in his mouth behind the tape. They'd run the tape all the way around his head a couple of times. I figured out where the missing sock was and decided I would be quiet.

"You know him?" the one with the gun said to Lane.

"He works for Asshole's lawyer. He's the one with the truck you fixed this afternoon. He's nobody, just hired meat."

"Scum," she said sadly. "What would make somebody take a job like that?"

"Money," the woman with the coat hanger said. "It's all about money. Even Asshole there, women are just property to him. Right, Asshole? Like cattle or something. You can do anything you want to them."

That was when I finally got it. "He's the one," I said.

The woman with the gun gave me a funny look. "I think Dr. Watson over here just figured something out."

"Javier," I said. "He's the one that . . ."

"Raped me," Lane said. "That's right. He raped me. Do you mean to sit there and tell me you didn't know?"

"I didn't know. But . . . I saw him here the other night. You called him by name . . ."

"Jesus," said the woman with the coat hanger. She sounded disgusted.

"Yeah, I know his name," Lane said. "I knew him before he raped me. So what? Because I know who he is, does that give him the right? I bought some coke from him, okay? And now my lawyer says he'll probably get off because of it. Even though he raped me. You want to hear about it? He pulled a knife, and he cut my clothes off, and he made me lie on my stomach, and he fucked me up the ass." She took two steps and kicked Javier in the face. She was wearing boots and she caught him on the cheekbone.

The woman with the coat hanger said, "Careful. Break his nose and he'll suffocate."

The woman with the gun said, "That'd be a real pity."

"Kind of misses the point, doesn't it? If we just *kill* him?" She had the hanger straightened out now and she was twisting one end into loops. It looked like a letter at the end of the straight piece of wire. It was a letter. It was the letter R.

"What are you going to do?" I said. Nobody paid any attention to me.

The woman with the coat hanger took it into the kitchen. I could see her through the breakfast bar. She took an ice bucket out of the freezer and set it on the counter. Then she bent the long end of the hanger double to make a handle. Then she got down a potholder, it was a red potholder, quilted in little diamond shapes, it fit over her hand like a mitten. Then she turned on a gas burner, turned it up to high. The flames were blue and the potholder was red.

Suddenly Javier started to spasm and make choking noises. There was a sour smell and he snorted a fine spray of vomit onto his clothes.

The woman with the coat hanger put it down on the stove and hurried over to take his gag off. The woman with the gun knelt on his legs and shoved the silencer into his crotch. "Don't make a sound," she told him. "Or you'll never fuck anybody again."

They were all looking at Javier. I got the Colt out. I was shaking again. It seemed like it was a million degrees below zero in that apartment. Javier spit puke on the floor and Lane ran into the kitchen for paper towels. She ran right past me and didn't even see the gun in my hand.

I stood up and the woman with the gun turned around. "What do you think you're—" She saw the Colt. Her face didn't change hardly at all. "So you want to play cowboy."

"I just want out of here. Let me walk out the door and you'll never see me again."

"I'd rather kill you," she said. I could tell she meant it. "I don't do anything with a gun pointed at me. So you can either use it or you can put it away."

We stayed like that, just looking at each other, pointing our guns at each other, Javier on his side, gasping, Lane with a handful of wet paper towels, the woman in the orange sweater standing to one side with a look on her face like she was only mildly interested. I tried to imagine myself pulling the trigger and knew I couldn't do it. It was the first rule my daddy taught me, that you don't pull a gun unless you're willing to use it, and here I'd gotten it wrong. I wondered how much noise her gun would make, with the silencer and all. I wondered if it would hurt.

"That's better," the woman with the gun said. I looked at my hand, saw my daddy's Colt now pointed down at the floor. My legs had gone weak and I eased down onto my knees and put the Colt on the cheap brown carpet between us.

I said, "Now what?"

The woman with the gun said, "Good question."

The woman in the sweater taped Javier's mouth shut again and went back in the kitchen. Lane went over to Javier and wiped up the mess on the floor. Then she got up and opened the front door.

The woman with the gun said, "Are you crazy?"

Lane looked at me, crooked her finger toward the door. "Get out of here."

The woman with the gun said, "Lane—"

"Let him go," Lane said. "Maybe he learned something."

I stood up. It didn't look like the woman with the gun was going to stop me. I took one careful step toward the door, and looked back. The woman with the coat hanger was holding it over the burner. A bright yellow flame was coming off it and the metal was turning red hot. I took another step and then I was walking, fast, and then I was outside and the door slammed shut behind me. I ran for the stairs and I was just to the corner of the building when I heard Javier, right through the tape, let out one long, muffled scream.

* * *

I just wanted to finish it. I stopped at the Diamond Shamrock on Airport and called Dennis' house. The rain was still falling, slower now, and I turned up the collar of my jacket while I listened to the phone ring. His wife answered and told me he was at the office. Fine, perfect.

I parked next to his Mercedes in the lot. I had to knock on the glass door of his office for him to come unlock it. He was working at the copier and there was a big stack of what looked like tax forms on the table next to it.

"What's up?" he said. He fed another form into the machine.

"Lane Rochelle's dropping the case," I said.

"You're kidding."

"That's what you wanted, isn't it? I mean, that's why you'd hire a big, stupid guy like me in the first place, right?"

"Maybe you're not so dumb as you look."

"Maybe not."

"I think this calls for a bonus. I expect my client could afford a couple hundred on top of your hourlies."

I expected it was worth a lot more than that to Dennis, not to have to put Javier on the stand, not to have him talk about his cocaine customers. But all I said was, "Why don't I get that bank bag for you?"

"Sure. It's in the desk there."

I went into Dennis' office and got the bank bag out of the side drawer. I guess I was just looking for something. I didn't know what it was going to be until I found it. I looked back into the waiting room and Dennis still had his back to me, feeding papers into the machine. I eased open the top drawer and there it was, a fat plastic bag full of cocaine. I figured it must have been about a quarter of a pound. I flattened it out and put it down the front of my pants and tucked my shirt back in around it.

I took the bank bag in to Dennis and he counted out three brand new hundred dollar bills. "Not bad for a day's work, eh?" he said. I couldn't do anything but nod. "You did good," he said. "There's plenty more where this came from. Just let me know, okay?"

I even shook his hand.

I went downstairs and jimmied the lock on the gas tank of his Mercedes. Then I took off the gas cap and poured the entire baggie of cocaine inside. When I closed it all back up I could hardly tell the difference. Then I threw the baggie in the dumpster. I don't really know what cocaine does to an engine, but I figure there's at least a lot of sugar in whatever it's cut with. Any way you look at it, it's just bound to be expensive.

I was still kind of pumped up when I got in the Pinto, but it wasn't like I thought it would be. I didn't feel any better. In fact I felt worse, I felt like hell. Lane said maybe I learned something, but if I did then maybe I learned the wrong thing. I got turned around and headed north on the I-35 access road, and I must not have been paying attention, because when I went to get on the freeway there was suddenly this car behind me that I never saw, his tires screaming on the wet road. I kept waiting for the thump as he hit me and it didn't happen, there was just his horn as he whipped around, leaning over in his seat to shake his fist at me. And there was nothing I could do except sit there and hold onto the wheel. Because there are all these millions of gestures for anger and not one to say I'm sorry.

Ron Kelly is a Southerner who's beginning to be recognized in the small press as an innovative and powerful writer on the rise. He has a fine sense of place and gives the reader a feeling that underneath all the darkness he writes about is . . . more darkness.

# BENEATH BLACK BAYOU

## Ronald Kelly

Reuben Traugott set off into the swamp in search of his brother, Lemuel. He took his most water-tight pirouge, a canteen of fresh water, a quarter pound of possum jerky, and a 12-gauge Mossberg pump. But even as he headed across the dark waters, Rube knew deep down in his soul that he would never find his troublesome sibling alive.

Most who ventured into Black Bayou after nightfall never were.

The bayou held a dozen different dangers; perils that shunned the light of day, yet emerged at twilight to swallow its careless victims whole. There were quicksand pools, poisonous snakes, and wild animals weary of rabbits and weasels, eager for a change of menu. The Cajuns even whispered of the evil La Sanguinaire, a species of demonic spider that trapped wayward swampers in its misty web and fed upon their life's blood.

And then there was Ma Gator. Old Ma was Black Bayou's resident man-eater. It wasn't known if the alligator was indeed a female or not, but the sheer fury of her constant attacks reminded the men in the area of a wrathful woman with an axe to grind. Ma was said to be well over fifteen feet long from toothy snout to scaly tail and close to eight hundred pounds in weight. There was no record of precisely how many men had been killed by the gator, but there was speculation that the number had grown to nearly thirty-five since the mid-1950's. Usually the only thing found to mark a Ma Gator attack was the ruin of a canoe or pirouge floating upon the still waters and, occasionally, an arm or leg that had been severed by Ma's massive jaws and forgotten as she dragged the remainder of her catch to the muddy bottom of Black Bayou.

Rube headed out at daybreak, hoping to find some sign of Lem's whereabouts by afternoon and allowing him enough time to make it back to Point Bleau before darkness fell. His brother had been a damned fool for taking his canoe across the bayou the night before, but then such behavior was to be expected of a man like Lem Traugott. The trapper was a notorious drunkard and wife-beater, and his indiscretions were what drove him from his home twelve hours before. Lem had come in all liquored up and angry over having lost at poker. He had decided to take out some of the misery of his misfortune on his children rather than his long-suffering spouse. But Harriet Traugott had not taken kindly to that. She had grabbed an old scattergun from the corner and peppered Lem's britches with rocksalt. Lem had lit out of there like a scalded hog. Cursing to the high heavens, he had untied his canoe and set off across the bayou. Harriet had expected him to show up in time for breakfast the next morning, shame-faced and sore-tailed, but he had not.

So Rube was on the bayou looking for him. The swamper rowed his low, wooden boat slowly through gnarled columns of water-logged cyprus. Sunlight was sparce, scarcely able to penetrate the upper layer of dense foliage and stringy Spanish moss that hung from the limbs overhead. By noon, Rube had drank half his canteen and nibbled away most of the possum jerky, and still he hadn't discovered hide or hair of old Lem.

It was nearing three in the afternoon and Rube was seriously considering turning back, when he spotted a gleam of sunlight on bare metal a hundred yards ahead. He rowed up next to a sandbar and found the rear half of Lem's canoe beached there. It looked as if it had been cut in half with a chainsaw. But Rube knew exactly what had done it. Only the snaggle-toothed jaws of Ma Gator could have torn the narrow boat so violently asunder.

He made a slow circle of the sandbar, looking for more evidence of poor Lem, but all he found was a splintered oar and his brother's soggy hat with a couple of crawdad's walking around the brim. He yelled Lem's name several times, but to no avail. He found himself feeling a little foolish calling to a man who was probably in the process of being digested at that very moment.

"I am sorry, my brother," apologized the Cajun after uttering a silent prayer. "But I must head on back without you. One Traugott for supper is quite enough for dat wicked bitch."

But Ma Gator wasn't so sure.

As Rube steered his pirouge north and started back for Point Bleau, he felt the boat rise below him. It lurched a good two feet into the humid Louisiana air, then hit the water's surface with a resounding splash. Rube forgot the oars and grabbed for his shotgun. He was in the act of jacking a shell into the breech when a great, leathery tail, as thick as a tree trunk and covered with algae and barnacles, rose from the swamp and lashed out. It hit the barrel of the Mossberg, sending the 12-gauge spinning from his hands and into a dense clump of cattails. Then the tail continued to fall. Like an unyielding pillar of stone it struck the pirouge squarely in its center, parting the sturdy dugout as if it was made of flimsy papier maché.

Abruptly, Rube found himself in the water. He kicked off his knee-high boots and began to swim for the sandbar he had just left. He was halfway there when he felt a heavy tug at his right leg. His heart played a symphony of dread as he felt himself sinking. A crushing pain gripped his lower body as a fifteen-foot demon began to haul him to the very depths of hell.

But, unlike the hell of his upbringing, it was not one of fire and brimstone. This hell was a decidedly liquid one, as cold and black as the womb of a dead woman.

Rube Traugott awoke . . . but not in the belly of Ma Gator.

He found himself lying in two inches of rank swamp mud, surrounded by total darkness. He reached up and his hand touched slimy stone three feet overhead. He was in some sort of cave, an underwater cave from the sound and motion of water lapping at the narrow opening to his left.

Trembling, he ran his hand down his belly toward his lower body and the sharp pulse of agony that had brought him back to consciousness. Relief flooded him as he discovered his right leg intact. It was cocked at a strange angle and broken in a place or two, but was still attached to his hip. But what was he doing here? And why hadn't Ma Gator gorged herself on him during their frantic struggle near the sandbar?

Slowly, Rube's mind cleared and he found that he had a pretty good idea. Gators rarely ate large game at a single meal. While the reptiles gulped down bullfrogs and swamp coons like popcorn, they preferred to take their time with larger critters. It was well known to the Cajun that a gator would sometimes drag a wild boar or small deer down into the depths of the bayou and stash it away in its underwater lair. There it would remain in storage, safe from rival predators, until the gator returned to consume it at leisure.

But there was something particularly odd about Ma Gator's latest catch. It was still very much alive.

Rube sat up and bumped his head on the cave's low ceiling. The man cussed and laid back down, propping himself up by an elbow. He breathed raggedly in the darkness and gagged on the cloying smell of stagnant mud and something else. He had to concentrate for a moment before he realized that the offending odor was that of decay. The creeping decay of something that had not been dead for very long, but was turning sour mighty fast.

The swamper rummaged through his trouser pockets. All he had with him was his lucky buckeye, a black plastic Ace comb, a three-bladed Case pocketknife, and the old Zippo lighter he had carried around with him since the Army. He sat there for a moment, as if waiting for his eyes to adjust to the darkness, but no dice. There was no light to separate shadow from contrast, not even from the narrow mouth of the cave.

Almost reluctantly, he opened the lid of the lighter. He didn't really want to see the cramped conditions of his predicament or the putrid thing that shared it with him. But Rube Traugott was not a man to pussyfoot around when things looked bleak. He placed his thumb on the roller and struck the flint.

The flame licked up, casting a pale glow on the surroundings. The depth of the cave, from mouth to back wall was about eighteen feet. Gator dung and old bones lay scattered across the muddy floor. In the corner there was a broad nest constructed of wilted ferns and thick moss. Amid the hollow of the nest were six leathery eggs. The unhatched young'uns of Ma Gator.

Then Rube turned around and the flickering light of the Zippo revealed the source of that godawful stench.

It was the body of his lost brother. Lem laid on his side, arms gnarled into fighting claws of fruitless rebellion, his pale face stretched taut in a rictus of horrible fear. Rube directed his light downward and found that his brother's body ended just below the ribcage. Ma Gator had bitten the poor bastard clean in half.

Rube was overcome with shock and nausea. He doubled over and vomited up that afternoon's jerky, as well as the sorghum molasses and biscuits he had eaten for breakfast. He tossed the Zippo aside and the blue-yellow flame winked out as the lid snapped shut on impact. Merciful darkness embraced him once again. But the smell—oh dear Lord, that confounded smell was still there, stronger than ever.

His brain boiling hot with panic, Rube scrambled for the narrow opening of the cave and squeezed through. Abruptly, he was surrounded by cold, black water. He struggled against the chill blanket of liquid limbo, bubbles of oxygen flooding from his mouth and nostrils. His eyes caught a glimmer of soft light from above and he knew that he was looking at the surface of Black Bayou. He kicked against the muddy bottom, pushing himself upward. An explosion of white-hot agony shot through his shattered leg, sending a wave of sickening dizziness through him. It seemed as though he surged toward the growing light for an eternity. Then his head broke through the barrier and he was back into the world of the living, back into *his* world.

But not for very long.

The first thing he saw when he reached the surface was Ma Gator. She laid on the sandbar, sunning herself in the last crimson rays of the Louisiana sunset. The splash of his emergence drew the reptile's attention. With a snap of horrid beartrap jaws, Ma bellied toward the edge of the sandbar and slid smoothly into the water after him.

Rube had no choice but to return to the dungeon from which he had escaped. He kicked and flailed wildly, diving deeper, ever deeper into the pit of murky darkness. He could feel Ma Gator behind him, getting closer, her huge tail propelling her forward like a leathery torpedo. On his way down, Rube wondered if he would even be able to find the cave again. He struggled with the twisted roots of a sunken cypress for one maddening moment, escaping from its tangle only seconds before the gator's jaws could grab hold.

Then there it was—the narrow mouth of the underwater lair. He pulled himself through and skittered across the mud and excrement to the back wall. His hasty entrance was followed by that of Ma Gator. She poked her huge head through the slit of stone, snapping and bellowing like an angry bull. He could not see the monster coming for him; it was much too dark. For some reason that was much worse than experiencing the horror close up and personal—the thought of not knowing when violent death would come to claim him.

He cringed against the rear wall, squeezing into a thin crevice that ran from ceiling to floor. He held his breath. He could hear the wet sounds of Ma Gator crawling through the muck toward him. Rube felt something blunt and alive press against the foot of his injured leg and he knew that it was the reptile's probing nose. He cried out in fear and pain, and pressed himself further into the crevice. As he did so, his hand brushed a long, hard object laying near the nest of eggs. His fingers enclosed the bludgeon. With a snarl of desperation, Rube struck blindly at the stalking gator, catching it across the nose. Ma bellowed with surprise and began to back away. He struck out again and again, driving the gator toward the mouth of the cramped cave. His other hand came into play and grabbed hold. Swinging the object like a baseball bat, he laid a stunning blow between Ma's beady eyes, or the spot where he assumed they were.

It did the trick. The alligator had had enough for now. She slid back through the opening, into the freedom of the open bayou. "Git yourself on away from here, you ugly she-bitch!" sobbed Rube. He collapsed against the floor of the cave and listened to the fading sounds of Ma Gator's retreat.

After a while, he gathered the will to get up. He scrambled around the cave for a time, searching for his discarded lighter. He finally found it. Once again he snapped it on. The fluid-fed wick revealed the true nature of the weapon in his hand. The thing he had chased Ma Gator away with was the denuded legbone of a fullgrown man.

Rube laughed until he cried. "Looky here, dear brother," he cackled, waving the femur above his head. "Now, wasn't dat a good one pulled on de old gator, do you not think so?"

Lem Traugott gave no reply. He only laid there and grimaced grotesquely at his living brother. Death had done nothing to improve Lem's sense of humor, which hadn't been much to begin with.

Despite the stink of the decaying body, Rube tenderly propped Lem's upper torso against the back wall and secured the Zippo in the fingers of one of his rigored hands. He frowned in disapproval at the state of his brother's appearance. He pulled a couple of bloated leeches from Lem's unshaven cheeks and combed the mud-plastered hair carefully into place with the Ace comb. It helped to promote the illusion of life, but not very much. There was still that frozen mask of unspeakable terror seizing his brother's lard-white face. A terror that would remain, transfixed, for as long as the flesh was intact.

Hours passed. Exhausted, Rube slept, dreaming of he and Lem as children, of the coon hunts they had taken through the marshland and the Huck Finn raft of cut saplings they had constructed and poled all the way down to Baton Rouge.

When he awoke he was hungry. The stench of decay had intensified, but that didn't seem to ruin his appetite. He lit the Zippo again, aware that the flame was growing shorter and dimmer with each use. He had no earthly idea whether it was morning or evening, noonday or night. He had no timepiece to consult with. His father had passed his pocketwatch down to the elder Lem upon his deathbed. Whole lot of good it had done his brother, though. The big railroad watch was probably ticking its way through the maze of Ma Gator's bowels by now.

His stomach grumbled, pleading for nourishment. Slyly, he turned his eyes toward the nest in the far corner.

Rube crawled over and took one of the leathery, gray eggs in his hand. His fingers dug into the soft shell and a slimy residue erupted through the punctures. He could feel the small, warm body of a gator embryo loll against his fingertips.

"Eat me, will you, Ma Gator?" grinned Rube. "Maybe so. But a condemned man, he must have his last meal. And while you have a taste for man-meat, I have my own . . . for gator."

And, with that, he split the shell in half and swallowed the fetus in a single, savory gulp.

* * *

Existence in the gator's lair drew on, changing the shape of Rube Traugott's life, twisting it into something less than that of a human being.

By his estimate—which was distorted and imprecise given the circumstances—he had been holed up there for nearly four days. He had set his broken leg the best he could, using the discarded bones of Ma Gator's victims as splints and strips of cloth from his shirt to bind them with. The limb was crooked and stiff, but the sickening pain had reduced considerably, leaving only a dull throbbing.

He found himself sleeping often, like an animal burrowed into hibernation. He had plenty of water to sustain him and outside air filtered from the narrow crack at the rear of the cave. While awake, he kept a fire burning using the Zippo and dry tender from the nest. Sometimes he sang the old songs and told the corny jokes that he and Lem had traded around campfires during their youth. But his was the only voice that rang through the cramped cave. Lem simply sat there, silent in his slow but steady decomposition.

Sustenance was the biggest problem. He had finished off the last of the gator eggs, as well as any slugs, insects, or leeches he could find in the cave. Despite the severity of his broken leg, he had tried several times to reach freedom. Each attempt, however, had proven futile. Ma Gator was always somewhere around; either laying on the muddy bottom near the entrance or swimming along the bayou surface, always aware of what stirred above and below her. Each time he would regain the safety of the cave, he would find his brother sitting there waiting for his return. And, as his hunger grew from nagging urge to cramping pain, Rube began to regard Lem not as a silent cellmate, but more and more as a side of meat that was rotting needlessly before his feverish eyes.

Once, Ma Gator had come visiting, gathering the nerve to return to the lair after the sound beating she had received at the end of a legbone. Rube had been napping, when a great splash and a hoarse bellow shocked him from his slumber. He awoke just as Ma's massive jaws shot forward and clamped down. But it wasn't he who suffered the gator's attack, but his brother. The reptile snagged Lem's left arm and began to drag the corpse toward the mouth of the cave. With a scream of angry defiance, Rube reached for his brother's half-body, grabbing it around the neck. Man and gator fought for a solid minute, subjecting the carcass to a grisly tug-o-war. Finally the rope gave out. Lem's arm tore away at the shoulder with a moist rip. Satisfied for the time being, Ma Gator slipped back into the watery darkness, taking the limb with her.

Rube sat there, cradling his rescued brother before the smoldering fire. He held him close and sobbed with the abandon of a frightened youngster.

Rube tried desperately to recall memories of he and Lem in the years past, the happy times they had shared along the mossy banks of Black Bayou. But no such recollections surfaced. There was nothing but the encroaching of primitive emotion, eroding away the remaining layers of civilized behavior from his weary mind. Soon, he feared, those dark emotions would grow so powerful that they would drive him toward total madness.

He hugged his brother's body closer, snuggling against it like a child to a battered teddy bear. As his tears began to play out and he drifted to sleep, Rube noticed that the awful stench didn't bother him nearly as much as it had before.

Rube knew that he must try for freedom once more—before the fine black worms of insanity burrowed too deeply into the tender meat of his brain and gained complete control.

"Farewell, my brother," he said, eyeing the pale form at the rear of the cave with genuine affection. Then he took the folding knife from his pocket and extended the longest and sharpest of the bunch. He would have much rather had a harpoon to defend himself with, but the lockblade would have to do. Taking a deep breath of stagnant air, Rube plunged into the dark waters and began his slow journey to the surface.

Halfway there, he met up with his nemesis. Ma Gator emerged from out of the murky darkness. She swept past and struck him a powerful wallop with a swipe of her tail. He felt ribs crack beneath the force of the blow. The impact and pain drove the reserve of air from his tortured lungs and he felt nasty water begin to snake its way into his nostrils and down his throat.

The gator made a sluggish U-turn and, again, came for him. He knew that there was nothing to do now but kill the monster, or die trying. Motionlessly, he floated there, playing possum, lulling Ma Gator into a false sense of triumph. Then, as the gator's mouth opened to receive its prize, Rube surged up and over the lengthly snout. He found his intended target—the creature's left eye—and, with both hands, drove the blade of the pocketknife downward. The honed blade slid smoothly and without error into the gator's orb. Ma thrashed and snapped, but to no avail. Rube wasn't about to withdraw the knife from the fatal wound. Instead, he pushed harder, bearing down with all his strength, sending the blade past the occipital bone and into the brain.

Ma Gator jerked in a final, rolling spasm, then grew limp and still. Slowly, she began to sink downward toward the murky depths of Black Bayou.

*Free!* thought Rube Traugott. *Free from the fiend who imprisoned me!*

He began to work his way upward, toward the surface of the bayou and the bright warmth of daylight beyond. There life reigned eternal, full of love, hope, and laughter. Birds sang from leafy branches, hounds bayed and barked joyfully as they chased fox and coon, old men joked and gossipped on the porch of the general store, and young men asked demure ladies to share a dance at the tune of a Cajun fiddle and a squeezebox accordian. Rube Traugott would go back to his family and fish and trap and live the remainder of his years as a happy and contented man.

But the closer he grew to the shimmering surface, the more that idyllic life seemed impossible, even perversely absurd, in nature. His life beyond Black Bayou had ended in the depths of the gator's lair. It had come to a close with insanity's dark victory and the hideous acts he had performed by the light of a tiny fire.

Rube's heart pounded with panic, his brain swelling with horror as he came within a foot of bursting through. He swam there for a long moment, then began to ease back down into the comforting black depths. As the light of day faded into memory, he drifted to the soft mud bottom, letting the cold currents engulf him, letting the blind catfish and slithering swamp snakes caress his doubts and fears away.

Letting the loving embrace of Black Bayou welcome him home once again.

Emery DeBossier set off into the swamp in search of the Traugott brothers. He took his john-boat with the big 75-horsepower outboard, his Winchester .30-30, and a Coleman lantern. He had no great expectations of finding Reuben or Lemuel, however. He knew Black Bayou and its reputation well enough to have his doubts.

Unlike most men in Point Bleau, though, Emery was not one who feared the twilight hours. He searched throughout the day and, when dusk passed into night, he didn't seek the safety of the locked door or the comfort of the woodstove. Rather, he ventured further into the far reaches of the dreaded backwater bayou.

It was well after midnight when he made his discovery. Fragments of both brothers' boats laid scattered upon a sandbar, like a graveyard of ships that had chanced a perilous reef and fallen victim to its hidden dangers.

He lit the lantern and steered his john-boat closer to the wreckage.

Suddenly, a gorge of water broke to his right and a long, leathery tail arched through the night air. It hit the glass chimney of the lantern, shattering it. Flaming kerosene splashed across Emery's face and hands. Quickly and without a second thought, he plunged into the cold waters of the bayou, dousing the burning flames before they could do much damage.

The shock of the sudden dive cleared his head, bringing him to the realization that he was in a very dangerous situation. He was about to climb back into the boat, when something grabbed him by the foot. He fought the best he could, but he was an old man and not as strong as he had once been. He felt his fingers slipping from the smooth fiberglass hull, betraying him, surrendering him to the thing that grappled with him from below.

The cold black water rushed up to swallow him. He kicked and flailed as the creature pulled him under. His knife! He had nearly forgotten about it! Emery reached for the eight-inch skinner he carried on his right hip. But it wasn't there. It had been—only moments ago. It was as if someone had grasped the staghorn handle and pulled it from the sheath mere seconds before he could get to it.

Deeper into the depths of Black Bayou he sank, the smothering cloud of watery darkness engulfing him. Soon, he could fight it no longer and found himself blacking out.

Emery DeBossier didn't expect to awaken, but he did. He laid there for a while, disoriented and confused. He seemed to be in some sort of cave—a cramped and dank cave underwater. But, strangely enough, it didn't seem like the lair of some marauding reptile. A small fire burned in the corner, casting an eerie glow upon the slimy walls of the cave, upon his shuddering and soaked form, and on the thing that sat nearby.

It was a skeleton. Or, rather, half a skeleton. Its bones were stark white and clean, as if it had hung in some college biology lab instead of moldering in the depths of a dark and muddy cave. Something about it disturbed Emery to no end. It was *too* clean. No animal could have done that. No animal could have picked the bones of flesh so meticulously and with such cunning precision.

Then, abruptly, the emphasis of Emery's terror shifted. The water at the mouth of the cave began to ripple and churn as his captor arrived. He cringed against the far wall as the great, toothy head poked its way into the cave. Emery could only watch, mortified, as the alligator crammed itself into the limited space. There was something vaguely strange about the way the gator moved, about the way its pebbled skin hung loosely on its body. But the Cajun did not give much thought to such things. All that concerned him at that moment was the dead-meat stench of the creature's breath and the mixture of malice and hunger that gleamed in its single, reptilian eye.

"Ma Gator!" he gasped as the horrid thing shambled closer.

"No," a familiar voice rasped in reply. "But you may call me Pa."

A hand appeared from a slit in the reptile's belly, an undeniably *human* hand, and in its grasp was the old man's missing knife.

It was then that Emery DeBossier looked into the gator's open maw and, from the innermost darkness, saw a grin within a grin.

Norman Partridge is a new writer whose stories are beginning to show up in a variety of markets, both semi-professional and professional. His contribution to *Dark At Heart* shows that his work will be around for some time to come.

# DEAD CELEBS

## Norman Partridge

The woman who answered the door had on a wispy chiffon dress that reminded Ray of the gowns those busty bitches wore in those old Hammer horror movies. Ray loved all that stuff—big breasts and Hammer horror movies and women with chiffon dresses and pinched British accents—and he would have been really excited but for a couple of things that didn't seem right.

The woman's skin was blue.

The dress was cinched around her middle with a rope of seaweed.

Her blond hair was soaking wet and a dead crab was tangled in it.

And worse than all that, she didn't have an accent. She greeted Ray in a flat, whiny voice that reminded him of the time he'd spent the night in a Sioux City bus station.

"What kind of wood doesn't float?" she asked.

Ray's eyebrows squirmed like two perplexed caterpillars. "Huh?"

She looked hurt. "You don't get it."

"Guess I don't."

"Natalie Wood. I'm Natalie *Wood*." She sighed. "Now do you get it?"

Ray squinted at her. This was some strange shit. This bitch wasn't Natalie Wood. Why, Natalie Wood was the wife of that guy who played that real cool TV crook who worked for the government. Ray remembered that, because that show was one of his rerun favorites, one of the best things to come off the Universal back lot in the sixties. And Natalie Wood had drowned years ago . . .

Ray laughed and tugged the rope of seaweed. "Natalie Wood!" He howled. "Shit. I get it! What kind of *wood* doesn't float!"

She looked him over, and it was her turn to look confused. "Who are you supposed to be?"

"Ray," he said, and he shifted the hatbox he was holding from right hand to left and shook her blue hand. "Raymond Meleski."

"Oh yeah?"

"No one told me it was a costume party. Really. I'm here to see the man of the house."

She rolled her eyes. "C'mon in, Ray Meleski."

Ray followed her down a hallway decorated with posters from silent movies. Excellent color, no fading, only the slightest hint of age. Some of the damn things were worth a good piece of change. Ray made a mental note to ask Cardell's friend if he wanted to unload any of them, because Ray was acquainted with a collector out in Thousand Oaks who would go apeshit over a couple of the Charlie Chaplin posters.

At the end of the hallway, Natalie brushed past a potted fern that was big enough to be used for a prop in a jungle picture. Before Ray could follow, a fat guy stepped in front of him.

It was Elvis Presley.

Well, it wasn't Elvis. But the guy was done up just like the King circa 1976, long after Big E had discovered carbohydrates. Big pillow for a gut. Bushy sideburns. White jumpsuit.

The zipper of the jumpsuit was lowered to the man's solar plexus, and there was a fake autopsy wound glued to his sternum. It was a good makeup job, and Ray wondered if Cardell had done it. If he had, Ray would bust the big soul brother a hard one.

Ray had grown up in Memphis.

"That's sacrilegious," he said.

The man thumbed the scar. "The record shows, I took the blows," he sang, waddling up a staircase to the right. "The record shows, I'll snort some blow, and snort it *myyyyyy wayyyyy . . .*"

From the spacious living room, Natalie gave Ray the old come-hither with her index finger. "Everyone's out on the pier," she said.

She opened a smoked-glass door and slipped outside.

Ray shifted the hatbox back to his right hand. The prize that he had brought for the man of the house rolled around inside.

Probably should have bought some of that popcorn stuff to keep it from getting messed up, he thought.

But there hadn't been enough time. The meet had been arranged at the last minute, and that was okay with Ray because he wanted to get the damn thing out of his apartment, out of his life. The sooner, the better.

Ray thought about money and he thought about Cardell.

"Nobody told me it was a costume party," he said.

Cardell called them fartlicks, though he didn't know why. They were easy for Cardell, hard for Ray, and a daily ritual for both on the beach near Cardell's apartment.

Run from one end of the beach to the other, like a sprinter. Then walk back. Then sprint again, then walk again. Basically, that's all there was to the fartlick game. Ray didn't much care for the whole thing, but he knew that he had to keep trim if he ever wanted to break into the movies, and he didn't like the idea of giving up desserts.

Ray Meleski had met Cardell Word on a construction job, and they'd hit it off right away because they both collected movie memorabilia. Cardell wanted to get into the movie business too, but he wanted to work behind the scenes. Makeup. FX. All that gooshy stuff you see in horror pictures. His dad was a successful mortician back in Chicago, and Cardell had developed his skills the hard way, reassembling faces that had been battered against car windows, plugging bullet holes with mortician's wax, and worse.

Ray moved in with Cardell when housing starts took a downturn and Ray got laid off, and he hadn't forgotten Cardell's generosity during that tough time. He got back on his feet with a union job as a gravedigger at a Hollywood cemetery, and he did well enough between that money and the money he earned selling memorabilia to get his own apartment again. He worked from four in the morning till noon, and spent his afternoons answering casting calls. After that, he ran fartlicks with Cardell, ate dinner, and crashed out until it was time for work.

Things were clicking right along. Then the cemetery pink-slipped him. Two weeks' notice.

Cardell was sympathetic. He could afford to be. He'd sold a fully articulated Ray Harryhausen dinosaur to a well-known horror movie producer, and he was negotiating with the guy to do the makeup, prosthetics, and radio-controlled mechanicals for a TV series featuring one of the few movie monsters that wasn't suffering from Creeping Sequelitis.

"You sure he's not just giving you a song-and-dance routine?" Ray asked as they walked on the beach.

"I don't know. The guy is nuts, though. Might do anything. So I'm gonna wait around and see. And my chances might improve if I can help him get a couple of things for his collection. I've been stringing the bastard along with some slightly illicit bait, and I think I might have him ready to bite, big time."

"Yeah? What's he looking for?"

Cardell stopped and gazed at the ocean. "Look, man, we can both make some money off this guy. You know that you can trust me, and if everything works out the deal might lead to some acting work for you. But I'll be straight with you, Raymond. We have to get this business done real soon, and if things go wrong, you'll be the one taking the heat."

"I don't much like the sound of that."

"Yeah. But how do you like the sound of five hundred grand, tax free?"

Ray stepped outside. *Five hundred grand. Tax Free. And that's just my cut.*

Ray walked across the deck. It was built to look like an old pier, real rustic, with lots of fishing nets and harpoons and petrified starfish and those glass floats used by Japanese fishermen. Beyond the pier, the sun was glinting off the waves. Ray reached into his pocket and got his sunglasses.

They were out here all right, just like Natalie had promised. Over by the railing, a blue-skinned Marilyn Monroe danced to a Jim Morrison tune with a man dressed in a Clark Gable "Gone With the Wind" outfit. Clark was pretending to have a heart attack at the very sight of her gyrations. Behind them, a guy in a Superman costume shimmied and shook with a battered Jayne Mansfield clone. Supes pulled a cap pistol from the band of his tights and gave himself a couple of good pops in the head.

Jesus. Cardell hadn't been kidding about the producer being a quart or two low. Ray could just imagine the party invitations: COME AS YOUR FAVORITE DEAD CELEBRITY. TASTEFUL RECREATIONS DISCOURAGED.

Ray got a beer from the bar and looked for Cardell, but his friend was nowhere in sight. He elbowed his way to the railing, set down the hatbox, and stared out at the surf. The tide was coming in. Not much beach left in sight.

Ray didn't know much about architecture—his construction experience was with hammers and heavy equipment, not blueprints—but he could see that the pier was more than just a clever decoration. It helped support the house. The entire structure was up on stilts, and at high tide the water was most likely directly underneath. It reminded Ray of a couple of restaurants he'd visited when he'd done a sportswear commercial up in Monterey.

He imagined the equipment they'd used to sink the big pilings. Must have been something to dig so many deep holes. And then he thought about the cemetery and all the goddamned holes he'd dug with the big yellow backhoe, and as he shook away the memory he knocked his beer off the railing.

It fell to the beach.

A wave kissed it.

Shit. At least it wasn't the hatbox.

*Get a hold of yourself, Raymond.*

Ray picked up the box and went for another drink.

At the bar, a guy wearing a pin-striped suit and a black fedora poured Stolichnaya into a tall glass jar. The jar contained a huge dildo, so long that it had been folded over in order to fit inside. He toasted Ray and took a big gulp of vodka.

Ray laughed. "John Dillinger, right?"

"On the first guess," the guy said.

Dillinger elbowed past a couple of guys disguised as the Kennedy Brothers. Shiny suits and lots of blood. Ray almost expected to see Cardell standing behind them, impersonating Martin Luther King.

But Cardell wasn't there.

Ray helped himself to a South Pacific Lager, found an opener, and popped open the green glass bottle. He headed for the railing, then turned back when he realized he'd forgotten the hatbox.

Natalie had it. She saw him and dodged through the crowd and into the house.

Laughing.

"C'mon," Ray said. "Open the door. I really need to have my box back."

"What's the password?" Natalie giggled.

Ray shook his head. First Cardell, who'd obviously come to the party disguised as Jimmy Hoffa or Judge Crater. Now this shit.

She said, "You haven't gone away, have you?"

The door opened an inch, just enough so Ray could see her smile.

Just as he considered ramming the door, it opened a little wider.

Blue skin. Lots of it.

"You're not mad at me, are you?" She glanced at the hatbox which sat on the corner of the bed. "I mean, I had to lure you up here somehow."

Ray smiled. Sky-blue breasts. Navy-blue nipples. Hell, even her trim was dyed as blue as a sapphire.

"Everyone's out on the pier," she said, stepping back from the door.

Ray moved forward and cupped a breast with his left hand.

Cardell wasn't around.

The hatbox was safe.

Hell, it *was* a party.

He took the dead crab out of her hair.

It wasn't until she had him on the bed, pants down around his ankles, that he looked up and spotted the Vampire hovering at the window.

Ray tried getting up from the chair, but James Dean whacked him real good with a steering wheel.

The Vampire laughed.

Ray glared at James Dean. What a sick fuck. He wore pigskin racing gloves and his long, bony fingers were wrapped around a twisted steering wheel that belonged in a junkyard. His blond hair spiked up from his skull, which was cracked on the right side, revealing a runny gob of brain matter that stained the collar of his red windbreaker. The rest of his face was like a weird jigsaw puzzle—torn, bloody, and missing a piece or two.

And the bastard seemed to enjoy his work. Ray started for him and got whacked again.

Steering Wheel Fu. Shit. Ray eased back in the chair.

"Ready to listen now?" the Vampire wanted to know.

Nodding, Ray looked at the producer's dead-white vampire face. Red lipstick had been applied to the man's generous lips with feminine care. He was gaunt in an androgynous kind of way, but the blue steel .45 that he held in his right hand went a long way toward defining his masculinity.

He stood before a wall that was cluttered with movie memorabilia: autographed stills, lobby cards, a pair of manacles hanging from a peg above a poster for "Murders in the Rue Morgue." A mahogany armoire stood on the wall to his left, and masks and expensive Japanese monster models were housed in glass cases that lined a wall-length bookcase to his right. Ray saw that one of the cases contained a rubber bat, old and mostly rotted. In another case was a wooden stake, along with a brass plaque that read DRACULA 1931.

The producer undid the string that was tied around the hatbox.

Ray remembered his last shift as a gravedigger. Dark. Quiet. The kind of dark quiet that only comes at four o'clock in the morning.

The producer lifted the lid.

Ray heard the creaking sound the casket had made when he'd opened it, remembered placing the shovel blade against the neck of the dead actor resting inside. Remembered Cardell's words: "If things go wrong, you'll be the one taking the heat." Remembered feeling sick and ashamed, but excited too, thrilled by the prospect of a steady television job.

He remembered thinking about five hundred grand.

He remembered the pink slip.

He remembered his booted foot stomping down on the shovel.

The producer lifted the head of Hollywood's most famous blood-sucker out of the hatbox. He raked his fingers through the dead man's hair. "Thank you, Mr. Meleski," he said. "My collection is all the richer for your assistance."

"Great," Ray said. "Now if we can just take care of the remuneration end of things, I'll be on my way."

The producer grinned, a perfect imitation of the mirthless expression that had sent shivers up the spines of so many moviegoers. He raised the severed head to eye level and stared at the sunken eye-sockets. "There *was* a stake in his heart, wasn't there?"

Ray almost laughed.

The producer's eyes widened. "Dear Christ, you mean to say there wasn't a stake?" He tipped the Vampire's head back and glanced at the ruined neck. "And there's no garlic stuffed in the neck cavity!" He ran a finger over the Vampire's yellow teeth. "Why, if the legends are true, he might just open his mouth and . . ."

"BITE!" The producer jerked his finger away from the Vampire's mouth and laughed hysterically. He pointed at James Dean, who had retreated to the door. "I had you going. Admit it. I had you going!"

James Dean lowered his battered head.

The producer placed the severed head on a mahogany desk that matched the armoire in style and color. "So," he said, "we'd be in real good shape if not for one little thing."

Ray asked what that was.

"You chopped my beef, you little asshole!"

The producer nodded at James Dean.

The rim of the steering wheel smashed Ray's nose.

"No two-bit actor chops my beef and gets away with it!"

Ray's head lolled dizzily. He wanted to say that he'd only done what the producer wanted him to do. He'd chopped the dead guy's head off. That was all. But then he realized that the producer was talking about Natalie, and the funny thing was that he hadn't even chopped her, because she'd had his pants down around his ankles and her plum-colored lips around his . . .

Again, the producer nodded.

"I didn't know she was your girl," Ray began. "I thought it was just a party, y'know? Open season . . ."

James Dean hesitated.

The producer waved his .45. "By Christ, you'd better do it if you want to get paid!"

The steering wheel spun forward and split Ray's lower lip.

Then the manacles came off the wall.

Ray cursed The Beach Boys. Such fucking liars. The California surf was nothing but cold. Miserable cold and advancing quickly, and there wasn't a resourceful surfer girl in sight.

Ray's mouth was full of blood. His feet were numb and his calves were cramping, and no matter how hard he tried, he couldn't straighten up. A wave threw him off balance and he butted the piling that stood before him. He swallowed hard and coughed against the gag jammed in his mouth.

Between waves, he could see the source of his predicament through the glassy, green-tinged water. There was a heavy eyebolt set in the base of the piling, and the chain that connected the manacles was looped through it. Ray could sit down, in which case the water rose to his Adam's apple when the waves washed in, or he could stand, hunched over, straining the muscles of his shoulders and lower back as he fought against the chain.

He settled on the latter. His head was clearing now, though his ears still rang from the beating he'd taken, and he used all his strength to pull at the eyebolt. But his feet sank into the sand, and the manacles cut his wrists, and the eyebolt didn't budge.

He could hear the party above. Music. Laughter. Dead Elvis, singing his special version of "My Way."

Another wave hit Ray, and a rope of seaweed lassoed his waist.

Stupid stupid stupid. Five hundred thousand bucks. There for the taking. Just like the fucking head was ripe for the plucking.

And he'd felt so bad about stealing it. Like a little baby. Jesus. What was his taking it next to what that sick fuck in the big house above was going to do with it? What was his momentary indiscretion next to the *years* of warped fun that that crazy shit was going to enjoy?

The producer made his own rules. That's how he'd got to where he was. Big house. Big deals. Ordering people around. He didn't give a shit about what anyone thought of him. He lived on his own terms.

Not like me, Ray thought. Not like a guy who gets laid off once, laid off twice, all the while scraping by like a bug because he doesn't have the guts to make the world give him what he wants. Doesn't have the stones to fuck people over, doesn't have the brains to realize that the absence of same is not an admirable trait in a town like Hollywood.

Maybe in Sioux City, but not here.

The tide washed forward. Even standing, straining for height, the waves were up to Ray's nipples.

Upstairs, someone turned off the music. Ray heard the distant breakers rolling in. Loud, pounding things. The party sounds waned and died. The light that broke through the slatted pier evaporated as the floodlights above were extinguished.

Now the waves were shoulder level. A good splash and Ray would get a mouthful of saltwater. And with the gag nearly jammed down his gullet, he'd be unable to spit out the water.

He could drown standing up.

Ray imagined he heard Natalie Wood's ghost laughing in the surf.

He strained against the manacles.

*If I get out of this, I'll change. If I get out of this, I won't be a loser ever again.*

A yellow circle bobbed between two pilings set high on the beach. A flashlight. Someone sloshed into the water and disappeared under a wave.

A jack handle scraped Ray's thigh.

The eyebolt was pried loose.

Ray raised his arms.

A ruined face appeared next to his own. "Man, your pecker really fucked us up this time, didn't it?"

The woman who answered the door screamed.

Ray stumbled forward, his eyes wild, seaweed coiled around his arms and waist. He grabbed Natalie by the hair and spun her against the wall, hard, but not so hard as to knock the expensive movie posters off their hooks.

She looked at him, her right eye bright and blue, her left eye swelled shut.

"I'm giving you a chance," he said. "Get gone."

He didn't have to tell her twice.

The producer was asleep in his bed. Without his makeup, he looked much older, withered.

Like the severed head that lay on the pillow next to him.

Ray grabbed the collar of the man's silk pajamas and jerked him to a sitting position. The producer's heavy eyelids fluttered open, but not before Ray had wrapped the manacle chain around the bastard's scrawny neck.

"Christ, no! You're dead! You're drowned!"

Ray grinned. "You should have pounded a stake through my heart. Should have stuffed my mouth with garlic."

Ray tightened the chain. He nodded.

James Dean came forward.

The twisted steering wheel came down hard. Again, and again.

They were in the trophy room, filling pillowcases and boxes with memorabilia.

Cardell had peeled off his James Dean mask and his black gloves.

"Ray, man, I can't say how sorry I am. I hated to hit you like that, but the way things came down I would have earned a bullet if I hadn't done what he said."

"It's okay." Ray lowered the glass-encased rubber bat into a box. "We're going to make it worth our while. We'll net a hell of a lot more than a hundred thow from this stuff." He set the box aside and opened a pillowcase. "I only wish I'd have known it was you behind that makeup. Dressing like a honky teen idol—I'd have guessed that was against your general principles."

Cardell shook his head and flipped through a neat stack of hundred dollar bills. "I wanted to let you know it was me. I wanted to meet you downstairs when you came in, but the sick bastard wouldn't have any of it. I think he wanted to split us up, divide and conquer, save himself some money. So he jerked me around up here, showing off his private collection."

"Private collection?"

Cardell smiled. He stepped to the mahogany armoire, twisted two brass handles, and opened its doors.

The severed heads peered out at them.

Hers. Jaw crumbled. But hair still platinum blond.

His. Eyeless. But the moustache still black, still pencil thin.

Hers. Cracked. Broken and battered in a car crash. But still, hers.

His. The twisted lips. The bushy sideburns.

Thinking of money, Ray smiled.

A winner's smile.

Bill Crider is best known for his series of novels about Sheriff Dan Rhodes, who presides over a small Texas town. Bill's work is wonderful at evoking small towns and small town thinking. The series is perfect for film or a television series. Starring say, James Garner or Dennis Weaver.

Bill has also written other novels, Westerns and Mysteries, and is beginning to build up a body of short fiction work of some note. Like the following.

# AN EVENING OUT WITH KARL

## Bill Crider

The bitch was asking for it, he thought. She was *really* asking for it.

He was in one of those dance clubs that were so popular with the kids, the kind where you had to watch your step on the dance floor because if you didn't you might step on a tab of Ecstasy or one of the other hot designer drugs that had popped out of somebody's shirt pocket in the midst of a spectacular Lambada move.

Now and then you might even crunch down on a vial of crack, though that wasn't nearly so common in these places. The kids didn't go for it. They were too affluent for ghetto shit, wanted designer drugs to go along with their designer jeans. In fact, most of them didn't give a damn if you stepped on their fucking drugs. They were generally too ripped to care. Or know.

It was the kind of place Karl really liked.

He had never been to this particular one, of course. He never went twice to the same place. His peculiar inclinations made that impractical. No matter how wired the patrons were, there was always the chance they would remember something about him if he went there more than once.

Like his appearance.

He might as well have been there before, however. As far as he could tell, all those places were the same place. It was like they loaded the fucker up on a big truck and just moved it from one location in the city to another.

There were the same colored lights flashing on and off and running up and down the ceiling, the same music played so loud that it reverberated in your rib cage like someone was beating your heart with a bass drum stick, the same crowd of teenyboppers, yuppies, and middle-aging housewives shaking their asses off with every new dance cut the dj slapped on the turntable. And the same smoke curling white and gray up there in the lights.

There was the same dance floor, no bigger than a good-sized dining table, where you had to be on the look-out at all times for flying elbows and flopping heads. It was like the management begrudged taking up valuable floor space that could be used for tables where the drinkers could sit and slurp up the over-priced drinks that contained barely enough alcohol to get a flea drunk if he could afford ten of them.

So what Karl liked wasn't the atmosphere and the conversation.

No, what he liked was the feeling of anonymity that he could achieve there. In the grotesque light, faces tended to take on odd planes and angles of shadow that made them difficult to recognize in normal illumination. There were so many people sweating and drinking and dancing and hitting on the unaccompanied women that one more strange face was hardly noticed at all.

And of course every now and then you came across someone like the bitch who was asking for it.

It was like she thought she was some vestal virgin. White top, white skirt, white shoes, even a white ribbon in her black, black hair.

She was no virgin, though. That was abundantly clear. The skirt hit her about mid-thigh, highlighting long, showgirl legs that were brown and seemed almost to glow with promise. The heels were five inches if they were one, and they pumped up the calves of those wonderful legs, not to mention the way they set up the gorgeous ass on which the skin was surely as tight as that on the head of a snare drum. And the white top was stretched over a pair of D-cups that measured forty-two inches at the bare minimum. Emphasis on the bare.

It was enough to make a man drool, especially a man like Karl.

He walked over to her table. Somehow she had one all to herself, though nearly everyone else in the place was having to share.

"Dance?" he said.

She gave him a speculative look with large dark eyes under long lashes that Karl were sure must be real.

"Sure," she said.

She had a husky voice that carried just below the level of the music and made the hairs stand up at the base of Karl's spine. She flowed up and out of the chair to take Karl's hand. With those heels, she was slightly taller than he was, but he didn't mind.

The dj was spinning some 12-inch dance version of something by Janet Jackson, and Karl showed his moves. They were pretty good ones, even he had to admit. Maybe not as hot as that fag shit's in SATURDAY NIGHT FEVER, but still damn good.

But they weren't as good as the woman's. She shook, slithered, bounced, and generally got with it in a way that Karl had rarely seen. In the middle of the record she seemed almost to go into a trance, her eyes half closed, her mouth slightly open, her tongue caught between small white teeth.

Definitely asking for it, Karl thought. For fucking sure. Just like the rest of them.

He almost had to laugh aloud when he read about them in the newspapers. They always sounded like they were just coming home from a Girl Scout meeting when the "ski mask rapist" got them. Or like they had been over at their mom's house baking cookies for invalids in the nursing home.

It was all bullshit, as Karl well knew. They were all exactly like the woman in white, practically begging for someone who was man enough to give it to them.

And Karl was man enough for all of them, the eleven reported in the newspapers and the other nine who hadn't said a word about their experience. Probably, Karl thought, because they'd enjoyed the hell out of it. So had the eleven who'd squealed, of course. They were just too chickenshit to admit it.

"What's your name?" he said, as he walked her back to the table as the Janet Jackson record segued into the latest from Prince. There was a fine sheen of sweat on her brow and arms that reflected the flashing lights.

"Donna," she said. "What's yours?"

"Roger," he said. He never gave his real name. He knew what the cops were like. If she reported it, they'd ask her for the names of the men she'd danced with.

"Roger what?" she said.

"Roger Loomis. Thanks for the dance." He never danced with them more than once.

"Thank you . . . Roger," she said, sitting down at her table with feline grace.

He went back to his own table, which he was sharing with two spaced-out and horny young men who had confided that they were attending a local university on tennis scholarships. He thought their vacant eyes boded ill for the future of intercollegiate tennis, not that he gave a shit. They were the perfect table companions, their minds so much on their own dicks that they wouldn't remember him beyond the club's closing time. If they remembered even that long.

She left around one-thirty. Karl had danced with any number of other women, some of whom were begging for it almost as much as Donna, but he had already made his choice. He was a lot of things, but he wasn't fickle.

Karl waited until she was out the door. Then he followed.

She was easy to spot in the parking lot, dressed in white like that. Hell, it was like she was advertising.

She slipped into a white Toyota Celica, and Karl jumped into his anonymous navy blue Ford Escort. He could have afforded a more expensive car, but this one was best for his purposes. Who ever noticed an Escort?

Following her was a snap. She wasn't trying to hide from him. She didn't even know he was back there.

Their cars swooped down FM 1960 under the long line of lights that reflected off their hoods and tops.

Karl's car windows were tinted with plastic so as to be nearly black. He liked the feeling of driving along with the traffic, knowing that no one could see him, much less suspect what he was up to.

The other cars, he was sure, contained sleepy shift workers going home to cold suppers and warm beds, or maybe philandering businessmen who were going to creep into their suburban palaces ("Priced from the $90s to the $150s!") while praying that the wife and one point five kiddies didn't wake up screaming at them when they slipped in the door.

The drivers of the other cars gliding along in the cool blue light would think that Karl was just like them, if they thought of him at all.

But they would be very wrong.

* * *

Karl had known he was special since the first one.

She had been asking for it, too, and so on impulse he had followed her home. He'd just gotten back from a winter vacation to Colorado, and the ski mask was in the car. He pulled it on at the last minute before he climbed over her condo fence and tried the sliding glass door, which of course had been unlocked. So many of them were careless like that, if you could call it careless.

Begging for it, that's what Karl called it.

He remembered how it had felt, stepping into the darkness behind the curtain that covered the glass door, hearing the water running in the bathroom, knowing that she was right there, probably taking a shower, the water running down her taut, soapy skin and out the drain.

He didn't have a weapon; he never needed one. Just his hands, in gloves, of course. The gloves were in the car, too, but wearing them wasn't an impulse. He'd known that he needed to wear the gloves.

He waited by the wall and grabbed her when she came out of the bathroom, clamping his left arm around her throat, his right hand over her mouth. He could smell the powder on her skin.

He threw her on the bed, knelt on her back, and tore off his belt, tying her hands with it. Only then did he take his hand off her mouth.

"One word," he said. "One word, and I'll kill you. Understand?"

She nodded, her head against the bedspread.

His pants were around his thighs. He slipped down his underpants.

"You were asking for this," he said.

"No!" she said, shaking violently. "No!"

"Yes, goddammit!" he said, slamming his fist into her temple. "Say yes!"

For a minute she lay still, not saying anything at all. Then she said, "No."

She shouldn't have said that. If she'd only said yes, then he wouldn't have had to hit her again, and it would have been more fun for both of them.

As it was, he did have to hit her, and she lay still and didn't say anything at all, even when he was finished.

But she loved it, he knew that, because she didn't even report it to the police.

He'd done three before one of them turned him in.

* * *

Donna got onto the Loop from 1960 and then got off at Westheimer. Turned left a few blocks later and stopped in front of a huddle of expensive townhouses. They had to be expensive, in that area of town.

Karl drove on by, made a quick U-turn at the next corner, and parked in time to see Donna standing contemplatively by her car. Karl wondered what she was thinking about. Under the street light she looked almost ghostly in the white skirt, top, and shoes. The black, black hair was stirred by the late-night breeze.

Just as Karl cut his lights, Donna pushed away from her car and started toward one of the townhouses that was squeezed right between two others. She got a key out of her purse and opened the door. She went inside and the door closed behind her.

Karl waited for five minutes before he got out of the Escort. The ski mask was in the left back pocket of his jeans. The gloves were in the right.

He walked past Donna's door to a long driveway. Sure enough, the driveway led to covered parking for the residents. It also led to the back entrances of the townhouses.

The area was lit up by a blue mercury vapor lamp on the light pole, but there was no one back there. There were just the empty cars, the light, and the shadows.

Karl stepped into a shadow and pulled on the ski mask and the gloves.

Then he went to the back door of the townhouse Donna had entered. He couldn't see a light in any of the windows, but that didn't mean anything. She was probably in the bathroom by now. That was the first place women generally went, and that was why he had waited. She wouldn't be likely to hear him come in.

It didn't bother Karl a bit that Donna had neighbors who shared her walls. Not one of the women he'd serviced had ever screamed, not after he'd warned them.

*Asking for it,* goddammit.

He smiled, his mouth stretching under the fabric of the mask.

He tried Donna's back door, but the knob didn't move.

Locked.

He wasn't worried. There was no deadbolt that he could see, just the cheap kind of lock that was part of the doorknob. The kind you always saw some guy slipping with a credit card in movies and on TV. The funny thing was that it really worked like that. He'd practiced on the one at his own apartment until he could slip it in ten seconds.

Donna's took him eight.

He palmed the knob and turned it slowly, pleased that it didn't make a sound. The hinges, too, were silent as the door swung inward to a dark kitchen.

Karl could make out a table and chairs. To his left was a cabinet with a sink in it, and beyond that a stove and oven. He took a step into the room and began to close the door.

Then his head exploded.

* * *

He came to in a bedroom.

He knew it was a bedroom because he was lying spread-eagled on a bed, his head turned to the left. His head blazed with pain, expecially just behind and below his right ear, the ear that was next to the bed.

He tried to move, but he couldn't, not much, and he gradually became aware that his hands and feet were tied to the bed by some kind of silky fabric.

As his eyes began to focus, he saw that Donna was sitting across from him in a gold metal chair, her back to a make-up table surmounted by a lighted mirror. All the lights around the mirror were on, and he could see the make-up strewn over the table. There were blush brushes, mascara brushes, lipstick, powder, different shades of make-up base, other things Karl couldn't identify. There was also an ashtray.

## AN EVENING OUT WITH KARL

Donna was sitting calmly, her right leg crossed over her left, smoking a cigarette.

"Hello, Roger," she said. "So nice of you to drop in on me."

It took Karl a second or two to figure out that she was using the name he'd given her at the club; he didn't see any reason to tell her that the name was wrong.

And then he realized that he was no longer wearing his ski mask or his gloves. He wasn't wearing anything at all.

For the first time, he felt a tinge of fear.

He ignored it. Maybe the bitch was kinky, but what the hell. Karl didn't mind a kink now and then.

"Hi, Donna," he said. "Anything for a good time, huh?"

Donna smiled. She uncrossed her legs and crushed out the cigarette. Her nails were long and red.

"Sure," she said. "Anything for a good time." She got slowly out of the chair and walked over to the bed.

She stood where Karl could see her, hands on hips, legs spread.

"Like what you see?"

"You bet," Karl said, wishing his damn head didn't hurt so much. "You didn't have to hit me, Donna."

"Yes I did."

"You were waiting for me, though. How'd you know I'd come?"

"I hoped you would," she said. "You or someone. It's happened before."

"It has?"

"You'd be surprised." She kicked off the high heels. They thumped against the side of the bed, then dropped to the floor. "Want to see a little more?"

"A lot more," Karl said, thinking that this might not be so bad after all. Hell, she was not only asking for it, she was going to help him. Maybe she would even untie him. "I want to see all you've got."

"Oh, you will," Donna said. "I think you can count on that. Where shall I start?"

"How about untying me?" Being tied was a real problem. Karl wasn't sure that he could even get an erection if he were tied. *He* had to be the one in control. That was the best part of it, being in control, making them know that he could kill them if he wanted, that they had to obey him implicitly, do whatever he demanded.

Donna laughed huskily. "I can't untie you yet, Roger. I meant, what do you want me to take off first."

Karl looked at her bulging breasts. "Start at the top," he said.

"A wonderful idea," Donna said. "I'm sure you're going to be surprised, Roger."

Karl wished his head didn't hurt so much. "I don't think so," he said.

"I do," Donna said, pulling off the black, black hair and dropping it to the floor.

"Shit," Karl said. He liked long hair.

"You *were* surprised, weren't you," Donna said.

He was, he had to admit it, and he was even more surprised at the timber of Donna's voice. It was much lower, no longer husky.

He was even more surprised when Donna took off the white top and revealed a smooth, flat, muscular chest.

And when the skirt dropped to the floor, Karl saw—

"Jesus!" he screamed. "Oh Jesus, no!"

"I'm afraid so, Roger," Donna said, peeling off the jock strap and looking down at his/her rampant erection. "I'm afraid so."

Karl was crying now, sobs racking his body, the whole bed shaking.

"Don't be such a baby," Donna said. "You're going to love it."

"No!" Karl wailed. "No!"

Donna walked over to the bed, the erection jiggling, clamped a hand over Karl's mouth and kidney punched him.

Twice. Hard.

"Not another sound, Roger. You might disturb my neighbors. You understand?"

Karl understood, but he couldn't say so. He was in too much pain.

It didn't matter anyhow. Donna reached down to the floor and came up with the ski mask, then shoved it in Karl's mouth.

"That's much better, Donna said. "I believe I told you my name was Donna. As you may have guessed, it's really Don."

He walked over to the make-up table, opened a drawer, and took something out. Karl watched with fear-crazed eyes.

Don came back to where Karl lay. There was a small bedside table, and Don lay the items he was carrying on it.

A package of condoms. A tube of K-Y jelly.

"You see, Karl? Nothing to worry about. I believe in safe sex."

Karl thrashed on the bed, jerking at the ties that held him bound until they bit into his skin, but he could do nothing more.

Don opened the package, took out a condom, slowly rolled it on. "Do be a good boy, Roger. You know you're going to like this." He picked up the tube of K-Y jelly. "You're going to like this a lot."

* * *

It was a couple of hours later when Wallace, Don's roommate, came in. Don was naked, sitting in the gold chair, smoking a long, thin cigarette.

Wallace looked at the unconscious man on the bed. There was blood smeared across his buttocks, blood on the bed covers. There was even still a little blood on Don.

"Jesus, Don," Wallace said, shaking his head. "This is the worst one yet."

Don didn't say anything. He blew a thin stream of smoke through his red lips.

"He'll yell for the cops," Wallace said. "He's bound to."

"No he won't," Don said. "No one's done that yet. He's just like them. Maybe worse. He'll be much too ashamed."

"Maybe," Wallace said. "But I'm not taking any more chances with you, Don. I told you what would happen if you did this again. I'm leaving."

He went into the other bedroom. Don didn't try to stop him. Later he came back, carrying two heavy leather bags. "I just don't understand, Don. I just don't understand why you do these things."

Don extended the cigarette he was smoking over the ashtray and tapped it with a long red nail. He sighed. He was tired of the argument already.

"The bitch was asking for it," he said.

Steve Rasnic Tem is a school of writing unto himself, and I suspect he'll stay that way. Any label given him rolls right off his back. He never does the same thing twice. What follows here is a story that is dark and suspenseful in the tradition of, none other than, Steve Rasnic Tem.

# RAT CATCHER

## Steve Rasnic Tem

Jimmy hadn't caught four hours sleep all week. Normally he was a dead man about five seconds after he hit the sheets. In fact he liked telling people "I work like a bastard for my sleepeye." Not that he didn't lie there staring at the ceiling a few hours now and then, but not like this, not for days, not for a week. Sometimes he might lie awake counting the tiles because he was trying to remember something, even though he might not know he was trying to remember something. Some special butt-saving part of his brain would nag at him until he'd think of that anniversary, birthday, or special favor for his boss that he'd completely forgotten. "Ah, Jimmy, thank you," he'd say when he remembered these things, flat on his back in bed. Sometimes Tess would nudge him with her elbow a little when this happened, pretending to be asleep but still letting him know he'd saved his butt by just a hair this time (she figured he'd forgotten something having to do with her and most of the time she was right).

But not this time. He didn't think his lack of sleep had anything to do with her. Not this time. What he forgot this time, he knew, came from somewhere deeper than that, from somewhere further back, off where the dog bled in the dark and the rats gathered round to lick the blood.

"Ah, Jimmy, thank you . . ." he said, but quietly, not wanting Tess to hear. *Off where the dog bled in the dark . . .*

Maybe he felt the scratching before he actually heard it. Later he'd wonder about that. He felt it up in his scalp, long and hard like fingernails scratching through a wooden door, the fingers bleeding from the effort and the mind spinning dizzy from the pain. Jimmy raised his head and looked toward the bedroom door—they always kept it open half-way and the hall light on because Miranda was just down the hall and at five years old she still *hated* the dark, almost as bad as Jimmy used to hate the dark. Almost as bad as he hated it now. They kept the door open because Jimmy wanted to be sure and hear her when she screamed, which she still did about once every two weeks. He didn't want to lose any time getting into his little girl's room.

Tess was always telling him that he coddled the kids. That was a funny word—he didn't think he'd ever heard anyone else use it besides his grandma, back when he was a kid. And maybe Tess was right. He'd never been able to talk much about what it is you do with kids—being a dad to them, disciplining them, that kind of thing—not the way Tess could. Sometimes she gave him these books to read, books on parenting by experts. He never got much out of them.

All Jimmy knew was to pay attention to them, love and protect them. And tell them when they did wrong, though after a while you couldn't stop them from doing wrong, just slow them down a little. Just doing that much wasn't easy, not like it sounded. The kids would find out soon enough that the world was worse than they'd ever imagined, and maybe they'd hate him a little at first because of that. But all he could do was try to keep them alive and teach them a few things that would help them keep themselves alive. And maybe someday they'd figure out he'd loved them and that he'd meant the best for them, even with all the mistakes he'd made. He figured love was mostly mistakes that turned out okay. And maybe he'd get lucky. Maybe he wouldn't be dead when that someday came around.

A small black dog, maybe a cat, came racing by the open door, in and out of the little bit of light like a shadow pulled by a rubber band. On its way to Miranda's room, looked like. But they didn't own a dog, not since they put old Wooly to sleep. And their cat was white as a clean pillowcase.

Kids scream for all kinds of reasons. But even for the silly ones Jimmy had never been able to stand it. When Miranda's scream tore so ragged out of the dark he was up and heading out the door without even pulling down the covers. Tess made a little gasp of surprise behind him as the headboard rocked back and banged the wall. The whole house was shaking with his legs pounding down the hallway and Miranda screaming.

As soon as he reached his little girl's door he caught the sharp smell of pee, and when he slammed the light switch on he fully expected to find the rat up on the bed with her, marking her with his teeth and claws and marking the bed with his pee just to let Jimmy know whose was whose.

But there was just Miranda huddled by herself, her face red as a beet (how do little kids make their faces go that color?), and the damp gray flower opening up all around her tiny behind.

"Daddy! A big mousy! Big mousy!" she screamed, words he would have expected from her two years ago but not now (Dad! I'm a *big* girl now!), pointing a whole pudgy and shaking fist toward her open closet door. Jimmy ran back into the hallway and Miranda started screaming again; he could hear the baby squalling in the back room and Tess and Robert were out in the hall, Tess shouting *What's wrong!*, but Jimmy could hardly hear her over Miranda's *Daddy!*. He waved a hand at Tess trying to get her to stay back, jerked open the hall closet door and grabbed the heavy broom, and ran back into his daughter's room.

Where he slammed her closet door as far back as it would go and held the broom up, waiting.

Miranda's screams had choked off into hard, snotty breathing. He could feel Tess and Robert behind him at the door, Tess no doubt holding Robert's jaw in that way she had when she wanted him to know he shouldn't talk just now. Daddy's real busy.

Suddenly there was movement at the bottom of the closet: Miss Raggedy Ella fell over and Jimmy could see that half her face had been torn away into clouds of cotton and he just started waling away with the broom on Miss Ella and Barbie and Tiny Tears and Homer Hippo and the whole happy-go-lucky bunch until they were all dancing up and down and laughing with those big wide permanent grins painted on their faces (except for Miss Ella, who now had no mouth to speak of) and screaming just like Miranda did. "Daddy, stop! You're hurting them!"

"It's a rat! A rat, goddamit!" He didn't know who he was yelling at; he just didn't know how they could be bothering him when there were rats in the house.

Eventually he stopped and when there wasn't any more movement he used the straw end of the broom to pull out Miranda's toys from the bottom of the closet one by one until it was empty.

He found a flap of loose wallpaper along the back wall above the yellowed baseboard. He lifted the flap up with the broom handle and discovered a four-inch hole in the plaster and lathe.

It took Miranda a long time to go back to sleep that night. She was trying to forget something but that part of her brain expert at saving your butt wasn't letting her forget so easily. Instead Jimmy knew that memory was getting filed back there where the rats lick the blood off the wounded dog.

Tess kept telling him, "It's all over now. Go to sleep, honey." And finally he pretended he had.

And thought about the rats he didn't want to think about living in his house, sniffing around his kids. He wasn't about to forget that one. He wasn't about to forget any of it.

He'd never thought that his momma had a dirty house, and he didn't think the other ladies in the neighborhood thought so either else they wouldn't have kept coming over to the house, drinking coffee, eating little cakes his momma made and getting icing all over the Bicycle cards they played with. But this was Kentucky and it was pretty wet country up their valley down the ridge from the mines and half the rooms in that big old house they didn't use except for storage, and fully two-thirds of all those dressers his momma kept around were full of stuff—clothing, old letters, picture albums, bedding—and were never opened. His momma never threw away anything, especially if it came down from "the family," and she had taken charge of all of grandma's old stuff, who had never thrown away anything in her life either.

So it was that he found the nest of hairless little baby rats in that dresser drawer one day. He wasn't supposed to be messing with that dresser anyway. His momma would have switched him skinny if she'd have caught him in one of her dressers.

Back then they'd looked like nasty little miniature piglets to him, squirming and squealing for their momma's hairy rat-tit, but not quite real-looking, more like puppets, a dirty old man hiding inside the dresser making them squirm with transparent fishing line. He'd slammed the drawer shut right away and good thing, too, because if he hadn't then maybe that dirty old man would have reached his burnt arm out of the drawer and pulled him in. Jimmy's momma had never told him to be scared of rats but she sure as hell had told him about the ragged, dirty old men who stayed down by the tracks and prowled the streets at night looking for young boys to steal.

He never told his momma about the rats either and they just seemed to grow right along with him, hiding in their secret places inside his momma's house. Like the rats he'd heard about up in the mines that grew big as beavers because they could hide there where nobody bothered them. He'd heard that sometimes the miners would even share their lunches with them. Then the summer he was twelve the rats seemed to be everywhere, in all the closets in the house and you could hear them in the ceilings and inside the floors running back and forth between the support beams under your feet and his momma got pretty much beside herself. He'd hear her crying in her bed at night sounding like his dear sweet little Miranda now.

He remembered feeling so bad because he was the man of the house, had been since he was a baby in fact and he knew he was supposed to do something about the rats but at twelve years old he didn't know what.

Then one day this big rat that should have been a racoon or a beaver it was so big—a *mine* rat, he just knew it—came out from behind the refrigerator (that always felt so warm on the outside, smelling like hot insulation, perfect for a rat house) and ran around the kitchen while they were eating, its gray snake tail making all these S's and question marks on the marbled linoleum behind it. Jimmy's momma had screamed, "Do something!" and he had—he picked up the thick old broom and chased it, and that big hairy thing ran right up her leg and she screamed and peed all over herself and it dropped like she'd hit it and Jimmy broke the broom over it, but it started running again and he chased it down the cellar steps whacking it and whacking it with that broken piece of broom until the broom broke again over the rat's back and still it just kept going, now making its S's and question marks all over the dusty cellar floor so that it looked like a thousand snakes had been wrestling down there.

Jimmy kept thinking this had to be the momma rat. In fact over the next year or so he'd *prayed* that what he had seen down there had been the momma, and not one of her children.

The rat suddenly went straight up the cellar wall and into a foot-high crawlspace that spread out under the living room floor.

"You get it, son?" His mother had called down from the kitchen door, her voice shaking like his grandma's used to.

He started to call back that he'd lost it, when he looked up at the crawlspace, then dragged an old chair over to the wall, and climbed up on the splintered seat for a better look.

Back in the darkness of the crawlspace there seemed to be a solider black, and a strong wet smell, and a hard scratch against the packed earth that shook all the way back out to the opening where his two hands gripped the wall.

The scratching deepened and ran and suddenly his face was full of the sound of it as he fell back away from the wall with the damp and heavy black screeching and clawing at his face.

His momma called some people in and they got rid of the nests in the dressers and closets but they never did find the big dark momma he had chased into the cellar. At night he'd think about where that rat must have got to and he tried to forget what wasn't good to forget.

There was one more thing (isn't there always, he thought). They'd had a dog. Not back when he'd first seen the big momma rat, but later, because his momma had felt bad about what happened and he'd always wanted a dog, so she gave it to him. Jimmy named it Spot, which was pretty dumb but "Spot" had been a name that had represented all dogs for him since he was five or six, so he named his first dog Spot even though she was a solid-color, golden spaniel.

Just having Spot around made him feel better, although as far as he knew a dog couldn't help you much with a rat. Maybe she should have gotten him a cat instead, but he couldn't imagine a cat of any size dealing with that big momma rat.

Jimmy didn't think much about that dog anymore. Ah, Jimmy, thank you.

They had Spot four years. Jimmy was sixteen when the rats came back, a few at a time, and quite a bit smaller than the way he remembered them, but still there seemed to be a lot more of them each week and he'd dreamed enough about what was going to happen to him and his momma when there were enough of those rats.

Then he was down in the cellar one day when he saw this big shadow crawling around the side of the furnace, and heard the scratching that was as nervous and deep as an abcess. He ran upstairs and got his dead daddy's shotgun that his momma had kept cleaned and oiled since the day his daddy died, and took it down to the dark, damp cellar, and waited awhile until the scratching came again, and then that crawling shadow came again, and then he just took aim, and fired.

When he went over to look at the body, already wondering how he was going to dispose of that awful thing without upsetting his momma when she got home, he found his beautiful dog instead.

He'd started crying then, and shaking her, and ran back up the steps to get some towels (but why had she been crawling, and why hadn't she just trotted on over to him like she'd always done?), and when he got back down to the cellar with his arms full of every sheet and towel he could get his hands on, there had been all these rats gathered around the body of his dog, licking off the blood.

And now there were rats in his house, around his children.

The rat catcher, Homer Smith, was broad and rounded as an old Ford. Tess called Jimmy at work to tell him that the "rat man" had finally gotten there and Jimmy took the time off to go and meet him. When Jimmy first saw him the rat catcher was butt-wedged under the front porch, his big black boots soles out like balding tires, his baggy gray pants sliding off his slug-white ass as he pushed his way further into the opening until all of a sudden Jimmy was thinking of this huge, half-naked fellow crawling around under their house chasing rats. And he was trying not to giggle about that picture in his head when suddenly the rat catcher backed out and lifted himself and pulled his pants up all in one motion too quick to believe. Homer Smith was big and meaty and red-faced like he'd been shouting all morning and looking into his face Jimmy knew there was nothing comical about this man at all.

"You got rats," Homer Smith said, like it wasn't true until he'd said it. Jimmy nodded, watching the rat catcher's lips pull back into a grin that split open the lower half of his bumpy brown face. But the high fatty cheeks were as smooth and unmoved as before, the eyes circled in white as if the man had spent so much time squinting that very little sun ever got to those areas. The eyes inside the circles were fixed black marbles with burning highlights. "Some call me out to look at their rats and it comes up nothing but little mousies they coulda chased away their own selves with a lighter and a can of hairspray. If they had a little hair on their chests that is." Miranda's "mousies" sounded lewd and obscene coming from Smith's greasy red lips. "But rats now, they don't burn out so good. That hair of theirs stinks to high heaven while it's burning, but your good size mean-ass rat, he don't mind burning so much. And you, son . . ." He raised his fist. "You got rats."

Jimmy stared at the things wriggling in the rat catcher's fist: blind, pale and constantly moving, six, maybe eight little hairless globs of flesh, all alike, all as blank and featureless as the rat catcher's fingers and thumb, which now wriggled with the rat babies like their own long-lost brothers and sisters. "How many?" Jimmy asked, glancing down at his feet.

"How many what?" Smith asked, gazing at his fistfull of slick wriggle. He reached over with a finger from the other hand and flicked one of the soft bellies. It had a wet, fruity sound. Jimmy could see a crease in the rat skin from the hard edge of the nail. A high-pitched squeak escaped the tiny mouth.

Jimmy turned away, not wanting to puke on his new shoes. "How many rats? How many days to do the job? Any of that," he said weakly.

The rat catcher grinned again and tossed the babies to the ground where they made a sound like dishrags slapping linoleum. "Oh, you got *lots*, mister. Lots of rats and lots and lots of days for doing this job. You'll be seeing lots of me the next few weeks."

And of course the rat catcher hadn't lied. He arrived each morning about the time Jimmy was leaving for work, heavy gauge cages and huge wood and steel traps slung across his back and dangling from his fingers. "Poison don't do much good with these kind o' rats," Smith told him. "They eat it like candy and shit it right out again. 'Bout all it does is turn their assholes blue." Jimmy wasn't about to ask the rat catcher how he'd come by the information.

If he planned it right Jimmy would get home each afternoon just as Smith was loading the last sack or barrel marked "waste" up on his pickup. The idea that there were barrels of rats in his house was something Jimmy tried not to think about.

If he planned it wrong, however, which happened a lot more and often than he liked, he'd get there just as the rat catcher was filling the sacks and barrels with all the pale dead babies and greasy-haired adults he'd been piling up at one corner of the house all day. Babies were separated from the shredded rags and papers they'd been nested in, then tossed into the sacks by the handsfull, so many of them that after a while Jimmy couldn't see them as dead animals anymore, or even as meat, more like vegetables, like bags full of radishes or spring potatoes. The adults Smith dropped into the barrels one at a time, swinging them a little by their slick pink tails and slinging them in. When the barrels were mostly empty, the sound the rats made when they hit was like mushy softballs. But as the barrels filled the rats made hardly a sound at all on that final dive: no more than a soft pat on a baby's behind, or a sloppy kiss on the cheek.

Jimmy had figured Smith was bound to be done after a few days. But the man became like a piece of household equipment, always there, always moving, losing his name as they started calling him by Tess's name for him, "the rat man," as if he looked like what he was after, when they were able to mention him at all. Because sometimes he made them too jumpy even to talk about, and the both of them would stay up nights thinking about him, even though they'd each pretend to the other that they were asleep. A week later he was still hauling the rats out of there. It seemed impossible. Jimmy started having dreams about a mine tunnel opening up under their basement, and huge, crazy-eyed mine rats pouring out.

"I don't like having that man around my kids," Tess said one day.

Jimmy looked up from his workbench, grabbing onto the edge of it to keep his hands from shaking. "What's he done?"

"He hasn't *done* anything, exactly. It's just the way he looks, the way he moves."

Jimmy thought about the rats down in their basement, the rats in their walls. "He's doing a job, honey. When he's done with the job he'll get out of here and we won't be seeing him anymore."

"He gives me the creeps. There's something, I don't know, a little strange about him."

Jimmy thought the rat man was a lot strange, actually, but he'd been trying not to think too much about that. "Tell you what, I've got some things I can do at home tomorrow. I'll just stick around all day, see if he's up to anything."

Jimmy spent the next day doing paperwork at the dining room table. Every once in a great while he'd see the rat man going out to his truck with a load of vermin, then coming back all slick smiles and head nodding at the window. Then Jimmy would hear him in the basement, so loud sometimes it was like the rat man was squeezing himself up inside the wall cavities and beating on them with a hammer.

But once or twice he saw the rat man lingering by one of the kid's windows, and once he was scratching at the baby's screen making meow sounds like some great big cat, a scary, satisfied-looking expression on his face. Then the rat man looked like the derelicts his momma had always warned him about, the ones that had a "thing" for children. But still Jimmy wasn't sure they should do anything about the rat man. Not with the kind of rat problem they had.

When he talked to her about it that night Tess didn't agree. "He's weird, Jimmy. But it's more than that. It's the way the kids act when he's around."

"And how's that?"

"They're scared to death of him. Miranda sticks herself off in a corner somewhere with her dolls. Robert gets whiny and unhappy with everything, and you *know* that's not like him. He just moves from one room to the next all day and he doesn't seem to like any of his toys or anything he's doing. But the baby, she's the worst."

Jimmy started to laugh but caught himself in time, hoping Tess hadn't seen the beginnings of a smile on his lips. Not that this was funny. Far from it. But this idea of how the baby was reacting to the rat man? They called their youngest child "the baby" instead of by her name, because she didn't feel like a Susan yet. She didn't feel like anything yet, really—she seemed to have no more personality than the baby rats the rat man had thrown down outside the house. Tess would have called him disgusting, saying that about his own daughter, but he knew she felt pretty much the same way. Some babies were born personalities; Susan just wasn't one of those. This was one of those things that made mommies and daddies old before their time: waiting to see if the baby was going to grow into a person, waiting to see if the baby was going to turn out having much of a brain at all.

So the idea of "the baby" feeling anything at all about the rat man made no sense to Jimmy. He felt a little relieved, in fact, that maybe they'd made too much out of this thing. Maybe they'd let their imaginations get away from them. Then he realized that Tess was staring at him suspiciously. "The *baby?*" he finally said. "What's wrong with the baby?"

"Susan," Tess replied, as if she'd been reading his mind. "Susan is too quiet. Like she's being careful. You know the way a dog or a cat stops sometimes and gets real still because it senses something dangerous nearby? That's Susan. She's hardly even crying anymore. And you try to make her laugh—dance that teddy bear with the bright blue bib in front of her, or shake her rattle by her face—and she doesn't make a sound. Like she knows the rat man's nearby and she doesn't want to make a noise 'cause then he'll figure out where she is."

In his head Jimmy saw the rat man prowling through the dark house, his baby holding her breath, her eyes moving restlessly over the bedroom shadows. "Maybe he'll be done soon."

"Christ, Jimmy, I want him out of here! And I know you do, too!"

"What reason could I give him? We're just talking about 'feelings' here. We don't really know anything."

"What *reasons* do we need? We hired the man—we can fire him just as easy."

"Easy?"

"You're scared of him, Jimmy! I've never seen you so scared. But these are our *kids* we're talking about!"

"He makes me a little nervous, I admit," he said. "What you said about Susan makes me nervous as hell. And I am thinking about the kids right now, and how I can keep things safe for them around here."

"So we just let him stay? We just let him sneak around our kids doing god-know's-what?"

"We don't know he's doing anything except acting a little eccentric. We could fire him and the police could force him off our property, but that doesn't help us any with what might happen later."

"Later," she repeated. Jimmy couldn't bear how scared she looked. "What are we going to do?"

"I'm staying home again tomorrow. I'll park the car down the street and hide in the house. If he's doing anything he shouldn't he probably figures he can avoid your one pair of eyes. But tomorrow you'll be following your normal schedule and I'll be your extra pair of eyes. Between the two of us we shouldn't miss much." Jimmy looked down at the floor, thinking of the beams and pipes and electrical conduit hidden there. He listened for the rats, but the only scratches he heard were the ones inside his head.

The rat man came out exactly at nine in the A.M. like always. You could set your clock by him. He started unloading all his equipment, including the sacks and the metal barrel he threw the adult rats in. Jimmy crouched low by the master bedroom window, watching for anything and everything the rat man did. The first sign of weirdness, he thought, and he'd be hauling his kids' asses out of there. Tess went to work in the kitchen; they agreed it'd be best to pretend she was having a normal day.

The rat man disappeared around the corner of the house with the big metal barrel. Jimmy was thinking about shifting to another room when he came back, holding four stiff rats by the tails, their black coats grayed with dust. *No way he could've caught and killed them that quick,* he thought. The rats appeared to have been dead a good day at least. Jimmy watched as the rat man waddled up to the corner where the house turned into an "L," the corner with the window to the baby's room. He watched as the rat man dangled the stiff rats against the rusting screen, clucking and cooing, rubbing his fingers up and down the smooth, hairless tails, talking to Jimmy's baby through the screen and smiling like he didn't realize where he was, like he was off in another place entirely.

*Off where dogs bleed in the dark and the rats gather round to lick the blood.*

All day long Jimmy watched as the rat man sneaked dead adult rats and hairless baby rats out of his rusted green pickup and planted them in the crawl spaces under the house only to haul them out again and replace them in the barrel and the sacks. The same ones, over and over. Jimmy wondered how many rats they'd actually had in the first place. A dozen? Six? Four? Just the one, trapped back under Miranda's bedroom, and coming into the rat man's hand easier than a hungry kitten?

Now and then the rat man would come out with something wrapped in a towel or a rag, cradling it carefully in his arms like it was his own baby. Jimmy couldn't quite credit the gentleness he was seeing in the rat man; he looked silly, really. Jimmy wondered why the rat man would want some of the rats bundled up.

Right after the rat man left for the day Jimmy told the whole story to Tess. "I wasn't about to confront him on it here," he said.

"Well, if he's just a con artist then we can call the police."

"He's a helluva lot more than that—I think we've both figured that one. That little office he has in town is closed and there's no home phone number listed. So I'm going to have to go out to his place tonight. I'm going to tell him not to come around here anymore."

"What if he says no?"

"He's not allowed to say no, honey. I'm not going to let him."

"What if I say no, Jimmy?" Her voice shook.

"I don't think you're going to say no. I think you're going to be thinking about the kids, and that crazy man dangling rats in front of their faces like they were baby toys." He stroked her shoulder. After a few seconds she looked away. And Jimmy grabbed his coat and went out to the car.

The rat man lived out past the empty industrial parks on the north end of the city. Here the municipal services weren't so good, the streets full of ragged holes like they'd just run short of asphalt, the signs faded, with a permanent, pasted-on look to the trash layering the ditchlines.

It wasn't hard finding the right house. "The rat catcher man? He lives down the end of that street don't-cha-know." The old man was eager to tell him even more information about the rat man, but these were stories Jimmy didn't want to hear.

The rat man's house didn't look much different from any other house in that neighborhood. It was a smallish box, covered with that aluminum siding you're supposed to be able to wash off with a hose. A small porch contained a broken porch swing. There were green curtains in the window. A brown Christmas wreath hung on the front door even though it was April.

Two trash cans at the curb overflowed with paper and rotten food. And the foot-high brown grass moved back and forth like a nervous shag carpet.

What was different about the rat man's yard was all the tires that had been piled there, stacked into wobbly-looking towers eight or nine feet tall, bunches of them sitting upright like a giant black snake run through a slicer, tangled together in some parts of the yard like a slinky run through the washer. Some of the tires were full of dirt and had weeds growing out of them. Some of the tires looked warped and burnt like they'd had to be scraped off somebody's car after some fiery journey.

But it was the nervous grass that kept pulling at Jimmy's gaze. It wiggled and shook like the ground underneath it was getting ready to turn somersaults.

When Jimmy moved through it on the way to the rat man's door it scratched at the sides of his boots. When Jimmy climbed the porch steps it slicked long, trembling fingers up around his ankles, making slow S-curves and question marks that set him shivering almost—it was crazy—with delight.

When Jimmy actually got to the door he could hear the layers of scratch and whisper building behind him, but he didn't turn around. The scratching got louder and Jimmy found himself angry. He started to knock on the rat man's door but once he got his hand curled into a fist he just held it there, looked at it and made the fist so tight the fingers went white. The scratching was in his ears and in his scalp now, and suddenly he was in a rage at the rat man, and couldn't get that picture out of his head: the rat man dangling those dead monster babies in front of Jimmy's baby's window.

He held back his fist before he punched through the rotting door and instead moved to the dingy yellow window at the back of the rat man's porch. He let go of the fist and used the open hand to shield his eyes from the late afternoon glare when he pressed his face against the glass.

He saw the rat man's back bobbing up and down like a greasy old sack moving restlessly with its full complement of dying rat babies. The walls of the room were lined with a hodge-podge of shelving: gray planks and old wooden doors cut into strips and other salvage rigged in rows and the shelves full of glass jars like his grandmother's root cellar packed with a season's worth of canning.

Jimmy couldn't tell what was in those jars. It looked like yellow onions, potatoes maybe.

The rat man was taking something out of a sack. He moved, and Jimmy could see a small table, and little bundles of rags on it. The rat man picked up the bundles gently and filled his arms with them. Then he headed toward a dark brown, greasy-looking door at the back of the room.

Jimmy stepped off the porch and moved toward the side of the house. The rat man's grass seemed to move with him, pushing against his shoes and rippling as he passed. He looked down and now and then saw a gray or black hump rise briefly over the grass tops before sinking down inside again.

The first window on that side was dark and even with his face pushed up into the dirty screen he could see nothing. A tall dresser or something had been pushed up against the window on the other side.

The second window glowed with a dim yellow light. Jimmy moved toward it, through grass alive with clumps and masses that rubbed against his boots, crawled over his ankles, and scratched at his pants legs.

A heavy curtain had been pulled across the window, but it gapped enough in the middle to give Jimmy a peep-hole. Inside, the rat man was unwrapping the bundles. Around the room were more shelves, but here they had been filled with children's toys: dolls, teddy bears, stuffed monkeys and rabbits, tops and cars and jack-in-the-boxes and every kind of wind-up or pull-toy Jimmy had ever seen. Some of them looked shiny brand-new as if they'd just come out of the box. Others looked as old as Jimmy and older, the painted wood or metal dark brown or gray with layers of oily-looking dust.

The rat man put his new toys up on the shelf: a Miss Raggedy Ella doll, Tiny Tears, Homer Hippo, GI Joe, a plastic Sherman tank, a baby rattle, and a teddy bear with a bright blue bib. Toys that belonged to Jimmy's kids. And then the rat man picked up the last, slightly larger bundle, and placed it in a pink bassinet in the middle of the room, where he unwrapped it and rearranged the faded blankets.

Suddenly Jimmy felt the rats clawing at his ankles, crawling up his legs.

He turned so quickly—thinking he'd run to the porch and break through the door—that he stumbled and fell on his knees. Instantly he had rats crawling up on his back, raking at his legs, several hanging by their claws and teeth from the loose front of his shirt. He stood and brushed them off him, finally grabbing one that just wouldn't let go with his hands around its belly and squeezing until it screamed and dropped.

All around him the towered and twisting mass of tires was alive with dark rats, scrambling over each other as they climbed and tumbled through the insides and over the outsides of the black casings. He didn't make it to the porch without losing a few hunks of skin here and there. *The rats gathered round to lick the blood . . .*

The rat man's door disintegrated the second time Jimmy plowed into it with his shoulder, but not without a couple of hard splinters lodging painfully into the top of his arm. He stumbled into the front room and crashed into the far wall where the shelves of old wood began pulling away from the wall, dumping row after row of Mason jars onto the floor.

His feet slid on the spilled gunk. He could feel soft lumps smashing under the soles of his shoes. He staggered and grabbed the edge of a shelf, bringing down more of the jars. He started moving toward the greasy brown door at the back of the room as if in slow-motion, looking down at his shoes and moving carefully so that he wouldn't slash himself on the broken glass, but all the time screaming, yelling at himself to get his ass in gear and get to that bedroom at the back of the rat man's house.

He saw, but didn't think about, the bodies of the hundreds of hairless little rat babies bursting open under his shoes and smearing across every inch of the wooden floor.

He felt himself sliding, beginning to fall, as he jerked the door open and headed down a pitch black hallway toward a dim yellow rectangle of light at the other end. He pushed at the invisible walls of the hallway to keep himself upright and raced toward that rectangle, the walls going away around him as in a dream.

He wasn't aware of pushing open the door to the back room. It just seemed to dissolve at the touch of his hands.

Homer Smith, the rat man, was bent over the pink bassinet, cooing and making little wet laughing sounds. Later Jimmy would wonder why it was the rat man hadn't paid any attention to the ruckus in the front part of his house.

Homer looked up, his hands still inside the bassinet, as Jimmy hit him across the face as hard as he could. He fell to his knees with a noise like thunder, then looked up at Jimmy, then looked around at all his toys, smiled a little, like he wanted Jimmy to play with him. *Off where the dog bled in the dark* . . . Jimmy kicked him in the ribs this time, with boots still smeared and sticky.

Homer doubled over without a sound, then he looked up at Jimmy again, and his face was as soft and unfocused as a baby's.

Jimmy thought about his baby in the bassinet, but couldn't quite bring himself to look yet. He glanced around the room instead and saw the broom propped in one corner. He stepped over to it, still aware that Homer wasn't moving, picked it up and brought it down across Homer's left cheekbone. The straw-end snapped off like a dry, dusty flowerhead and Jimmy used the broken handle to whip Homer's face until it was a bloody, frothy pudding, Homer's head snapping back and forth with each blow but still Homer stayed upright, leaning forward on his knees. Jimmy couldn't believe it, and it scared him something terrible.

He kept thinking about the baby, but couldn't keep his eyes off the baby catcher, the baby snatcher. Finally he took the ragged, broken end of the broom handle and held it a couple of feet from Homer's throat. Jimmy could feel the weight of the pink bassinet behind him, and the thing wrapped up inside it, not moving, not crying, keeping still as if watching to see what would happen, but Jimmy knew it wasn't just keeping still. It was dead. Susan was dead. He hadn't checked on her before he came out here after the rat man and he should have known, watching the rat man carrying all those swaddled objects out of his house like that. He should have *known.*

At last Homer Smith raised his bloody head and stared at the sharp stick Jimmy had poised at his throat and seeing what Jimmy was ready to do Homer began to cry a wet, blood-filled cry, like a baby, just like a baby Jimmy thought, and it reminded him of lots of things, not all of it bad, as he drove the sharp end of that stick as hard as he could into the soft skin of Homer's throat.

The dying took a few minutes, Homer trying to pull the stick out but not being able to. Jimmy threw up over by the bassinet until he had nothing left to heave. Finally he got to his feet again and stood over his baby, hesitated, then slowly unwrapped the blanket from around her.

And found two dead black rats there, curled around each other like Siamese twins. Homer had dressed each in baby doll clothes.

Jimmy felt the scratching up in his scalp, long and hard like fingernails clawing through a wooden door, long before he actually heard it. And then the sound of hundreds of pale tongues, lapping.

He turned and looked *off where the dog bled in the dark* at Homer Smith's body, and the hundreds of rats gathered round to lick the blood.

Robert Petitt has the same sort of steel-toed boot approach to writing that Robert E. Howard had. Powerful. Fast-paced. Sometimes crude. Always interesting, and very often disturbing. He's a maturing talent and talent to watch.

# I'LL ALWAYS LOVE YOU

## Robert Petitt

Pain.

Pain like nothing he could have ever imagined. Hot Roman Candles exploding behind his eyes/pain. Molten lava dripping like acid into his brain/pain.

Excruciating pain.

But behind the harsh red haze of shimmering agony, a vision of her blurred, cleared, focused, cleared, focused, clarified. And that was all that was necessary to keep him at task. For death was not a task to be taken lightly. Especially when it was his own.

His death had to be perfect, or the bitch would never know how much he truly loved her. And he really did love her, though that didn't keep him from calling her a bitch. Or worse. Like, that fucking cunt.

For now, since the bitch had walked out—left him—his goal in life (death) was to show her how much he did care. Prove his love, let her know how much he suffered, force her to see with her own eyes what he had endured, see how he had suffered for her. For her . . .

And she would be forced to see, because the police would want a positive I.D. on the body. They would bring her in here, right smack dab into the middle of this bathroom, right goddamned in the middle of all the blood, stink, shit, and gore of his fucking bathroom, and ask her point-blank if what she was looking at was the remains of her late husband.

And it would have to be her; there were no other next of kin. She would see him, read his suicide note, and his only regret would be that he wouldn't be here to see the look on her face.

The pain was but a dull ache by the time everything was in place. The bathtub was half-filled with gasoline, the .44 Magnum lay on the rim of the tub. He lit the match, felt the whoosh! as the blast of superheated air singed his face. Watched in grim fascination as the flames ate into his best tux, the one he had worn at his wedding.

Everything was perfect. He placed the gun in his left hand, the one with the wedding band that she had slipped on his finger right after she had said until death do us part. He grimaced as another wave of agony swept over him. The stench of burning flesh assailed his nostrils.

He lifted the gun, imagined it was her he was aiming it at, gently squeezed the trigger. The recoil slammed his left hand to the tile floor, fingers curled in a death grip around the butt.

The body continued to burn.

Tori Porter stood before the graveyard marker; her dark eyes, tinged with sadness but untouched by tears, moved slowly over the words carved so meticulously into the smooth gray granite. The wind, tainted by a hint of the rains to come, played at her auburn hair which only recently had become plagued with strands of silver. Idly she brushed aside a wisp that tickled at her forehead.

She sighed, thinking that Rick had been every bit as dramatic in death as he had been in life.

His epithet epitomized that thought; the words were like a slap in the face. They stung, numbed her, those carefully chiseled words: Every Man Destroys That Which He Loves The Most, Here Lies Proof To That Testament.

She sighed again, her small breasts rising slightly with the effort, and sarcastically laughed to herself.

Fifteen years of marriage to Richard Porter, who endowed more women with new, larger, firmer, and shaplier breasts than any other surgeon in New Orleans, and his wife was still packing the same set of fried eggs she had had since puberty. Ironic? Poetic justice? She didn't know, didn't care to dwell on the thought, for Rick had been a tit man in more than one sense.

At parties and other affairs, she had often found him giving unsolicited examinations and offering his opinion on the improvements needed to make each pair of mammary glands a perfect match. She could live with that aspect of their marriage, and did, because it was his job.

But when she had caught him with Georgia Hanson—the wife of her boss, for chrissakes—kneading and squeezing her breasts . . . well, that had been it, as far as she was concerned.

He had claimed they had both drank a teesy-weensy bit too much, and that things had gotten out of hand. He had said that he was sorry, and nothing like that would ever happen again.

She knew he was sorry, all right. Sorry he had forgotten to lock the bathroom door. Sorry Tori had walked in, sorry his pants and shorts were down to his ankles, sorry Georgia Hanson had her three thousand dollar original tucked up around her waist, with her lace and silk panties lying in a guilty red pile on the white tile floor. He was sorry as hell, he had said.

And that was exactly where Tori had told him to go: straight to—do not pass go—Hell! Her words, verbatim. And she had left, right there and then, without bothering to pick up a damn thing.

And now, this. This great, gray stone standing silent sentinel over a slight mound of dirt and decayed flowers. And she wondered, as she read the inscription one last time before leaving—did he do what she had told him to do?

*Did* he go straight to Hell?

The dingy sky had darkened and a light drizzle had begun falling by the time she drove through the gates of the cemetery. As the car moved down the winding asphalt road outside the graveyard, flashes of intermittent lightning illuminated the monuments to the dead, lending to the real world a surrealistic effect of intermingled night and day. A twilight world of dancing shadows and swaying branches; the embedded tombstones leaning toward the receding tail-lights of the station wagon like winter-stricken trees stretching for that last tinge of warmth from a waning sun. That last faint touch with the living that the dying know only too well.

A grim and determined, jealous reluctance to let go.

"Yes, ma'am. Go about four miles down this road and you'll come to a bridge. Cross that, then take a right on the other side of the bayou. Follow that drive until you can't go no more and that's the place you're looking for. You can't miss it."

Tori thanked the service station attendant for his directions and drove away. She spied the turnoff as she crossed the bridge and immediately regretted the station wagon as a means of transport even though she needed the room in the back for art supplies, canvasses, and her personal effects. She had planned to spend most of her time doing some painting, and mouthed a quick prayer that none of the jars of paint would break when she saw what she had gotten herself into.

The trail to Henry Hanson's summer camp was narrow, with muddy potholes galore, and broken vines and paint-peeling bushes lining the barely passably drive.

At least she hoped it was passable, as the wagon bounced and scraped itself along the tiny slit of mud, leaves, twigs and roots of Louisiana river bottom. The sunlight, what little there was, as the rain wasn't far behind, filtered between tremendous spreads of oak tree canopys and gleamed off the windshield, sending pinpricks of light dancing across her pupils and making her sleepy.

Suddenly she was there, staring in awe at the imposing edifice that Henry referred to as a camp. If this was a camp, she opined, then the quarter million dollar townhouse that Rick and she had owned was a shack.

And that shack was up for sale now, as was all of Rick's things. She wanted nothing left to remind her of him. Nothing. And that was the reason why she was here now: therapy. Time to get away, time to forget, time to forgive. Forget Rick, but mostly, to forgive herself.

Though she was constantly told it wasn't her fault, she couldn't help but shoulder the blame for Rick's suicide, and had therefore gone through nine weeks of consultation, evaluation and therapy. Until, at her doctor's insistence, therapy consisted of her getting away from it all. Not running away, he had explained, just getting away.

And what Henry had, as he had told her, was the perfect place. He, too, had insisted she make use of his camp for the summer. After half-hearted attempts of thank-you's-but-I-just-can't, she finally relented, for two reasons.

One, Georgia Hanson had accepted Henry's offer of money, and had gone to Rio, where she waited for the divorce to be final. Two, Henry would be gone to Europe for the summer to purchase, at various auctions, quality works of art for his New Orleans gallery. She knew that Henry was more than a little in love with her, and she would have been adamant in her refusal to use his place if she knew he would be so close as to feel the need to check in on her every so often. It was her feeling that both of them had just been taken on an emotional roller coaster ride, and that something could happen should they be together, too often, too soon after . . .

And she just wasn't ready for any type of physical or emotional involvement with anyone. Not right away. Maybe later, when the wounds had healed and the scars weren't so visible. But not now.

The mush and mire abruptly ended and gave way to a concrete drive and she eased the wagon to a halt directly outside the front doors of the mansion. For mansion it was; Tori had toured several antebellum plantations, including Parlange in New Roads, built in 1750, and both the Cottage and the Myrtles in St. Francisville. The Myrtles was reputed to be haunted, and Tori believed it; the place had given her chills, and she had been glad to leave the tour group and get back outside, into the welcome sunshine.

She stepped out of the car, stretching the kinks out of her tight muscles, but not taking her eyes from the house, with its huge Doric columns, and countless Dormer windows like blank unseeing eyes spaced around the perimeter of the third floor. She was so engrossed that she jumped when the voice came from behind her.

"Do you like it? Oh, sorry, I didn't mean to startle you, but I guess you didn't expect me to be here."

Tori had jerked around, surprised more than frightened, then confused when she saw it was Henry standing there with a frozen half-smile on his face.

"Henry . . . I thought you had flown to London yesterday. What are you doing here? I mean it's your place, but I didn't really expect to see you until August."

Henry moved toward her a step, his blue eyes flashing as brightly as the gleam of his white teeth. He was handsome, she thought, what with that shock of red hair and Huck Finn grin. She felt weak in the knees and lightheaded. Giddy was the word, but she shook off the sensation as best she could and listened as he explained.

"I put it off for a few days. I wanted to get up here and make sure that you were provided with everything you might need. And to make sure that the phone and electric services were functioning properly, as I didn't want you doing without any essentials. But, to be honest, I guess I wanted to make sure that you were all right, and I suppose I just wanted to see you, period."

The grin left his face, to be replaced with a look of concern and caring. A jumble of responses collided in her head, none of them the right one, and she was trying to stutter an answer when a bright flash of lightning shattered the ever-darkening sky. An instant later the ensuing clap of thunder shook the ground. Her mouth was still open when Henry grabbed her arm and quickly moved them up the steps and into the house. The roar of the rain was only seconds behind.

"My things," she managed to stammer once she was safely shivering in the hallway, "they're still in the car."

"I know," Henry was serious, "and they can stay there for a while. I don't mind the rain so much, but lightning is something no sane person fools with. We can wait; we don't really have a choice."

Tori could only agree.

The tour of the house took almost two hours. Henry explained that almost everything in the house was a replica—meticulously crafted—but replicas nonetheless. He told her it just wouldn't do to leave anything valuable in the house; even with the year-around guard who lived in a small house a few hundred yards away, and who monitored the road for anyone driving in. They were in the library, leaning against the window sill and watching the downpour, when he mentioned the guard.

"Which reminds me, Tori, what did you think of old man Bradley, anyway? Isn't he something else?"

She looked puzzled. "Who?"

"Bradley. The guard. The man I've been talking about. Didn't he stop you on the way in?" It was Henry's turn to be confused.

"No. I didn't see anyone. Why, was he supposed to stop me?"

"Yes. I told him when I arrived earlier to be on the lookout for you, and to introduce himself. But, with this weather . . ."

As if on cue, another flash of lightning sizzled across the sky, causing them both to jump back from the window.

Reflex. That was what she told herself later, when she lay naked under the crisp, clean sheets of Henry's bed, listening to the faint, soothing sound of rain intermixed with the gentle breathing of Henry lying beside her. Just natural reflexive action.

She had jumped into Henry's arms when the lightning struck. And from there to the bedroom had been just as natural and reflexive as that small leap into Henry's arms. She smiled, sighed, the first sigh of happiness that had passed her lips since she had been told of Rick's death. Then she knew nothing; sleep claimed her thoughts.

And came awake stifling the scream on the verge of escaping her throat. The nightmare. Again.

A heavy film of perspiration had covered her body, drenched the sheets; she was hot and sticky, even with the overhead fan circulating the humid air. She would have to get up, wake Henry, change the sheets . . . but not just yet. First, she had to shake the residue of the nightmare.

She knew she hadn't had to identify Rick's body; the police had told her it wasn't necessary that she do so. Whereas, she later found out, the fact was that the body was unidentifiable, burned beyond any form of recognition. Only the left hand and part of the arm was intact, and that was good enough to lift prints and match them. The suicide note ruled out foul play, so the case was cut and dried. Rick was dead, very, very dead, but the nightmares came, just the same:

He is burning, clothes blazing, face melting from the bone. And she stands, transfixed, unable to move. Blood, and bone, and brain tissue is scattered over the white tile; one tile is spider-webbed from the hole created by the heavy slug passing through. It is almost like a surrealistic painting, but with sound and action. The dancing flames, the billowing smoke, the snap of bone, the crackle and tear of rupturing flesh . . . all there.

In slow motion the hand holding the gun lifts, points it at her. The hole in the muzzle is the size of a cave opening, it centers between her eyes. The melting mouth opens, lips and gums hissing and popping in the blaze, teeth falling out. And the words, words of damnation from the very Pits of Hell: "I'll always love you."

The finger tightens on the trigger. The flash, the bullet coming out, right at the itchy spot on the bridge of her nose. The scream starts somewhere deep inside . . .

. . . and that was when she woke up, heart pounding, body bathed in sweat.

As soon as she had controlled her breathing and her emotions, Tori flicked on the nightstand lamp, eased herself from the bed and padded lightly toward the bathroom. The wind from the fan was cold on her naked flesh; she shivered, then her heart stopped in her chest when something wrapped around her calf, clung to her flesh. Goosebumps sprang up over every inch of her body, and she was afraid to look down, didn't want to know what had her.

But she had to, she had to. She forced her eyes down, using every iota of will to keep them open. Then broke into a nervous laugh when she saw what it was: the window curtain, the damn window curtain! Her walking by, creating static electricity from the carpet, plus the action of the fan blades, had caused the bottom of the drape to cling to the sticky sweat on her leg. She breathed a sigh of relief, bent down to untangle herself, and froze again when something outside the window caught her attention.

Henry's bedroom overlooked the old cemetery, the one he had told her was the final resting place of family members, as well as a great many blacks who had worked the fields near the turn of the century. He had also explained that the plantation was built after the Civil War, so there had never been slavery. The Hanson money had not been achieved through the blood and suffering of others, a fact that Henry took great pride in relating.

But Tori had seen something move out there, amid the grave stones, something that wasn't supposed to be there. She stared at the spot where she had seen (imagined?) some subtle shift in what should have been frozen scenery. Nothing. The floodlights mounted at the corners of the house barely penetrated to that distance, and was weak, at best, at the edge of the wrought iron fence surrounding the small graveyard. What she had thought herself witness to had been in the middle.

Trick of wind, rain, lightning, bad light, and imagination fired up by nightmare. Okay, that's that, she thought, and began to turn away. And that's when logic, reason, and sanity proved themselves the lies they had to be.

Because, that was when a hand thrust through a mound of muck that had once been called a grave. The sludge began to move, part, and a tall thing lurched to its feet—rain turning mud into streaming mire that cascaded down its blackened body—and stared directly up at her. Its mouth opened like rusty hinges on a mausoleum door, and the wind shrieked the words through her ears: "I'll always love youuuuu . . ."

Tori collapsed to the floor in a dead faint, the billowing curtain drifting over her naked form like a pale gossamer shroud.

The aroma of fresh brewed coffee woke her; she stretched her body, curled the unoccupied pillow tightly to her breasts, savoring the feel of taut cotton against her skin. She lay still, attempting to bring back the horrors she had dreamed about the night before. The mental images were fuzzy-edged and only slightly clearer in the center. The sunlight entering through the windows were diffusing the terrors that had stalked her night, and were relegating to the shades of darkness all thoughts of Rick, and things rising from the grave.

From outside the bedroom door came the tinkle of a breakfast bell, which chased the last of her moribund mood into the shadows of her mind, and brought a smile to her face. A moment later Henry entered the room, wearing his Huck Finn grin, and carrying a steaming silver tray loaded with all kinds of wonderful smelling things.

She had donned jeans, t-shirt, one of Henry's plaid shirts to cover her arms, and comfortable walking boots. The rains had abated and Henry was taking her on a tour of his property, with one of his goals to tell Bradley about a vehicle coming into plantation property without being seen, a situation that should never occur again. Henry was in the shower, singing, and she was tying her hair up in a pony tail when the phone rang. She stared at it, glanced back to the closed bathroom door. It rang again, insistently. She shrugged and reached for the receiver, thinking it was probably Bradley checking in with his boss. She picked it up, said: "Hello."

Nothing but the crackle of static.

"Hello. Is there anyone there? Hello?"

Hiss and pop of static, like the call was being made from a long way off. She was about to hang up when a flat, emotionless voice finally spoke: "What you and Henry did last night was wrong. He knew better. You, I forgive, because I'll always love you."

Tori slumped to the bed, letting the phone strike the carpet. She paled, the blood draining from her face. Though, not exact, she felt that she recognized the voice on the line. She pinched her arm, knew the pain was real, knew she wasn't dreaming. Though, she had to be!

"Is something wrong? Are you all right?" It was Henry, wearing a towel wrapped around his waist, but not his usual grin. Instead his features were etched with concern. "Was it bad news?" He indicated the phone on the floor, which was now beep-beep-beeping, signifying a dead line on the other end.

She looked into Henry's face, found his blue eyes, and said as calmly as she could manage: "It was Rick. He sends his love."

"Thank you, I appreciate all the help, and your time." Henry hung the phone up, glanced at Tori sitting on the sofa, wringing her hands and staring expectantly at him. He shook his head, came and sat down next to her, separated her nervous hands and covered them with his own strong, yet gentle ones. He sighed.

"Look, it has to be someone with a sick sense of humor, someone who read about this in the papers, or saw the news coverage; hell, it could be any of a million weirdos out there. But—and get this in your head—it wasn't Rick. Rick was a good surgeon, could do wonders with the skin and tissue, but he couldn't duplicate fingerprints. No one can.

"Tori, look at me. Rick is dead and buried, and whoever it is that's playing this disgusting trick on you will be caught and stopped soon. I'm having that call traced and I have the police working on this right now. So, lighten up, take it easy. Okay?"

Tori pulled her hands free, stood, paced back and forth, finally paused in front of Henry. "Then, what did I see last night? What did I see in the cemetery? When I fainted, before you put me back in bed? Explain that, please."

Henry was startled; she could see it in his eyes. He reflexively half-rose, sat back down just as quickly, spread his hands as if he could feel something tangible with his fingertips, something solid he could touch and grasp hold of. He found nothing, dropped his hands and shook his head.

"I'm sorry, Tori, but I didn't—don't know what you saw, or think you saw. And I didn't put you in bed. As far as I know you were asleep all night, and in the same spot on the bed. Maybe you were dreaming . . ."

"Yeah, maybe, I guess," she interrupted, "though I think it's best to drop the subject for now." She smiled, a false mask of bravery, reached for his hand. "Come on, let's take that tour."

The ground was blanketed in a thick layer of fog, drifting calve-high; though thin tendrils of the mist, in random pockets, wafted thigh-high like phantom fingertips, the longing caress of a ghostly lover. Tori felt as if she were asea: the vaporous mists were like waves tugged by an unseen moon on a smoke-white ocean; the probing tendrils were tentacles waiting to grasp and pull down into the depths any foolhearty and fragile creature who dared trespass its surface.

The house, seen from the front lawn, seemed as if it were a ship afloat, precariously tethered to its moorings by an invisible anchor, slowly swaying to feeble wave and tired tide. She felt as if a pirate flag should be flying atop the main mast and looked up; the blank eyes of the myriad Dormers stared back at her, and she quickly lowered her gaze. It reminded her too much of the Myrtles Plantation, and she shivered, tightened her grip on Henry's arm and let him lead her along the fog-hidden path of stone, and around the corner of the house.

The spires of the wrought-iron fence surrounding the tiny family cemetery greeted her gaze, and she abruptly stopped, almost causing Henry to stumble. He looked down, saw what held her eyes.

"Whoops, sorry. I wasn't thinking. Let's go the other way." He tried to turn, but Tori didn't budge.

"When did it start, Henry? When did Rick go off the deep end?"

She hadn't averted her gaze, and Henry understood the mental trauma she was experiencing, the self-blame, the not comprehending. He felt she was ready to talk it out, right here, right now. He pulled his arm free, took her hand; this time she didn't struggle as he moved toward the latticed gazebo in the center of the graves. He knew that to understand death, sometimes it was necessary to get as close to it as possible; hence the gazebo, where he often sat and communed with the spirits of his ancestors, expecially his mother.

As they walked, she talked. "Richard was emotionally disturbed since he was a child, and he never got better, he just learned to hide it. He was an over-achiever, he was self-indulgent, he was selfish and self-orientated. He came up out of the slums, poor but proud, broken home, raised by his mother, his father never came around after he was eight years old. He had to prove that he was as good as anyone else, intensely felt the peer pressure around him. You know what I mean, the look-at-me syndrome, see-what-I-can-do . . . the whole nine yards.

"He was always alone; even in a crowd he was the only one there. Worse, and contradiction it is, he couldn't tolerate being alone, he had to be with people, impose his will on everyone. Especially me. Sadly enough, I was his favorite target, his personal whipping girl. Not in the physical sense; he didn't abuse me that way. No, it was verbal, and mental . . . a lot of mental torture.

"Then, finally it all caught up with me. I just couldn't take it anymore. And don't say a word, Henry, but it wasn't because of the thing with Georgia. There were plenty of women before that. No, that incident was simply one more drop in the bucket. And I had toted that bucket a long time, watched the steady drip, drip, drip, as it filled up, got heavier. Then, the proverbial straw that broke the camel's back, and the bucket was just too heavy for me to lift anymore.

"I tried, tried my damnest, but it wouldn't budge. Not an inch, not one iota. And I knew then that the well had dried up. My well. I had no feeling for him left inside of me. And I think that's why he did what he did—because I was something he had owned, a prized possession taken away. He couldn't stand that; that's what destroyed him, too. I know that, just as surely as I'm standing here."

She laughed, self-deprecatingly. "I just thought of some morbid graveyard humor. Fits the mood, wouldn't you say?" She indicated with a sweep of a hand the stones and markers before them. "Do you know what's inscribed on Rick's marker? Every man destroys that which he loves the most. He had that done so he could take one final stab at my heart, thinking that I'd take it to mean that he had destroyed me, and his death was atonement for that imagined sin. The humor is that he was right, he did destroy what he loved the most.

"He destroyed himself."

Then she was crying, and Henry was holding her, and it was no longer a humid, overcast day, with tornado and flood watches, no stink of insect repellent, no humming of mosquitos. Everything was perfect, and the world was once again a beautiful place in which to live.

Henry was carrying her as if she were weightless, back to the house, back to the bed. Her eyes were closed tightly, she was seeing nothing, feeling only inner peace and serenity.

She didn't see the grave next to the gazebo, ripped open like a black wound in the green grass.

When she woke it was dark, and though there had been no nightmare, the humidity had taken its toll again. She was soaking wet, sticky, and Henry's leg across hers had numbed it; probably the tingling was what had woke her. At least Henry had put in a shower, even if he hadn't had the house air-conditioned, insisting that human comfort wasn't as important as keeping the house as original as possible. But a shower was in order.

She slid her leg from under Henry's, gasped slightly when the needles of returning circulation stabbed into her flesh, sat up on the edge of the bed and quickly began to knead the dead muscles back into enough semblance of life so she could walk again. God, but she was sticky! Even her hair was matted with sweat. She groaned and got up, favoring her right leg as she padded into the bathroom, refusing to acknowledge the existence of the window, let alone consider looking out of it. She flicked on the light switch . . .

. . . and every nightmare she had ever had, if they were combined, would not have prepared her for the sight that greeted her in the mirror.

She wasn't drenched in sweat . . . she was covered with blood. Wet, glistening blood, dripping from her skin, spattering on the linoleum floor covering. Her hair, breasts and pubic area were smeared with the stuff, as if an erotic body painter had experimented on her while she lay sleeping.

And as her leg had earlier gone to sleep, so did the rest of her body. She went numb, shock setting in, shutting down conscious thought, not letting her mind comprehend what was happening. Shock: that marvelous mental defensive mechanism that takes over and prevents the brain from short-circuiting, like a computer that has been fed too much information shuts itself down to avoid damage to vital functions.

Behind her, something rustled. In a trance, she turned from the mirror, her movement the slow motion quality of dream-state. Though it was a nightmare that met her eyes.

The shower curtain parted and a rotting hand, oozing a viscous black fluid, penetrated the slit, began sliding the white plastic farther apart. The hand was clawlike, greenish-gray, with dirt and squirming maggots imbued in the flowing liquid putrescence seeping to the floor. She was mesmerized, couldn't tear her eyes from the sight.

But the horror had only begun.

Like a gunshot, the metal rings slammed together and the curtain opened completely. Rick lay there, face and flesh of his naked body black, wrinkled, besmeared in blood and muck. He was grinning, his yellowed teeth flashing dully, but there was no smile in his dark and dead eyes. His voice was hoarse, gutteral, but recognizable as the same one that she had heard on the phone earlier.

"Honey, I'm home." He spoke the phrase like he had just walked in the door from a long day at the office. And not like a man who had just come back from the dead.

Somewhere, deep inside herself, something snapped, something overrode the shock, something even more inherently related to the basic human instinct for survival. A whimper escaped her throat, rose in scale and volume until it could have been the anguished ululation of a timber wolf, a howl of such pure animalistic regression that the hairs actually did rise on the nape of her neck, though she was totally unaware of the sensation.

Whatever it was, that power surge, rush of adrenalin, whatever, she went beyond shock, she reverted to animal. A frightened animal. Even as Rick was rising from the tub, reaching for her, she was moving out the door. The blood-soaked bed, the lifeless body, briefly seen in the pale throw of light from the bathroom, didn't register as she rushed past. The only thing that mattered was that she was moving away from the horror she knew to be in pursuit.

Hurried plans of action grew root, then died as she realized her predicament. The car keys were in her purse, upstairs—no going back for them. She had descended the stairs, momentarily held in check as she decided which way to go. Henry's Jeep was in the garage, but the garage door was locked; even if the keys were in the ignition she would have to fumble for the right one to open the garage—no time.

A weapon, then. She had seen no guns on the premises, nor did she know how to work one—that was out. Then what? What?

It dawned on her at the same time she heard the creak of stair above, and she was sprinting for the kitchen, hitting the light switch as she flew through the swinging door, grabbing a large meat cleaver from a rack near the back door. Then she was outside and running, her heart pounding in her eardrums, her breath coming in rapid gasps.

Unconsciously, she headed up the narrow road she had driven down only yesterday, though it seemed as if years had passed since then. At least it was dark, for which she was grateful; she could hide in the woods if she got winded, watch for Rick to pass, double back and get her keys, something to cover her nakedness, drive for help.

Suddenly the road lit up with lights for as far as she could see, coming on so quickly and brightly that she stumbled, lost her balance. The meat cleaver flew from her hand as she slid in the mud, scraping her leg and painfully banging a knee against a tree root.

A door slammed and the slapping of running feet resounded from the concrete pavement behind her. Rick had turned on the lights and was coming after her pretty goddamn fast for a dead man. She scrambled to her feet, remembered the cleaver, stooped to pick it up while trying to run at the same time. The slosh of mud told her he was off the concrete and closing the gap. She reached full stride in seconds, fear lending wings to her heels.

* * *

The pain was gone, had been gone for a long time; he ran easily, feeling nothing. The physical form he occupied knew no sensation; it was as if it didn't exist. Only his mind, only his thoughts existed. Thoughts of revenge. The bitch was going to pay, and excruciatingly slow. And incredibly painful.

She was as stupid as he had always believed. She was running for the highway and the bridge. He slowed, savoring the anticipation of the kill. The hunt was over, as far as he was concerned; his prey was running itself into a corner.

The blood and salty sweat had drawn mosquitos and flies; she slapped them away as best she could while she ran. Her legs were giving out, her lungs laboring with every breath, yet she forced herself to keep going. The river couldn't be too far away, the road was sloping downward. Not much longer. Then across the bridge and into the small town on the other side, to safety.

The last of the string of spotlights had ended, and only the pale glow from a cloud-shrouded moon lighted her way, through patches of ground fog, ducking under water soaked, low hanging branches, around tangles of vines and the stabbing thorns of briar bushes. The roaring in her ears grew louder; she thought it to be the pounding of her heart, until it dawned on her that the sound came from an external source. The river!

She burst into the opening where she had made the turn with her car, and stopped abruptly. She stood on the last rise before the land dipped low, and began to quiver in rage and frustration. She had heard it all on the radio, but it had never registered. Though now, seeing it up close and first-hand, it did. Flash flood alert for the following Parishes, the announcer had said. Blood River was right in the middle of all the rain.

And Blood River was running high, fast, mean, and nasty. Its waters were already over the bridge, nearly to the top of the last rung of the hand-rail. She could make out the glimmer of metal from the halogen lights placed at each end of the bridge and from the flashing yellow lights atop the barricades the Highway Department had set up to prevent anyone from trying to drive across.

Tori cast a nervous glance back over her shoulder; she saw nothng but fog and shadows, yet she knew that Rick was back there, and coming her way. She had no choice. The overflow from the river bank had made even the ramp in front of her deep and treacherous with muddy roiling water. Still, there was only one way out and that was it.

She hesitated no longer, began to wade out, her feet slipping and sliding but gaining enough purchase on the rough asphalt to keep her from losing her balance. The unwieldy meat cleaver didn't help but there was no way she was going to drop it. She didn't have any idea what good it would be against a dead man; she only knew it made her feel better.

She was midway across and chin high in water, when a loud splash came from behind her, followed by an insane laugh and Rick calling to her.

"Hey, baby, it's a nice night for skinny dipping, isn't it?"

Maniacal laughter trailed behind her, closer. She lunged forward, the water now waist high. Thigh. Calve. Ankle. Scrambling for footing, when her left foot slipped in the mud and she fell. Before she could get up, something grabbed her ankle. She spun over, saw Rick grinning up at her.

"Gotcha. Now, how about a little kiss, just for old times sake?"

It happened in a blur, then, like the striking of a snake. She whipped the cleaver down, about a foot below where Rick's right hand tightly grasped her ankle. Quick as she was, he was faster. He threw up his left arm, and an instant later, the hand, neatly severed at the wrist, flew out to splash in the water. Foul smelling liquid spurted out, landing on her belly and thighs, causing her to retch violently.

Rick simply looked puzzled, then shook it off.

"Well, the gratitude you get these days. Offer a lady your hand and she takes it literally. But, easy come, easy go. See, I got another." He released his hold on Tori, held up his right hand to prove that he did, indeed, have another.

She used the opportunity to kick him in the face, felt a certain grim satisfaction when she felt the gristle of his nose give way. He fell back into the water, and she was up again, dropping the cleaver, running to the bridge.

The turbulence she had experienced fighting her way across the waters of the boat ramp were as nothing compared to the ferocity of the river itself. The current almost swept her off her feet and she needed both hands to hang onto the railing, to keep from being swept away.

Slowly, foot by foot, she made her way, hanging on for life. Once both feet were knocked out from under her by a branch and it was all she could do to retain her grip before she could get her legs back under her. Her strength was rapidly fading; she didn't know when the next slip of foot or hand would be her last. She was almost tempted to just let go, end the nightmare she found herself trapped in. However, she didn't, couldn't; some inner strength of character, or the simple will to survive, wouldn't allow her such recourse. She kept moving.

"Has anyone ever told you that you're beautiful when you're naked? I'll bet Henry did. Didn't he?"

Tori jerked her head. Rick was standing less than two feet away, the elbow of his bad arm locked over the railing, his good hand clutching the cleaver she had dropped. The idiotic grin was fading, to be replaced by an insane leer. Tori was too far gone to move. She could only hold on and wait.

Wait for the end, and hope it was quick. Silently, she began to pray.

"You didn't answer me. You don't have to. I know. I could have killed the both of you last night. Henry's a sound sleeper. And you had fainted when you saw me. I picked you up from the floor, put you back into bed, with him. Rehung the curtain you dragged down when you fell. Yes, I could have killed you both then." Rick's eyes glazed over, as if remembering something long ago and far away. Instantly they cleared, came back to the present.

"But I didn't. I waited. I called you. I wanted you to remember me. Me, the man who will always love you. Henry didn't love you; he only used you. I listened to him this afternoon, listened to you. Moaning while he did things to you, whispering into his ear words I couldn't hear because of the slap, slap, slap of sweating naked flesh!

"And you did this after I called. After. You fucking cunt!"

The cleaver glistened, shimmering in alternating reflections of yellow as the blade mirrored the flashing lights, lifted higher, ever higher. His voice was a banshee's shriek as it rose above his head.

"Here's that tit job I've been promising you!"

Tori screamed.

But not because her eyes had followed the hypnotic blade. Instead her eyes were on the river. Her peace had been made; she wouldn't have given him the satisfaction of seeing her scream.

The arm began to come down, the cleaver seemed to whistle . . .

The pine tree had been struck by lightning, its top was a broken lance, and though shattered, it was a lance nonetheless. Two hundred pounds of pine, propelled by a sixy mile per hour current, was one hell of a juggernaut of a lance.

Rick's stomach exploded when it ripped right through him. That was all Tori saw, because, by the time her scream ended, the tree and the impaled Rick were gone. Long gone.

"Tell me, Henry, I've got to know. No more side-stepping. I mean it; I'm serious."

Tori was sitting up in the hospital bed, Henry sitting beside her, her small hand in his larger one. She gave his a hard squeeze.

"Okay, okay, just no more torture, please. I'll fill you in on all I know. Most is fact, but there is some speculation involved.

"Richard wasn't a dead man back from the grave, for one. As I said before, he was an excellent surgeon. He proved it, fooled the police, the coroner, us . . . everyone. He found someone—we don't know who, probably never will—some wino, maybe, that was a close match to his own physical build and size.

"Richard drugged him, and when the time was right, amputated both of their arms between the elbow and the wrist. He transplanted his arm to the drugged man, using his mastery of stitches and a new ecto-plastic product to hide his handiwork. Excuse my morbidity, but using the gasoline in a controlled burning area was ingenious. He knew that ceramic tile and the porcelain tub were virtually fireproof. Even the amount of gasoline was pre-measured. The silk tux would burn wonderfully, ensuring that the ectoplast would fuse with the flesh and make it almost impossible for even close scrutiny to detect that the hand and arm were from two separate individuals.

"He felt that the body would burn beyond recognition, therefore he was careful to leave *his* hand, with *his* fingerprints, as far from the flames as possible. Recoil from a large caliber handgun would make the most plausible explanation. Toss in the suicide note and the recent loss of his wife, whom everyone knew he loved dearly, and no one wants to do any more paperwork than they have to. Case closed.

"And that's all you need to know for now, so get some rest."

He leaned over to kiss her, but she pulled her head away.

"Unh unh, none of that until I hear all of it."

"Okay, but then you have to promise to sleep. And remember, most of this is conjecture.

"For whatever reason, to frighten you, or who the hell knows, he grafted the dead man's arm onto his own. He didn't do a good job, and gangrene set in, which explains his insane behavior, on top of his definite mental unbalance. He shot himself up with morphine to kill the pain. He got crazier and crazier as the disease affected his brain. He somehow found out where you were going, got there ahead of you, but behind me. He tied Bradley up in the woods. He found some roofing tar in one of the sheds, coated himself with it, then buried himself in one of the old graves.

"The afternoon when we—er—took an early nap, I got up after you fell asleep and went to Bradley's cabin. He hadn't answered the phone and hadn't been around, so I was worried. Well, Richard was waiting for me. He knocked me out, and tied me up. I guess it was right after that when he got Bradley—poor soul—and cut him to pieces in my bed, while you slept.

"Now you really do know everything. Wait, except for the State Trooper who went out on that bridge and rescued you. Brave man. He is now the new guard at the camp, at twice the salary, and he and his wife are very happy people. So, now will you get some sleep."

"Okay, but first I deserve a kiss."

Henry smiled, leaned down. Her lips were soft, sweet.

"Ooops. Excuse me, I didn't know this was the honeymoon suite."

A nurse came in, wearing a warm smile and carrying a large bouquet of roses. Both Henry and Tori grinned at her friendly joke.

"Well, more flowers. My, but aren't you the most popular lady in the room," Henry jested.

"Definitely the loveliest," the nurse agreed, "where in the world am I ever going to put these? This room has more plants and flowers than a greenhouse."

"Just toss them on the floor," Tori quipped, "but let me have the card, please; black roses are what my mother always sends me."

The nurse handed Tori the card, and somehow found a vase empty enough and large enough to hold the roses.

Tori opened the envelope, read the one line: I'll always love you. Then she was falling, falling into blackness . . .

She lay on the bed, eyes wide and staring, vacant orbs, seeing nothing. Catalepsy, the doctors had diagnosed, usually a temporary state, but in Tori's case they just weren't sure. Henry turned the word over and over in his mind, trying to puzzle it out. At the same time he turned the card over and over in his hand. The one she had been reading when she had phased out of the real world.

It, too, was a conundrum to Henry. How could just those few words do something like that to someone, so suddenly? How?

Through tear-stricken eyes he read it again.

I'll always love you,<br>
Yours,<br>
Henry.

(For Teri Petitt)

Steve Gallagher is a Brit and a writer of some popularity in England. A popularity that's beginning to expand to America. His novel VALLEY OF LIGHTS is a fine place to start sampling his work, or you could start with the following droll story, inspired, gulp, by a visit to my house, and by the Lansdale kids and the Gallagher kid.

Steve, buddy, what have we wrought?

# HOMEBODIES

## Stephen Gallagher

Right away, we could see that there was going to be trouble.

We could see it the minute that he brought her into the house, the two of them stumbling and giggling and Daddy saying Hush, and how they'd wake up the kids and everything. But he never came up to see if we were asleep. She missed the peg and dropped her coat in the hallway, and then the two of them just went on through into the other room where the booze and the big couch are. He didn't even close the door all the way behind them.

I looked at Kathy and Elaine, and they looked at me. We knew what was coming, and nobody even had to put it into words.

There was something about her. Big. Loud. Like a lady wrestler, gone to fat. She had blue eyelids and red lips and she laughed like a man. The last one had been the same and Kathy had reckoned that she probably *was* a man, underneath, but I wouldn't let her sneak downstairs to look. I'm the oldest, I have to show a sense of responsibility.

'What are we going to do?' Elaine said.

'We'll wait,' I told her. 'It may not be so bad, this time.'

They wanted to believe it, I could see as much in their eyes. But they didn't, and neither did I.

As quietly as we could, we got to our feet and went into my room.

We'd emerged at the sound of the car, wondering if he'd be coming home alone tonight or with company. My room was on one side of the hall, Kathy and Elaine were just across from me. We knew that if we kept our lights off and laid ourselves flat with just our faces up against the banister rails, it would be almost impossible to see us from down below. Not that it had mattered, because neither of them had even glanced upward. Just lurched in, goosed each other like they were both squeezing cushions, and lurched on.

If that's what passes for fun when you're a grownup, I'm of the opinion that it isn't much to look forward to.

Elaine wanted to play Nintendo but, regardless of the fact that I wanted to as well, I had to say no. Because there were three of us, and you can't get more than two on a game, and we needed to be strong and together. So I put on the TV instead, and we all sat together in a nest made out of the pillows and bedding and watched the late movie. It was one of the *Omen* movies, the one where Damien's grown-up and rides a horse. You must know it, it's the one with the wimp ending. We were just at the part where the lady TV reporter finds Damien lying curled-up and naked under a back-to-front cross and starts to wonder if there's perhaps something he hasn't been telling her about himself, when the noise started up again from downstairs.

This was after about half an hour. It was a pattern, of a kind. First slam the car door, then into the house giggling and tiptoeing, some clumsy sounds of glass against glass, and then about twenty or thirty minutes of silence before the argument started. And she could shout, could this one. Kathy looked at me and I could see the apprehension in her eyes, so I just leaned forward and turned up the sound on the TV. It wouldn't matter if they could hear us downstairs, not by now. It was like a flight plan. You reach a certain point, and beyond it you know there's no turning back.

Downstairs there was some banging and crashing, and we heard a couple of screams. Then there was some sobbing and then everything went quiet again. We all kept our eyes on the TV screen, and we all pretended we heard nothing.

And only then when the movie was over did we get to our feet and go downstairs.

It was now after one in the morning. We switched on the stairway light because we didn't want to trip and fall. There wasn't much danger of being seen or heard by the neighbours; the house is in woodland with its own creek and about three acres all around it, and there's no direct line of sight with anybody. When it's dark you can just about make out a single streetlamp at the end of the driveway on the ridge road, but that's all.

Kathy pushed open the door. We all stood in the doorway and looked into the room.

Daddy was on one end of the couch, his head thrown back and his arms flung wide like he'd been caught in the act of belting out an Ethel Merman song. Except that he was snoring, and his head was bobbing slightly with the vibration. Every time he reached the end of a breath, his fingers twitched as if his hands were trying to make little claws.

The woman was at the other end. Or rather she had been, and now she'd slid down onto the floor and was lying there like a whale on a beach. Her face was all mottled and her tongue was sticking out further than it had any right to.

'Uh-oh,' said Elaine.

We saw to Daddy first. We tipped his head forward and sat him there for a few minutes until the two girls were able to take an arm each and get him to stand. He could just about help himself when he was like this, but he moved like a sleepwalker and didn't really know what he was doing. They manoeuvred him toward the doorway and he complied, a kind of unguided missile.

'Get him upstairs to the bedroom,' I told them. 'I'll make a start down here.'

I put the Scotch away. One of the glasses had got broken on the floor, so I first had to get together all the pieces and then mop up the spill. Then I straightened the cover on the couch and took a cloth and wiped around everywhere that she might have touched. I had to step over her a few times while I was doing this. I was never certain where Daddy picked up his women, because it was hardly something that I could ask; but I had a suspicion that he found them crying in dark corners in bars. She was even bigger than she'd looked from upstairs. Stretching to step over, I almost fell on her. I know for a fact that big women weren't Daddy's type, and yet he always brought the same kind home. Mother wasn't big at all, so doesn't that prove it?

I crouched down by her head and looked into her face. Her eyes were slightly open and there were clusters of blood spots unders the makeup, as if tiny fireworks had burst inside her skin. I said, 'Lady, I can see you're going to give us a problem,' and just then I heard Daddy start to shout incoherently.

So I ran out to help. Kathy and Elaine had managed to get Daddy about halfway up the stairs, but now he was shouting and fighting them off. It wasn't serious fighting because he was moving like a man in a dream or under water, but it was making life hard for them. I came up behind and said 'Easy, Daddy, easy,' and he turned and looked at me. The turn was like old clockwork, and the look was a heartbreaker. One eye was wide open and the other was half-closed, and the half-closed eye was a red ball. He stared at me with no recognition at all, but at least he'd calmed down and I was able to take one of his arms and guide him onward.

We put him on his bed and stripped off his trousers and his tie, and then we left him in his shirt and his underwear and covered him over. He just lay there, eyes closed and snoring again. There wasn't anything else that we could do for him, so then we went back downstairs for another look at his lady friend.

Nothing had changed since I'd left her. I don't know what we'd have done if she'd moved or shown some sign of life; after all we could hardly let her go off and tell anyone of what had happened, not now. I didn't like to picture myself putting a cushion over her face and sitting on it until she went still again. The notion seemed kind of cruel.

We stood around her and we stared for a while.

'Jesus, she's fat,' Elaine said.

'I know,' I said. 'I know.'

I'm the oldest, but I can't say I'm the strongest. There were two years when I was small that I spent going in and out of the hospital for one thing after another, and I don't think I ever fully caught up. Kathy, now . . . Kathy was a tank. She didn't look much, but she could hit harder than any boy I knew. Nobody ever picked on me because they couldn't stand the thought of having to run in fear when a girl came after them, which she most certainly would. We stuck together. Even without Mother we were a family, after all.

Kathy took one of the woman's arms and Elaine and I took the other, and we heaved. She shifted about an inch.

'This is going to take a while,' I said. 'Let me think about it.'

I went back to the hallway and got her coat. It was red, and like her it was heavy. I took it through and spread it on the floor beside her, and then the three of us all got together and rolled her onto it. That wasn't easy, either. She kept getting halfway and then flopping back, and for a while I was thinking that we'd never be able to do it. But then we gave one last big heave-ho, and she rolled over like a ship.

I was gasping. But Kathy patted me on the shoulder.

'She might be easier to handle when she's stiffened up a bit,' she said.

'I know,' I said. 'But that won't be for hours.'

We at least had to get her out of the house before morning. Once outside we could drag her into the shed or even just cover her with an old tarpaulin until Daddy was out of the way and we could finish the job, but the simple fact is that there's no easy way to hide a dead fat lady indoors. Put her in a chest or a closet, and she'll go rigid on you and you won't be able to get her out again until she loosens up after a good twelve hours or more.

And who knew *what* could happen in those twelve hours?

We all lined up and got a grip on the coat, and we started to drag. The coat collar began to tear at first, so we had to stop and rearrange everything before we tried again. It was slow progress but we got her across the floor to where a doorway led through to the kitchen, and there we had a problem because the three of us all got bunched together and we couldn't squeeze through.

Something moved upstairs, and we all froze.

'Only Daddy turning over,' I said.

The woman had lost a shoe, and Kathy went to retrieve it while I sat on the kitchen floor and got my breath back. Details like that can really mess you up if you don't keep on top of them. She tossed the shoe onto the coat and stepped over the woman to rejoin us.

'Better move the table,' she said.

We moved the kitchen table to give us a clear run to the back door. Once through the door we'd be outside, but then there would be two steps to manage. But at least we'd be going down them, and not up.

Getting her across the kitchen floor was a lot easier. The floor was tile instead of carpet, and it made a difference. Even so it was a considerable strain, and when we got there Elaine sat down heavily and said, 'That's it, I've had enough.'

It isn't only that Elaine's the baby in the family. She's also something of a complainer. You have to know that, and you have to manage her or else she'll just throw up her hands on everything and say, 'Well, *you* do it.' You always know when she's come into a room because she announces her presence with a heavy, exasperated sigh. Then you're supposed to ask what's wrong so that she can tell you.

I said, 'Now, everybody listen. We're going to do this and we're going to do it *tonight*. Just us and nobody else. Because Daddy's going to wake up and come down for breakfast in the morning, and if he sees her lying here by the door he's going to get a pretty good idea there's something wrong.'

What we're talking about here is impeccable logic and there was nobody there in that kitchen who could give me an argument, mainly because the one who'd probably be most inclined to was elsewhere bending the ear of Jesus. I looked at Kathy and Kathy nodded, and I looked at Elaine and Elaine stuck out her bottom lip and looked dark. But for once she didn't argue.

'Here's how we'll do it,' I said. 'Kathy, you and me are going to go to the shed and get the boards. Elaine's going to stay here and listen out in case Daddy starts wandering around again.'

'With *her?*' Elaine said, eyeing the body distastefully.

'Yeah, with her,' I said. 'Don't worry, she isn't going to bite.'

'She's really ugly,' said Elaine.

'Try not to let it depress you,' I said.

Kathy and I went out to the shed. It was a cool night and there was a starry sky, and most of the leaves had fallen from the trees by then so there was a clear view of the stars through the woodland all around the house. We could hear the running of water in the creek and the cry of some far-off animal and, just for a moment, the passing of a car on the main road about a quarter of a mile away. We stopped and waited, but nothing turned down the ridge road toward us.

The boards were two shelves on the shed wall. They weren't fixed on their brackets but before we could get them down we had to take off a number of half-empty paint cans and gluepots and bottles and a lot of other dusty stuff that seemed to have been there forever. We didn't worry too much about where anything belonged, we could put it all back afterwards in any order and Daddy wouldn't know. He kept his stock in here and that was his only use for the place; otherwise it was mostly a dump for kid stuff like my old bike or Elaine's play house. Daddy's stock was of industrial vacuum cleaners and vacuum cleaner parts, the kind that they use mainly in hotels and office blocks. You can use them in houses too, but not many people do because they're so expensive. They're cast in solid metal instead of plastic, and they look like their design hasn't changed since about 1945. One of the tricks that he'd use when he was demonstrating would be to let the people run their own vacuum over a room and then redo it with one of his machines with a white handkerchief across the tube like a filter. Then he'd show them the handkerchief so that they could see what their machine had missed, and if they'd any shame at all he'd get to make a sale.

That was on the good days. He had maybe a couple of those every month.

Otherwise, he never had much call to come in here.

We got the boards and we took them back to the kitchen doorway, and we laid them outside over the steps like a ramp and that's how we got her out. It was nearly three in the morning by then, and Elaine was yawning and this time it wasn't just for effect. Even Kathy looked dead on her feet, although nobody looked quite as much so as the fat lady.

I'd planned to get her across the yard area behind the house and in amongst the trees where we could cover her over, but I could see that it wasn't going to happen . . . at least, it wasn't going to happen tonight. The troops were exhausted. So instead we kept up with the coat trick and dragged her past the sandpit and into the shed, where we then hauled out a few of the sample boxes and built them into a wall to screen her from the door. I checked, and you couldn't see her at all. It wasn't ideal, but it would do for now.

It was after four. We went inside, cleaned ourselves up, and all went to bed. I don't remember what I was thinking about as I went off to sleep.

I only know that it didn't take long.

* * *

I woke late in the morning. I knew that I'd overslept but all the same I just lay there, vaguely remembering the night before but not quite able to grasp the relationships between the events. Then suddenly it all came together with a bang, like a jet-propelled jigsaw, and I jumped out of bed. I could hear movement from downstairs as I got into yesterday's clothes, and I hoped that I wasn't going to be too late.

I checked on Daddy's bedroom on the way past. His bed was empty.

Everyone was in the kitchen. Daddy was at the table and Kathy was right behind him, and as I froze in the doorway she was making frantic signals to me that he couldn't see. *It's okay,* she was signing. *Everything's okay.*

Daddy looked up from his cereal, and he smiled.

'Morning, Charlie,' he said.

The bad eye was closer to normal. It was just ordinary bloodshot, now. He looked pale and the lines on his face had a look as if they'd been dusted-in with grey powder, but otherwise he was the same old Daddy again. Elaine was bringing him an Alka-Seltzer from over by the sink.

As she set it down beside him, he rumpled her hair as a kind of thanks and said, 'Did anybody notice what time it was when I got in last night?'

We all shrugged and shook our heads.

He sighed. 'These late business meetings,' he said. 'Sometimes I wish I could dodge them altogether.'

We all sat around the table and we talked about the things that we'd been doing and the things that we still had to do, when the fact of it was that the only thing on three of our minds was the problem of the corpse out there in the shed. Daddy seemed to have no memory of the previous night at all.

But that was usual.

After a while he slammed both hands flat onto the table and, rising, said in a bright voice, 'You know, I don't know what it is, but I'm feeling lucky today. I think I'll just get myself made presentable and then I'll make a couple of calls and then I'm going to hit the road.'

Something went cold inside me.

I said, 'Do you want us to bring any of your stuff out of the shed?'

'Well, thanks for the offer, but I've told you before about you kids not handling the stock. I'll see to it myself.'

He went upstairs, whistling lightly. And I can tell you, the moment he was out of earshot we nearly panicked.

'What are we going to do? What are we going to do?'
saying, until I had to tell her to shush because Daddy was going to hear her voice through the floor.

'You and me are going to go out and move her,' I said, 'while Elaine keeps a watch right here.' I turned to Elaine. 'You hear him coming, you get him over to the other side of the house and keep him busy there until we're done.'

'How?' she said.

'You can be thinking of that while you're waiting for him,' I told her.

Kathy and I went out to the shed. When Daddy went for a wash and a shave he could usually be counted on to be missing for half an hour, at least. He liked to play the bathroom radio and take his time and make a real production out of it. Surely we could get her out and into the trees in that time; we could pile sacks or leaves over her, or even truck out all of the sand from the sandpit and bury her in *that* . . . anything to keep her out of Daddy's sight until he was out of the way, when by the sound of it we'd have the entire day in which to finish the job properly.

'We'd better put the boxes back too, or he'll know,' Kathy said.

So first we rearranged the stock as we'd found it, uncovering the fat lady as we did. She didn't look any better or worse than she had the night before, but now she looked it in daylight. I checked my watch. We'd lost ten minutes so far, we had another twenty. There'd be no more than fifty yards to cover, but it would be over rough ground and there were only two of us now.

'Let's do it,' I said.

We got her by the arms again except that by now, of course, she was a statue. She seemed to weigh like marble, too. Imagine trying to haul a dead cow around your living room and then push it out of the doorway; that was the kind of problem we faced. We tried dragging her, we tried dragging the coat she still lay on.

I checked my watch again. Fifteen minutes gone. And the half-hour was an optimistic estimate anyway.

Kathy let go.

'I've got an idea,' she said.

She dived behind Elaine's upended playhouse at the back of the shed, and after about a minute's rummaging she came out with a skipping rope.

'A skipping rope?' I said.

'We loop this under her arms,' Kathy explained, 'and then we take an end each and pull. Like Wagon Train.'

'Let's try it,' I said.

We ran it under her shoulders then around her armpits. One side was easy, but on the other we had to work it through and touching her flesh was like handling a chicken fresh out of the 'fridge. I had to wipe my hands on my shorts and then the two of us each took a handle of the skipping rope and leaned back like we were in a tug-o'war and pulled.

She moved, just a little. We braced our legs, we put our backs into it . . .

And she moved again.

Slowly but surely, we were getting her toward the door. That was only a matter of a few feet and I'm not pretending that it was easy, but we were doing it and that was encouraging. We got out of the doorway, she slid up to it and stopped. Stopped dead, if I can say as much.

'She's stuck,' I said.

'She can't be stuck,' Kathy said. 'We got her through there last night, didn't we?'

'Her arm's in the way,' I said.

And it was, too. It must have been the way that she'd been lying; whatever the cause, her arm was sticking out like a toppled mannequin's and was refusing to give.

'I'll fix it,' Kathy said, and she pushed me aside and took a hold on the doorframe for balance and then raised herself and put one foot against the arm and pushed. Nothing seemed to happen.

'If this doesn't work, I'm taking the shovel to it,' Kathy said, and she started to use her entire weight to rock the arm back and forth like a car on its springs.

She never needed the shovel. I knew that the moment that I heard the arm go with a crack.

We got back into position and then we turned our backs to the fat lady and leaned into the skipping rope like a couple of oxen, and with a lot of hugging and straining we got her over the threshold and began the long, slow journey across open ground toward the trees. I couldn't check my watch now. I didn't dare break off from what I was doing. Did you ever see those pictures of Egyptian slaves dragging the big stones that went to make the pyramids? Well, I know exacttly what they felt like.

We'd gone less than halfway when Elaine came running out of the house.

'Get back in,' I gasped, losing my footing at the same time. 'Get back in before he comes out and see us!'

But Elaine only said, 'There's a police car coming up the ridge road.'

I dropped the rope.

'Oh, shit,' I said.

There's a useful expression I've learned since, and it's *hoist with one's own petard*. Essentially as I understand it, it means all fucked up and all your own fault. We'd dragged her right out into the middle of the yard and put her on open display, where only a blind person with no dog could miss her. There wasn't the time to go forward, there wasn't the time to go back. We couldn't even stick a few feathers on her and pretend that she'd fallen out of a tree.

'Do what you can here,' I said. 'I'll try to keep them away from the windows.'

I ran for the house. My mind was racing, but I can't honestly say that it was achieving much. As I entered the kitchen, I could hear Daddy coming down the stairs to open the front door and any hopes that I'd had of the police car heading on for somewhere else just went. I could hear muffled voices now, and I turned and looked out of the kitchen window. The woman lay there like an anthill with legs. Kathy and Elaine were nowhere to be seen, and I honestly couldn't say that I blamed them.

The muffled voices were coming my way, and getting less muffled with every stride.

I did the only thing I could think of. I grabbed the rod and turned the slats on the Venetian blind so that the light was still coming in, but you couldn't take a straight look out.

Daddy came into the kitchen first. He was saying, 'If the kids didn't turn the coffee machine off, there ought to be . . .' and then he stopped, and said, 'Oh,' because the coffeemaker wasn't on and hadn't even been working for weeks.

'Doesn't matter, Mister Philbin,' the man behind him said, and the room seemed to fill from wall to wall with the terrifying aura of authority that came in through the door with that police uniform. His hat was in his hand, but that made no difference. And his voice was like an elderly uncle's, almost kind, but that made no difference either. I was awestruck, dwarfed in his shadow.

The policeman saw me, and winked.

He was older than Daddy, and bigger. I can imagine that under any other circumstances I might even have liked him on sight, but today most definitely wasn't the day for it.

He said, 'Don't take this wrong, but we've got to eliminate. Women out on their own go missing, it's something you've got to check up on. You don't remember talking to her at all?'

Daddy shook his head. 'I don't remember talking to *anyone*. I pretty much keep to myself when I go . . .' he looked at me then, and there was a barely perceptible hesitation. 'When I go into town.'

'Do you remember what time you left?'

Daddy frowned, and looked at me. 'Charlie?' he said. 'Did I already ask you this?'

'You got home around ten-thirty,' I said, hazarding a guess and hoping.

It would seem that I got it just about right, because it appeared to be what the policeman most wanted to hear.

'Well, that takes care of that,' he said, brightening. But as quickly as the light touched his features, it gave way to something more serious.

He said, 'I'm sorry to be bothering you with this at all. I know what a rough year you've had, what with . . .'

And the two of them kind of nodded, acknowledging their way around the unsayable.

'A terrible way to go,' the policeman said. 'For her, and for everybody. Especially when you have to watch them heading downhill for so long.'

Daddy said, 'I've been luckier than some. At least I've had the kids to look after me and keep me going. I don't know how I'd ever have handled it without them.'

'Yeah,' the policeman said. 'A family's blessing, all right. Of course, mine are all grown up and gone now.' And my heart soared as he put his hat on, obviously making ready to leave.

'We can get out this way,' Daddy said, moving to the back door.

I gagged.

I was trying to speak.

The problem was, I couldn't think of a single thing that I could possibly say.

'Everything all right, Charlie?' Daddy said with a puzzled, half-smiling look of enquiry as he opened the door to the yard and stood back for the policeman to precede him outside. 'Anything wrong?'

I smiled what had to be the most stupid smile in the history of goofiness, and shook my head.

They went out.

I stayed there, waiting for the bomb to burst.

I heard Daddy say, 'Those are my other two.' And the policeman say, 'Nice kids.'

Nice kids?

I waited for the next part, something along the lines of Hey, I see you have a dead fat lady in your garden, mind if I just go over and see if it's the same one we're looking for? And then maybe Daddy would say No, help yourself, we get a lot of that around here.

But all I heard was Daddy calling, 'If you're going to play with that thing, don't go leaving it outside all night.' And then a chorus from Kathy and Elaine of, 'Yes, Daddy.'

I couldn't believe what I was hearing. I snapped open a gap in the blind and peered through.

Daddy and the policeman were just disappearing around the side of the shed, heading around to the driveway at the front of the building. Out across the yard, Kathy and Elaine had spread out a dolls' picnic before Elaine's playhouse. I stared stupidly at the scene for several moments before I realized what they'd done.

The playhouse was a printed cloth tent over a frame of lightweight plastic tubes. For all its size, Elaine could just about carry it on her own as long as there wasn't a strong wind. Two of them together could have lifted it into place in a matter of seconds. You were supposed to break it down and pack it all away when it wasn't in use, but it was much easier simply to stick it on its side in the shed until the next time that it was wanted. At least that way, pieces didn't get lost.

It hadn't covered the woman perfectly, but you couldn't see that from the house. It only became apparent as I walked across the yard toward them and saw her top end sticking out at the back. She looked as if she was trying to crawl out from under. Only she wasn't, of course, she hadn't even moved. The skipping rope was still in place around her shoulders, the wooden handles lying on the ground to either side of her head.

Kathy and Elaine were looking up at me.

I said, 'I stalled them for you as long as I could. You should have heard me in there. I was brilliant.'

I don't know what it was; perhaps it was the policeman talking about Mother. But when Daddy came back inside he went down to his office in the basement and picked up the phone, and that's how I found him when I went down about twenty minutes later—sitting there with the receiver in his hand gazing blankly at all the unpaid bills in their clip on the wall, and with that faint howling noise coming out of the earpiece. You know the sound, it's the one they put on after a minute or so when you've forgotten to dial. I took the receiver out of his hand and set it down, and he looked at me. I was scared then.

But he knew me.

He didn't go out after all. His bright mood was gone, and he seemed to have forgotten any plans that he'd made for that day. He just hung around the kitchen, which in turn meant that the three of us had to hang around that stupid playhouse in order to keep a guard on what we had hidden inside. Sometimes he'd watch us from the window, which meant that we couldn't even take a shot at moving her again.

Only when it had started to go dark were we able to leave it and come inside. Elaine was happy. She'd spent all day in her element, organising tea parties and handing out the plastic food.

Daddy said to me suddenly, 'Did somebody come to the house this morning?'

'I don't think so, Daddy,' I said.

And then he walked away again with a puzzled, uncertain look on his face as if he was trying to remember a dream.

At around seven he reappeared in his good clothes and said, 'I have to go into town tonight. It's one of those late business meetings, something I can't avoid. I want you to lock up and look after your sisters.'

And I said, 'I will.'

As soon as his car was gone, we put on the yard lights and went out to finish the job. With three of us on the skipping rope, we had her there in less than half an hour.

I took the lid off the tank, and we used one of the boards to lever her up and tip her in. What a strain. For a moment it looked as if she wasn't going to fit through, but we all stamped on her together and she went through with a pop. It wouldn't have been so easy if the tank hadn't been buried in the ground. All of the waste from the house was supposed to go in at one end and clean water was supposed to flow out into the creek at the other, but don't ask me how it worked. Kathy dropped the loose shoe in after.

We'd a flashlight with us, of course. I shone it through the hatch just to be sure that she hadn't got jammed halfway down. But she hadn't. In the beam I could see the faded prints of old dresses and odd bits of mildewed jewelry and some hair and some bones. Whatever this tank process was, it seemed to be taking its time.

The light caught on something that grinned.

'We've brought a new friend for you,' I whispered. 'Now, you've all got to be nice to her.'

And then I put the lid back onto the tank, and we all went into the house to watch some television.

David Schow is the author of two novels, THE KILL RIFF, and THE SHAFT, as well as two volumes of short stories. He's written several screenplays and edited a fine anthology of film horror stories called SILVER SCREAM. The following is a disturbing little chiller that shows Schow in top form.

# ACTION

## David J. Schow

D.W. stepped out. The door had been opened for him. The county sheriff was huge, bristle-cropped, with mean piggy eyes. He had just slugged D.W. with his baton. The bailiff was bigger—6'6", all starched blouse, body armor and attitude. Both packed 9mm autos. Hardly a cop in LA would shame image with a revolver anymore. They had been easily legalized. A snip of red tape. Bang.

D.W. stepped into the light.

The judge's nameplate soberly proclaimed HER HONOR FRANCES McCLANAHAN. D.W. caught her eye and smiled a matinee idol smile. She was robed, sexless, a turkey neck above all-business wire-rims in gold. Brown hair, chopped short, graying more with each verdict. Dying a little every day.

Cops with auto pistols. Lady judges. Things had changed.

"Action."

D.W. had whispered the magic word to himself. *Lights, camera . . .*

All his life, more than anything, D.W. had aspired to be a good actor. Since he was nine. Before that it was paleontologist, then paramedic. Actors knew what to say. A quip for every crisis. They could pretend to be paleontologists and paramedics and get paid for it. Actors got girls effortlessly. D.W. presumed actresses could get guys with equal casualness. But they were all called actors now, both sexes. More progress.

Actors knew how to hit their marks and pick up their cues. Actors were in the public eye. *People* Magazine. *Entertainment Tonight.*

D.W. saw lights, cameras, an audience. He was conducted to a seat next to his defense attorney, Rupert the Lawyer. D.W. took short steps because of the ankle cuffs.

"Howdy, Rupert."

"Reino," said Rupert, giving a discreet thumbs-up. Rupert was wearing his gray pinstripe today. Rupert had known the TV people and news crews would be in attendance. Rupert owned twelve lawyer uniforms and D.W. knew them all. Tomorrow, if there were cameras again, Rupert would brush off his black three-piece.

Several yellow index cards lay face-down at Rupert's spot. Last-minute notes and updates. As he sat, he flashed his killer smile for the cameras. The audience rumble stirred up. Magic.

Her Honor Frances McClanahan called for order.

The prosecution had set up its charts for Blackwood Avenue. That was one reason the media had poked up their snouts. Coffin was present at the enemy desk; that was two. Gardner Coffin was the masthead go-getter for Coffin, Boles, Thatcher, Grimes and Halliday, P.P.C. His firm had undertaken the successful imprisonment of seven of LA County's more notorious mass murderers and serial killers, including the Jigsaw Ripper fiasco.

That had been before D.W.'s time.

He flipped up the top card, handcuff links clinking. All the cards were in Rupert's post-Harvard scrawl.

*Rumors of hung jury #2. Appeals.*

Another reason for the news folks. Next:

*Blanchard's evidence ruled contradictory.*

Remove enough lugs and the wheel falls off and the car won't go no more. Blanchard's key testimony had sprung a leak. Three:

*Coffin to step in personally.*

Oh well. D.W. would follow script regardless. If his accusers pulled bigger guns, it might signify a panicked fortification of an already wobbly case. Public opinion would shift if there were the slightest whiff of wrongful arrest.

The judge droned. D.W. checked out the spectators. A redhaired woman in the second row was mopping tears and fighting to keep a stiff upper. That would be the mother of Number Five, Ruth Ann Fowler.

Who had been abducted from Blackwood Avenue.

Ruth Ann Fowler's corpse was not discovered until May 11th, dumped off Mulholland Drive to cook in the spring sun for four days after her murder. She had been tripped over by a sitcom writer chasing a lost Porsche hubcap downhill. She had been naked except for the tennis ball duct-taped into her mouth. She had evacuated fluids but bloated with bacterial gas.

Her wrists were tightly bound with coathanger wire. She had been cut with a scalpel, long incisions from armpits to wrists, plus similar cuts from the inside thigh to the ankle on each leg. A pathologist testified that the same scalpel had been used to remove her lips and labia. Semen tracks were identified in her throat, her anus, and on the flathead screwdriver they pulled out of her. The obvious C.O.D. was massive hemorrhage. The coathanger marks indicated that she had lived for at least four hours after being bound. Ruth Ann Fowler had been 14, a nail biter. She had many more friends at school after she died, when the TV cameras showed up to provide human interest at 4,5,6 and 11.

D.W. turned to his public long enough for lenses to zoom in on the three sixes tattooed on his forehead. He shot his smile at Ruth Ann Fowler's mother. "I love you," he said. "Baby, I need you so bad."

Chaos.

Two days later, Ruth Ann Fowler's mother wept in the courtroom as Rupert the Lawyer's prediction of a hung jury came shockingly to pass. The cameras ate up her breakdown.

"I want you. I *need* you."

Ruth Ann had been Number Five. Five out of eleven. Other mommies and daddies present erupted in rage or grief. They could do little about D.W. because another bailiff had scanned them all with a metal detector prior to entry.

Two cameramen cranked in contrary directions and cracked lenses. D.W. laughed—a shrill, fluting giggle that was one of the trademarks of Reino Salazar, the Meat Man.

Another day, another trial, a new jury. D.W. hit the #1 slot on the news consistently. He was more exciting than the freeway snipers or the gang hits.

They shot him being hustled from the courtroom. They freeze-framed a shot emphasizing the 666 on his forehead. He looked as lethal as a cobra, as compelling as a TV star.

He had an interview at five.

* *

The setup was a tad grotesque.

D.W. had been looking forward to fucking with Mario Escovar's head. Mario was the top-rated news anchor on LA's #1 independent station. His producer had decided to hurl in Tracy Whitmore at the last minute. Tracy was darkhaired, with a weird frost job and a pretty dead-ahead set of legs. It was an angle—woman quizzes sex killer—and much better showbiz. Mario Escovar would have asked penetrating questions. Multi-leveled. Tracy would lean into frame, representing an entire sex against whom this maniac was destructively devoted, and try to probe *why* for her viewers. In post, editors could insert shots of her leaning, crinkling her surgically perfect brow, pursing her lips and nodding importantly as though she actually comprehended. They put her on a barstool to mold her calves and had a keylight especially for her legs.

Grotesque.

D.W. sat shadowed by bars in his interview cell. Dark killer versus the shed light of prime-time reportage. There was a good nine feet of dead space between his bars and her stool. You never knew; nobody really wanted to see Tracy get snatched while tape was running. Nobody except maybe her producer and Mario Escovar. And the audience that would make the show a ratings giant.

Still, this was a matter of serial killer decorum.

"So, Reino . . . is it true your mother abused you as a child? Hit you? Made you wear a dress?"

*Why I Hate Women 101A*. Jesus.

"You honestly believe that you've done nothing wrong, that you haven't hurt anyone, Reino?"

First-name familiarity with each interrogative. That clumsy have-you-stopped-beating-your-wife entrapment. Christ, what a tyro!

"Ms Whitmore." He consciously drew out the *mizzz*. Tape ground away, loop upon loop of three-quarter-inch gold grade, capturing everything. "Are you attempting to help the media convict me for something I did not do?"

That rattled her leash.

"How do you feel about being imprisoned, then, if you're . . . innocent?"

No first name now. That tiny pause before she said *innocent*. She did not believe Reino Salazar was innocent. Time to shake her up and give the viewers what they wanted.

"Not thirteen," he said. Sly.

"I beg your pardon?"

"Only eleven. Not thirteen. An error. Thirteen is a perfect number, you know."

Eagerly, as if programmed, she asked him why. And he told her. From that moment, he owned their exchange. He played her the way gangbangers play ghetto blasters. In minutes her skin was acrawl and she could not meet his eyes directly.

"Who's your buddy? Satan's your buddy." He had almost forgotten to pitch in the devil reference. "Satan's your pal."

According to censors in the know, an upturned thumb, plus index and pinky fingers, signifies denial of the Holy Trinity, as well as the infamous triple-six.

D.W. looked the camera in the eye. It did not turn away from him. *Cut.*

* * *

Seated around the conference table in the judge's quarters were Her Honor Frances McClanahan, Rupert the Lawyer, Gardner Coffin and a crony, and Edward Truex, to whom D.W. referred affectionately as Emerald Ed. D.W. was escorted in by a quartet of armed bulldog guards, chains and cuffs aplenty.

"Are you positive you don't need at least one of us to stay in here with you, Your Honor?" It was the sheriff's deputy with the piggy eyes, like shiny glass beads, the one who had nightsticked D.W. He did not approve of this due process shit.

"I think these men should be adequate to the task if the prisoner does anything untoward," said Judge Frances. The sheriff left without a Milk Bone.

Once the sheriff was gone, D.W. said, "That motherfucker hit me in the stomach with his baton."

Her Honor went bloodless. "Did he speak to you?"

"He said, and I quote, 'I'm waitin for ya, rapist scumbag. I'll cut off your *cojones*.' Then he struck me. Twice." D.W. nailed the judge with a glare. "Muzzle that asshole, Frances, and I do mean *now*."

Emerald Ed spoke up. "My client is not supposed to be subjected to physical abuse. This has occurred more than once. I think it's time to discuss a little extra compensation."

There was no one responsible enough to deserve scorn, so Ed helped D.W. out of his restraints and brought him a club soda with lime.

"D.W., what can I say? I'm sorry." Frances frowned.

D.W. waved it to insignificance. "Didn't see it coming, is all. Let's get it on."

"The hung jury got you the fever pitch you asked for," said Coffin, a fortyish man who looked like a graduate of aftershave commercials. "Time to drop the blade and let 'em see a little blood."

"Especially since you'll be the executioner," said Rupert the Lawyer. "You bag the glory of nailing the Meat Man in court."

Nobody needed to remind Rupert that Coffin's media-hog image was precisely the reason he had been hired.

"Think the copycats will come through for us?" Emerald Ed was musing again.

"Be nice if they capped some poor shmuck inside one of the original hit zones." Coffin fired up a cigarillo, one of his many eccentric trademarks. "Maybe Blackwood Avenue. Did you *see* that lady in court?"

Judge McClanahan nodded. Mrs. Fowler's had been a stellar collapse, fraught with raw sympathy and parental anguish. Emmy material. They'd gotten it for free. On all channels, all timeslots, D.W.'s grinning mug had almost been crowded out by those choice-cut closeups of that red and weeping face.

"We need to turn that into an advantage," said Rupert.

"Rupert, I think that shot will mold public opinion the way we want *without* some foggy reliance on a copycat," said Judge McClanahan.

"Unless you farm out the copycat job to take advantage of the news." It was D.W.'s first commentary.

"We're not in the business of taking human life." They all turned to the judge when she spoke; they all saw there was no room to wiggle on this particular issue.

Emerald Ed was quick to crack the tension. "Besides, D.W.'s contract expressly forbids violation of his exclusivity." He could quote whole clauses from his eidetic memory, and beyond his banker's soul lurked an instinct for blood that would shame a tiger shark. "No add-ons. D.W.'s the star."

"Just a notion," Coffin said defensively. He had forgotten it had been Ed who raised the idea of the copycat hit in the first place.

Ed was talented, no lie.

Judge McClanahan rose magisterially. "All right, gentlemen. We proceed with the new jury. Cull the primary list." Jurors for the first two abortive passes had been carefully selected to hamstring the trial, and they had come through like the TV-mesmerized nincompoops they were. "Third try, we pitch a no-hitter. So, D.W., it looks like your contract with us will be satisfactorily discharged in, oh, approximately—"

"Say six months," said Coffin. Rupert the Lawyer nodded approval. Just enough time to make the docket shenanigans appear authentically rigorous.

Her Honor addressed prosecuting and defense counsels respectively. "Pool your notes. Let's give them a good show."

"Yes *ma'am*," Rupert said happily. He gathered up the chain restraints from the table and untangled them. "Time to keep the public safe from you," he said to D.W.

"What about that sheriff?" D.W. could confer with Emerald Ed later; find out what was on tap for their next gig.

Judge McClanahan nodded. "When D.W.'s gone, walk that officer in here. He strikes my prisoner again, I'll cornhole him a wind-tunnel."

"That guy'd probably enjoy it," said Coffin.

D.W. smiled and willingly extended his hands toward the waiting cuffs. He was a trouper.

That night, he watched himself on the news. Rather, the rerun of the news in the wee hours. He videotaped each broadcast onto a scrapbook cassette. He squinted at his own closeup. He contemplated the tears of Ruth Ann Fowler's mother, and reassured himself that he was a force for good in the world.

Somewhere out there in the bad old LA smogscape, the genuine Meat Man was probably face-down in a landfill, chopped apart by a gang shotgun. Gone underground. Blown town. Schizzed out. Working a new identity as a mushroom picker upstate.

It did not matter.

What mattered was that the bad old LA TV-watching public felt security due to the capture of the Meat Man, a gruesome killer of white urban females. What mattered was that they were confident that their police forces and judicial machinery actually functioned for the good of the people. They could sleep at night, knowing the Meat Man was max-locked.

D.W. removed his nose, his chin cleft, and tilted out his brown contacts. He shampooed his hair from black to auburn, with streaks of gray. He washed the three sixes off his forehead.

His jail togs were bagged; he'd done the right thing and changed in Rupert's car. That was why Rupert's car had black mirror windows.

He showered, almost to scalding, and irrigated away his assumed persona. His role.

Towelling his hair, he heard the news video playing back, talking about Reino Salazar and all the bad things he had done to women in Los Angeles. He had turned off the VCR before showering.

There was a burglar watching D.W.'s television. He had helped himself to a bottled beer from D.W.'s fridge. As D.W. entered, the intruder kept his eyes mostly on the screen, and his short-barrel .357 mostly on D.W.'s crotch.

"Don't bother to tell me, man—I already know this is a security building."

The guy wore glasses and had mangey, scouring-pad patches of beard bristle. Teeth too big for his head, horsey and uneven. His eyebrows had tried to grow together. Acne pits and big, oily pores. He looked as though he had mugged some Brentwood yupster and wrestled in a trash dumpster for his clothes. And won.

"What . . . are you doing here?" D.W. was off-guard and out-of-character. He was still dripping. His penis tried to telescope up to hide between his lungs.

"Sit on down," the burglar said. "Check out the news. Man, there's murderers everywhere out there tonight. You're safe in this place. You're smart, am I right?"

D.W. sat where the gun told him to.

"Whackos from hell." The burglar chuckled; stayed conversational. He indicated the Meat Man playback. "Now, this home, check him out. He fucks them, he cuts them up, he kills them, and everybody tries to figure out why."

D.W. felt he should stand tough despite his nudity, wetness, and lack of a suitable equalizer. The shocked yet resilient urban dweller. Reasonable in the face of crisis. "I don't have much money. But you're welcome to what there is. I don't want any–"

"Will you *relax?*" D.W. was overridden. "Let me talk for a minute. You want a beer?"

Thousands of responses scrolled in D.W.'s head. "No."

"Okay, so shut up and don't interrupt. Check it out." Onscreen, the Meat Man glowered at his accusers. "Man, I love it when he gives, like, the devil-stare, you know?"

"I've already seen it."

Ruth Ann Fowler's mother came unhinged. Tight shot, intimate. In D.W.'s head, Reino Salazar was wondering what this thug would look like with a screwdriver jammed up his fundament.

"Okay, so you *know,* man."

"Know what?"

"That's entertainment! The devil made him do it! Whoa, look out, heavy metal made him do it! Porno, handguns, Bud Lite and the Texas Chainsaw Massacre made him do it. Poor dude's just a victim of our Constitution, am I right?"

As the tape winked to static, the burglar launched from his seat with such viper speed that D.W. could only track his wake. By the time D.W. registered the foam and spilled beer on the throw rug, the burglar was pressed right into his face, one hand preventing a block, the other aiming the gun. D.W. was shaking. When the burglar touched his chin—gently—D.W. opened his mouth. He kept it open as he felt the .357's front sight bump past his teeth.

"Let me educate you, amigo," the man said in college-lecture tones. "The only way to know, is to do it for real." He inclined his head back toward the snowy TV. "Those donkey-butts, they don't know. I know. I can see right through you, man. But that's okay. Are you scared? Nod your head."

His mouth full of gun, D.W. nodded. Gently.

"You think you're gonna die now, right? That's okay, too. Listen: The money in your wallet? I already got it. I already got the cash from the phony peanut butter jar in the kitchen. What, is that supposed to fool me? Don't ever offer a crazy person *anything.* He'll take what he wants anyway. Don't negotiate. You paying attention? Scared people, they always try to parley. You still scared?"

He cocked the hammer of the pistol. D.W. felt it all the way to the base of his spine. Sweat had rinsed away his shower.

"Okay, good. Listen to me: This guy Reino Salazar, they say is the Meat Man, you know what I think? I think they're gonna nail him with this new jury. Put his ass away, max-lock, everybody relaxes. The cops get raises, the

Suits get re-elected, everybody's smiling, right? Am I right? Answer me or you're gonna die."

There was no play to make. D.W. nodded.

"Good."

The burglar snapped the trigger. He sprang back from D.W. No gunshot. D.W. was still tasting metal and feeling the impact on his teeth and fearing the bright light as his heart thuddingly urged him to have a coronary. He bleated and thrashed spastically on the couch . . . until he finally understood that he was still alive.

The burglar cocked the hammer again. "Okay, okay, calm down, it was a crummy trick, okay? Next chamber up is for real, just so you don't get Western. People watch too much TV; they think they can be heroes, am I right?"

All D.W.'s moisture was outside his body. His tongue was an emery board, his mouth, a dry well. He managed one line: "What do you want from me?"

"I don't want nothing from you, man. I love you. I *need* you. What you did for me—no price. I just want to tell you that I thank you from right here." He thumped his fist against his chest. Then he moved behind D.W.

Behind the couch, he hovered close enough for D.W. to feel the .357 teasing his earlobe. His whisper was the sound of ghost relatives, calling in favors.

"Okay, listen to me: You're all messed up now, so what I need you to do is go take another shower, all right? You wash up. I'll take another beer, and that's all I'll take, other than the cash, which I genuinely need. I'll rewind your little archive tape, and when you come out, I'll be history. Like I was never here, am I right?"

D.W., certain a bullet was next, closed his eyes. He wanted to weep but didn't have the juice for tears. He just couldn't summon up Reino Salazar while this guy was in the room.

"Always remember: I love you, man. Who's your pal, right? But this is important: To *know* it, you've gotta *do* it. The rest is all horseshit and circuses. Go take your shower."

*Take Two.*

D.W. padded into the living room after an invigorating hot-and-cold. He replayed the video and watched one commentator after another talk gravely of the Meat Man and all the bad things he had done to women in Los Angeles.

D.W.'s video editing needed polish.

Reino Salazar was old news. All that awaited the Meat Man was an ironclad conviction, a unanimous verdict. Tracy Whitmore would write a paperback with a lurid cover, emphasizing Reino's 666.

Past that guy on TV that gave the public their safe little chills, there was no Meat Man. D.W.'s nighttime visitor had murdered the Meat Man long ago.

*Who's your buddy?*

D.W. got his robe and whipped up a brandy espresso. It was time to smoke one of the six Havana cigars he permitted himself annually. Beyond the high windows of his security building, the people of Los Angeles watched TV and got murdered, among their other normal pursuits.

He reran the tape and watched it again, with the attitude of a student winnowing data. He assessed each of the news anchors, each personality.

Nah, too easy, he thought.

After contemplation, he pulled down a phone book, and picked a name and address at random.

Ed Gorman is one of the most underrated writers working today. Crime fiction is only one of the literary avenues he pursues, but it's to my way of thinking, his best traveled avenue. His work is thoughtful and strong on characterization. And though the following story isn't suspense of the thriller school, crime of the sluggem school—it's quiet, in fact—it hangs with you well after reading; clings like a deadly alien creature to the back of the skull, where slowly, ever so slowly, it sips from your soul.

# THE LONG SILENCE AFTER

## Ed Gorman

The flight from Baltimore was bumpy. Not that Neely cared much. Not now.

At Hertz he asked for a city map. The counter woman, oddly sweet in her chignon and early evening exhaustion, smiled sadly. As if she knew why he'd come here. She gave him the map and a brand new Buick that did not yet smell as if somebody had barfed in it and then covered up the stench with Air-Wick.

He had one more stop to make. The Fed Ex office near O'Hare. A package waited there for him. He did not unwrap it until he got back in the car.

Inside the red white and blue wrapping, inside the well-lined box, he found what he'd sent himself here last night: a snub-nosed .38. From the adjacent small box he took the cartridges. He would never have gotten this stuff through airport security.

Finally now, he was ready.

* * *

He spent four hours driving. Street names meant nothing. Sometimes faces were white, sometimes black. He wanted a certain section. Three times he stopped at gas stations and described the area. How there was this drugstore on one corner and a Triple-XXX theater directly across the street and (cheap irony here) a big stone Catholic church a couple blocks down.

Finally, one guy said, Oh, yeah, and told him where he'd find it in relationship to Rogers Park (which was where he was now).

Around nine, just before he saw the drugstore and the XXX-theater, it started raining. Cold March rain. Beading on the windshield, giving all the neon the look of watercolors.

He found a parking garage. A black guy who had a big jaw of chewing tobacco kept spitting all the time he was taking the keys. And kind of glaring. Fucking suburban white dudes. Motherfuckers anyway.

In the front of the XXX-theater was a small shop where you could rent videos and buy various "appliances" (as they are called). He had never been comfortable in such places. Probably his strict Lutheran upbringing. Places of sin.

The man behind the counter had bad teeth and a wandering left eye. Somehow that was fitting in a place like this.

He described the woman he was looking for but the counterman immediately shook his head. "Don't know her, pal."

He described the woman a little more but the man shook his head again. "Sorry," he said exhaling Pall Mall smoke through the brown stubs of his teeth.

He didn't expect to get lucky right off, and he sure didn't. He started at the west end of the street and worked down it: three bars, a massage parlor, a used clothing store, a tiny soup kitchen run by two old nuns, and a bar with a runway for strippers.

And nothing.

Sorry, my friend. Sorry, buddy. Sorry, Jack.

Never seen/heard of her. You know, pal?

And so then he started on the women themselves.

Because of the rain, which was steady and cold, they stood in doorways instead of along the curbsides. The thirty-four degree temperature kept them from any cute stuff. No whistling down drivers. No shaking their asses. No jumping into the streets.

Just huddling in doorways instead. And kind of shivering.

And it was the same with them: no help.

He'd describe her and they'd shrug or shake their heads or pretend they were thinking a long moment and go "Nope, 'fraid not, friend."

Only one of them got smart-mouth. She said: "She musta really been somethin' special, huh?" and all the time was rubbing her knuckles against his crotch.

Inside his respectable suburban topcoat, the .38 was burning a fucking hole.

Around midnight he stopped in this small diner for coffee and a sandwich. He was tired, he already had sniffles from the cold steady rain, and he had a headache, too. He bought his food and a little aluminum deal of Bufferin and took them right down.

And then he asked the counter guy—having no hopes really, just asking the guy kind of automtically—and the guy looked at him and said, "Yeah. Betty."

"Yes. That's right. Her name was Betty."

Through the fog of four years, through the fog of a liquored-up night: yes, goddamit that's right, Betty was her name. Betty.

He asked, "Is she still around?"

The counter man, long hairy tattooed arms, leaned forward and gave him a kind of queer look. "Oh, yeah, she's still around."

The counter man sounded as if he expected the man to know what he was hinting at.

"You know where I can find her?"

The counter man shook his head. "I don't know if that'd be right, mister."

"How come?"

He shrugged. "Well, she's sort of a friend of mine."

"I see."

And from inside his respectable suburban topcoat, he took his long leather wallet and peeled off a twenty and laid it on the counter and felt like fucking Sam Spade. "I'd really like to talk to her tonight."

The counter man stared at the twenty. He licked dry lips with an obscene pink tongue. "I see what you mean."

"How about it?"

"She really is kind of a friend of mine."

So Sam Spade went back into action. He laid another crisp twenty on the original crisp twenty.

The tongue came out again. This time he couldn't watch the counter man. He pretended to be real interested in the coffee inside his cheap chipped cup.

So of course the counter man gave him her address and told him how to get there.

Fog. Rain. The sound of his footsteps. You could smell the rotting lumber of this ancient neighborhood now that it was soaked. Little shabby houses packed so close together you couldn't ride a bicycle between some of them. One-story brick jobs mostly that used to be packed with Slavs. But the Slavs had good factory jobs now so they had moved out and eager scared blacks had taken their place.

Hers was lime green stucco. Behind a heavy drape a faint light shone.

He gripped the gun.

On the sidewalk he stepped in two piles of dogshit. And now the next-door dog—as if to confirm his existence—started barking.

He went up the narrow walk to her place.

He stood under the overhang. The concrete porch had long ago pulled away from the house and was wobbly. He felt as if he were trying to stand up on a capsizing row boat.

The door opened. A woman stood there. "Yes?"

His memory of her was that she'd been much heavier. Much.

He said, "Betty?"

"Right."

"Betty Malloy?"

"Right again." She sounded tired, even weak. "But not the old Betty Malloy."

"Beg pardon?"

"I ain't what I used to be."

Cryptic as her words were, he thought that they still made sense.

"I'd like to come in."

"Listen, I don't do that no more, all right?"

"I'd like to come in anyway."

"Why?"

He sighed. If he pulled the gun here, she might get the chance to slam the door and save herself.

He had to get inside.

He put his hand on the knob of the screen door.

It was latched.

Sonofabitch.

"I need to use your phone," he said.

"Who are you?"

In some naive way, he'd expected her to remember who he was. But of course she wouldn't.

"Could I use your phone?"

"For what?"

"To call Triple-A."

"Something's wrong with your car?"

"The battery went dead."

"Where's your car?"

"What?"

"I asked where you car was. I don't see no new car. And you definitely look like the kind of guy who'd be driving a new car."

So he decided screw it and pulled the gun.

He put it right up against the screen door.

She didn't cry out or slam the door or anything. She just stood there. The gun had mesmerized her.

"You gotta be crazy, mister."

"Unlatch the door."

"I ain't got no money, man. I ain't got nothing you'd want. Believe me."

"Just unlatch the fucking door or I start shooting."

"My God, mister, I don't know what this could be about. I really don't."

But she unlatched the door and he went inside.

He closed and locked both doors behind him.

He turned around and looked at the small living room she stood in. The first thing he noticed was that she had not one but two velvet paintings of Jesus above the worn and frayed couch. There was a 17-inch color tv set playing a late movie with Sandra Dee. There was a pressed wood coffee table with only three legs, a stack of paperback books substituting for the missing leg.

She sat on the couch.

He pointed the gun at her.

She said, sounding exhausted now, "You look crazy, mister. I can't help but tell you the truth. You really look crazy."

And now he had some idea of how much weight she'd lost. Maybe forty, fifty pounds. And her facial skin was pulled drum-tight over her cheekbones. And her pallor was gray.

There was a bad odor in the place, too, and he didn't have to ask what it was.

"You fucking bitch," he said, waving the gun at her. She'd been right. He heard his words. He was crazy.

She looked up at him with sad and weary eyes. "I'm so tired, mister, just from walking over to the door that I can't—What do you want anyway?"

"You know this is pretty god damn funny."

"What is?"

He started pacing. For a time he didn't talk. Just paced. She watched him. The floorboards creaked as he walked over them.

"You destroy me and you don't even remember who I am? That's pretty god damned good."

And then she said, seeming to know everything suddenly, "Oh, shit, mister. Now I know why you come here. And all I can say is I'm sorry."

He turned on her, seized with his fury. "I've got a wife and two children. I've got a good business. I'm not gay or some junkie or—"

She said, and now her breathing was ragged, and she looked suddenly spent: "How long have you known?"

But he didn't want to answer questions.

He wanted to shake the gun in her face, the gun that signified how trapped and outraged he felt.

And so he shook it. He went right up to her and shook it in her face and said, "You fucking bitch, couldn't you have had yourself checked out before you went on the streets?"

Because that was how it had happened. Him visiting Chicago for an insurance convention. Some executive friend of his from Milwaukee who really liked slumming bringing him down here for a little "black poontang" and—

And a week ago his family doctor, just as incredulous as he was, told him, "David, Jesus Christ, these tests can be wrong sometimes but right now it looks as if—"

Only once in eighteen years of marriage had he been unfaithful.

In Chicago.

Insurance convention.

Black woman.

And now he stood above her. "I can't tell you how badly I want to blow your fucking head off, you bitch."

She looked up at him and said, "Maybe you'd be doing me a favor. I got maybe six months to go myself, mister, and this is some hard way to die, let me tell you." Again, she sounded completely spent.

"The worst thing is, I may have infected my wife."

"I know," she said. "My old man left me when he found out. But it's probably too late for him, too."

"You fucking bitch!" he said, no longer able to control himself.

He brought the gun down hard across her jaw.

Almost immediately she started sobbing.

And then he couldn't hit her any more.

He heard in her tears the inevitable tears of his wife and children when they found out.

And he couldn't hit her at all any more.

She just sat there and sobbed, her whole body trembling, weaker with each moment.

He said, "I'm sorry."

She just kept crying.

He started pacing again.

"I can't believe this. I keep thinking that there's no way I could—"

He shook his head and looked over at her. She was daubing at her nose with an aqua piece of Kleenex.

"Do you get help?"

She nodded. She wouldn't look at him any more. "The welfare folks. They send out people."

"I'm sorry I was so angry."

"I know."

"And I'm sorry I hit you."

"I know that too."

"I'm just so fucking scared and so fucking angry."

Now she looked at him again. "The anger goes after awhile. You get too tired to be angry anymore."

"I don't know how I'm going to tell my wife."

"You'll do it, mister. That's the only thing I figured out about this thing. You do what you've got to. You really do."

He dumped the gun in the pocket of his respectable suburban top-coat. And then he took out his wallet and flicked off a hundred dollars in twenties.

"You really must be crazy, mister," she said. "Leavin' me money like that."

"Yes," he said. "I really must be crazy."

She started crying again.

He closed the doors quietly behind him. Even halfway down the walk, even in the fog and even in the rain, he could still hear her crying.

There was a three o'clock to Baltimore. He wasn't sure he had nerve enough to tell her yet but he knew he would have to. He owed her so much; he certainly owed her the truth.

He walked faster now, and soon he disappeared completely inside the fog. He was just footsteps now; footsteps.

Dan Lowry is a relatively new writer with three sales under his belt. This is his first solo effort. Simple, but memorable. Dan lives and works in the Dallas area, and is, we hope, at work on more stories.

# BLADE

## Dan Lowry

I bet no one in this fern bar restaurant is thinking about lovely young women being torn to shreds but me. Least of all the tall voluptuous brunette four tables down. She looks like the only thing on her mind is the obnoxious ass hole she's sitting with.

"Here's your order sir. Is there anything else I can get for you?"

"Maybe another beer in a while, but I'm fine now, baby."

"Ok, are you going to need any help with that, sir?"

"No I'm just fine. That's all I need right now." But I got something you need and you're going to get it if you don't go away now.

"I just thought we've got a stack of phone books. If you want me to I'll get a couple for you to sit on. It might make it easier for you."

I got something you can sit on bitch that will make it easier for both of us. And if you don't leave me the fuck alone, I'm going to take that button nose of your and sew it to my fucking underwear!

"That's really kind of you but I can manage just fine." Great, now the redhead behind me thinks it's so fucking funny she just couldn't suppress that giggle. Every mindless cunt in the joint is looking and laughing at me now. Including the brunette four tables down.

For all the attention I attract in what for anyone else would be everyday anonymity, I can stalk the prey undetected. If they don't hear my whine I can manage just fine. Tonight everybody in Bennagen's could heard me whine my way out the door. I'm sure that's what they were all laughing about when I left.

Later I thought about the brunette as I stroked my Blade. She and the geek never suspected they were followed back to her apartment. Never knew I was still there watching at two in the morning when he finally left. Just thinking about her makes me stroke the Blade harder. She needs to meet the Blade but it hasn't been long enough since the last one.

## Second Evening

Maybe it has been long enough. Three weeks ago that paper she's reading would have had headlines announcing the discovery of more mutilated remains. There is so much violence these days it's hard to dwell on one scene of one act of such a large production. That's fine with me. What I want to do with the brunette is private. A personal matter.

I could never escort her to the outdoor restaurant across the street where she's sucking down margaritas and the fashion section. But the Blade and I can take her places no one else would dare to escort her. Take that black haired babe beyond the pale, through the veil and cut a path right over the mists of time. We can put her on the razor's edge of adventure, right on the very cutting line of heart rending action. We can kill the sneering little bitch. And that's about as personal a matter as I can think of.

I still think it may be too soon since the blond screamer. Boy what a set of lungs that one had, in more ways than one. I've still got one set in the freezer too. I may thaw those out tonight and cleaver the cleavage. Tease the Blade a little.

## Evening Three

Ok, what the hell I might as well. This morning's paper brought the news of another so-called serial killer on the West coast. Our very own government announced the latest generation of nuclear weapons. The good news is these mega ton babies can wipe out twice as many people with half the radiation. The killers can bask in their killing without wearing lead lined jumpsuits. The exciting world of modern science. If the biggest and best democracy on earth can plot, plan, and build to kill why can't I?

I've got my Blade with me today. On the van seat next to me sits the conqueror of cunts, vanquisher of the vain, and dicer of the dames. My best friend, the Blade. The Blade wants that brunette. We talked it over last night. I'd already told old Blade about her of course. But I hadn't said anything to insinuate that she might be right for the two of us. Blade knew all along though. I just can't hide anything from the Blade. I guess that's the way real friends are.

Now comes half the fun. Stalking her. You can attack the first chance you get like a punk mugger, and get caught. You can skulk around like a jackal trying to build up nerve, and get caught. Or you can take the prey with stealth, the honed cunning of a true master of the predatory arts. Artist, that's what I am. I'm the artist, the Blade's a brush, bloods the paint, and the world's a canvas.

Damn it, she's exiting out the other side of the lot. That's ok, I know she'll stop at that little store before she goes back to the office. Her patterns are already starting to fall into place.

The Blade and I get the old scrapbook out after supper again. Looked at all the pictures of the old me. Standing there with Mother and Aunt Gladis. Standing there with Mother and Aunt Ethal. All the women glaring into the camera. I remember the photographer was a man. Then all the medical photos from an infant till I stopped going to the crippled children clinics. All the doctors agreed mine was the most unusual case of its kind they had ever seen. I remember Mother telling one of the doctors when I was six or seven if I was that precious why didn't they just keep me. The look of disgust that crossed his face was the same one that stayed on Mother. Then the newspaper accounts of Mother's tragic murder, slaughter as one of the headlines put it. "The only witness was the victim's afflicted son who is unable to give police any details yet due to shock." Ha, ha. More clippings taken over the years of terrible murders.

And then a new chapter. "Case of mistaken identity leaves handicapped man in i.c.u. The victim of a terrible birth defect was the victim of an accidental police shooting last night. Officer Betty Johnson pulled over a car for a defective taillight. At the driver's window she states she clearly saw the driver's hand reach for a pistol in a shoulder hoster. Doctors at Urban Hospital where the man was taken said he was wearing a metal and leather harness custom designed for his unusual physical deformation. This, experts say could have been mistaken for a shoulder holster in dim light." And a small clipping from the back pages of a month later that read, "Grand Jury does not bring indictment on female police officer in shooting. Motorist is not expected to fully recover." Not expected to fully recover. The Blade and I have a good laugh at that as we go over the latest entrees. Reports of the series of "brutal" attacks on women. "Body parts still not found." "These murders were done by a vicious animal." How right you are.

* * *

## DARK AT HEART

### Evening Four

She's actually going to make this easy. Walking over to the next apartment complex this afternoon she probably didn't mean to stay after dark. If she stayed that late she probably didn't plan on being alone. But now it's late, dark, and she's alone. Well, she thinks that she's all alone. We know better. I know the Blade and I should wait. But we can't. We'll have to make this fast, but we want to take our time. I guess you can't have everything, right?

Good, she's going back home the way she came through that little green belt area. We got time to drive around to the other side and meet her in the middle. I wonder how many wine coolers she had. Looks like she's a sheet and a half in the wind.

Like I said, I attract a lot of attention in public. Fear however is not one of the emotions the sight of me elicits. The brunette trudging along the walk toward me only hesitated a second when she heard me whining toward her. Then dismissed me with a little snort. She didn't know I had the Blade behind me. When the Blade stepped out in her path it was a different story.

"Wow, is that yours?"

"Yes."

"Does he bi . . ."

"Yes."

It's hard to talk when your throat has just been torn out. It's a crying shame we didn't wait till we could have had more privacy, but Blade's not wasting a second.

"That's it Blade, tear that stuff up boy. Nobody can say we can't give a girl an exciting time." The Blade is just playing with her.

"Ha doll, maybe I'll call you floppy. I like that. Your flopping all over the ground."

Ah, that Blades beautiful in action. Thrust, parry, slashing with a muzzle full of little ivory knives.

Born deformed and having what's left paralyzed by a woman cop made it hard on a born slasher like me. Electric wheelchairs and prosthetic limbs alone can't get me where I need to go. No, for that I needed a blade. So now I have the Blade. Who would have thought you could turn a hundred and five pounds of Doberman pinscher into a prosthetic knife. Where there's a will there's a way.

"That's the way, get her face again Blade. Shred that sneer off it. Leave the legs alone though. I'll put them in the doggie bag and you can have them tomorrow."

Chet Williamson is a wonderful writer worthy of greater attention. And he'll get it. You can't be this good and not get it. Check out his novels REIGN and DREAMTHORP and you'll see what we mean. He's also a nice guy. The following story is a fine slice of dark crime. Enjoy.

# MUSHROOMS

## Chet Williamson

When 3-Ball and X-Too got on the train, they walked immediately to the last car, X-Too in the lead. 3-Ball was glad, since it gave him a chance to watch X-Too move, and X-Too moved about as def as any brother he'd ever seen, even with a piece on his hip. The piece made X-Too move even cleaner than usual, thrusting out his hip to the left as if to make up for the uneven balance the pistol caused.

They didn't pass any cops on the way, and there was nobody in the last car except a tall and stringy blind kid with shades and one of those long white canes with the red tip. He was sitting near the center of the car, his head back, blind eyes looking up. Looked a little like Stevie Wonder, 3-Ball thought, wondering if the blind brother could be a musician.

"Think he's a musician?" he asked X-Too.

X-Too gave him The Look. "Whatta fuck you talkin'?" he said.

"Blind homeboy. Look like Stevie Wonder."

"Well, I look like fuckin' Ice Cube, only badder, and I don't rap. Now stop talkin' shit."

They sat down at the very back of the car, which ran across a section of dead track, throwing the train into total darkness and stopping the noisy fans for five seconds. "Wonder if that home know when that happens," said 3-Ball when the lights and fans came on again.

"What?"

"When it gets dark in here."

"How he know? Homeboy's blind."

"Well, y'know, sometimes they can tell between light 'n dark."

X-Too didn't say anything, just kept looking at the door at the front of the car. Finally he spoke. "We ice that motherfucker soon's he come in. Don't give him no chance to grab his own piece."

"Yeah. Smoke 'im in the fuckin' feet."

"Not the feet *first,* asshole. Fuckin' *head* first, or chest. *Then* his feet." X-Too nodded. "Right in his goddam Air Jordans, home. Nail his feet to the cross with bullets."

Lord Jake-Ay was the man they were about to kill. Jake-Ay had been the one who had shot Luther JD dead, then shit in his suede Fila hightops and jammed them back on Luther JD's feet, leaving him lying in an alley with shoes full of crap. On top of that, Jake-Ay had pissed on Luther JD's colors. It had been stupid of Jake-Ay, but everybody knew that Jake-Ay was stupid, even Jeango, the Blews' main man, but he kept Jake-Ay around anyway, since Jake-Ay would smoke anyone anytime.

Well, now X-Too and 3-Ball would smoke Jake-Ay.

They knew that he got on every night at the third stop past where they got on, always at the same time, after he got done pushing rock in the Van Norris Street arcade, got on and headed uptown to chill with Jeango. 3-Ball thought they'd grab his take, but maybe not. It would be some def gesture, leaving the money on him, just banging his feet until they were bloody stumps of dirty white leather and muscle and bone. The Blews would get the message all right. All the boys in the hood would know it was The Chillin Crew. And no shit and no piss. That kind of jive was for animals like Jake-Ay.

David heard the voices at the end of the car. Two young black men. They spoke seldom, and although they made no attempt to talk quietly, the sound of the train prevented his picking out more than the occasional word.

He felt the train begin to stop, and knew they must be just below the theatre district, although he could not see the walls of the tunnel pass by more slowly until the individual bricks and the name of the station were discernible. When he felt the train stop and heard the doors slide open, he started to loudly whistle, "Stop in the Name of Love."

"What the motherfuck . . ." he heard one of the young men say, but kept whistling, thinking about Nancy and how hard it was going to be for her. He had been blind from birth, but to learn what it was like when you were in your twenties—damn, that was tough.

He kept whistling, heard the door at the front of the car rasp open, heard the scrape of a cane on the floor, heard her call his name, tentatively, and with no little fear. "David?"

"Here, Nancy," he said. "Fifth seat back on the right."

The cane stuttered along, and he felt the vibration as she grasped the edge of each seat, counting. "That's right, here," he said when he heard her beside him.

Just as she sat, the train lurched and started, and she fell against him. He felt something strike his thigh and clatter to the floor. Unerringly he leaned forward and skimmed his fingers just above the linoleum, immediately contacting her sunglasses. As he lifted them, he could feel that they were the type with side panels, allowing no one to peer in. He took her hand and placed the left stem into it.

"Thanks," she said.

"Get down okay from your apartment?"

"Yeah. But God, it was rough. Getting down the street to the station was scary, but once I was down here, finding the right platform . . ." She sighed with a shudder. "I must have asked half a dozen people. I feel so much at the mercy of just anybody."

"You'll get over it," he told her. "It's rough at the start."

"I don't know how it could get any rougher," she said.

"Fuck, man," X-Too said.

"What?"

"Thought that blind fuck be off by now. 'Stead he meet some bitch."

"She fly, though," 3-Ball said, then added, "'Cept she blind."

"Wouldn't stop me. Fly's fly. Head down, butt up, don't matter they see or not. Bust her butt."

"We do that?" asked 3-Ball, trying not to sound anxious.

"Shit, no. We bangin' Lord Jake-Ay tonight, not pussy. Wish they get off, though."

"Got another stop. Maybe they will."

"They don't, we tromp 'em down we have to. They just mushrooms."

"Yeah." 3-Ball chuckled. "Mushrooms." He thought it would be a pity, though, to burn a bitch that good looking. "You know, I seen her somewhere," he said after a moment's thought. "Ain't she that bitch inna commercial—for that, what the fuck, secretary school or somethin'?"

"What trash you talkin'? Blind secretaries?"

"Nah . . ."

"How them bitches type? Got Braille typewriters?"

"Nah, nah, they ain't *blind* secretaries."

"Then what that bitch be sellin' for 'em? Motherfucker, but you dumb."

"She fly enough to do commercials," 3-Ball insisted.

"Yeah, fuck, sellin' canes." X-Too glared at the couple. "They don't get off the next stop, they need more than canes. Fuckin' mushrooms. Smash 'em. Cold smoke 'em."

The lights and the fans went off, started again. The train began to slow.

"You hear those guys?" David asked Nancy.

"What guys?"

"Two homeboys in the back of the car. Left side."

"How do you know that?"

"Heard them talking. You'll hear when we stop now."

The train shivered to a halt. The doors slid open, but David heard no one get on or off. The men in the back were silent, and David thought he sensed a tension in them. When the doors closed, he heard only a few words, one of which was "mushrooms."

Mushrooms. They were hardly talking about fungi, David thought, so it must have been innocent bystanders they were referring to. But what the hell, it was probably just gang talk, bravado. He had heard enough of it growing up in the projects. If the two had been planning to do anything to him and Nancy they probably would have done it by now.

David had little fear of the trains. He'd been robbed before, but he had always been cooperative and never been hurt. He always carried twenty dollars with him. It was no more than he could afford to lose, and just enough to satisfy a mugger.

"I hear them now," Nancy whispered.

David heard them too. Their voices were pitched lower now, and from their tone he knew he had been right about the tension he had sensed. But he had heard it all before, and if he had left a subway car every time he heard those tight, choppy tones, he would have had to cab everywhere. Maybe they were on their way to a drug deal, or, hell, maybe just a date. People could get edgy about a lot of little things.

"I hear them," Nancy repeated, "but I can't tell exactly where they are. How do you know?"

"Same way I knew where to get your sunglasses. Get a sense from the sound of things. I know—aurally—what a subway car's like, how the sounds bounce off the walls, how many rows, how many seats. And something close, like your glasses, well, that's easy. Most sighted people could do it, they put their mind to it. They drop things in the dark, they poke around for a while. But if they'd just listen to it hit, even something little, they could reach right for it."

"Um. That's neat. I really appreciate you helping me like this, David."

"No problem." David smiled, and hoped she could sense it. He had helped a lot of people like Nancy who came to the Blind Association. He always enjoyed it, showing people the ropes, fascinating them with his abilities and teaching them to do the same kind of thing. He just hoped it would do her some good.

The train jerked, and began to move.

"Shoulda told 'em to get off, maybe," said 3-Ball.

X-Too frowned even deeper than before. "Hell, we make 'em get off, they's a cop at the next stop. They don't get off in time, fuck 'em. Maybe we bust caps on 'em, they don't get smoked before."

3-Ball sat back and tried to relax, but it was hard. He heard that Lord Jake-Ay had an Uzi, though Luther JD had been smoked with a .38. X-Too had an Uzi too, but only used it to cap homes from cars. It was too big to carry around. What X-Too had tonight was a .44 magnum, its six and a half inch barrel jammed down his pants leg next to his dick. It was still a big gun, big enough to tear off Jake-Ay's feet once they smoked him dead.

'Course maybe they could shoot him so that he didn't die right away, but could feel his toes being blown off. 3-Ball grinned at the thought, and his hand went inside his bright red jacket, to his waistband and his own pistol, a sweet little Colt Cobra that X-Too called a pussy gun. That hadn't stopped 3-Ball from capping three Blews with it in as many months. And tonight, Jake-Ay.

Then he looked at the man and woman sitting halfway up the car, and thought he should tell them, tell them now before the train stopped, so that they could get off right away, before Jake-Ay got on and the shooting started. He knew mushrooms were mushrooms, but damn, there was no point in blind people being hurt. After all, they hadn't seen him or X-Too, couldn't make any I.D.,

He stood up and started to walk toward them, but X-Too's shout stopped him. "3-Ball! Whatta fuck you doin'?"

"I'm just—"

"Get yo' ass back here. *Sid*down!"

3-Ball shambled the few feet back to where X-Too sat. When he looked behind him, he saw that the man and woman were cocking their heads as if listening to the rebuke. 3-Ball sat down and said softly, "Man, don't dis me in front of them people, okay?"

"Fuck, they can't see, they don't know I dissed you."

"Still, man . . . I just wanted to tell them to get off fast, the train stop.

You know, 'fore Jake-Ay get on."

"Well, that was dumbfuck. What you care? They start walkin' off, Jake-Ay use 'em for cover comin' in, now that's fuckin' brighta you. Just leave 'em where they sittin'." X-Too looked out the window at the dark rushing past. "'Sides, we gotta cap 'em anyway."

"What? Why?"

"They heard your name. I call it."

3-Ball could only see X-Too's reflection in the dirty glass, but thought that the dark line of X-Too's mouth was smiling. Maybe X-Too called his name on purpose. Sometimes 3-Ball thought that X-Too just liked smoking people, it didn't matter who. Yeah, maybe he did it on purpose.

"Damn," 3-Ball said. "Thassa shame, have to waste a fly piece of pussy like that."

"Accidents happen," said X-Too, still looking out the window.

When the train started to slow, X-Too and 3-Ball didn't wait until it stopped to take out their pistols. X-Too slid his .44 from his pants slow, a smooth smile on his face, like he was slipping out his dick to show a bitch. 3-Ball just tugged his Cobra from his waistband, and out it came, the grips getting wet fast from the sweat on his palms. "Watch the side," X-Too said. "I take the front."

Finally the train stopped, and the doors opened, but no one came in. After half a minute the doors closed again, the train started rolling. "Ain't comin' in the side," said 3-Ball.

"Shut up," X-Too said, his yellow glare fixed on the window of the door at the front of the car. "I see 'im."

Now 3-Ball saw him too, and they both slouched down so that only the tops of their capped heads were visible over the seat in front of them. Jake-Ay slammed a fist against the door, smashing it open, and came into their car. He was wearing a heavy leather coat and a Kangol whose brim hid his eyes.

X-Too's first shot took him by surprise, giving him no time to draw his gun. It hit him in the left shoulder, slamming him back against the edge of the door.

The sudden motion made 3-Ball's shot miss, and he saw blood and more splatter from the rip in Jake-Ay's leather coat. Then Jake-Ay dove into the corner, flipped back his coat with his good arm, and 3-Ball knew why Jake-Ay's coat was so huge. It had to be to keep an Uzi under it.

X-Too stood up to get off a second shot just as Jake-Ay let loose with the Uzi. It spat a trail of bullets across the width of the car, and 3-Ball ducked down behind the seat. The last thing he saw had been the blind man and woman dropping, and he wondered if they had been hit, then decided they hadn't, because he would have seen their heads pop.

Then he heard X-Too's .44 roar again, and X-Too's voice screaming, and the Uzi stop chattering, and when he looked he saw X-Too falling down on top of him like a big black tree, and he caught him, one Crew catching another, and felt a hot wetness in X-Too's belly, and heard X-Too moan, "Fuck, fuck, *mother*fuck," over and over like some dumb, simple rap.

3-Ball staggered to his feet, his Cobra up and pointing toward the end of the car, but Lord Jake-Ay's face beneath the Kangol looked like grape jelly, and he wasn't moving. The Uzi lay silent across his lap.

Now X-Too was saying something that 3-Ball couldn't make out, something that sounded like X-Too was trying to whistle through his teeth. 3-Ball leaned across, and X-Too grabbed him with the hand that wasn't holding his insides.

"*Feet,*" X-Too said. "Feet . . . shoot his . . . motherfuck . . . feet. Use the Uzi . . ."

3-Ball nodded, climbed over X-Too, and ran down to the end of the car, his Cobra trained on Jake-Ay just in case. As he passed their seat, he saw the man and woman crouched behind the seat, probably wondering what the hell was happening.

He grabbed the Uzi, stuck the Cobra in his belt, stood over Jake-Ay's body, and fired into the dead man's feet. The bullets went through the floor of the car, and blood, ripped muscle, and bone shards spattered his own clean hightops, but he kept smoking until the Uzi was empty, and Jake-Ay's right foot was only pink pulp. There wasn't even that much left of the severed right foot, most of which had been smashed down through the floor onto the tracks.

Then 3-Ball put the empty weapon under his arm, and trotted back to X-Too. X-Too's face was ashy, and blood and something yellow was seeping through his fingers where he held them against his stomach.

"Now . . . cap the mushrooms," he rasped. ". . . then get me out . . ."

The train was starting to slow for the next stop, and 3-Ball knew he'd have to be quick. He set the Uzi next to X-Too, yanked the Cobra from his belt, walked up to the seat, and lifted the gun to fire.

But when he saw the girl's face, so pretty even though masked by sunglasses, he hesitated for just a moment, just long enough for the train to cross a rough switch and lurch savagely, so that he nearly fell, and the pistol slipped from his sweating, trembling hand. He saw it spinning down into the dark space between the man and the woman, and the image locked in his sight as they hit dead track, and all the lights in the car went out.

David had heard the shots, the running footsteps, then the same coming back, had heard them stop beside him and Nancy, had heard the gun hit the floor and slide across it.

He reached down, to the right, and grasped it with his right hand, took Nancy's hand with his left, pressed it against her palm, said, "Do it," praying that she would.

Then he felt the gun wrenched away from him, and heard her sunglasses clatter again on the floor. This time he didn't reach down to pick them up.

In three seconds, when the lights came back on, 3-Ball found himself unarmed, and the bitch with the gun in her hands, swinging it in his direction. Blind or not, he wasn't taking any chances. If he grabbed it, she'd sure as hell pull the trigger, and the way the damn piece was waggling in his direction, he didn't want to risk it. So he moved back slow, watching the black muzzle like a blind eye.

Then he heard a voice roar, "*Geddown!*" and he hit the floor, scuttling back toward X-Too, thinking that if he got X-Too's .44 he could smoke the bitch. But then he heard his gun go off in the bitch's hand, and saw X-Too's gun come thudding down into the aisle, along with X-Too's shoulders and head, part of which had been blown away by the crosscut bullets with which 3-Ball kept his Cobra loaded. Damn, he thought, not bad cappin' for a blind bitch.

3-Ball kept crawling toward the .44, now only eight feet away, moving as silently as he could so the bitch wouldn't hear him. He had halved the distance between himself and the gun, when he heard footsteps behind him. He turned, looked, and froze when he saw the woman standing, her face and the Cobra pointing in his direction. Her sunglasses had come off, and he could see her eyes now, blue and real pretty for blind eyes.

But it was all right. As long as she didn't hear him, he could grab that gun, take sweet, slow aim, and drop her like a sack of shit. He made himself look away from her, and kept crawling.

"Stop," she said. Her voice was real pretty, even shaking like it was, but he just smiled and kept crawling toward the gun, now nearly within his reach.

"Stop," she said again. "*Stop,* red jacket!"

*Red jacket?* The words froze him. How'd the bitch know what he had on, unless . . .

He turned and looked up at her, at her bright, blue, pretty eyes that he damn well *knew* he'd seen on the TV, staring at him, seeing him . . .

Yeah. Really *seeing* him.

"Stop," she said again, in the voice he'd heard telling all about that secretarial school.

But he couldn't stop. Not this close. And he turned and reached for the gun, grabbed it, brought it around, and then the bullet smashed into him and he went blind and deaf and dumb for always.

When the police got on at the next stop, they found three dead men and two people alive, one blind man, one sighted woman. One of the cops helped the woman pick up the things that had fallen out of her bag. The last thing he found was a script of a play entitled *Wait Until Dark.*

"Did you get enough of a lesson for tonight?" David asked Nancy when they finally left the hospital.

"Yes," she said, holding his arm in hers, guiding him down the strange steps, over the strange sidewalk, toward a corner where they could catch a cab.

"Sedative helping?" he asked her, thinking that he felt a lot calmer now. But he hadn't killed anyone.

"I think so. I'm still shaky. God, what a nightmare. A bad dream that got worse. Let's sit down. Just for a minute. My knees are still trembling." They sat on a bench, but she still held David's arm.

"I thought I was playing, you know?" said Nancy, almost to herself. "Like a game. Sensually slumming. But now I feel like being blind is . . . as much of a craft as acting. Even an art. How you ever found that gun, just grabbed it so fast . . . I never could have found it in the dark that way."

David turned toward her. "Mushrooms were meant for the dark," he said, and she gave a little laugh, then stopped, as if angry with herself for being flippant after what she had done.

"I found it." David said, then added slowly, softly, "But I couldn't have shot them."

"No. No. You couldn't see them."

Now he was even quieter. "I didn't say that."

She said nothing, then released his arm. When she spoke again, her words were chill and distant. "God. It must be hard to be blind."

"Maybe we should all be blind," David said. "It makes it a lot harder to kill people."

Nancy looked at him for a long time. Though he couldn't see her, he felt her eyes on him. By the time a cab drove by, it had grown colder, and no less dark.

Ardath Mayhar has written over twenty novels, some under pen names. She has written Young Adult novels, Westerns, Science Fiction, Fantasy and Non-fiction, and no telling what I've left out. She is also the author of numerous short stories, and is an award winning poet. And though Ardath is a very nice lady, her fiction is often quite unlady like. Read "Aunt Dolly", and enough said.

# AUNT DOLLY

## Ardath Mayhar

Outside the tightly closed window, the ivy leaves were beating against the small panes in the first real storm of winter. Even though the house was tight, the windows closely fitted, Dorothy shivered, feeling that the heavy draperies, only half drawn as yet in the last light, should be billowing in the fury of the wind.

Snug in her rose-shaded room, safe in the bed in which she had been born, Dorothy should have been content, but in the last month that had been lost to her. The hearty old woman who had broken wild horses, reared her three great-nephews to adulthood, if not to responsibility, and managed the horse farm she had built up from the tatty farm her father left her seemed lost in the past.

Now she was an invalid, wrapped in plush blankets, confined to this room that had never fitted her personality. The pale rose blankets, the deep rose velvet of the draperies, the charming flower pattern of the sheets, those were matters that had appealed to her mother.

Dolly was a farmer, a horse breeder, a tough-minded, tough-bodied creature who had never been ill in all her sixty-seven years. This terrible thing that had happened to her frightened her for the first time she could recall.

A small stroke—what nonsense! You stroked a cat or the nose of a horse. This was more like a blow, aimed not only at her mind but at everything she had ever stood for. Aimed, worst of all, at the independence she cherished above anything else.

There came a stir in the hallway outside her door. A timid tap told her that Cynthia, her third nephew's wife, stood outside with a cup of chocolate and the afternoon paper.

Dolly sighed. "Come on in," she grunted. "And close those damned drapes. That wind wants to come right through the glass, it seems like, and at my age I don't need that for a bedfellow."

Cyn set the tray just so, its legs straddling Dolly's lap, and moved to tug at the velvet rope that shut out the chill pewter of the evening. The delicacy of her motions, the finicky precision of everything she did grated on the old woman's nerves like diamond on glass. She suspected that in private Cynthia was far less ladylike than she appeared now.

"Do sit down!" she commanded. "And don't fiddle! I like my room messy. Makes me feel at home."

She stirred the marshmallow into the steaming cup of chocolate and took a tentative sip. Ah! The warmth relaxed her a bit, and she settled back against the piled pillows behind her, holding down her irritation at the frills edging the cases.

"Tell me about the mare—did Mr. Winlow find out what ails her? She's too valuable to risk, let me tell you, and if we need another vet we've got to get one. Winlow isn't bad, but he's an old fogey in a lot of ways."

"Oh, Auntie, don't worry yourself about the horses. Jerry is taking the most splendid care of everything . . ."

"Don't give me that! Jerry never took splendid care of anything but himself, and that includes taking care of you. He's checking out every salable item on the place with an eye toward sneaking it out to a pawnshop is more like it. He'll rob his brothers, if they're not careful." She watched the young woman closely, but Cynthia had learned to hide her feelings when Dolly went on a tear.

Rather disappointed, Dolly drank down the chocolate and poured another cup from the rosebud-sprigged pot. That was Haviland that she had bought to please her mother, once there was money for that sort of nonsense.

She wondered if any of the pieces had been sold, downstairs, by her rapacious kinsman. The stuff was worth a mint, the antiques-dealer had told her when she made the purchase.

She always rolled her food and drink around her tongue, these days, trying them for any odd taste. She wouldn't put it past Jerry and his nasty-nice wife to try poisoning her. Then they'd have a free run at everything while Ed and Charlie traveled the long miles from England and Africa to protect their interests.

Cynthia turned even paler than usual, but she held her peace. The old saying, "Wouldn't say boo to a goose" applied nicely to her, Dolly thought.

"Winlow," she said again, her tone stern. "Tell!"

"The mare was only bloated. He tended to it and gave her something to help. Jerry says he thinks she'll be fine tomorrow." The words came out slowly, precisely enunciated, spent grudgingly as if they were dollars instead of breath.

"Good." Dolly finished the cup, placed the thin china in its saucer with a decisive clink, and motioned toward the door. "Now go and do whatever it is you find to do all day and all night. I'd as soon talk to a parrot!"

When the door closed behind the thin behind and the sharp elbows of her great-niece-by-marriage, Dolly sighed. She had tried. She truly had!

But those boys were a handful, and no matter how she worked them and taught them and made them toe the mark, they kept breaking out wherever she wasn't expecting it. If she'd had a husband it might have helped. A man would have understood them better.

But as it was, she was a better man than any of the three, and they all knew it. They all resented it, too, which was why Ed had gone to London as soon as his paper had an assignment there. Charlie had taken himself off to Botswana or some such godforsaken place to write a book.

Jerry had been closest, and that only because the chemical firm for which he was a sales rep was based on the west coast. They gave him leave and here he was, complete with baggage and wife, who was also a pretty fair baggage herself.

She listened sharply as the crisp steps descended the uncarpeted stair. The kitchen door gave its usual definitive thunk as it closed, and she smiled. Time to practice walking again.

She didn't intend to be a bed-ridden invalid for the rest of her years, that was certain. But every time she suggested that Jerry help her stand and walk he fussed and worried and all but said that he wanted her flat on her back.

There was no way she was going to put up with that, and his refusal was motivation enough to drive her to secret exercises that by now had strengthened her legs considerably.

"How is the old . . . darling?" Jerry asked, as Cynthia entered the kitchen. "Bitchy as ever?"

She sighed, her thin face pinched. "I think she's a lot stronger than she was. It wouldn't surprise me if she got out of that bed one day and went back to running the farm."

Her husband turned pale. "That's impossible. At her age, with a stroke . . ."

"It was a minor one, with no permanent damage, Dr. Armworth said. "Sixty-seven is not old. Not any more. I warned you to take your time and be certain, but no, you had to sell those two fillies when you had that offer from the breeder in Kentucky. If she takes hold again, you're going to have to buy them back, whatever it costs, and you know we haven't a dime between us."

She glared at him. "We could both go to jail, Jerry, if she gets back to normal."

The man dropped into the rockingchair behind the long table where the family had always eaten informal meals. His sallow face was still pale, and his dark hair drooped dispiritedly over his forehead.

"When Ed and Charlie come, the fat's going to be in the fire. You thought she was a lot worse off than she was, or you never would have risked going ahead with those sales. Now what do we do?"

"We think," he said, putting his head into his hands.

"Think!" she muttered, clanging pans together as she started supper. "With what, I'd like to know?"

"I can't get that money back. Arnie will turn his bruisers loose on me if I don't get another fifteen thousand within the next two weeks. The boys will be here next week, as well. I've just got to sell the gray stallion and use that to clear my account."

She turned on him, red spots glowing in her cheeks. "That's my Jerry—just keep going ahead, even when you know you're going to fall over a cliff in the dark. The old woman's going to get *well*, you fool!"

"Maybe . . . not." He looked up from the rocker, a gleam dawning in his eyes. "Maybe not. Armworth is a lot like the vet—he doesn't keep up with the times, and he all but said that someone her age was likely to pop off at any time. He won't be surprised if she does, and he'll sign her death certificate without any question."

She in her turn, went pale. She turned back to stir the pot on the stove, into which she had been slicing carrots, turnips, potatoes, and cold roast with vicious precision.

Back turned, she said, "You mean to kill her?"

"No, no. Not strangle or anything violent. There's some stuff they prescribe for her that should do it. Just give her her regular dose and put a double-sized one in her supper. She's supposed to have it in her system anyway, and Armworth will never think to do an autopsy."

Cynthia's skinny shoulders sagged suddenly. It was the only way, and she knew it as well as Jerry did. She didn't like the old biddy, anyway.

Jerry rose and went upstairs. She knew he was visiting the bath that connected their bedroom with that of Aunt Dolly. There was a new vial of medication there, along with a few tablets in the old one.

Like it or not, they were about to become murderers.

Dolly heard the heavy steps coming up the stairs. She had gained a lot of mobility in the past couple of days, and she managed a pretty fair sprint back into bed before they reached the top and came down the hall. To her relief, Jerry went into the bathroom, instead of looking in on her.

She picked up a mystery novel and turned a page, staring at the lines without reading them. She had, she felt, to pretend to be a coddled old lady, helpless, weak, unable to get about. Some instinct told her that her life might depend on it.

Water ran. The toilet flushed. There was a tap on her door, and she glanced about to make sure everything was normal before responding. Her slippers, shed in her flight back to the bed, lay in the middle of the floor. She reached for the cane she used in going to the bathroom and raked them close beside the bed.

"Come in," she said, in her most unoffending voice.

"Cyn's making her special stew tonight," he said. "You'll like it a lot, I think. Should be ready about six-thirty. How are you getting on, auntie?"

"As well as can be expected," she said, her tone dry. "I'm not twenty, Jerry, but I seem to be holding up pretty well, considering." She felt a sudden pang, recalling the thin, tanned little boy who had brought his troubles to her.

He had been the youngest of the three, hit hard by the loss of both parents to a virus infection while they were abroad. He had seemed wary of everyone, as if fearing that they, too, might go away and never return.

She sighed. "That's nice. I like a good stew. But I'm tired now, and I think I'll take a little nap before suppertime."

He nodded and crept out, looking entirely too satisfied with himself. She knew him too well to believe that such a look could possibly be innocent.

When his steps had died away in the distance, she waited. Usually he walked around the place before supper, and when that was something that could be left to simmer Cynthia went along. Perhaps the cold wind would keep them inside, but she hoped they might at least check on the animals in the barn some three hundred yards from the house.

When she had heard nothing from the lower floor for fifteen minutes, Dorothy swung her feet to the floor, slid them into her slippers, and rose unsteadily. The cane propped her nicely, as she donned her robe and headed for the closet.

This was a very old house, and rooms, stairs, even the floors had been altered time and again, over the years. There had been a back stair, once, and her closet was the head of it, using the space between the inner and outer walls to make a walk-in space.

The steps were still there, leading down into blackness and emerging in the back entryway as a deep supply cupboard beside the kitchen door. The well was narrow enough to allow her to brace one hand against the wall while bracing the cane on the other side, securing her slow downward steps.

She paused from time to time, resting, listening for any sound from the kitchen, now just on the other side of the partition. But no hint of movement came to her ears other than the slap of wind-blown shrubbery against the outer wall.

Then her descending foot found no further steps. She was in the cupboard, her right shoulder brushing the shelves stacked with preserves and canned goods, some of them years old. She opened the door a crack and peered into the hallway, finding that after the darkness on the stair even this dim passage was visible.

Nobody.

She crept along the hall and into the kitchen, finding one light burning over the stove and the stewpot simmering obediently, its contents smelling delicious. She was tempted to take a taste before doing what she came to do, but she pushed the impulse away.

She took a vial, salvaged from her stash of medications for healing—and killing—animals, from the pocket of her robe and dumped its contents into the stew, stirring it vigorously with the spoon conveniently placed in the flower-shaped holder. When the last hint of oily liquid was gone, she turned away and made her painful trek back up into her room.

When she dropped into bed again she was genuinely exhausted. Jerry, checking on her before bringing her supper, found himself wondering if he needed to trouble himself to doctor her food, but he knew it was better to be safe.

"She doesn't look good at all," he said with great satisfaction, as he helped Cynthia dish up the stew into rose-sprigged Haviland bowls. He piled crackers on the plate under the bowl, and his wife added a salad to the tray as he assembled his aunt's supper, complete with special seasoning.

Dorothy had to be helped into a sitting position, and he almost felt a qualm, remembering all the times she had nursed him through childhood illnesses. But he placed the tray across her lap, folded the napkin over her chest, and asked if she needed anything else.

"No, no, I'm quite all right. You go and eat your supper. I'll manage by myself. And when I'm done I'll set the tray on the table, here. This does smell good . . ." she inhaled greedily, and he smiled as he closed her door behind him.

Cynthia was waiting for him. She was very persnickety in many ways, he had to admit, but she was an excellent cook. They dug into their meal with good appetite, his enjoyment augmented by relief at the solution of his immediate problem.

Dolly set the tray aside on the bedside table, the stew untouched. That was bad—she had to get rid of it, and the best way was to flush it, if she could make it that far.

She didn't want to risk the Haviland, her footing being as unsteady as it was, so she dumped the stew into the emesis basis kept in the drawer and carried it cautiously into the bathroom. The stew went down without leaving untidy fragments in the bowl, and she rinsed out the basin and set it in the bathroom cabinet before turning toward her room again.

The cane hit a slick spot on the tiled floor and skidded. Dorothy flung out both hands to catch herself as she went forward toward the tub, but even before she hit the hard edge she felt that familiar blackness engulfing her again.

Dr. Winlow rapped on the door. "Miss Pelling? Mr. Danvers? Is anyone there?"

He rapped his heel irritably against the flagstone walk as he waited. Surely, so early in the morning, there would be someone stirring. He had taken the trouble to check again on that mare, and here they were lying slug-abed, neglecting their work.

He rapped again. "It's the vet! Come on, now, I'm a busy man."

He touched the knob and it turned. They hadn't locked the door last night? That was odd, in these days of vandalism and pilfering.

He pushed and went into the wide, inviting hall at the front of the house. Lights were on at its other end, in the kitchen, and he went that way, calling at intervals.

The Danverses were there, all right, convulsed, soiled, and quite dead beside the cold remnants of their meal. On the stove a scum of scorched stew smoked nastily on the low-set burner. There was an odd tang there, even amid the smell of burning.

He turned to find the phone, which he knew was in the hall. Then it occurred to him that the old lady might be upstairs, helpless, hungry, wondering what had happened. He called the sheriff and Dr. Armworth; then he climbed wearily up the dark walnut stair, clinging to the banister and feeling very old and tired.

There was a line of light below Dorothy's door. He tapped softly. "Miss Pelling? Miss Pelling? It's Dr. Winlow."

There was no reply, and he turned the knob and thrust his grizzled head into the room. The covers were tumbled back, but the bed was empty. The door into the bath was, however, open.

He felt something tighten in his throat. He stepped to the door and tapped again. "Do you need help, Miss Pelling?"

Still there was no sound.

He flipped the switch and light blazed from the old-fashioned white ceramic tiles. Dorothy lay sprawled, face down, against the tub, her cane caught beneath her hips, her legs at ungainly angles.

Dead? He touched her wrist, found it cool but not with the chill of death. She was alive, he thought.

Catching her as gently as he could manage in the cramped space, he turned her onto her back, straightening her limbs and pulling her nightgown down over her knees. Her face was drawn down on the left side, the eyes wide, staring up into his, trying, he could feel, to convey something to him.

But this stroke was a major one, unlike the earlier. This time Dorothy Pelling would never ask the question or say the words that burned on her frozen lips.

# A Necessary Author's Preface

The story you are about to read exists *only* because of Joe Lansdale. It is a clone to an earlier story of mine, "The Francis File," nearly identical in structure, basic content and headings, although all of the interior wordage is new.

Here's how it evolved . . .

In 1989, at the World Fantasy Convention in Seattle, I did a reading of some of my newer short fiction, including "The Francis File." Joe Lansdale was in the audience that afternoon and was greatly impressed with the story. However, as he declared after the reading, he *hated* the ending, claiming that it cheapened a stark, savage murder tale by turning it into a fantasy. "Take out the fantasy element and redo the ending," he said, "and I'll buy it for *Dark at Heart*. It's just what I'm looking for."

Sorry, I told him, the story was already sold—to *Whispers*. Besides which, I happened to like the fantasy element, *and* the original ending.

Joe couldn't get "The Francis File" out of his mind. A month later he phoned me: "I've got to have that story in the book. Could you do a new version, with a realistic ending?"

The idea intrigued me. I'd be telling the same story from a wholly new perspective. "If I do it," I told Joe, "I'd want to let my readers know that this one has been deliberately cloned from 'The Francis File.' Otherwise, they'll think I steal from myself."

"Sure, go ahead and write a preface explaining the whole thing," said Joe, "and I'll print it with the story."

So I did.

And he did.

Joe still hates the fantasy element in "The Francis File."

There's no fantasy in "Hi, Mom."

Me, I like *both* versions.

W.F.N.

William F. Nolan is the author of short stories, teleplays, screenplays, novels, biographies, and he has edited a number of anthologies, including the Dark Harvest anthology, URBAN HORRORS. He is best known for LOGAN'S RUN which was made into a successful movie that bore only the faintest resemblence to Nolan's excellent and poetic novel, but his real strength is in his shorter work, and "Hi, Mom" is one of his best.

# HI, MOM!

## William F. Nolan

Among items found by police in the apartment of William Charles Kelso, 4200 E. Ivy, Hays City, Kansas:

ITEM: A pair of recently severed human hands. Female. Each fingernail lettered in red nail polish. B-I-L-L-Y (on left hand) K-E-L-S-O (on right hand). Lettering identified as by subject, William Charles Kelso.

ITEM: A baby's plastic rattle, pink. Apparently belonged to subject, W.C.K., when infant.

ITEM: A Sportsman's hunting knife with yellow bone handle, human hair adhering. Bloodstains on blade from victims, various.

ITEM: A photo, undated, of W.C.K. as young boy (five? six?) standing in back yard of unidentified house next to his mother, Mrs. Ella Patrick Kelso. Mother's features (Caucasian) defaced by knife cuts across photo. Word, "SLUT!" written in blue ink by subject at margin of photo, with arrow pointing to Mrs. Kelso.

ITEM: A scrap of what appears to be butcher's wrapping paper, undated. Written (in pencil) on paper by subject:

I am a void
I am not part of this planet
There is no Billy Kelso

ITEM: A snapshot (faded, n.d.) of Mr. and Mrs. Kelso seated on cement steps of apartment house (location unknown) with subject as infant in arms of Ella Kelso. Father is black. Full name: Leonard Edward Kelso. Written across back of snapshot (blue ink) in subject's hand:

> This is only photo I have of my goddam father. The bastard split when I was four. Used to beat up Mom a lot when he was drunk. She's deaf in one ear because of a table fork he stuck in there. I hope he got cancer. Hope it hurt a lot and that he rots.

ITEM: A typed school report sent to Mrs. Kelso from grade school teacher Catherine Vanne in 1966 when subject was eight years old:

> Your son Billy is a very difficult child to control in class. He openly rebels against all forms of discipline. On the playground today he attacked a smaller boy with a wooden bat and had to be physically restrained. Billy is aloof, and has made no friends among his classmates. If his behavior does not show a marked improvement over the remainder of this semester he will be expelled.

Subject added, in blue ink, at bottom of this page:

> Mom whipped me plenty bad for this with her leather belt. Later, I was real dizzy and started spitting blood. Mom says maybe I've got an ulcer.

ITEM: A membership card in an organization known to be on Anti-American list by FBI. Card is marked:

> Cancelled. Non-Caucasian.

ITEM: A human ear. Female. Found in ziplock bag in subject's refrigerator.

ITEM: A poem, undated. Pencil. In subject's adult hand:

## HI, MOM!

Moonlight eating
  severed flesh
  in dreams
of icy death

ITEM: A loose news clip from the *Daily Register*, Benford, Illinois, dated July 10, 1968:

CAT MYSTERY SOLVED

Local Boy Admits Killing Felines

In response to a neighbor's phone call, local police entered the home of Mrs. Leonard Kelso, 1222 Vincent Avenue, to discover the decomposed bodies of some two dozen cats listed by owners as missing over the past year. The animals were buried in the dirt in one corner of the Kelso basement. They were headless.

Mrs. Kelso's 10-year-old son, William, told police that he was responsible for slaying these animals, but could not remember what he'd done with the heads.

The boy was taken to Juvenile Hall.

ITEM: A child's sketch (by W.C.K.) done when subject was attending grade school in Benford. In colored crayon, sketch shows a row of downtown office buildings with red-and-yellow tongues of flame coming from the windows. At bottom of this sketch, in child's hand:

FIRE IS NICE

ITEM: An untitled story, written in pencil by W.C.K. (when schoolboy) in blue-lined tablet, n.d.:

Once upon a time there was a littel boy named Billy who had a Daddy that was called a niger who used to hit his Mom before he went far away to another place. Billy was also called a littel niger but his Mom told him he was white like her so he didn't know which he was and he wanted to run away with a circus and get his face painted all colors like a klown's is.

ITEM: A plastic bag found in subject's bedroom, stuffed with human hair, used as pillow.

ITEM: A copy of the Benford High School Yearbook for 1975. On page 79 is a student graduation photo of subject, with description beneath:

> "Billy." Independent. Quiet. Not one of the crowd. A nut for boxing. (Don't get him sore at you!) Odd sense of humor. Likes small animals. Ambition: "to be an undertaker." (He's *got* to be kidding!)

ITEM: A private reel-to-reel tape recording:

*TAPE BEGINS*

*Voice of young woman:* What *is* this shit? Are you recording us?

*Voice of William Charles Kelso:* That's right.

*Woman:* Well shut it the fuck off! I didn't come here to be put on some fucking tape.

*Kelso:* Watch your mouth. I don't like to hear a lady talk like that.

*Woman:* And who says I'm a lady? Okay . . . are you going to shut it off or not?

*Kelso:* No, I'm not.

*Woman:* Then I'm splitting. Since we didn't do anything I'll just charge you ten bucks. For coming over.

*Kelso:* You're not leaving.

*Woman:* The hell I'm not! I don't dig freaks. Get out of my way, damn you!

(SOUNDS OF STRUGGLE)

*Kelso:* You're never going to leave me again, Ella.

*Woman:* (terrified) I'm not Ella? . . . who the fuck is Ella?

*Kelso:* Time to die, slut!
(STRUGGLE INTENSIFIES.
SOUND OF BLOWS.
A HIGH-PITCHED SCREAM.
GASPING. SILENCE.)

*TAPE ENDS*

ITEM: A pair of initialed white-silk underpants. Initials: E. K. (Thought to have belonged to subject's mother.) Slashed repeatedly with knife.

ITEM: Letter, hand-written, dated November 7, 1984, from ex-convict Alvin P. Stegmeyer to subject (then living in Indianapolis):

> Dear Billy,
>
> Hey, old buddy, how are things? You promised to keep in touch when you left the joint. How come I never hear from you? As for me, just like I told you, I am back in K.C. in the plant, working as a meat packer. Job is okay, and I am back with my girl Nancy and get laid regular. You getting any? I hope you are, because a guy needs his pussy! (ha, ha) Why not come out to K.C. and visit an old pal? Have you watched one of those 500 Indy races yet? I hear they are great to see with lots of crashes into the wall. (ha, ha) Well I'd better go. Take it easy, buddy, and let me hear from you.
>
> Your friend Al
>
> P.S. Still looking for your Mom? As for me, I never want to set eyes on my old lady ever again. She never done nothing good for me. Or for my sis or brothers either, that's for sure. Maybe because you don't have sisters or brothers your Mom treated you better. Anyway I hope you find her.
>
> See you, Al

ITEM: A magazine article, torn from a copy of *Psychology Today*, dated October 3, 1985. Titled: "Portrait of a Compulsive Killer," by Anne Franklin. Following paragraph underlined in red by subject:

With each subsequent murder, this type of maladjusted individual compulsively repeats his ongoing pattern of violence. He is unaware of *why* he must kill since the elements leading up to his acts are usually deep-rooted in childhood and he has no conscious realization of what motivates him.

He is satisfied only with the death of his latest victim (usually chosen at random). This pattern remains unbroken until he is either apprehended or commits suicide. (Between killings he may experience severe guilt or remorse for his aberrant behavior, but these periods are not constant.)

ITEM: A list, scribbled in subject's hand, on sheet of lined notepaper:

Kill her dog
Break into her house
Kill her
Get momento (maybe her thumbs ???)
Burn house

ITEM: A scrapbook of news clips (collected by subject) relating to murders ascribed to William Charles Kelso:

COED FOUND FATALLY STABBED IN UNDERGROUND PARKING LOT

MOTHER AND BABY SLAIN IN HOME

TEENAGERS BEATEN TO DEATH ON HIGHWAY

PATTERN OF KNIFE MURDERS POINT TO SERIAL KILLER

ITEM: A postcard from subject (sent from motel in Jasper, Wyoming) to Kelso's mother in Chicago, dated December 15, 1984. (Card was returned, stamped "Address Unknown"):

Hi, Mom

Plenty cold this time of year in Wyoming. In Chicago too I know! The wind sounds like people screaming. How are you? I am pretty good except for the bad dreams that wake me up sometimes at night. You can write me care of the postoffice here in Jasper in case I leave this motel. Working as a frycook at a burger place. I'm doing okay but I need to see you.

Your son,
Billy

ITEM: A poem, written on back of a large brown mailing envelope in subject's hand, n.d.:

Teeth of acid
tear my flesh.
Young flowers bleed
and worms of fire
consume me.

ITEM: Final section of a printed transcript from a televised interview with subject. Show, titled "Insights," telecast over KRRO-TV, Missoula, Montana during August of 1988. Interviewer: Dean Hawkins.

HAWKINS: . . . and despite the fact that you warned the psychiatrist that you were still a danger to society and could not function outside prison, the parole board nevertheless released you?

KELSO: They did, yes. The prisons in this country . . . they're very overcrowded and don't care much who they let out on the streets. I kept trying to . . . trying to tell them that I wasn't fit to leave . . . that . . . I didn't want to leave.

HAWKINS: Are you telling us you *like* living in a prison environment?

KELSO: No, I'm not really saying that . . . I . . . well, in a way I guess I do . . . like being in prison better than outside where there's . . . no control.

HAWKINS: What is it you're trying to control?

KELSO: Things I do . . . that I don't like doing.

HAWKINS: Then why do them?

KELSO: Because I *have* to. I don't seem to . . . to be able to have any choice.

HAWKINS: Just what things are you talking about?

KELSO: (mumbles—not audible) . . . can't say them. I don't want to talk about them. I got put in prison for robbing a store to get some food after I lost a job I had. But I never got caught for . . . for doing what bothers me.

HAWKINS: Are you, as of today, a danger to society?

KELSO: Yes . . . I am. That's true.

HAWKINS: What is it you want to do with your life, Billy?

KELSO: Get it stopped. End it. I just . . . think it's better if I'm dead. That would be better for everybody.

HAWKINS: But what about your family? Don't you have people who care about you?

KELSO: I got no brothers or sisters. Pop left us when I was real small, and Mom split when I was ten. Said she . . . couldn't handle me anymore . . . and she put me in a home where I ran away. I looked for her but I could never find her. Now I don't care.

HAWKINS: Maybe she's ill and can't contact you. A mother's love is a strong force.

KELSO: Mom never loved me. She used to . . . to beat me with a belt of hers that had a metal buckle that cut me up pretty bad. I got lots of scars on me from that buckle . . . (Pause) I'd get . . . terrible headaches after she beat me. I just couldn't even think straight. That's when I got a cat from the street and . . .

HAWKINS: And what, Billy?

KELSO: I'm not going to talk about that. I needed to find Mom and tell her . . . about how much she hurt me as a kid. But I guess she doesn't care.

HAWKINS: I see. (Long pause) Why did you volunteer to come here today, Billy?

KELSO: To let people know about how these parole boards let you out of prison when you're not ready to be outside. It's a bad thing for them to do . . . very bad.

HAWKINS: We . . . uh . . . certainly thank you for your honesty. There's no doubt that our overcrowded prison system is in severe need of adjustment . . . Thank you for coming here today to tell your story.

KELSO: I didn't tell a lot of it. I left out the . . . the worst parts. I'd really like to be dead now.

NOTE: With regard to the case of William Charles Kelso: Conclusion, computer transcript of signed statement from Ella Patrick Kelso, freely given in presence of Chief of Police Darren Arnwood and police stenographer Philip Eston, at police headquarters, Hays City, Kansas. Dated June 21, 1990:

. . . and when I got here to his apartment I found all this blood. Billy was on the couch in his sweatshirt, drinking a beer and watching TV. There was blood on his hands and all over his pants and shirt and I knew he'd killed somebody else. I'd been reading about him and I knew it was my boy, Billy, doing all these killings.

He was rotten, like his father. Just no damn good, ever. Didn't give me a minute's peace all the time I had him with me. I never wanted to be the mother of some freak kid like he was. I prayed to the Good Lord to deliver me from such a burden. Billy did sick things from the start, and whipping him didn't change him any. Just made him meaner. Maybe it was his mixed blood. I never should have married no black man, that's for sure. One summer Billy set six fires downtown, but nobody knew it was him.

I heard he'd been looking for me a long time, and then I heard he was here in Kansas working in a bakery. So I drove out here to Hays City, to Billy's apartment, and when he looked up real surprised to see me, and said "Hi, Mom," I shot him. Six times. In the head and chest. With a boy like that you just have to do your duty as a mother. So I did that.

I did my duty.

John Keefauver is rare in that he is a professional short story writer. No novels. No films. Just short stories. And he survives. His work has appeared just about everywhere. He is primarily known for his off-the-wall tales of fantasy and satire. The following is a bit more traditional, but lacks none of the wild Keefauver imagination.

# DEAD VOICES LIVE

## John Keefauver

Mark had numbly got out of his car and started across the rain-dark yard toward his living quarters above the old grocery store when a light flashing on in his mother's room there stopped him. Robotlike, he stared up at the window; it seemed to stare back at him like an unblinking square eye, or like a spotlight pinning him to the soggy yard. Through the glass he could see the ceiling of the high old-fashioned room and part of a light fixture, and he thought that if he listened he would hear the squeak-squawk of her ancient rocker begin. Or if he watched long enough he would see her come to the window with a needle in her hand.

Then, still numb, he began to move across the yard toward the back door of the store again. A quartered moon, momentarily appearing between ash-colored clouds, deepened the shadows beneath his eyes and sharpened the line of his nose and the high cut of his cheekbones. It made him look older than his twenty-seven years.

He was almost to the door that led upstairs to the living quarters when a rhythmic chant came from the shrubbery near a fence that enclosed the yard. "Yes-s-s-s, Mr. Nelson," the voice wailed. "Yes-s-s-s, Mr, Nelson." Mark shook his head in disgust and, turning, started toward the wail. George was at it again. And as he approached the fence he saw the man jerk up his cabbagelike head. "Mr. Nelson?" George whimpered, his voice piously simple.

"It's me, George. Mark."

"Oh." The word was heavy with disappointment.

Mark stopped in front of him and he knew immediately that George had entered a new phase with Nelson. He had never seen the man's face so calm, so peaceful. Then, as he watched, George's gaze dropped and he began to pat a small mound of earth near the fence, at the top of which was a potted plant.

"I thought you was Mr. Nelson 'cause he's gonna come see me tonight," George mumbled. "He told me. It was plain."

Slowly the man stood up. He was taller than Mark, and burly. "And he told me that Mrs. Gribe was after you." The peacefulness in his face had disppeared. "But I already knew that. She's all mad 'cause you didn't stay home." His sausage fingers dug into his shaggy hair. "He don't want you to go in the house."

"Mother's not after me, she's asleep. Or she was."

George's cabbagelike head spun. "Not asleep. She's been running around the house with that needle in her hand, yelling at me, like she does when the devil's talking to her."

"Oh, come off it, George."

"The devil *does,* too! Like Mr. Nelson talks to me. Like now."

"Oh, for God sakes, George. I've got enough on my mind without having to listen to you and your Nelson talk again."

And Mark started toward the door. It was times like this that he'd like to kick George out of the house. But the stoop had been living with him and his mother for years now as sort of a handyman. He was almost part of the family . . . if you could call what they had a family. Actually, though, of course, he couldn't *let* George leave. He might talk.

"Don't go in there, Mark, don't go!" George lumbered after Mark. "No!" He grabbed Mark's shoulders with his huge hands. "She's acting just like she used to when Mr. Nelson was here."

Mark whirled. "I've told you to shut up about dad! It's hard enough as it is, without your yelling his name around."

"But I heard him," George whimpered. "I hear him all the time. He just says, 'George, George, George.' He won't stop, Mark. No time! He's trying to tell me something, something he wants me to do. He's gonna tell me tonight."

"For Christ sake's, George, shut up." He watched the man sink to the ground again, hands to his head, whimpering. "You and your voices! You'll drive us all crazy. Crazy enough now." Audry was gone, he was thinking. Audry . . . gone.

Gone. He had driven to her apartment tonight, but she wouldn't let him in. Wouldn't let him in, and they were supposed to get married in less than a week. He had knocked on her door . . . knocked and knocked . . .

until she had finally said from behind hit, "Go away. Go away, Mark."

He had thought he had misunderstood her, of course, and he'd said, "Audry, it's me . . . Mark."

"Go away."

"What?"

"Go away. I don't want to see you again. Go away. Don't come back."

He still thought he was hearing things, but she had kept saying, "Go away," and when he'd finally asked her why in the name of God she was saying that, what in the name of God was going on, all she would say, finally, was, "I know what happened," half a whimper, half a sob.

That was when the numbness had begun. And he had asked her, "You know *what* has happened?"

But all she would say after that was, "Go away, don't come back." And then she wouldn't even say that. She wouldn't say anything, and she wouldn't open the door.

He had gone to the nearest phone and tried to call her. She wouldn't answer. And so he had driven home, thinking, his mother must have told her. His mother must have phoned her. His mother would do anything to break them up. Yes! After all, he had told his mother just this evening that he and Audry were going to get married.

But she wouldn't have told Audry *everything*.

Or would she? Was she that insane?

All he could do was hope until, confronting her, he found out, one way or the other.

He said to George, as calmly as he could, "Was Audry here tonight?" She could have come between the time he'd left the house and the time he'd arrived at her apartment. He'd been to a two-hour class at the college during that period.

"Just me and Mr. Nelson here. Me and Mr. Nelson, that's all. And Mrs. Gribe."

"Are you sure?"

"Yes."

His mother must have phoned her. He turned toward the door to the store and living quarters again. "Come on, George, let's go in. You'll get soaked out here."

"Don't act like Mr. Nelson. Only he tells me what to do. Just him."

"Oh, George, shut up that talk! Let's go in."

"I can't help it," he whimpered. "He talks to me, and I got to talk back to him, else he'll get mad at me again." He stared up at Mark, his face once again peaceful. "Mr. Nelson ain't mad at me no more. Him and me been talking a lot tonight. Just him and me, all alone out here." He looked back at the fence. "Haven't we, Mr. Nelson? Haven't we, huh?"

"You better get that plant back in the house before mother finds out."

"I was inside at first. But I couldn't hear Mr. Nelson good in there. So I come out here where him and me are closer together."

"Yeah, I know all about that, George. Now, let's go in."

"No."

Mark made a movement toward the store. "Okay, stay out here all night if you want to, but I'm going in."

"No!" He lifted up straight on his knees. "Don't go in there!"

George was up on his feet as Mark started for the house. He grabbed Mark by the arm, his huge hands like a vise.

"For Christ sakes, George, stop acting like a maniac."

"Stay out here with me and Mr. Nelson, Mark. He don't care. He likes you now." George's face shone with pride. "He likes you almost as much as he likes me. He told me so." His voice rose, excited. "He told me! He don't like Mrs. Gribe at all. Don't like her at all, he said. He don't what you to go in there!"

He began to yank at Mark's arm, jerking him back toward the fence and the potted plant, pulling the lighter man behind him.

"Stop it! George. I'm not in any mood to play around!"

"Mr. Nelson don't want you to go in the house!" he shouted. He held Mark tight at the fence, arms around his waist.

"Goddamn it! George, let me go!" He kicked out and jammed his elbow in George's stomach, almost slivering away.

"No! Mr. Nelson says no!"

Mark's foot slammed around and clipped the potted plant, scattering broken parts on the ground.

George moaned and let Mark go. "Oh-h-h. All busted. Mr. Nelson's flower, all busted." He dropped to his knees and clumsily began to scrape bits of the broken pot together and tried to set the plant upright. He moaned again and looked accusingly up at Mark. "You ruined it for him. Now I'll have to . . ."

His voice broke off. As Mark watched, he whispered and dropped the plant and the bits of pottery, and collapsed on the ground.

"Yes, Mr. Nelson," he moaned. "Yes, sir. Yes, Mr. Nelson."

"George?" Mark said, irritated yet worried.

George stirred, and his head came up from the ground. A moan, and he looked at Mark, his face glazed and trancelike. "Did you hear him?" he mumbled.

"Come on in the house, George."

"Did you?" quickly, eagerly.

Mechanically, Mark's head moved in a no.

"That was Mr. Nelson." He smiled happily and slowly nodded. "He said, 'George, let Mark go in the house now.' That's what he said. 'Let Mark go in the house now.' It was plain. You didn't hear him at all?" incredibly.

"No, George."

"You ought to have. It was plain. He said to let you go in the house now so he can go looking out here." He glanced at the remains of the plant, childishly happy. "He won't tell me who it is he's looking for. But when he does I'm gonna get that person for him. That's how I'm gonna help him." Quickly, he swiveled his head up toward Mark. "He didn't tell you who he was looking for, did he?" he said anxiously.

"No, George," softness in his voice now. "Mr. Nelson didn't tell me."

He smiled, relieved. "He won't tell nobody 'til he tells me." He shook his head in emphasis. "Nobody!"

"All right, all right."

"I bet I know Mr. Nelson better than you do. Or Mrs. Gribe. I bet that. He won't talk to you or her, I bet. None at all." He proudly puckered his bottom lip. "Just me."

"Okay, now come on, let's go in."

"I'm going to stay out here, Mr. Nelson told me to."

"Aah, for God sakes," Mark said as he went toward the store.

"I'm not aah!" Mumbling, mad, he puffed out his lips. "I'm not aah 'cause I'm really helping Mr. Nelson find somebody and he comes up out of his grave and tells me, too. Every night. It's plain! And he don't want nobody acting like him, neither. Like that ol' girl did tonight."

Mark was nearing the porch when he heard George's words. He stopped and spun around. "What girl, George!?" His voice shot across the yard.

"Nobody."

George lowered his head. He began to moan and whimper as Mark ran toward him.

"You told me Audry wasn't here!" he yelled, grabbing the man by the shoulders.

George whimpered. "Don't hurt me, Mark. I didn't mean to do anything bad."

Mark felt his nerves snap and twitch. He had an almost overpowering desire to scream, to ram his fist into George's face. Everything seemed to be crushing him—his mother, Audry, George. He raised his hand to slap George, but at the man's flinch, his frightened expression, he calmed himself, he lowered his arm.

"I didn't mean to tell her," George whined. His head whirled. "I didn't mean it, Mark. Honest I didn't."

"Tell her what?"

George groaned. "Bad. Awful. Oh-h-h-h." He gagged. "Bad."

He had George by the collar now and was shaking him.

"Tell her what! George?"

"I didn't mean to, I didn't mean to."

Mark stared at the anguished man. He had to be calm now. He had to relax. He had to be sure of what George had told Audry. He felt weak and syrupy. Everything was drained out of him now. Everything, gone.

"George," he said, "when Audry came here tonight you told her something. Is that right?"

George shook his head in a moaning yes.

Mark steadied himself. He heard his voice come whisper-dry out over his lips. "You told her about dad's murder, didn't you? That I was . . . involved. Didn't you?"

George sobbed.

"Didn't you!"

George nodded.

Mark turned, he felt himself move, the store was in front of him and he was putting one foot down, then the other, moving toward the door. Walking over the yard, walking up to the porch. He felt his hand move out and turn the door knob, and then he was inside the house, the dark stairs reaching up over his head. He heard the sound of his feet on the steps. Up. He was so tired, he wanted to drop down and go to sleep. Sleep. If he could just go to sleep. Just sleep and sleep and sleep.

When he came up over the head of the stairs and saw the white splotch of light in the hall from his mother's room and heard the squeak! squawk! of her rocker, he stood still for a moment. The light seemed almost friendly now, beckoning. It was somehow calling to him, it seemed, this puddle of light from his mother's room. His mother was in there. She was waiting for him. Always waiting. He pondered, his face in a twisted smile, then shrugged and walked toward the light, squish! clump! squish! clump! rain water coming out of his shoes. He'd leave tracks, he thought, and wanted to laugh because that was a crazy thing to be thinking about, when really what he wanted to think about was Audry. Audry was gone. Audry . . . gone.

He walked into his mother's room and said, "Audry's gone," and it sounded so natural and the right thing to say that he said, "Audry's gone." again.

Squeak!

Her staring eyes, rocking with the motions of the chair.

Squawk!

He gazed at her, this thing, this rocking mother. She was a funny thing. He wondered if she were alive and how she would be if she were dead, and at that he had to smile, for in a way he was dead and so was Audry, and his mother might as well be, too. He felt a second smile curl through his lips; but this one twisted into a smirk.

Squeak!

He saw the thick, blue-veined ankles and dark-striped skin at the top of her bedroom slippers. And the twirling darning needle rolling between her forefinger and thumb. The needle that she always had stuck in the front of her blouse or dress or sweater, ready to be pulled out and played with, or worse. Her needled eyes. She was smiling at him. Smiling. Ugly-pretty smile, layered on her face, a gloating smile.

He took a step toward her.

His voice sounded strange to him when he spoke; it seemed to come from a distance. Hollow. Empty. As if he were hearing it from someone else's lips. Audry's lips. Audry. Heavy on his mind, he felt her.

"Mother," he had murmured.

"I heard George and you screaming out back. Was Nelson after him again?"

The needle spun.

"It must be awfully frustrating," she said, "sitting out there on a grave trying to talk to a corpse. But George can be quite a conversationalist. At times." With a quick flick of her hand, she straightened her housecoat over her knee. "I heard you shouting Audry's name at him." Smirking, she glanced up at her son. "Tell me, Mark, did you actually expect to marry that Barrow woman? . . . as if you think you're a grown-up man?"

The mole on her cheek was withered and brown; it danced obscenely in the light from the lamp at her shoulder as she talked. Her face was the color of wet ashes now.

"If I was that hard up, I'd just pick up one of the local whores. But I suppose Miss Barrow had something special about her. She was pregnant, I suppose. You either had to marry her or pay for an abortion."

"Shut up!"

"Sharp wires are effective, Mark. Much cheaper, too." Her eyes glittered. "I wish I had known about wires and such when I was carrying you." She shrugged. "But I suppose Barrow knows all about that sort of thing."

"Audry's gone!"

"Gone? My word, where? To heaven?" She chuckled. "Too bad Nelson isn't there to enjoy her company. He'd enjoy that—sleeping with an angel." She sighed. "His soul might be enjoying hot females, but what's left of his body surely isn't."

Mark heard her chuckle splinter into a shriveling laugh—an insane laugh.

"But at least Nelson's good for something," she went on. "Fertilizer. Did you see how well the grass next to the fence came up this spring?"

"Shut up!"

Squeak! squawk! sang the rocker.

"Don't talk to me like that, Nel . . . Mark," she said in pretended fright. "I'll sic George on you."

"You mention dad's name again, mother, and so help me God I'll kill you!"

"Kill me. My word, how horrible. Kill your own mother?" She snickered.

"But if you do, get George to help you. He's good at it, with the hands he has. As you know. As Nelson knows. As George knows—after I told him about what they could do, what they had to do if he wanted to keep living here, if he wanted a home, if he wanted to eat."

Mark felt a dry hard laughing knot begin at the bottom level of his stomach, then snowball up as if it were something separate from him. The laugh exploded, short and piercingly shrill.

"Mark, stop it. And sit down," she said coldly. "You remind me of Nelson with that insane cackle of yours."

The darning needle whirled as she smiled and motioned for him to sit beside her. He didn't move.

"That woman of yours isn't going to come here anymore, Mark." Her voice was restrained and concise, yet with cutting strength. "I've had enough of her sucking around you."

"You have?" The words were flat.

"She puts her foot in this house again, I'll mash that pretty face of hers in. Or have George do it. Or worse. The bitch will find out about George's hands too."

"Shut up, mother," he said calmly.

"Don't tell me to shut up. Your father used to do that. I just told you not to remind me of him that way."

"So you did."

"You know just the thought of him frightens me—in certain ways . . . his . . . his hysterics."

"I know."

A flush swept her face. "I don't like your attitude, Mark. You held your tongue until that Barrow woman started influencing you." Her voice snapped at him. "From now on you're going to stay in your place!"

Mark felt another knotted laugh burst out of him. He saw his mother recoil from its shrillness.

"Mark, stop it! And sit down."

He did not move.

"Stay in my place," he murmured bitterly. "Sure. Stay in my own little hole." He laughed again; he couldn't stop it. "If I try to climb out you'll push dad's murder in my face. You'll go to the police. If I move out, you'll go to the police. You don't care. You don't care if it's found out that you planned to have him killed, arranged it, that George killed him. You don't care if I'm found guilty of hiding it, of not going to the police myself. If only I had gone right after it happened. But I wanted to protect you. *You!* You who just don't care one way or the other. I realize that now. The only thing you care about is making my life miserable. And you can do it either way: by going to the police or not going. One way I go to jail, the other way I live with you the rest of my life. I'm miserable either way, which is what you want—just why only your screwed-up mind knows, but I bet a . . . needle it's because I was fathered by a man you came to hate. You're insane!"

A squeak and the rocker stopped, and he saw her come up toward him, then hesitate, then reach out for his arm. "Mark," she said softly.

"Yeah, Mark. That's all you have to say and I'll come running. But I'll never do enough running, enough of anything. You've made sure of that with your threats to turn me in. And there's nothing I can do about it."

Deliberately he brushed her reaching hand away. She stiffened. The rocker began to move, rapidly. The needle spun.

"Of course there isn't," she said.

"When someone else tries to get into my life, you'll get rid of *her*."

"No," she said, so soft, so cuttingly soft. "I won't. *You* will."

He bent over her and let his fingers flick through her hair. "You're so sweet and kind."

She knocked his hand away.

"Why, mother, am I upsetting you?"

"Go to bed," she snapped. She spun the needle once, then glared up at him. "You won't be able to get up in the morning . . . to open up the store." She smirked.

"That son-of-a-bitching place!"

Squeak!

He jumped. He grabbed the chair and held it still.

"Old gray-haired mother," he said.

"Don't make fun of me, Mark." Her smirk and sarcasm were gone.

"How can I?" His fingers were playing with her hair. "You're much too sweet . . . and kind."

"Mark! stop it!"

He chuckled. A strange chuckle. He listened to it a moment, his hand on her arm, squeezing the old flesh, slowly, so soft between his fingers. Insane old mother, it would be better if she were dead.

"Mark! stop it!"

"Don't tell me *I'm* scaring you? Only dad could do that."

She twisted. "Please."

"Please. What a strange word for you. Say it again."

"Mark, don't."

"You're sure you're talking to Mark? Remember that dad was the only one who could . . ." he squeezed ". . . scare you." The needle, glinting in the lamplight, caught his eye. "That goddamn thing. I'd like to run it through your neck," and he gave a short, brittle laugh and grabbed for it and missed.

She half rose out of her chair, her arm still in Mark's grip. "Let's go in the kitchen and have a cup of coffee," she said.

But his hand was on her forehead, pushing her back.

"Mark!" She jerked her arm free and sprang up and ran for the door. He caught her by the wrist.

"I believe you're afraid, mother," he said, softly sarcastic. "I couldn't hurt you. Only dad could do that. Only dad could make you scream. You remember dad, don't you? Dear, sweet dad."

She whimpered. "Mark, stop it! Get away from me! Stop! You're hurting me!" She twisted and pulled at him.

"Just like dad."

He hit her.

She fell to the floor and he stood there staring at his fist, puzzled at the sting in his knuckles. Then he looked down. She was twisting up on one knee and trying to get up. He pulled her to her feet.

"Son," she whimpered. Her head flopped as he shook her. "Son."

"Son," he echoed, then exploded a laugh. "I'm not your son!" shouting now, flopping her head back and forth. "I'm not your son! I'm Nelson now, your husband!"

She sagged against him, whimpering.

"You understand! I'm *Nelson* now!"

"Nelson," she moaned. "Nelson." Her eyes flew wide. "Nelson!" she screamed. "Nelson, don't . . ."

"NELSON!

Nelson!

Nelson.

"Stop it! My dearest husband, don't! In God's name, Nelson, don't!"

She tore out of Mark's arms and ran, the needle still in her hand; stumbled out into the hall and down the back stairs, screaming hysterically, "Get away from me, Nelson! Get away . . ."

Huddled next to the fence, George looked up at the sound of her screams. "Stay away from me, Nelson!" he heard her shout. She was running toward him through the rain. Ponderously, he rose to his feet. "George!" she screeched, "Nelson's after me!" She stumbled and almost fell, then swaying, sagged against him and clawed at his shoulders. "Help me, George," she moaned. "Nelson's chasing me!"

"You?" he mumbled.

She nodded, making frantic bumps on his chest. "He's after me," she whimpered.

"Mr. Nelson . . . after *you?*"

"Yes. Me."

George's face was puzzled and amazed and frowning; then slowly his expression began to clear. "Mrs. Nelson, he was looking for *you* all the time," he murmured, smiling in understanding, nodding up-down, up-down. "After *you.*"

Then, suddenly, he tilted his head, attentive, listening, his face tranquil and trancelike. "Yes, Mr. Nelson, sir," he mumbled. "Yes, sir."

He felt Mrs. Gribe trembling against his chest, her head so little on his shoulder, her hair so soft. He lifted his ham hands and patted her cheeks. "Mr. Nelson says I got to," he said, voice cloud-soft. He clumsily caressed her arm. "Got to do it, he says. It's plain."

"Help me, George." She glanced back at the house.

"I'm helping Mr. Nelson."

His fingers rose to her neck.

"He told me to, and I got to do what he says."

His fingers tightened on her neck.

"George!" she sputtered. She tried to jerk away. But his hands like hooks held her.

His face lifted. Rain splattered on his forehead and ran down his thick jaw, his bristled chin. "Yes, Mr. Nelson, yes, sir, Mr. Nelson," he chanted, voice humbly pious.

His fingers squeezed.

Mrs. Gribe gagged and squirmed and twisted; she clawed at George's fingers, she jabbed at his hands with the needle; but his huge hands only tightened and squeezed as his blood trickled down to his wrist.

"Yes, Mr. Nelson, sir, I'm doing it, sir."

Mrs. Gribe choked, she weakened; her weight sagged against George.

His face was glowing, mystically ecstatic. Mrs. Gribe, rag-limp, dangled from his hands.

"Yes, Mr. Nelson."

His fingers loosened.

"Yes, sir."

He let her go and she crumpled onto the ground.

A tear of happy pride rolled down George's cheek as he turned and walked toward the house. His hands had done it. His big, strong hands had helped Mr. Nelson and he was happy with them—now, this time. His own hands. Mrs. Gribe had told him about them, how big they were, how strong. Yes, they were very good hands. He was very proud of them now.

He went up the steps talking to Mr. Nelson. When he got in the hall he saw the light coming from Mrs. Gribe's room. He ought to turn off the light. Ain't no use having a light on now.

He was surprised when he saw Mark flopped on the bed. This wasn't his room. This was Mrs. Gribe's room.

"Hullo, Mark," he said.

Mark stirred and opened his eyes.

George smiled. "Mr. Nelson told me to do it, Mark." His voice was kind and proud. "Mr. Nelson told me to help him." He nodded in quick jerks. "Yes he did, he told me."

Wearily Mark turned on the bed, his back to George. "All right, George."

“He was after Mrs. Gribe tonight and he told me to help him. That’s what Mr. Nelson said, Mark, that’s what he told me. He was after Mrs. Gribe all the time. All the time, he was.”

“All right, George. Now go on in your room and go to bed. I’m waiting for mother to come back.”

“It was plain, Mark, what Mr. Nelson said.”

“I’m simply going to tell her that I’m going to marry Audry, regardless. If she’ll have me now, that is.”

George bubbled happily and looked down at his hands.

“It was plain.”

Thomas Sullivan lives in Michigan, writes with tremendous grace. His stories have appeared in Omni, Midnights, Best of The West, edited by Joe R. Lansdale (his ownself), and other top markets. His novels are THE PHASES OF HARRY MOON and BORN BURNING. "Deep Down Under" gives one the sense of glimpsing behind the veil of life's shadows, and seeing things we'd rather not see.

# DEEP DOWN UNDER

## Thomas Sullivan

Darkness, as all children know, is vast. Kill the lights and it rushes out to infinity. Kill the lights, and the borders of space collapse. Even ebony corners become free zones for things without shape and hunters without mercy. And hunger. Hungry things are always there. Darkness and hunger were Allison's nightmare.

She was six when they left La Paz. And an hour later she was sixty. But until the end of that hour she had no inkling of what would happen, even though the objects of her darkness were illuminated for a time.

There was the airliner itself, like a furnished and carpeted tunnel, and the thirty-three passengers murmuring drowsily in different languages, and her mother, warm and smiling. There was the strangely flat smelling air and the taste of chocolate covered mints in her mouth. And there were the two men.

The one that looked like Bluto frightened her. He didn't have any mouth and he sat right across from her, and when she stared at his big hands and the funny beard that went around where his lips should be, he turned suddenly and hated her with his eyes. They were big eyes. Dark and hungry.

But then she discovered the second man, and he was nice. He sat right behind the first. He wasn't so big and he had twinkling blue eyes and a smile that almost connected his ears. He waggled his fingers at her when she peeked around the edge of the seat. Nice men waggled their fingers.

The hour was up then, and the first thing that happened was that it began to snow like she had never seen it snow before. One moment the sky outside was blue along the jagged mountain, the next it looked like boiling milk. It got darker and darker until they had to put the cabin lights on. And that was about the time the sound the plane made changed.

The people on the other side of the aisle up where the wing was leaned toward the window. There were gasps and someone began to cry. A woman screamed. The man with no mouth said: "*Fuego.*" She heard it distinctly and thought what a funny thing to say when everyone was screaming. Even the plane was screaming as it started to plunge.

But the little girl did not scream. She wanted to but didn't. She looked at her mommy, and her mommy was struggling to get the seat belt around her. That was all before one of the trays tumbling through the air hit her. The crash never came.

She didn't scream when she woke up again, either. It was dark, very dark, and silent, and the cabin smelled like fear. She had no way of knowing that the nose of the plane was a hundred feet beneath the snow on a plateau high in the Andes. But her chest hurt. And it was absolutely dark. So she didn't scream.

She felt for her mother. First the seat, then in front of the seat. The safety belt kept her from touching the next row. She remembered the safety belt being fastened while the plane was tilting. That was why her chest hurt, and why she was here, and why mommy wasn't. And when she realized that, the borders of her space collapsed again and hungry things rushed in.

The next time she came around the silence was profound, as if the molecular echoes of thirty-odd passengers had subsided. The cold bit into Allison along her downy forearms and the back of her neck. It was one of the hungry things of the darkness. And now she really wanted to scream, but she didn't dare because the darkness was listening. She wished everyone else would hurry and wake up. But deep down under she knew that her mother and everyone else was dead and she was alone. Entombed in a hundred foot drift near the summit of the Andes, a little girl screamed and screamed and screamed.

* * *

## DEEP DOWN UNDER

The length of time it takes a tightly sealed airline fuselage locked in a hundred foot snowdrift to drop five degrees farenheit, that was how long she remained in shock this time. And when she emerged, as though from a chrysalis of ice, she did so with a pang of hunger and the certain knowledge that she had to act or die.

The seat belt lock released like a cavalry unit unsheathing, and the sound froze her in place again. It might have been five minutes, it might hve been an hour, before she stood up. Time seemed to have stopped along with everything else, and the only measures she had were degrees of numbness and hunger. But then she stood and stretched her arms out in front of her and took tiny steps in what she hoped was the direction fo the aisle. On the third, her foot landed on something. Slowly she stooped down. It had a hard irregular shape. Her finger found ripples. Ripples and curves and—*suddenly she realized that her fingers were between teeth!* With a little gasp of disgust she flung the dentures into the void.

Her child's imagination conjured up a mouth torn out by its roots, a mouth that had coated her hands with gore, and of course it must belong to the man who had none. No mouth. And bulging eyes. Bluto.

Whirling, she tried to remember in which direction the false teeth had gone, so that she could dart the other way. She took a step, colliding with a seat, a body in fact. And a face. Her trembling fingers splayed over the skin like water dancing on a griddle. She could feel the eyes. Bulging eyes. *Eyes that snapped open when you touched them.*

Her fingers recoiled as if from fire, but she knew it was too late. It was Bluto, and he knew she was there. She fell to the floor, tried to crab-walk away. But her back was up against something unyielding.

"*Madre de Dios!*" his groaning voice lunged after her.

The sounds came forth in agony, a great longing for relief. The man was wounded. Even now he breathed in gulping lungfuls that were mixing with something bubbly. She wished fervently that each breath would be his last. But they grew stronger, more violent.

He wasn't going to die. It was just the effort of awakening and the shock that had stirred him. He was hurt, but he wasn't going to die. And now he was croaking, and she could hear his hand groping along the carpet a few inches away. If it touched her she was going to scream the loudest scream of her life. Already it was swelling in her chest, getting ready to leap into her throat the moment those fingers dropped on her. And that was when she heard the cough. Which wouldn't have made any difference, except that it came from *behind* the man with no mouth.

He was the nice man, and he would waggle his fingers and try to help.

"I'm here," she murmured.

But all she got was more coughing.

The man with no mouth said something leaden with pain then, and the man who waggled his fingers began to speak, dazedly at first but with a gradually clearing voice.

"How . . . Oh, god. Anyone? Who is that?"

"It's me."

"Little girl? Is that you?"

She nodded, even though she knew he couldn't see.

"Anyone else?" he called.

The man with no mouth moaned, and the other man seemed to understand for the first time who it was, where it was. "Can you help me, Mister? I can't move. Something is pinning my legs." No answer. "Little girl? Are you okay?"

"My mommy's gone."

"But are you okay? Can you move?"

"I don't know."

"Do you think . . . you can help me?"

"I'm scared."

"I'm scared, too, but if you don't help me—" He broke off. "What's your name?"

"Allison."

"Allison. I'm Mr. Cleary." His voice was edgy now. "Allison, I want to help you, but I'm trapped under something. If you could move it, why then I could help us both."

To get to him she had to go by the man with no mouth. "I'm *scared!*" she asserted, and the strength of this seemed to drain the man.

It was quiet for a while. The plane got colder.

"I'll help you," she said finally.

"Good girl." He sounded weaker. "Just come straight toward my voice. Straight toward me and everything will be alright."

She came straight toward him.

But she only got a couple of steps, and then the hand shot out and began fumbling for her arm. It almost seemed like more than one little girl screaming this time. The plane turned red with sound, and when it was over she was back in the seat she had started in, and the man with no mouth was chattering in his funny language like an animal angry at having missed a meal.

"Allison?" Mr. Cleary was demanding urgently.

"He grabbed me!" she blurted.

"Are you sure?" The cadence of her whimper began to rise and he added quickly that he believed her. "But I don't think he speaks English, Allison. I think he's pretty badly hurt, and I don't think he can communicate. Maybe he was just trying to let you know. I don't think he wants to hurt you, Allison."

But she had seen him in the light and felt him in the dark, and she knew he was a hunter.

"Allison, can you help me now?"

The cold pinched her voice, and she only made a quavery sound.

"It's alright," he said. "You couldn't lift this off me, anyway."

They didn't speak for a long time after that. The plane grew colder still, the darkness more brittle. Eternity joined infinity. And there was an odor. Allison knew it had something to do with the plane—not the bodies but the plane itself. It was aviation fuel. It had been growing stronger by the hour as it saturated the snow outside and began to waft through the breeches in the fuselage. The headache from breathing the vapor mingled with the headache from hunger and roused them both from lassitude.

"Allison."

"What?"

"We're going to be rescued."

Little girl sniffle.

"For sure. They're looking for us right now. Maybe they've already spotted us. Only thing is . . . it may take awhile." He gave that a few moments to sink in. "We must be pretty high in the mountains. I don't know how long ago we crashed, but a rescue team might take days to reach us. It's cold, and we're not in the best of shape. You know what we need, Allison?"

"What?"

"Food and water. And maybe a fire."

"I'm hungry," she said dully. Her voice was as thin and airy as a dog whistle.

"We've got to hang on until the rescue team gets to us. We've got to search the plane."

The cue gnawed at her, but each time she imagined herself groping through the dark a wave of terror quenched it.

"I could help you, Allison," he said then.

"How?"

"I know where the food is. There's a little galley somewhere behind me. That's where they keep it. You could go back there." Pause. "Okay?"

"I can't."

"Well then, damn it, we're all going to die!"

The vitality of that left them both stung, but in a few seconds it had been absorbed by the chill and the stillness of the plane, which seemed to be solidifying, nibbling away at their energy. It was the little girl who was doing the listening now, the man whose breathing became a funny stanza of frustration and fear. But that, too, passed. He must have come up on one elbow then, because his breathing was louder and closer. "What is it you're afraid of, Allison, is it just this man here? Would you come back here if I showed you how to stay away from him?" Pause. "Listen. All you have to do is climb over your seat. He's hurting or something. In fact, I think he's pinned by the same thing that's pinning me. If you climb over your seat, he can't reach you. Then you can go to the galley and get us food and water. Maybe there's even a flashlight back there. Okay?"

"What's a 'galley'?" she asked slowly.

"Like a kitchen. A tiny room with cupboards and drawers. And maybe a faucet and a refrigerator."

She wiggled around and stood in her seat, swung one leg over, cautiously stretched out. Already she felt the tingle. This was the border. Any second now the man with no mouth would come surging back to life. She let her feet dangle. And that was when she heard him move. The tingle rushed up her legs in a searing wave. She kicked. But it was too late. Like a daub of mud on a wall, she slid down.

And waited.

But there was no clawing hand. Suddenly she sprang up and over that seat as well, and then she sidled to the aisle where Mr. Cleary lay.

"Good . . . good, Allison. We're going to make it. Thanks to you we're going to make it." He laughed in a loose way. "Come here, now. Put your hands on this . . . push. There. Again. Once more." Pause. "I guess it's no use. Well. The galley, then. Straight back. Just walk up the aisle."

She took a few steps. "There's something in the way."

"Well, go around."

"I can't."

"You haven't *tried* yet. For heaven's sake, *try!* You can *try*, can't you?" Silence. "Allison, you've got to try."

"I'm trying!"

"Did you try going around it on this side of the aisle?"

"Yes."

"You couldn't climb on the seats there?"

"There aren't any. There's a thing over them."

"And the other side of the aisle. What's over there?"

"The same thing."

"Did you try going over it?"

"I can't."

Silence.

"Well then, we'll have to look somewhere else."

She stood there in the dark, disenfranchized from the order and warmth of her world. Her legs ached and still she stood.

"Allison?" he said at last, and it was as if the long silence had been edited out of the conversation and a clock had resumed ticking.

"What?"

"There are cigarette lighters and candy bars all over the plane."

"Where?"

"The people have them." He said it with a tremor, knowing what he was asking of her. "The passengers . . . in their pockets. Some of them."

"The dead people?"

He didn't answer.

"I think my mommy's dead," she said, half asking.

There were gaps between their exchanges now, as if they were communicating from remote points with transmission delays.

"Your mommy would want you to look for food. No matter how hard it is, she'd want you to look for it. That's what you've got to think about, Allison. *My mommy wants me to look . . . my mommy wants me to live.* So go ahead. If you wait any longer, you'll be too weak, too cold."

Slowly she climbed over the seats.

*Mommy wants me to . . .*

"Where are you, Allison?"

"I'm here." Dreamily.

"Move to the other side of the plane."

The other side of the plane was away from her mother's side. She moved there.

"You've got . . . to find someone now."

*Mommy wants me to . . .*

She began to feel around. But there wasn't anyone. The seats were intact and empty.

She stood still in the dark for another minute, and then she cried forlornly: "They're gone!"

"No. They aren't gone, Allison. They're all together. Go forward a little."

She went forward a little.

*Mommy wants me, mommy want me to . . .*

And then she found them. And she began to make a noise, not quite a wail, not quite panic-stricken. Because they were all together. In pieces.

"They can't hurt you, Allison!"

—so many fingers.

"Go through the pockets, Allison!"

—so many shoes.

"Think about what you want to find in the pockets and purses."

She could not possibly pull that—*mommy wants . . . mommy wants me*—that jumble apart. The faces were cold. Like marble. But with hair hanging over them. It made her remember a pile of broken dolls in the basement of a church at Christmastime.

*"Allison!"*

Mr. Cleary was shouting so fiercely. Like she was falling out of the plane or something, falling through the sky like a broken doll. And then she knew that she really was going to fall, and that she must do the touching thing in the next few seconds before she collapsed. Breathlessly, she plunged her hands into the pile. Ankles and wrists moved furiously, heads bobbed. Her voice was gurgling in her throat, but she couldn't hear it. The unholy thrill of what she was doing sang in her mind, blocking out concrete thoughts, except that just before the final thing happened it occurred to her that her mother was in this terrible mound. She didn't really think about what happened next, either. But all at once it was in her palm—a piece of something wrapped in foil. Green foil. She knew it was green. A chocolate-covered mint wrapped in green foil. The stewardness had passed them out to all the children earlier. And this one was special. This one was hers. Because she had the distinct impression that a hand in the pile had placed it in hers. *And it had been in her mother's hand when the plane went down.*

"Allison!"

How long had he been shouting that? She got up then. Felt her way back. It could not have been what she thought had happened. Lots of mints had been in lots of hands.

"I found something," she said.

"Good, child! Bring it here."

She started to climb the seat, but suddenly the man with no mouth stirred and bellowed something in his predator voice. Allison stopped moving.

"It's alright," Mr. Cleary assured her. "Bring the food here."

But now the collected dread of the past few minutes had caught up, and it wasn't until he repeated his encouragement that she even managed to whisper tightly, "I . . . can't."

"Of course you can, Allison. You've come this far, you can't give up now."

*"I can't."*

"Come here, *damn it!*" Forced silence ate at the sting in the air. "Do you want me to die and leave you alone? It wouldn't take much, you know. I'm weak, I'm freezing—"

He let her cry for a long time. And then he said, "I'm sorry." It sounded like he was crying, too.

She banked back her tears and with adult compassion said, "I forgive you."

"It's just that we've got to share everything now," he said. "There's no telling how long this has to last. Did you find any blankets or a coat for yourself?"

"No."

"Well. I've figured out, you don't have to climb back here. If we both stretch toward each other, we can reach. The man you're afraid of won't even know what we're doing."

"Yes. He will."

"No, he won't. He doesn't understand us. And you'll be very quiet. He'll think it's just me. Come now. Reach over the seat. I'm stretching. Are you stretching yet? Don't answer that. Ah. There you are. Good. I've—" The mint exchanged hands. "Was that it?" His voice was hushed and incredulous. "Was that it?" Not so hushed. "My God, that was it!" He laughed harshly and swore and just as quickly reined it in. And now when he spoke, his voice croaked and fragmented. "Allison, Allison, it isn't enough. Not nearly enough. I thought . . . I thought. Dear God." He was quiet then. Quiet for several minutes. And this time when he spoke it came out gentle and sad. "You eat it, Allison. You eat it all. It's not enough for two."

"No," she said.

"Take it, Allison."

She could tell from his voice that he was straining toward her. Reluctantly she reached out over the seat. But just as the foil came in contact with her fingers, a third hand rived out of the darkness. The force of the second grasp sent pain all the way to her shoulder. She screamed and yanked. And remarkably broke free. But a ring on her captor's finger tore the back of her knuckles, and she lost the foil-covered mint.

"Damn you!" Mr. Cleary exploded. "Give it back! Damn your eyes!"

She heard him struggle in his seat and finally yield to exhaustion.

"Damn you," he said feebly. A few moments later he said: "He got it, didn't he, Allison?"

"I don't know."

"Did you drop it?"

"No."

"Then he must have got it. I didn't think he understood anything we said. I guess I was wrong."

And that really chilled her—that the man with no mouth had known. It spoke of terrors that hid in your mother's arms, where you thought you were safe, and phantoms and nightmares. Twice she had eluded him, but the man with no mouth was going to get her the next time.

"Allison?"

"What?"

"You've got to look some more."

"No," she said and meant it.

She could smell the mint being eaten, above the odor of the aviation fuel. After that it just got very quiet. Quiet and colder.

She didn't know how long it was until she heard the sound and sensed the others sitting up. It sounded like bells. Or clanging shovels.

"Thank God!" Mr. Cleary exclaimed, and then he began shouting and laughing.

The rescuers heard, shouted back. The ringing shovels centered above them. Muted thuds exploded over their heads. A fine debris rained down. Rescuers were coming through with pick-axes—pick-axes and an acetylene torch!

Rapidly a crimson line ate an arc in the ceiling. Light poured through, enough for them to see themselves. It was the luggage rack and the side of the fuselage which had bowed in, trapping the two men. A bloodied arm was all that emerged from the warp in the next row forward.

Quickly the arc became a circle, framing a rescuer.

"You okay?" he hollered down.

Mr. Cleary shouted back that they were pinned. The man with no mouth spoke then, and the rescuer answered in kind. A flashlight probed down.

"Little girl, are you trapped?"

"No," she said resolutely, and just at that instant a spark from the torch puffed into a blue, transparent flame, swiftly unfurling over the fuel-soaked inner wall of the plane.

Collective anguish went up like smoke from the flames, and someone shouted: "The girl! Hand up the girl!"

Arms came down toward her. But they stopped too far away. She was standing on the seat, the back-rest now, bobbing as best she could, and time which had moved with frozen sluggishness was dancing to a radiant maestro all around the burning plane.

"Allison!"

Mr. Cleary was beckoning her with one hand, reaching upward with the other. There was very little space between the arm reaching up and the rescuers outstretched palms. Still bobbing and straining toward her would-be rescuers, she moved closer to Mr. Cleary. Over one seat, onto the next, she clambered. She was maddeningly close. Close enough for a nice man—a man who waggled his fingers—to save her with a little boost. Except that the fingers suddenly did what she feared most.

It was the grip of the hunter, the grip that said "gotcha!" It was *Mr. Cleary's* grip. He had her by the wrist, and he was yelling at the men above. He was telling one of them to come down and pull him free—pull him free or he wouldn't release the little girl.

"There's no time!" the rescuer yelled back. "Push her up!"

There really wasn't any reason to hold her. She wasn't going anywhere. "They'll rescue us both if I hold out," he whispered desperately to her, easing his grasp.

She snatched her arm away and jumped back, but remained there, crying fearfully. That was when she saw the man with no mouth staring at her. He had the same look of fierce hate as before, but his arms were outstretched.

"Don't trust him, Allison!" Mr. Cleary warned. "There's something wrong with him."

She blinked away her tears, but the face stayed the same. A hunter's face. A foreigner's face. A face with no mouth and eyes that bulged hate. But the arms were outstretched.

"Come to me, Allison!" Mr. Cleary said.

She glanced back white-eyed. Mr. Cleary's arms were outstretched, too.

And that was when she saw the ring. Mr. Cleary had the ring. Mr. Cleary had snatched the green-foil mint from her with one hand while the other was giving it to her. Mr. Cleary had eaten the mint . . .

It would be a long time before she could weigh out the truth with an adult's sense of proportion. Did crises like the one aboard an airliner entombed deep, down under the snows of the Andes cause natures to reverse? Or had she simply come to terms at that moment with the false perceptions of her own?

Encroaching flames and noxious fumes made analysis moot. The cabin glowed an unearthly lavender. Death was at hand, and his spoils were arrayed in a hideous knot at the foot of the aisle. The remainder cowered before his lapping tongue, their fates ordained, except for a child's whose blue avenue of escape was blocked by phantoms of fear and mistrust.

And then she ran into the arms of the man with no mouth, and he lifted her up, his strong hands shackling her knees and thrusting her the final half foot to sanctuary, sanctuary, sanctuary . . .

David Morrell is best known as the creator of Rambo. The character appeared in *First Blood,* and has gone from there to several film incarnations, and David has gone on from there to write several bestsellers. He has also written numerous short stories. His short work is generally lean and fast and very dark. Witness the following gem of a tale.

# THE SHRINE

## David Morrell

Grady was in the mausoleum when the beep from his pager disrupted his sobbing.

The mausoleum was spacious and bright, with shiny marble slabs that concealed the niches into which coffins had been placed. In an alcove near the tall, wide windows that flanked the main entrance, glinting squares of glass permitted mourners to stare within much smaller niches and view the bronze urns that contained the ashes of their loved ones. Plastic, bronze-colored letters and numbers that formed the names of the deceased as well as their birth and death dates were glued upon the squares of glass, and it was toward two of those panes, toward the urns behind them, that Grady directed his attention, although his vision was blurred by stinging tears.

He'd chosen cremation for his wife and ten-year-old son, partly because they'd already been burned—in a fiery car crash with a drunken driver—but more because he couldn't bear the thought of his cherished wife and child decomposing in a coffin in a niche in the mausoleum or, worse, outside in the cemetery, beneath the ground, where rain or the deep cold of winter would make him cringe because of their discomfort, even though the remaining rational part of Grady's mind acknowledged that it didn't matter to his fiercely missed family, who now felt nothing because they were dead.

But it mattered to *him*, just as it mattered that each Monday afternoon he made a ritual of driving out here to the mausoleum, of sitting on a padded bench across from the wall of glassed-in urns, and of talking to Helen and John about what had happened to him since the previous Monday, about how he prayed that they were happy, and most of all, about how much he missed them.

They'd been dead now for a year, and a year was supposed to be a long time, but while Grady sobbed, he couldn't believe the speed with which the year had gone. His anguish remained as great as the day he'd been told they were dead, his loneliness, his *emptiness*, as extreme. Friends at first had been understanding, but after three months, and especially after six, most of those friends had begun to show polite impatience, making well-intentioned speeches about the need for Grady to put the past behind him, to adjust to his horrible loss, to rebuild his life. So Grady had hidden his anguish and pretended to take their advice, his burden made greater by social necessity. The fact was, he came to realize, that no one who hadn't suffered what he had could possibly understand that three months or six months or a year meant nothing in the case of infinite bereavement.

Grady's weekly visits to the mausoleum became a secret, their half-hour concealed within his Monday routine. Sometimes he brought his wife and son flowers and sometimes an emblem of the season: a pumpkin at Halloween, a Styrofoam snowball in winter, or a fresh maple leaf in the spring. But on this occasion, just after the Fourth of July weekend, he'd brought a miniature flag, and as he wiped his tears, unable to control the strangled sound of his voice, he explained to his beloved Helen and John about the splendor of the fireworks that he'd witnessed and that they'd so used to enjoy while eating hot dogs at the city's annual picnic in the sloped, wooded park near the river on Independence Day.

"If only you could have seen the skyrockets," Grady murmured. "I don't know how to describe . . . They reminded me of . . . Their colors were so . . ."

The beep from the pager on his gunbelt interrupted his halting monologue. He frowned.

The pager was one of many innovations that he'd introduced as standard equipment for the police force he commanded. After all, his officers frequently had to leave their squad cars, responding to an assignment or merely sitting in a restaurant on a coffee break, but while away from their radios, they needed to know whether headquarters was desperate to contact them.

The persistent beep from the pager made Grady stiffen. He wiped his tears, braced his shoulders, said good-bye to his cherished wife and son, and stood with effort, reluctantly leaving the mausoleum, locking its door behind him. That was important. Helen and John, their remains, by all means needed to be protected, and the cemetery's caretaker had been as inventive as Grady had been about the pager, arranging for every mourner to have a key to the mausoleum, so that only the privileged would be allowed to enter this sanctuary of mourning.

Outside, the July afternoon was bright, hot, humid, and horribly reminiscent of the sultry afternoon a year ago when Grady had come here, accompanied by friends and a priest, to inter the precious urns. He shook his head to clear his mind and stifle his torturous emotions, then approached the black-and-white cruiser and leaned inside to grab the two-way radio microphone.

"Grady here, Dinah. What's the problem?" He released the transmit button on the microphone.

Dinah's staccato response surprised him. "Public-service dispatch."

Grady squinted. "On my way. Five minutes."

Troubled, he drove from the cemetery. "Public-service dispatch" meant that whatever Dinah needed to tell him was so sensitive that she didn't want a civilian with a police-band radio to overhear the conversation. Grady had to use a telephone to get in touch with her at headquarters. After parking at a gas station across from the cemetery, he entered a booth beside an ice machine, thrust coins in the telephone's slot, and jabbed numbers.

"Bosworth police," Dinah said.

"Dinah, it's me. What's so important that—?"

"You're not going to like this, Chief," the deep-voiced female dispatcher said.

"It's *never* good news when you page me. It's even worse when . . . Public-dispatch message? *Why?*"

"We've got a combination one-eighty-seven and ten-fifty-six."

Grady winced. Those numbers meant a murder-suicide. "You're right." His voice dropped. "I don't like it."

"It gets worse, Chief. It's not in our jurisdiction. The state police are handling it, but they want you on the scene."

"I don't understand. Why would that be worse? If it isn't in our jurisdiction?"

"Chief, I . . ."

"Say it."

". . . I don't want to."

"Say it, Dinah."

"You know the victims."

For a moment, Grady had trouble breathing. Then he slumped against a dingy window of the booth and clutched the telephone harder. "*Who?*"

"Brian and Betsy Roth."

Shit, Grady thought. Shit. Shit. Shit. Brian and Betsy Roth had been the friends whom he'd depended upon for consolation after all his other friends had distanced themselves from Grady when his grief persisted.

And now one of *them* had killed the other?

And after that, the executioner had committed *suicide?*

Grady's pulse sped, making his mind swirl. "Who did what to . . .?"

The husky-throated, female dispatcher said, "Brian did. To Betsy. A forty-five automatic."

"Christ. Oh, Jesus Christ," Grady said. His mind swirled more intensely.

The puzzling directions Grady received took him not to Brian and Betsy's home, where he'd assumed the killings would have occurred, but instead through and past the outskirts of Bosworth into the mountains west of town. Pennsylvania mountains: low, thickly wooded, rounded at their peaks. Between them, primitive roads led into hidden hollows. In a turmoil, confused, Grady wouldn't have known which lane to take if it hadn't been for the state-police car blocking one entrance. A square-jawed trooper dropped his cigarette, crushed it into the gravel with his shoe, and narrowed his eyes when Grady stopped the cruiser.

"I'm looking for Lieutenant Crane," Grady said.

When the trooper heard Grady identify himself, he stiffened. "And the lieutenant's waiting for *you.*" With remarkable efficiency for so bulky a man, the trooper promptly backed his car from the entrance to the lane, allowing Grady to drive up the narrow draw.

Leaves pressed against Grady's side window. Just before the first sharp curve in the lane, Grady glanced toward his rearview mirror and saw the state-police car again block the lane. At once he looked forward and abruptly jerked the steering wheel, veering left, narrowly avoiding a boulder. Then, behind as well as ahead, he saw only forest.

The lane tilted ever more upward. It kept forcing Grady to zigzag and increased his anxiety as branches scraped the top of his car in addition to his windows. The dense shadows of the forest made him feel trapped.

Brian shot Betsy?

And then shot *himself?*

No!

*Why?*

I *needed* them.

I depended on . . .

I loved them!

*What on earth had made them come out here? Why had they been in the woods?*

The lane became level, straightened, and suddenly brought Grady from the forest to the unexpected view of a sun-bathed plateau between two mountains where an open gate in a chainlink fence revealed a spacious compound: several cinderblock buildings of various sizes on the left, a barbecue pit adjacent to them, and a swimming pool on the right.

Baffled, Grady parked behind three state-police cars, an ambulance, a blue station wagon marked MEDICAL EXAMINER, and a red Jeep Cherokee that Grady recognized as belonging to Brian and Betsy Roth. Several state troopers, along with two ambulance attendants and an overweight man in a gray suit, formed a cluster at the near rim of the swimming pool, their backs to Grady. But as Grady opened his door, one of the troopers turned from the cluster, studied Grady, glanced back down toward the rim of the pool, again studied Grady, and with a somber expression approached him.

Lieutenant Crane. Middle forties. Tall. Pronounced nose and cheekbones. At the same time, trim—Crane's doctor had ordered him to lose weight, Grady remembered—with short, receding, sandy hair. On occasion, Crane and Grady had worked together when a crime was committed in one jurisdiction and a suspect was apprehended in the other.

"Ben." Crane stopped before Grady.

"Jeff," Grady said.

"Did your dispatcher explain?" Crane looked uneasy.

Grady nodded, grim. "Brian shot Betsy and then shot himself. Why the hell would he—?"

"That's what we were hoping you could tell us," Crane said.

Grady shivered in spite of the afternoon heat. "How would *I* know?"

"You and the Roths were friends. I hate to ask you to do this. Do you think you can . . .? Would you . . .?"

"Look at the bodies?"

"Yes." Crane furrowed his brow, more uneasy. "If you wouldn't mind."

"Jeff, just because my wife and son died, I can still do my job. Even though Brian and Betsy were friends of mine, I can . . . Whatever's necessary. I'm ready to help."

"I knew as much." Crane fidgeted.

"Then why did you have to ask?"

"Because you're involved."

*"What?"*

"First things first," Crane said. "You look at the bodies. Then I show you what your friend Brian had in his hand, clutched around the grip of the forty-five. And then we talk."

* * *

The stench of decay constricted Grady's nostrils. A waist-high wooden fence enclosed the swimming pool. Grady followed Crane through an opening onto a concrete strip that bordered the pool. One of the policemen was taking photographs of something on the concrete while the overweight man in the gray suit suggested various angles. When the other policemen saw Crane and Grady arrive, they parted to give them room, and Grady saw the bodies.

The shock make him nauseous. His friends lay facedown on the concrete, redwood deck chairs behind them, their heads toward the pool. Or what was left of their heads. The .45-caliber bullets had done massive damage. Behind Betsy's right ear and Brian's, the impact wound was a thick, black clot of blood. On the opposite side, at the top of each brow near the temple, the exit wound was a gaping hole from which blood, brain, bone, and hair had spewed to spatter the concrete. Flies buzzed, a repugnant swarm on the gore. The .45 was next to Brian's right hand.

Grady wavered.

"Are you all right?" Crane touched his arm.

Grady swallowed. "I'll manage." Although he'd been the police chief of Bosworth for almost ten years, he'd seen few gunshot victims. After all, Bosworth was a modest-size town. There wasn't much violent crime. Mostly the corpses he'd viewed had been due to car accidents. That thought suddenly reminded Grady of the accident in which his wife and son had died. The thought reminded him of their grotesquely charred remains. And he felt grief upon grief, for his friends, for his family.

Determined not to lose control in front of these fellow policemen, Grady sought refuge in forcing himself to muster professional habits. Objectivity. Sure.

"These corpses"—Grady struggled to order his troubled mind—"they've started to bloat. Even as hot as it's been, they wouldn't be this swollen . . . Unless . . . This didn't happen today."

"Right," Crane said. "As close as we can tell, it was early yesterday."

The overweight man in the gray suit interrupted. "I'll know for sure when I do the autopsy."

The man was the county's medical examiner. He gestured for the trooper to stop taking photographs. "I think that's enough." He turned to the ambulance attendants. "You can move them now." He pivoted toward Crane. "Provided you don't object."

Crane thought about it and shrugged. "We've done as much as we can for now. Go ahead."

Sickened, Grady heard the zip of bodybags being opened. To distract himself, he stared toward the glistening blue water of the swimming pool while the attendants put on rubber gloves and went about their grisly business. He was grateful when Crane spoke, further distracting him.

"Brian and Betsy were expected home yesterday evening," Crane said. "When Brian's sister phoned them and didn't get an answer, she figured they must have changed their plans and decided to spend the night here. But when she called again in the morning and still didn't get an answer, and when it turned out that Brian hadn't opened the restaurant this morning, his sister got worried. This place doesn't have a phone, so she drove out here . . ."

"And found the bodies," Grady said, "and then called you."

Crane nodded. In the background, the attendants strained to lift a bulging bodybag onto a gurney and roll it toward the ambulance.

"It looks as if they were both sitting in these deck chairs, facing the pool," Grady continued. "The impact of the bullets knocked them out of the chairs."

"Right. That's how we figure it," Crane said.

"Which tends to suggest they weren't arguing, at least not so bad that it made Brian angry enough to shoot Betsy and then shoot himself when he realized what he'd done." Grady's throat felt tight. "People are usually on their feet when they're shouting at each other. But it's almost as if the two of them were just sitting here, enjoying the view. Then Brian goes to get the pistol, or else he's already got it on him. But why? *Why would he decide to shoot her?* And why would Betsy just sit there, assuming she knew Brian had the gun?" Grady's voice rose in frustration. "I don't understand."

The attendants stooped, struggling to lift the second heavy bodybag onto the gurney.

"He planned it," Crane said.

"Obviously, or else he wouldn't have had the gun."

"That's not the only reason I know Brian planned it. The gun." Crane pointed downward. "Look at it."

Grady lowered his gaze toward the concrete, avoiding the black clots of gore at the rim of the pool and the contrasting white chalk silhouettes of where the bodies had been, concentrating on the weapon.

Grady didn't reply for a moment. "Yes." He sighed. "I get the point."

The slide on the .45 was all the way back, projecting behind the hammer. The only time a .45 did that, Grady knew, was when the magazine in the pistol's handle was empty.

"Brian didn't load the magazine completely." Grady scowled. "He put in only two rounds."

"One for Betsy, one for himself," Crane said. "So what does that tell you?"

"Brian thought about this carefully." Grady squinted, appalled yet filled with a strange admiration. "He respected guns. He didn't load the magazine completely because he knew that the gun would selfcock after he fired the second shot, after he killed himself and the pistol dropped from his hand as he fell. He didn't want whoever found him to pick up the gun and accidentally fire it, maybe killing the person who held it. He tried to do this as cleanly as possible."

With force, Grady shook his head. *Cleanly?* What a poor choice of word. But that was the way Brian had thought. Grady had gone hunting with Brian often, and Brian had a habit of talking about clean kills as opposed to sloppy ones. Brian had always worried that an animal he shot might be hit in the stomach, escape to the forest, and suffer for several hours before the animal mercifully finally died. In that sense, the way that Brian had arranged to kill his wife and then himself was definitely clean. Two shots placed efficiently at the soft spot behind each victim's ear. A direct route to the brain. Instantaneous, non-painful death. At least in theory. Only the victims knew if the death was truly painless, and they couldn't very well talk about it.

Grady scowled so severely that his head ached. Massaging his temples, thinking of the bullets that had plowed through Betsy's skull and then Brian's, he studied Crane. "Usually someone does this because of marriage problems. Jealousy. One of the partners having an affair. But as far as I know, Brian and Betsy had a faithful relationship."

"You can bet I'll make sure," Crane said.

"So will I," Grady said. "The only other reason I can think of is that Betsy might have had a fatal illness, something they kept hidden because they didn't want to worry their friends. And when the disease got worse, when Betsy couldn't bear the pain, Brian—with Betsy's permission—*stopped* the pain, and then, because Brian couldn't stand the agony of living without Betsy, he . . ."

"That's something else I'll be checking for when I do the autopsy," the medical examiner said.

"And I'll be talking to her doctor," Crane added, sounding determined.

Grady drooped his shoulders, his sadness overwhelming. "So how does this involve me? You told me it was something about his hand. Something he clutched."

"Yes." Crane looked reluctant. "I'm afraid there's no good way to do this. Ben, I'm sorry. I'll just have to show you. Brian left a note."

"A note? I was going to ask if he did. I need answers."

Crane pulled a plastic bag from a pocket in his shirt. The bag contained a piece of paper.

Grady murmured, "If Brian left a note, there's no question. Combined with the way he loaded the .45, there's no doubt he made careful plans. Perhaps along with . . ." Grady shuddered. "I've got the terrible feeling Betsy agreed."

"That thought occurred to me. But maybe she didn't. There's no way we'll ever know."

Grady's hand trembled when he accepted the transparent plastic bag.

"He had this clutched around the grip of the pistol." Crane looked bleak. "When the .45 dropped from his hand, the note stuck to his fingers.

Grady studied it and once again shivered.

The note was printed boldly in black ink.

**TELL BEN GRADY. BRING HIM HERE.**

That was all.

And it was too much.

*"Bring me here?"* Grady moaned, on the verge of sobbing. *"Why?"*

"That's why I said we had to talk." Crane bit his lip. "Come on, let's get away from where this happened. I think it's time for a stroll."

They emerged from the swimming pool area and crossed a stretch of gravel, their footsteps crunching as they passed the barbecue pit as well as two redwood picnic tables and approached the largest of the cinderblock buildings. It was flat-roofed, thirty feet long and half as wide. A metal chimney projected from the nearest wall and angled upward above the roof. There were three dusty windows.

"Bring you here." Crane echoed Brian's note. "That can mean different things. To see the bodies, or to see the compound. I didn't know Brian well, but my impression is, he wasn't cruel. I can't imagine why he'd have wanted you to see what he'd done. It makes me wonder if . . ."

Grady anticipated the rest of the question. "I've never been here. In fact, I didn't know this place existed. Even with the directions you relayed through my office, I had trouble finding the lane."

"And yet you and the Roths were close."

"Only recently—within the last year. Only because we both shared grief. I met them at a meeting of The Compassionate Friends."

"What's . . .?"

"An organization for parents who've lost a child. The theory is that only a parent in grief can understand what another parent in grief is going through. So the grieving parents have a meeting once a month. They begin the meeting by explaining how each child died. There's usually a speaker, a psychiatrist or some other type of specialist who recommends various ways of coping. Then the meeting becomes a discussion. The parents who've suffered the longest try to help those who still can't believe what happened. You're given phone numbers of people to call if you don't think you can stand the pain any longer. The people you talk to try their best to encourage you not to give in to despair. They remind you to take care of your health, not to rely on alcohol or stay in bed all day, instead to eat, to maintain your strength, to get out of the house, to walk, to find positive ways to fill your time, community service, that sort of thing."

Crane rubbed the back of his neck. "You make me feel embarrassed."

"Oh?"

"When your wife and son were killed, I went to the funeral. I came around to your house once. But after that . . . Well, I didn't know what to say, or I told myself I didn't want to bother you. I suppose I figured you'd prefer to be left alone."

Grady shrugged, his spirit hollow. "That's a common reaction. There's no need to apologize. Unless you've lost a wife and child of your own, it's impossible to understand the pain."

"I pray to God I never have to go through it."

"Believe me, my prayers go with you."

They reached the largest cinderblock building.

"The lab crew already dusted for prints," Crane said. He opened the door, and Grady peered in. There were sleeping bags on cots along each wall, two long pine tables, benches, some cupboards, and a wood-burning stove.

"Obviously more people than Brian and Betsy used this place," Crane said. "Have you any idea who . . .?"

"I told you I've never been here."

Crane closed the door and proceeded toward a smaller cinderblock building next to it.

This time, when Crane unlatched and opened the door, Grady saw a wood-burning cook stove with cans and boxes of food as well as pots, pans, bowls, plates, and eating utensils on shelves along the walls.

"I assume," Crane said, "that the barbecue pit was for summer, and this was for rainy days, or fall, or maybe winter."

Grady nodded. "There were twelve cots in the other building. I noticed rain slickers and winter coats on pegs. Whoever they were, they came here often. All year round. A hunting camp in the fall. A place for Brian, Betsy, and their friends to have weekend parties, even in winter, as long as the snow didn't block the lane."

"Yeah, a beautiful location." Crane shut the door to the kitchen, directing Grady toward the final and smallest structure. "This was the only building that was locked. Brian had the key on a ring along with his car keys. I found the ring in his pants pocket."

When Crane opened the door, Grady frowned.

The floors in the other buildings had been made from wooden planks, except for fire bricks beneath the stoves. But this floor was smooth, gray slate. In place of the cinderblock walls in the other buildings, the walls in here had oak paneling. Instead of a stove, a handsome stone fireplace had a shielded slab of wood for a mantle, an American flag on each side, and framed, glistening photographs of eight smiling youngsters—male and female—positioned in a straight line above the flags. The age of the youngsters ranged. Grady estimated, from six to nineteen, and one image of a boy—blond, with braces on his teeth, with spectacles that made him look uncomfortable despite his determined smile—reminded Grady distressingly of his own, so horribly longed-for son.

He took in more details: a church pew in front of the photographs above the fireplace, ceramic candle holders on the mantle, and . . . He stepped closer, troubled when he realized that two of the smiling faces in the photographs—lovely, freckled, red-headed girls, early teens—were almost identical. Twins. Another pattern he noticed, his brow furrowed, was that the oldest males in the photographs, two of them, late teens, had extremely short haircuts and wore military uniforms.

"So what do you make of it?" Crane asked.

"It's almost like . . ." Grady felt pressure in his chest. "Like a chapel. No religious objects, but it feels like a chapel all the same. Some kind of shrine. Those twin girls. I've seen them before. The photographs, I mean. Brian and Betsy had copies in their wallets and showed them to me a couple of times when they invited me over for dinner. They also had larger, framed copies on a wall in their living room. These are Brian and Betsy's daughters." Grady's stomach hardened. "They died ten years ago when a roller coaster jumped its tracks at a midway near Pittsburgh. Brian and Betsy never forgave themselves for letting their daughters go on the ride. Guilt. That's something else grieving parents suffer. A lot of guilt."

Grady stepped even closer to the photographs, concentrating on the blond, vibrant, ten-year-old boy with glasses and braces that reminded him so much, so painfully, of his son. The resemblance wasn't exact, but it was poignantly evocative.

Guilt, he thought. Yes, guilt. What if I hadn't been working late that night? What if I'd been home and Helen and John hadn't decided to go out for pizza and a movie? That drunk driver wouldn't have hit their car. They'd still be alive, and it's all my fault because I decided to catch up on a stack of reports that could just as easily have waited until the morning. But no, I had to be conscientious, and because of that, I indirectly killed my wife and son. Inside himself, not showing it, Grady cringed. From a deep, black, torture chamber of his mind, he silently wailed in unbearable torment.

Behind him, Crane said something, but Grady didn't register what it was.

Crane spoke louder. "Ben?"

Without removing his intense gaze from the photograph of the young, blond boy who reminded him of his wonderful son, Grady murmured, "What?"

"Do you recognize any of the other faces?"

"No."

"This is just a hunch, but maybe there's a pattern."

"Pattern?"

"Well, since those two girls are dead, do you suppose—could it be?—is it possible?—that *all* the kids in these photographs are dead?"

Grady's heart lurched. The photographs suddenly chilled him.

Abruptly he whirled toward the sound of a splash.

"You look pale." Crane frowned. "What's the matter?"

"That splash." Grady moved toward the door. "Someone fell into the pool."

"Splash? I didn't hear any . . ."

Grady's eyes felt stabbed by sunlight as he left the shadows of the tiny building. He stared toward the state policemen at the concrete rim of the swimming pool. The medical examiner was getting into his station wagon. The ambulance was pulling away.

But the pool looked undisturbed, and if anyone had fallen in, the troopers didn't seem to care. They merely kept talking among themselves and didn't pay attention.

"What do you mean?" Crane asked. "There wasn't any splash. You can see for yourself. No one fell into the pool."

Grady squinted, shaking his head in bewilderment. "Yes."

He silently added, *But I would have sworn.*

Disoriented, Grady did his best to answer more questions ("I don't know.") and finally left the compound an hour later, shortly after five, just as Crane and his men were preparing to lock the buildings and the gate to the area, then secure a yellow NO ADMITTANCE—POLICE CRIME SCENE tape across the fence and the gate.

Troubled, numb with shock, aching with sorrow, Grady couldn't stop trembling. He used his two-way radio to contact his office while he drove unsteadily along the winding road through the looming mountains back to Bosworth. He had a duty to perform, but he couldn't let that duty interfere with his other duties. The office had to know where he'd be.

With Brian Roth's sister. The deaths of his wife and son—the rules he'd learned from attending the grief meetings of The Compassionate Friends—had taught him that. You had to do your best to console someone newly bereaved. Compassion was the greatest virtue.

But when he finally stopped at Ida Roth's home, a modest trailer in a row of other trailers on the outskirts of Bosworth, he didn't get an answer after he knocked on her thin, metal door. Of course, Grady thought. The undertaker. The cemetery. The double funeral. Ida has terrible arrangements to make. She'll be in a daze. How I wish I'd been able to get here in time to help her.

To Grady's surprise, a neighbor lady came over and told him where Ida had gone. But his surprise wasn't caused by the gossipy woman's knowledge of Ida's schedule. What did surprise him was Ida's destination. He thanked the neighbor, avoided her questions, and drove to where he'd been directed.

Five minutes away to the restaurant-tavern that Brian and Betsy had owned and where Grady found Ida Roth sternly directing waitresses while she guarded the cash register behind the bar.

The customers, mostly factory workers who regularly stopped by for a couple of beers after their shift was over, eyed Grady's uniform as he sat at the counter. They knew him both as a policeman and as a member of the community, but whenever Grady came in to say hello to Brian and Betsy, he was usually off-duty and in civilian clothes. For him to be wearing his uniform made this visit official, the narrowed eyes that studied him seemed to say, and the somberness of those narrowed eyes suggested as well that word had gotten around about what had happened to Brian and Betsy.

Grady took off his policeman's cap, wished that the juke box playing Roy Orbison's *Only the Lonely* weren't so loud—

—and who the hell had been morbid enough to choose *that* tune?—

—then studied Ida's gaunt, determined features.

Brian's only and older sibling, she was in her early fifties, but she looked close to sixty, partly because her hair had turned totally gray and she combed it back severely into a bun, thus emphasizing the wrinkles in her forehead and around her eyes, and partly as well because her persistent nervousness made her so thin that her cheeks looked hollow, but mostly because her pursed lips made her expression constantly dour.

"Ida," Grady said, "when some people tell you this, you've got every right to feel bitter. The automatic reaction is to think 'bullshit, get out of here, leave me alone.' But you know that I've been where you are now, a year ago when my wife and son"—Grady winced—"were killed. You know that I'm an expert in what I'm talking about, that these aren't empty words. I understand what you're feeling. With all my heart, I'm sorry about Brian and Betsy."

Ida glowered, jerked her face toward a waitress, blurted "Table five's still waiting for that pitcher of beer," and scowled at Grady while pressing her hand on the cash register. "Sorry? Let me tell you something. Brian shut me out after his children died. We visited. We spent time together. But things between us were never the same. For the past ten years, it's been like we weren't blood kin. Like"—Ida's facial expression became skeletal—"like there was some kind of barrier between us. I *resented* that, being made to feel like a stranger. I tried all I could to be friendly to him. You've probably been told how I got worried when he didn't come back on Sunday night for a dinner I'd made, how this morning I went out there and found . . . As far as I'm concerned, a part of Brian died a long time ago. What he did to Betsy and himself was *wrong*. But it might be the *best* thing that could have happened."

"I don't understand." Grady leaned forward, trying hard to ignore Roy Orbison's mournful song and the stares from the silent, intense factory workers.

"It's no secret," Ida said. "*You* know. The whole *town* knows. My husband divorced me eight years ago. After we were married, I kept having miscarriages, so we never had children. It *aged* me. How I hate that young secretary he ran off with. All I got from the settlement, from the greedy lawyers, from the God-damned divorce judge, is the rickety trailer I'm forced to shiver in when the weather gets cold. *You're* sorry? Well, let me tell you, right now as much as I hurt, *I'm* not sorry. Brian had it all, and I had nothing! When he shut me out . . . The best thing he ever did for me was to shoot himself. Now this tavern is *mine*. Finally I've got *something*."

Grady felt shocked. "Ida, you don't mean that."

"The hell I don't! Brian treated me like an outcast. I *earned* this tavern. I deserve it. When they open the will"—Ida's stern expression became calculating—"if there's any justice . . . Brian promised me. In spite of the distance he kept from me, he said he'd take care of me. This tavern is mine. And I bet you could use a drink." She stiffened her hand on the cash register.

"Thanks, Ida. I'd like to, but I can't. I'm on duty." Grady lowered his gaze and dejectedly studied his hat. "Maybe another time."

"No time's better than now. This is happy hour. If you can't be happy, at least drown your sorrow. Call this a wake. It's two drinks for the price of one."

"Not while I'm in uniform. But please remember, I do share your grief."

Ida didn't listen, again barking orders toward a waitress.

Disturbed, Grady picked up his cap and stood from the stool at the bar. A professional instinct made him pause. "Ida."

"Can't you see I'm busy?"

"I apologize, but I need information. Where Brian . . .? Where Betsy was . . .? What do you know about where it happened?"

"Not a hell of a lot."

"But you must know *something*. You knew enough to go out there."

"There?" Ida thickened her voice. "*There?* I was *there* only once. But I felt so shut out . . . so unwelcome . . . so bitter . . . Believe me, I made a point of remembering how to get there."

"Go over that again. Why do you think he made you feel unwelcome?" Grady asked.

"That place was . . ." Ida furrowed her already severely pinched forehead. "His *retreat*. His wall against the world." Her scowl increased. "I remember when he bought that hollow. His children had been dead five months. The summer had turned to fall. It was hunting season. Brian's friends made an effort to try to distract him. 'Come on, let's hunt some rabbits, some grouse,' they told him. 'You can't just sit around all day.' He was practically dragged from his bedroom." While Ida continued to keep her left hand rigidly on the cash register, she pointed her right hand toward the ceiling above the tavern, indicating where Brian and Betsy had lived. "So Brian . . . he had no energy . . . if it weren't for me, the tavern would have gone to hell . . . he shuffled his feet and went along. And the next day, when he came back, I couldn't believe the change in him. He was *filled* with energy. He'd found some land he wanted to buy, he said. He was . . . Frantic? Intense? That doesn't describe it. He kept jabbering about a hollow in the mountains. He'd wandered into it. He absolutely had to own it."

Ida gave more commands to her waitresses and swung her severe gaze toward Grady. "I figured that Brian must have had a nervous breakdown. I told him he couldn't afford a second property. But he wouldn't listen. He *insisted* he had to buy it. So despite my warning, he used this tavern as—what do they call it?—collateral. He convinced the bank to loan him money, found whoever owned that hollow, and bought the damned thing. That's the beginning of when he shut me out.

"The next thing I heard—it didn't come from him; it was gossip from customers in the tavern—was that he'd arranged with a contractor to put in a swimming pool out there, some buildings, a barbecue pit, and . . . The next year when construction was finished, he invited me into the hollow to see the grand opening.

"I admit the place looked impressive. I figured Brian was getting over his loss, adjusting to the deaths of his children. But after he, Betsy, and I and their friends—and my fucking soon-to-be, ex-husband—had a barbecue, Brian took me aside. He pointed toward the woods, toward the pool, toward the buildings, and he asked me . . . I remember his voice was low . . . hushed . . . the way people talk in church . . .

"He asked me if I felt anything different, anything special, anything that reminded me of . . . anything that made me feel *close* to his dead children. I thought about it. I looked around. I tried to understand what he meant. Finally I said 'no.' The camp looked fine, I said. He was taking a risk with the bank. All the same, if he needed a place where he could get away and heal his sorrow, despite the financial risk, he'd probably done the right thing. 'Nothing about the swimming pool?' he asked. I told him I didn't understand what he meant, except that his children liked to swim.

And with that, he ended the conversation. That was the last time he invited me out there. That was the real beginning of the distance between us. The *barrier* he put up. No matter that I saved his ass by taking care of the tavern back then, just as I'm taking care of it *now.*"

Grady knew that he'd exceeded the limit of Ida's patience, interfering with her compulsion to take charge of this tavern she was convinced she'd inherit. He searched his troubled mind for a final question that might settle his confusion.

"Do you know," he asked, "who owned that hollow, or why Brian suddenly felt compelled to buy it?"

"You might as well ask me who's going to win the lottery." Ida's expression became more severe. "He told me nothing. And *I* told *you,* I don't have time for . . . *Please.* I'm trying my best not to be rude, but I've got customers. This is the busiest time of the day. Happy hour makes all these people hungry. I've got to make sure the kitchen's ready."

"Sure," Grady said. "I apologize for distracting you. I just wanted . . . I'm sorry, Ida. That's why I came here. To tell you how painfully I sympathize with your grief."

Ida glared toward a waitress, blurting. "Table eight still needs those onion rings."

Grady stepped back, ignored the stares of the factory workers, opened the door, frowned toward the lowering sun, and left the tavern. As the screen door swung shut, as Grady trudged past pickup trucks toward his cruiser, he heard the customers break their silence and murmur almost loudly enough to obscure another mournful tune, this one by Buddy Holly: *I Guess It Doesn't Matter Anymore.*

Hollow, Grady radioed his office and told the dispatcher where he'd be—at his home. Then he solemnly drove along sunset-crimsoned, wooded streets to the single-story house he'd shared with his wife and son.

The house.

It haunted him. Often he'd thought about selling it to get away from the torment of the memories that it evoked. But just as he hadn't disposed of Helen and John's possessions, their clothes, the souvenier mugs that Helen had liked to collect, the video games that John had been addicted to playing, so Grady hadn't been able to convince himself to dispose of the house. The memories it evoked tormented him, yes, but he couldn't bear to live without them.

At the same time, he felt haunted by the house because it felt empty, because he hadn't maintained it since Helen and John had died, because he hadn't planted flowers this spring as Helen always had, because its interior was drab and dusty and in a few years might literally resemble a haunted house.

When Grady shut the front door behind him, there wasn't any question what he'd do next. The same thing he always did when he came home, what he'd done every evening since the death of his family. Back at the tavern, he'd told Ida that he couldn't accept a drink while on duty. Now, though, he walked directly to a cupboard in his cluttered kitchen and pulled out a bottle of Jim Beam bourbon, poured two inches into a glass, added ice and water, and drank most of it in three swallows.

He closed his eyes and exhaled. There. Yes, there. Grady had explained to Lieutenant Crane that The Compassionate Friends were emphatic in their advice that grieving parents should not seek refuge from their loss by relying on alcohol. Brian and Betsy had emphasized that advice as well. There'd been no liquor bottles or beer cans at the camp, Grady had noticed. Whatever the cause of the murder-suicide, anger caused by drunkenness had not been one of them.

Grady had pretended to follow The Compassionate Friends' advice. But at night, in the depths of his sorrow, he more and more had relied on bourbon to be his anaesthetic, what he'd taken to calling his amnesia juice. Except that it didn't really dispel his memories. All it did was blur them, make them more bearable, stupify him enough that he could sleep. As soon as the bourbon impaired him enough to slur his speech, he'd put on his answering machine, and if the phone rang, if the message was something important from his office, he'd muster sufficient control to pick up the phone and say a few careful words that managed to hide how disabled he was. If necessary, he would mutter that he felt ill and order one of his men to take care of the emergency. Those were the only times when Grady violated his code of professionalism. But just as he'd failed to maintain this house, so he knew and feared that one night he'd make a mistake and inadvertently let outsiders know that he'd failed in other ways as well.

At the moment, however, that fear didn't matter. Sorrow did. Shock did. The bourbon did, and Grady hurriedly poured another glass, this time adding less ice and water. He drank the refill almost as quickly. Brian and Betsy. Helen and John. Jesus.

Grady slumped against the counter and sobbed, deep outbursts that squeezed his throat and made his shoulders convulse.

Abruptly the phone rang. Startled, Grady swung toward where the phone hung on the wall beside the back door.

It rang again.

Grady hadn't put on the answering machine yet. The way he felt, he didn't know whether to let the phone continue ringing or . . . Brian and Betsy. Helen and John. All Grady wanted was to be left alone so he could mourn. But the call might be from his office. It might be important.

Wiping at his tear-scalded cheeks, Grady straightened, brooded, and decided. Inasmuch as the bourbon hadn't begun to take effect, he'd still be able to talk without slurring his words. Whatever this call was about, he might as well take care of it while he was still able.

His hand trembled as he picked up the phone halfway through its fourth ring. "Hello?"

"Ben?"

"Yes."

"Jeff Crane. I'm sorry to bother you at home, but this is important, and when I phoned your office, one of your men told me where you'd be."

"Something important?" Grady's tongue began to feel thick from the bourbon. "What is it?"

"I've got some names. Tell me if they're familiar. Jennings. Matson. Randall. Langley. Beck."

Grady concentrated. "I can't put any faces to them. No one I've met. At least they didn't impress me enough to make me remember them."

"I'm not surprised. They don't . . . they didn't . . . live in Bosworth. They all came from nearby towns, to the west, between here and Pittsburgh."

"So why are they important? I don't get the point." Grady's tongue felt thicker.

"They all died last Thursday."

"*What?*"

"After we finished at Brian's camp, we drove back to headquarters," Crane said. "We couldn't help talking about what had happened out there. One of my men who wasn't on our assignment jerked to attention at the mention of Brian and Betsy Roth. He'd heard those names before, he told me. Last Thursday. One of the worst traffic accidents he'd ever investigated. Ten people killed. All in one van. A driver of a semitruck had a tire blow, lost control, and rammed into them. The investigation revealed that the victims in the van had all been headed toward a Fourth of July celebration in the mountains. To a camp. And that's why I wanted to talk to you. The camp was owned by Brian and Betsy Roth."

Grady clutched the phone so hard that he thought it would break while he sagged against his back door. "All ten of them were killed?"

"They met at one place, left their cars, and went in the van," Crane said.

A traffic accident! Another God-damned traffic accident! Grady thought. Just like Helen and John!

"So on a hunch, I made some calls," Crane said. "To the relatives of the victims. It turns out, what I learned, was that Brian and Betsy got around. They didn't go to grief meetings just in Bosworth. They went to towns all around here. Remember, back at the camp when I wondered about the photographs on the wall of the smallest building? You called it a shrine?

Well, I had the notion that because two of the photographs showed Brian and Betsy's dead children, it could be there was a pattern and maybe the other photographs showed dead children, too."

"I remember."

"Well, I was right. Every one of the couples who were killed in that accident had lost children several years ago. Your description of that building *was* correct. That building *was* a shrine. According to relatives, the parents put up those photographs above the fireplace. They lit candles. They worshipped. And they sobbed."

"What a nightmare," Grady moaned.

"You know about that kind of nightmare more than I can ever imagine. All twelve of them, including Brian and Betsy. A private club devoted to mutual sympathy. Maybe *that's* why Brian lost control and . . . Maybe he murdered Betsy and then shot himself because he couldn't stand more grief."

"Maybe. Yes. It's possible." Grady shudddered.

"The pictures of the older children, the two in military uniforms, those young men were killed in Vietnam. That's how far back the grief of those parents went."

"Believe me, I understand," Grady muttered. "I've got a feeling it lasts forever."

"And I believe *you*. But Ben, what I'm getting at is, now we've got a motive. An explanation. Brian and Betsy were prepared for a weekend get-together. But it didn't work out that way. It turned out to be a weekend of brooding and depression and . . . With the two of them alone out there, Brian decided he couldn't go on. Too much sorrow. Too damned much. So he shot his wife. For all we know, he even had her permission. And then he . . ."

"Shot himself." Grady exhaled.

"Does that make sense?"

"As much as we'll probably ever find out. God help Brian"—Grady had trouble speaking—"and God help Betsy."

"I realize this is hard for you to talk about," Crane said.

Grady mentally added, You don't know shit. But he managed to control his thickening speech enough to say, "Yeah, hard, but at least you've made sense of what Brian did. Or at least as much sense as we'll probably ever learn. You did good, Jeff. I can't say I'm happy, but your theory holds together enough to set my mind to rest. I appreciate your call." Grady wanted to scream.

"I just thought you'd like to know."

"Sure."

"If there's anything more I hear, I'll call you back."

"Great. Fine. Do that."

"Ben?"

"What?" Grady asked.

"I don't want to make a mistake a second time. If you need me—someone to talk to—call me."

"Sure, Jeff. If I need to. Count on it."

"I mean what I said."

"Of course, you do. And *I* mean what *I* said. If I need to talk to you, I will."

"Good. That's all I wanted to hear."

"Later."

"Right."

"Good-bye."

Grady hung up the phone, pushed himself clumsily away from the back door, and desperately lurched across the kitchen, toward the counter, toward his glass, and most of all, toward the bourbon.

The next morning, early, at four, Grady coughed and struggled from his bed. The bourbon had allowed him to sleep, but as its effects dwindled, he regained consciousness prematurely, long before he wanted to confront his troubled existence. His mouth felt dry. His skull ached. His knees wavered. After stumbling into the bathroom, he swallowed several aspirins, palmed water into his mouth, and realized, squinting from the harsh light above the medicine cabinet, that he still wore his uniform, that he'd been so stupified that he hadn't removed his wrinkled clothes before he fell across his bed.

*Tell Ben Grady. Bring him here.* The note that Brian had clutched in his hand beside the .45 that he'd dropped after shooting Betsy and then himself . . . The dismaying note remained as vivid in Grady's memory as when he'd jerked his anguished gaze from their corpses and read the words on the plastic-enclosed piece of paper that Crane had handed to him yesterday at the compound. TELL BEN GRADY. BRING HIM HERE.

*Why?* Grady thought as his stomach churned and he leaned against the sink, tilting his head to the right toward the toilet bowl, trembling, straining to subdue the urge to vomit. *Why?* Everything Jeff told me last night—the ten people killed in the van, the motive for Brian's depression, the explanation for what Brian did—made sense. Brian had reached the end of his endurance. What *doesn't* make sense is the note and Brian's insistence that I be contacted, that I drive to the camp, that I see the bullet holes. The clotted blood. The swarming flies. The corpses.

Grady's mind revolted. He lurched toward the toilet bowl, convulsed, and emptied his sour stomach. Chest heaving, he clumsily straightened, leaned over the sink, turned on the cold water, rinsed his mouth, then repeatedly splashed his clammy face. Depressed, unnerved, he staggered from the bathroom, wavered into the kitchen, and slumped at the table.

The light there, too, stabbed his eyes. Alka-Seltzer, he thought. I need some Alka-Seltzer.

But Grady's impulse was canceled by the awkward feel of a pile of envelopes and mail-order catalogues upon the table. When he'd returned home last evening, he'd automatically grabbed his mail from the box outside his door while he'd fumbled for his key. He'd thrown the mail on the kitchen table, impatient to open the cupboard where he kept his bourbon. Now, having propped his elbows on the table, further spreading the envelopes and catalogues, he found himself staring at a letter addressed to him, one of the few letters he'd received since Helen and John had died, since Helen's relatives had stopped sending mail here.

The instructions on the envelope—BENJAMIN GRADY, 112 CYPRESS STREET, BOSWORTH, PENNSYLVANIA, then the zip code—had been scrawled in black ink. No return address.

But Grady recognized the scrawl. He'd seen it often enough on compassionate cards that he'd received, not only in the days and weeks after Helen and John had died but as well in month after month as the painful year progressed. Encouraging messages. Continuing sympathy.

From *Brian.* And the *postmark* on the envelope was *four days* ago. On *Friday.*

Despite Grady's increasingly torturous headache, he snapped to attention, grabbed the letter, and tore it open.

*Dear Ben,* it began, and on top of the nightmare that had fractured Grady's drunken sleep, a further nightmare awaited him. Grady shuddered as he read the message from his wonderful, generous, stubbornly supportive friend, who no longer existed.

*Dear Ben,*

*When you receive this, Betsy and I will be dead.*

*I deeply regret the sorrow and shock that will cause you. I don't know which will be worse, the shock initially, the sorrow persistently. Both are terrible burdens, and I apologize.*

*If our bodies are found before you read this letter . . . if the note I plan to write and place in my hand when I pull the trigger doesn't achieve my intention . . . if something goes wrong and you're not asked to come here . . . I want you to come here. Not to see the husks that contained our minds and our souls. Not to torment you with our undignified remains. But to make sure you see this place. It's special, Ben. It consoles.*

*I can't tell you how. What I mean is, I won't. You have to find out for yourself. If I raised your expectations and they weren't fulfilled, you'd feel guilty, convinced that you weren't worthy, and the last thing I want is to cause you more guilt.*

*Nonetheless that possibility has to be considered. It may be you won't be receptive to this place. I can't predict. For certain, my sister wasn't receptive. Others weren't receptive, either. So I chose carefully. My friends who died on Thursday were the few who understood the comfort that this place provided.*

*And now they're dead. And Betsy and I don't want to be alone again. Too much. Too fucking much. I've been watching you carefully, Ben. I've been more and more worried about you. I know that you drink yourself to sleep every night. I know that you hurt as much as Betsy and I do. But we've been lucky enough to find consolation, and you're still seeking consolation in a bottle. I'm afraid for you.*

*I had planned to bring you out here soon. I think you're ready. I think you'd be receptive. I think that this place would give you joy. So I left the note that instructed the state police to bring you here. And now that—I presume—you've seen it, I need to tell you that after I drive into town to mail this letter, I'll make a sidetrip to visit my lawyer.*

*I intend to amend my will. My final compassionate act on your behalf is to give you this compound. I hope that it will ease your suffering and provide you with solace, with peace. You'll know what I mean if you're truly receptive, if you're as sensitive as I believe you are.*

*Forgive me for the pain that our deaths will cause you. But our deaths are necessary. You have to accept my word on that. We anticipate. We're eager. What I'm about to do is not the result of despair.*

*I love you, Ben. I know that sounds strange. But it's true. I love you because we're partners in misfortune. Because you're decent and good. And in pain. Perhaps my gift to you will ease your pain. When you read this, Betsy and I will no longer be in pain. But in our final hours, we pray for you. We wish you consolation. God bless you, my friend. Be well.*

*Brian Roth.*

Beneath Brian's signature, Betsy had added her own.

Grady's chest heaved. His tear ducts swelled. He groaned, in torment. His tears dripped onto the page, dissolving the ink on the final words, blurring the signatures of his profoundly, sorely missed friends.

Jeff Crane frowned increasingly as he read the letter. Pursing his lips, he read it again, then again. At last, he straightened, leaned back from his desk, and exhaled.

Grady sat across from him, brooding.

"Jesus." Crane slumped. "That's certainly a hell of a way to start the morning."

"I'm sorry for waking you," Grady said. "I waited as long as I could force myself, till after dawn, before phoning your home. Really, I thought you'd be up by then. I wanted to make sure you were going straight to your office instead of on an assignment. I assumed you'd want to see that letter right away."

Crane looked puzzled. "What are you talking about? You assumed I'd want to see this letter right away? Of course. For damned sure. That isn't what I meant by 'a hell of a way to start the morning'. I wasn't referring to me. *You,* Ben. I was sympathizing with *you.* Dear God, I'm surprised you waited till after dawn. In your place, as close to Brian and Betsy as you were, barely awake, then shocked awake by this letter, I wouldn't have waited for dawn. I'd have called my friend . . . and that's what I hope you think I am . . . at once."

Grady shuddered.

"Hey, you don't look so good." Crane stood and reached toward a beaker of coffee on a warmer. "You'd better have another jolt of vitamins." He refilled Grady's cup.

Grady's hands trembled as he raised the steaming cup to his lips. "Thanks." He fought to subdue his hangover. "The letter. Jeff, what do you make of it?"

Crane scowled. "The most obvious thing is that Betsy's signature proves she agreed to Brian's plan. This wasn't a murder-suicide, but a double suicide.

Betsy just needed a little help is all."

"Christ," Grady said.

"The other obvious thing is that the letter has gaps," Crane said. "Brian insists it was necessary to leave the note at the compound, sending for you, but he doesn't explain why. Oh, sure, he says he wants you to see the place. But after you found out he'd given it to you in his will, you'd have gone up to see it anyhow. There wasn't any need for you to be forced to look at the bodies."

"Unless . . ." Grady's throat cramped.

"Unless?" Crane raised his eyebrows.

"Suppose I was so overwhelmed with grief that the last thing I wanted was to see where Brian had shot Betsy and himself. What if I was so repulsed that I decided to sell the compound without ever going up there? The truth is, I *don't* want the compound. Brian might have been afraid of that, so he left the note in his hand as a fail-safe mechanism—to make sure I *did* go up there."

Crane shrugged. "Could be. That leads me to another gap in the letter. He tells you he wants you to see the compound because it's . . ." Crane traced a finger down the letter. ". . . 'special. It consoles.' Brian refuses to tell you how, though. He says he's afraid he might give you expectations that won't be fulfilled."

"I thought about that all the time I was driving here." Grady's throat tightened. "Obviously Brian, Betsy, and those ten people who died in the van in the traffic accident considered the compound a refuge. A private club away from the world. A place to indulge themselves, to let out their grief. A beautiful setting where they could support each other. Brian might have understood that if, in his letter, he praised the compound too much, I'd be disappointed because the compound didn't matter as much as the company did. At the same time, the compound *is* special. It truly is beautiful. So he gave it to me. Maybe Brian felt guilty because he'd never included me in the group. Maybe he hoped that I'd start a group of my own. Who knows? He was under stress. He wasn't totally coherent."

"No shit." Crane studied him, then leaned forward. "So what are you going to do about it?"

"About . . .? I don't understand."

"The compound. You said you don't want it. Are you really so repulsed by what happened up there that you don't intend to go back, that you'll sell the place?"

Grady stared at the floor.

He didn't speak for several moments.

"I don't know," he finally murmured. "If he'd given me something else—let's say a watch, something that was special to him, as a momento—would I throw it away because I didn't want to be reminded? Or would I cherish it?"

* * *

Two solemn days later, Ida Roth helped Grady choose. Not that she intended to. Nonetheless she did. At the funeral. Or rather, after it, at the wooded cemetery where the mourners gathered to watch the coffins be carried from the hearses and set upon sturdy, burlap straps over the earth-rimmed graves into which they'd be lowered.

Grady had hoped to be one of the pallbearers, but Ida Roth—Brian's only family survivor, in charge of the arrangements—had disappointingly failed to ask him. Grady had tried to get in touch with her, at her home, at the restaurant-tavern, but he'd never been able to succeed. Sweating from the morning's heat and humidity, wiping the sweat from his eyes, reminded of the heat and humidity a year ago when he'd arrived at this same cemetery, carrying the urns of his wife and son into the mausoleum, he realized that the moisture that stung his eyes wasn't sweat but tears. When he finally turned, despondent, to walk back to his car, he abruptly felt a presence behind him, an *angry* presence, although how he sensed the presence, he didn't know. But the anger was inexplicably, eerily palpable, and he froze when Ida growled behind him, "You son of a bitch."

Confused, Grady pivoted. The glare in Ida's sunken, wrinkle-rimmed eyes was dismaying. He'd tried to get close to her before and after the funeral, but she avoided him. At the graves, he'd done his best to make eye-contact, frustrated at the stubbornness with which she'd averted her gaze.

Now, though, her gaze was disturbingly direct. "Bastard," she hissed. Her gaunt face, framed by her severely tugged-back hair, looked even more skeletal.

Grady winced. "I don't deserve . . . Why are you calling me that, Ida? I haven't done anything against you. I miss them. I'm here to mourn them. Why are you—?"

"Don't play games with me, you hypocrite! You know fucking well!"

"What are you *talking* about?" Grady demanded.

Mourners who passed them frowned.

"The compound, you leech!" Ida said. "Brian's attorney told me about the will! It wasn't enough that my God-damned brother had so much self-pity that he let the tavern go to hell. It wasn't enough that since he shot himself I've been scrambling to balance the tavern's accounts so his creditors don't take over the place. No, I have to find out that while he mortgaged the tavern which *I* inherited, the camp in the woods which *you* inherited, you bastard, is paid off, free and clear! I don't know how you tricked him. I can't imagine how you used your dead wife and kid to fool him into giving you the compound. But you can bet on this, you cocksucker. If it takes my last breath, I'll fight you in court. Brian *promised* me. He swore he'd take care of me! And by God, I intend to make sure he keeps his word. You don't deserve anything! *You* weren't there when his twins died. *You* weren't there to hold his hand. *You* came *later.* So count on this. If it's the last thing I do, I'll own that camp. I'm tempted to have the buildings crushed, the swimming pool filled, and everything covered with salt. But damn it, I need the money. So instead I'll have the will revoked and sell the place! I'll get the money I deserve! And you, you fuckface, won't get *anything!*"

Grady seethed. Ida's verbal assault, in particular her unforgivable accusation that he'd used his grief for his dead wife and son to manipulate Brian into willing him the compound, made him so furious that he inhaled and trembled and told her, "Fine, Ida. Whatever you want to do." He shook more fiercely. "Or try to do. But listen carefully. Because there's something you don't realize. Until this minute, I intended to give up the compound and transfer my title to you. I believed you deserved it. But you made a mistake. My wife and son. You shouldn't have . . . Jesus, no. I've suddenly changed my mind. That compound is mine. I didn't want it. But now I do. To spite you, Ida. For the insult to my wife and son, you'll rot in hell. And *I'll* rot in hell before you ever set foot on that camp again. You're a fool."

With Lieutenant Crane's permission, Grady angrily tore the yellow NO ADMITTANCE—POLICE CRIME SCENE tape from the chainlink fence at the compound's entrance. Using the key that Crane had given him, Grady unlocked the gate, thrust it open, and stalked bitterly into the camp.

The hollow between the mountains was oppressively silent as Grady flicked sweat from his brow and strode with furious determination toward the swimming pool, through the wooden gate, to the concrete border and the white chalk outlines of where Brian and Betsy's corpses had lain. A few flies still fluttered over the vestiges of blood, bone, and brain. Watching them, Grady swallowed acrid bile, then straightened, rigid, with indignant resolve.

Fine, he thought. I can clean this up. I can deal with the memories. The main thing is I intend to keep what Brian and Betsy gave me.

That bitch won't have it.

In outrage, Grady spun from the chalk outlines, left the pool area, ignored the barbecue pit, and approached the cinderblock bunkhouse. Despite his preoccupation, he was vaguely aware that he repeated the sequence in which Lieutenant Crane had taken him from building to building. He barely glanced inside the bunkhouse, gave even less attention to the cookstove in the separate kitchen, and stomped toward the smallest building that he'd described to Crane as a shrine.

Inside its gloom, Grady felt that the oppressive silence from outside was emphasized. The slate floor should have made his footsteps echo. Instead it seemed to muffle them, just as the oak-paneled walls seemed to absorb the intruding sounds of his entrance. He uneasily studied the church pew before the fireplace. He raised his intensely narrowed gaze toward the photographs of the eight, dead, smiling children between the candle holders and the American flags above the mantle. Knees wavering, he approached the photographs. With reverence, he touched the images of Brian and Betsy's dead, teenage, twin daughters.

So beautiful.

So full of life.

So soon destroyed.

God help them.

At last, Grady shifted his mournful eyes toward the poignant photograph of the ten-year-old, bespectacled, embarrassed-to-smile-because-of-the-braces-on-his-teeth boy who reminded Grady so unbearably of his own, so profoundly missed son.

And again Grady heard the startling sound of a splash. He stiffened, then abruptly reeled toward the open door from the shrine. He couldn't help recalling that the last time he'd been here, with Crane, examining the photographs of these dead children, he'd also heard a splash.

From the swimming pool. Or so Grady had been absolutely certain until he'd hurried outside and studied the policemen next to the swimming pool and realized that he'd been mistaken, that no one had fallen in, and yet the splash had been so vivid.

Just as now. With the difference that as Grady hurried from the shadows of the shrine into the stark glare of the summer sun, he flinched at the sight of a young man—late teens, muscular, with short brown hair, wearing swimming goggles and a tiny, hip-hugging, nylon suit—stroking powerfully from the near end of the swimming pool across its length, water rippling, muscles flexing, toward the opposite rim. The young man's speed was stunning, his surge amazing.

Grady faltered. How the hell? He hadn't heard a car approach. He couldn't imagine the young man hiking up the lane to the compound, taking off his clothes, putting on his swimming suit, and diving in unless the young man felt he belonged here, or unless the young man assumed that no one would be here.

But the kid must have seen my cruiser outside the gate! Grady thought. Why didn't he yell to get my attention if he belonged here? Or go back down the lane if he *didn't* belong? There weren't any clothes by the pool. Where had the kid undressed? What in God's name was going on?

Scowling, Grady overcame his surprise and ran toward the swimming pool. "Hey!" he shouted. "What do you think you're doing? You don't have any right to be here! I own this place! Get out of the pool! Get away from—!"

Grady's voice broke as he rushed through the gate to the swimming pool. The young man kept thrusting his arms, kicking his legs, surging across the swimming pool, rebounding off the opposite end, reversing his impulse, stroking with determination.

Grady shouted more insistently. "Answer me! Stop, damn it! I'm a policeman! You're trespassing! Get out of the pool before I—!"

But the swimmer kept stroking, rebounded off the near rim, and surged yet again toward the opposite edge. Grady was reminded of an Olympic athlete who strained to achieve a gold medal.

"I'm telling you one last time! Get out of the pool!" Grady commanded, his throat cramping. "You've got thirty seconds! After that, I radio for backup! We'll drag you out and—!"

The swimmer ignored him, churning, flexing, stroking.

Grady had shouted so rapidly that he'd hyperventilated. Dizzy, he groped behind him, clutched a redwood chair, and leaned against it. His chest heaved. As his heart raced and his vision swirled, he struggled to keep his balance and focus on the magnificent swimmer.

Seconds passed. Minutes. Time lengthened. Paradoxically, it also seemed suspended. At last, the swimmer's strength began to falter. After a final weary lap, the young man gripped the far end of the swimming pool, breathed hoarsely, fumbled to prop his arms along the side, and squirmed laboriously onto the concrete deck. He stood with determination, wavered, dripped water, and plodded unsteadily around the pool toward Grady.

"So you're finally ready to pay attention?" Grady asked and heaved himself away from the redwood chair with the same unsteadiness that the swimmer had stood from the edge of the pool. "Are you ready now to explain what the hell you're doing here?"

The swimmer approached him, ignoring him.

Grady unclenched his fists and shoved his anger-hardened palms toward the swimmer's shoulders.

But Grady's palms—Grady tingled, gasped, and shivered—passed through the swimmer.

At the same time, the swimmer passed through *him*. Like a subtle shift of air. Of *cold* air. And as Grady twisted, unnerved, watching the swimmer emerge from his side, then his swiveling chest, he felt as if he'd been possessed—consumed, then abandoned.

"Hey!" Grady managed to shout.

Abruptly the young man, his sinewy body dripping water, his cropped hair clinging to his drooping head, his taut frame sagging, vanished. The hot, humid air seemed to ripple. With equal abruptness, the air became still again. The swimmer was gone.

Grady's lungs felt empty. He fought to breathe. He fumbled toward the redwood chair. But the moment he touched its reassuring firmness, his sanity collapsed as did his body.

Impossible! a remnant of his logic screamed.

And as that inward scream echoed, he stared toward the concrete.

The wet footprints of the swimmer were no longer evident.

Grady trembled in the chair for quite a while. At last, he mustered the strength to raise himself.

The young man had been a stranger.

And yet the young man had somehow looked unnervingly familiar.

No. Yes. *Have to.*

Grady wavered, then lurched from the pool. Sweat streamed down his face. Obeying an irresistible compulsion, he managed to stagger toward the smallest building.

He listed within the shrine's brooding confines, stumbled past the church pew, clasped the mantle above the fireplace, raised his disbelieving gaze above the candles, and concentrated on a photograph to his right.

A young man in a military uniform.

A handsome youngster whom Lieutenant Crane had said had been killed in Vietnam.

The *same* young man who'd been swimming with powerful strokes in the pool, passed coldly through Grady's body, and suddenly disappeared.

As always, the bottle of Jim Beam in the cupboard of the shadowy kitchen beckoned. With unsteady hands, Grady poured, gulped, grimaced, and shivered. He didn't recall his frantic drive from the compound through the mountains into Bosworth and the sanctuary of his home, of his kitchen, and most important, of his bourbon.

I'm losing my mind, he thought in panic and tilted the bourbon over the glass.

But his amnesia juice wasn't allowed to do its work. Because the phone rang, making him jerk.

With quivering hands, he set down the bottle, grabbed a dish towel, wiped spilled bourbon off his sleeve, and grabbed the phone.

"Hello." His voice seemed to come from miles away.

"Chief, we've got trouble," the dispatcher said. "A robbery down at the truckstop near the highway."

"Is anybody hurt?" Grady's voice seemed even *farther* away.

"No," the dispatcher said. "Thank God for that."

"Did a witness get a license number?"

"Luckily."

"Then send our units to block the exits from town. Alert the state police. I don't understand why you wasted time phoning me, Dinah. You know the procedure. Do your job."

"There's no need to bark."

"Hey, two friends of mine were buried today."

"I'm sorry. I honestly am, but . . ."

Grady exhaled. "I'm sorry, too. Forgive me, Dinah. I guess the funerals must have got to me more than I realized. I apologize for . . . I can't talk right now." Grady set down the phone as quickly as he could without slamming it.

And now I've broken my final rule, he thought. I swore I'd never let my personal problems interfere with my work.

He pivoted toward the bourbon. But again the jangle of the phone interrupted him. Flinching, he fought to steady himself, then picked it up. "Hello." The effort to sound normal was excruciating.

"So you're finally home, you bastard," Ida Roth said. "I just thought you'd like to know that my lawyer agrees with me. My brother was obviously out of his mind! That will's invalid!"

"Ida, I'm not in the mood to argue." Grady's head throbbed. "We'll let a judge decide."

"You God-damned bet. I'll see you in court!"

"You're wasting your time, Ida. I intend to fight you on this."

"But I'll fight *harder*. You won't have a chance!"

Grady's left ear throbbed when Ida slammed down the phone.

Bitch, he thought and swung toward the bourbon. But again the phone rang.

Jesus.

Grady jerked the phone to his ear. "Ida, I've had enough! Don't call me again! From now on, have your lawyer talk to mine!"

"Ben?" A man's voice sounded puzzled.

"*Jeff?* Is that *you?* My God, I'm sorry! I didn't mean to shout. I thought it was . . ."

"You don't sound so good," Lieutenant Crane said.

Grady trembled.

"It must have been a rough day," Crane continued.

"You have no idea."

"The reason I'm calling . . . Do you need company? Is there any way I can help?"

Grady slumped. "No. But I appreciate your concern. It's good to know that someone cares. I think I can manage. At least, I'll try. On second thought, wait," Grady added. "There *is* something you can . . ."

"Name it."

"That's exactly what I want. *Names.*"

"I don't . . ." Crane's voice dropped.

"When you phoned me the other night, when you told me about the traffic accident, about the friends of Brian and Betsy who'd been killed . . ."

Crane exhaled. "I remember."

"The names of the victims. I was too upset to write them down. Who were they?"

"Why on earth would you want to . . .?"

"Please!"

Crane hesitated. "Just a minute." Crane made fumbling noises as if he sorted through a file. "Jennings. Matson. Randall. Langley. Beck."

"I need their addresses and phone numbers," Grady said.

Crane supplied them, adding, mystified, "I don't understand why you need this information."

"Which parents lost their sons in Vietnam?"

"Langley and Beck. But why do you . . .?"

"Thanks. I really appreciate this. I'll talk to you later."

"I'm worried about you, Ben."

"I'm fine." Grady hung up the phone.

Langley and Beck.

Grady studied the phone numbers. Both sets of parents had lived in towns between Bosworth and Pittsburgh. He pressed "1" for a local long-distance call, then the numbers for the Langley residence.

No one answered.

That wasn't surprising. Since the Langleys had been old enough to have lost a son in Vietnam, their other children—if they had any—would be in their thirties or forties, with homes of their own.

Grady urgently pressed the other numbers. He heard a buzz. Then another buzz.

He rubbed his forehead.

At once a man's husky voice said, "Yes?"

"My name is Benjamin Grady. I'm the police chief of Bosworth. That's about forty miles east of—"

"I *know* where Bosworth is," the thick voice said. "What do you want? If this is about the accident, I don't feel up to talking about it again. You picked an inconvenient time to . . . My wife and I have been trying to sort through my parents' effects, to settle their estate."

"This isn't about the accident."

"Then what *is* it about?"

"Your brother."

"Jesus, don't tell me something's happened to Bob!"

"No. I didn't mean . . . I'm referring to your brother who died in Vietnam."

"Jerry? But I don't get it. Why after all this time would you want to—?"

"It's too complicated to explain, but believe me, it's important. Was your brother a swimmer? A *serious* swimmer?"

"I haven't thought about that in . . ." The man swallowed thickly. "The coach in high school said that Jerry could have been a champion. My brother used to train every day. Three hours minimum. He could have made the Olympics."

Grady felt as cold as when the swimmer had walked along the side of the pool and passed through him.

"What did you say your name was?" the husky voice demanded. "Grady? And you claim you're the police chief over in—? What the hell is this? A sick joke?"

"No. If there'd been another way to . . . I deeply regret intruding on your grief. What you've told me is important. Thank you."

Grady hung up, chilled to his core. His legs felt so weak that he had to grab a kitchen chair on his way to the bourbon.

Despite the rising sun, Grady needed his headlights to see to drive up the bumpy, zigzagging lane through the shadowy trees to the compound. Finally at the top, he trembled and stared toward an eerie mist that rose off the swimming pool, spreading around it. Faint sunlight revealed the pines and maples on the dusky ridges that flanked the compound, but the compound itself was completely enshrouded. Grady's headlights glinted brilliantly off the thick, almost-crystalline mist.

He got out of his police car, stepped apprehensively ahead, and nearly bumped into the chainlink fence before he saw it. After fumbling to unlock the gate, he swung it open and nervously entered the haze-obscured compound. The silence around him remained as oppressive as the day before, so much so that when he stepped onto gravel, the abrupt crunch startled him. Clinging, the cold mist dampened his clothes and beaded on his hackled skin.

When he'd left the cruiser, he'd turned off his headlights. Now he wished that he'd kept them on or had thought to bring a flashlight because the mist became denser as he moved through it.

I ought to turn around and drive back to town, he thought. This is crazy. *What am I doing here?*

But Grady knew the answer. Last night, he'd again collapsed into bed after drinking too much. Again, as the alcohol's effects had dwindled, he'd wakened prematurely, around four. Jittery, confused, he'd roamed his house, and the more he analyzed it, the more the apparition from the day before had seemed impossible.

I *couldn't* have seen it. I must have imagined it! I was so upset by Brian and Betsy's funeral, by what they did, that I must have hallucinated!

Sure.

But Grady couldn't stop brooding. He couldn't resist the beckoning compound, and finally he'd told himself that he had to go back, to prove to himself that his imagination had gotten the better of him, that he hadn't seen . . . his mind balked, reluctant to complete the outrageous thought . . . the ghost of a young man who'd died so many years ago in Vietnam.

First Helen and John.

*Then Brian and Betsy.*

You've been thinking about death too much!

So Grady had cleaned up, changed his clothes, and driven with fierce resolve to the compound. I've got to get my mind straight! He intended to settle this right away, as soon as possible, before he was supposed to arrive at his office. Then he could put yesterday's nightmare behind him, do his work, and stop feeling haunted.

But Grady now wished that he hadn't come. The mist seemed unnatural. Too thick. Too . . .

Be careful, he warned himself. You're letting your imagination get control of you again. Mist often rises from swimming pools at dawn. It's something to do with the change in temperature. There's nothing unusual about . . .

Grady faltered, suddenly realizing that without the benefit of a visible object to aim toward, he might lose his bearings and wander in a circle. He felt disoriented. Bewildered. Confused.

He braved another step forward and winced as he bumped against the waist-high, wooden fence that bordered the swimming pool.

At the same time, he winced for another reason. Indeed he flinched. For as Grady rubbed his stomach from his sharp impact against an upright slat, he glimpsed a shadow that passed from left to right before him beyond the fence: the shadow of what seemed to be a man. The shadow's motion caused the mist to swirl. Then the shadow disappeared. The mist became still again.

When Grady heard a splash from the pool, he stumbled backward. The splash was followed by the echoing strokes of a powerful swimmer. Grady froze, paralyzed by conflicting impulses.

To charge through the gate and confront the swimmer.

(But he'd done that yesterday, and he was terrified that the swimmer would again pass through him.)

To stay where he was and shout to demand an explanation.

(But he'd done that yesterday as well, with no effect, and anyway if Grady tried to shout, he was certain that the noise from his mouth would be a shriek.)

To pivot and scramble desperately from the pool, frantic to find his way back through the gloom to the cruiser.

(But)

Grady heard a further splash. *Someone else diving into the water.* With increasing dismay, he saw *another* shadow—no, two!—pass through the haze beyond the fence. A woman, it seemed. And a child.

Grady screamed, swung, and recoiled as a *further* shadow appeared in the mist, this one approaching from the direction of the bunkhouse.

"No!" Grady wailed, seeing three more shadows!—two women and a girl!—approach from the haze-obscured kitchen. He lurched sideways to avoid them and suddenly found himself confronted by still *another* shadow, this one coming from the direction of the shrine. Grady's impetus was so forceful that he couldn't stop. He and the shadow converged. He lunged *through* the shadow, unbearably chilled, and despite the density of the mist, he managed to see the shadow's face. It was Brian Roth.

Grady's eyes fluttered. Something minuscule inched across his brow, making his skin itch. A fly, he dimly realized. He pawed it clumsily away, then opened his eyes completely. The stark sun directly above him made him squint. He was on his back, sprawled on the gravel near the swimming pool.

My God, he thought. I must have fainted.

As his consciousness focused, he groaned and managed to sit, peering around him, cringing, expecting to be confronted by ghosts.

But all Grady saw was the silence-smothered compound.

He hurriedly glanced at his watch. *Almost noon?* He pressed his hands against his throbbing head. Dear Lord, I've been lying here for . . .

Brian!

No! I *couldn't* have seen him!

Terrified, Grady squirmed to his feet. His vision blurred, then mercifully focused again. In place of the dampness from the mist, his skin was now clammy from sweat, his stained uniform clinging to him. He managed to straighten, then scanned the otherwise deserted compound.

I've lost my mind.

That's what it is. I'm having a nervous breakdown.

He stumbled toward his police car, anxious to contact his staff. They'd be wondering where he was. They'd have tried to get in touch with him, and their efforts having failed, they'd be afraid that something had happened to him. He had to let them know that he was all right.

More important, he had to think of an acceptable reason for his not having gone to the office, for his not having responded to their calls. He couldn't let them know how fucked up and out of control he was.

But as Grady reached the cruiser, about to lean in and grab the two-way radio microphone, he stiffened, hearing the drone and jolt of a vehicle as it struggled up the bumpy lane. Pivoting, he saw that the vehicle belonged to the state police, that it veered from the trees to stop beside his own car, and that Jeff Crane got out, glancing solemnly around, proceeding somberly toward him.

"Ben."

"Jeff."

The exchange of greetings was awkward.

"You've got a lot of people worried about you," Crane said, frowning.

"I'm afraid the situation's difficult," Grady said. "I was just about to—"

"Your uniform. What have you been doing, sleeping in a ditch?"

"Yeah, well, it's hard to explain."

"I bet. All the same, why not give it a try?"

"How'd you know I'd be here?"

Crane studied him with concern. "Process of elimination. After a while, the more I thought about it, the more this seemed the most logical place."

"Why *you*, though?" Grady persisted.

"I don't understand."

"How come *you're* out looking for me?"

"Oh." Crane shrugged, although his expression remained severe. "When your dispatcher kept failing to reach you, when she became concerned enough, she contacted all your friends. I'll say it once again. You've got a lot of people worried about you, Ben. Why didn't you check in?"

"The truth is . . ."

"Sure. That's a good idea. Why not? The truth would be refreshing."

"I . . ."

"Yes? Go on, Ben. The truth."

"I fainted."

"From booze?"

Grady's shoulders drooped. "What makes you think . . .?"

"The note Brian left makes it clear you've been drinking a lot. Because of your wife and son. But he's not the only one who noticed. Too many times when I phoned you at night, your voice was slurred."

"A couple of drinks."

"Don't bullshit me, Ben. Damn it, I can't help you if you lie."

"Okay. Sometimes a couple of drinks too many. But it never interfered with my work."

"Yeah. Like now. Like this morning."

"You're wrong. This morning had nothing to do with booze," Grady said. "I came up here early before I was due at work so I could . . . I guess I wanted to look around, to decide if I was going to keep this place. Then everything finally caught up to me. Brian and Betsy. My wife. My son. I felt dizzy. I passed out. Over there by the pool."

Grady turned and pointed.

And what he saw demanded that he use every remnant of his remaining willpower not to react. Because the area around the pool was crowded with people: six children including Brian's twins; the two young men who'd been killed in Vietnam; twelve adults, ten of whom Grady didn't recognize, although two were Brian and Betsy.

And I'll bet the five couples I don't recognize are the people who died in that traffic accident last Thursday, Grady inwardly moaned.

They were having a barbecue, eating, talking, laughing, although the scene was weirdly silent, no sounds escaping from their mouths.

Grady's cheeks felt numb as if he'd turned pale, and his body shook, but then it had been shaking when Crane arrived. He managed not to whimper.

I really ought to be congratulated, he thought. I'm seeing ghosts, and I'm not gibbering like a lunatic.

Crane who looked toward the pool showed no reaction either, and Grady stiffened with the shock of understanding. "Jeff, do you notice anything unusual?"

"What do you mean?"

Grady was amazed to discover that he repeated almost exactly what Ida Roth had said that *Brian* had said when he'd brought her to the camp. "Do you feel anything different, anything special, anything that reminds you of . . . that makes you feel close to Brian and Betsy?"

"Not particularly." Crane frowned. "Except of course the memory of finding their bodies here."

"Nothing at the swimming pool?"

"That's where the bodies were, of course." Crane debated, drawing his fingers through his short, sandy hair. "Otherwise, no. I don't notice anything unusual about the pool."

"I need help, Jeff."

"That's why I'm here. Haven't I been asking you repeatedly to let me help? *How?* Tell me what you need."

"A reason that my staff will accept for my not checking in. An explanation that won't affect the way they look at me."

"You mean like there was something wrong with your radio but you didn't know it? Or you had to leave town for an appointment that you thought you'd told them about?"

"That's it. Exactly." Grady's chest swelled with hope.

"I'm sorry, Ben. I can't do it."

Grady felt deflated.

"I won't back you up on this." Crane squinted. "The only explanation I'll help you with is the truth."

"And you keep saying you're my friend."

"That's right."

"So what kind of friend would—?"

"A good one. *Damned* good. Better than you realize. Ben, you've been fooling youself. You claim that your problems haven't interfered with your work. You're wrong. And I don't mean just the booze. I mean the reason for the booze. Your grief. Everybody's noticed it. Your nerves are on edge. Your temper's raw. You always look distracted. You have trouble concentrating. Your staff walks on tiptoes not to annoy you. The best way I can help you is to give you this advice. Take a month off. Get some psychiatric counseling. Admit yourself to a substance-abuse clinic. Dry out. Accept reality. Your wife and son are dead. You have to adjust to that, to try harder to come to terms with your loss. You've got to find some peace."

"A month off? But my job is all I've got left!"

"Ben, I'm telling you this as a friend. Keep acting the way you've been, and you won't even have your job. I've been hearing talk. Rumors. You're close to being fired."

"What?" Grady couldn't believe what Crane was saying. It seemed as impossible as the ghosts at the swimming pool, as the silent party that Crane couldn't see but Grady did. "Oh, Jesus, no!"

"But if you go along with my recommendations," Crane insisted. "No, Ben. Don't keep looking at the swimming pool. Look at *me*. That's right. Good. If you go along with what I recommend, I'll do everything in my power to make sure that your staff and the Bosworth town council understand what you've been going through. Face it. You're exhausted. Burned out. What you need is a rest. There's nothing disgraceful about that. As long as you don't try to hide your condition, as long as you admit your problem and try to correct it, people will sympathize. I swear to you. I'll make *sure* they sympathize. You used to be a damned good cop, and you can be one again. But only if you do what I ask. And *if* you do what I ask, I guarantee

I'll use all the influence I've got to fix it so you can keep your job."

"Thanks, Jeff. I really appreciate that. I'll try. I promise. I truly will."

Grady sat in the mausoleum, sobbing, blinking through his scalding tears toward the niches that contained the urns of his sorely missed, beloved wife and son.

"I've got trouble," he told them, his voice so choked he could barely speak. "I'm seeing ghosts. I'm drinking too much. I'm fucking up at work. I'm about to lose my job. And as far as my mind goes, well, hey, I lost that quite a while ago.

"If only you hadn't died. If only I hadn't decided to work late that night. If only you hadn't decided to go to that movie. If only that drunk hadn't hit you. If only . . .

"It's my fault. It's all my fault. I can't tell you how much I miss you. I'd give anything to have you back, to make our life perfect the way it used to be, a year ago, before . . ."

The pager on Grady's gunbelt began to beep. He ignored it, wiping at his tears, continuing to address the urns of his precious family.

"Helen, when I come home, the house feels so empty I can't stand it. John, when I look in your room, when I touch the clothes in your closet, when I smell them, I feel as if my heart's going to split apart, that I'll die on the spot. I want both of you with me so much I . . ."

The pager kept beeping. Grady pulled it from his gunbelt, dropped it onto the floor, and stomped it with the heel of his shoe.

When the pager beeped again, he stomped it harder, hearing it crack, feeling a satisfying crunch.

The pager went silent.

Good.

Grady peered down at its shattered frame, then blinked upward through the blur of his tears, and continued his torturous monologue.

"Perfect. Our life was perfect. But without you . . . I love you. I want you so much. I ache so . . . I'd give anything to have you back, for the three of us to be together again."

Grady finally ran out of words. He just kept sitting, sobbing, staring at the niches, at the names of his wife and son, at their birth and death dates, imagining their ashes in the urns.

A thought came slowly. It rose as if from thick darkness, struggling to surface. It emerged from the turmoil of his subconscious and became an inward voice that repeated sentences from the puzzling letter that Brian had written.

*I'm afraid for you. I had planned to bring you out here soon. I think you're ready. I think you'd be receptive. I think that this place would give you joy.*

*My final compassionate act on your behalf is to give you this compound. I hope that it will ease your suffering and provide you with solace, with peace. You'll know what I mean if you're truly receptive, if you're as sensitive as I believe you are.*

Grady nodded firmly, stood, wiped his tears, kissed his fingers, placed them over the glass that enclosed the urns, and left the mausoleum, careful to lock its door behind him.

The compound was enshrouded again, this time by a cloud of dust that Grady's cruiser had raised coming up the lane and that a breeze had caused to drift ahead of him. He stopped the cruiser, waited for the dust to clear, and wasn't at all surprised to see Brian and Betsy, their twin daughters, the other children, the young men who had died in Vietnam, the five couples who'd been killed in the accident.

Indeed he'd expected to see them, grateful that his hopes had not been disappointed. Some were in the pool. Others sat in redwood chairs beside the water. Others grilled steaks on the barbecue.

They were talking, laughing, and this time, even from inside the cruiser, Grady could hear them, not just the splashes but their voices, their mirth, even the spatter of grease that dripped from the steaks onto the smoking coals in the barbecue.

That had puzzled him: why he'd been able to hear the strokes of the swimmer but not the conversations of the ghosts whom he—but not Crane—had seen this morning.

Now, though, he understood. It took a while to make contact with the specters. You had to acquire sensitivity. You had to become—how had Ben put it in his letter?—receptive. Each time you encountered them, they became more real until . . .

Grady reached for the paper bag beside him and got out of the cruiser. He unlocked the chainlink fence and approached the compound, smiling.

"Hi, Brian. Hello there, Betsy."

They didn't acknowledge him.

Well, that'll come, Grady thought. No problem. I just have to get more receptive.

He chose an empty chair by the swimming pool and settled into it, stretching out his legs, relaxing. It was evening. The sun was nearly down behind the mountains. The compound was bathed in soothing alpenglow. The young man he'd first encountered, the potential champion swimmer who'd died in Vietnam, kept doing his laps. A delighted man and woman, gray-haired, in their sixties, kept blurting encouragement to him.

Grady turned again to Brian and Betsy who were over by the barbecue. "Hey, how have you been? It's good to see you."

This time, Brian and Betsy responded, looking in his direction.

Yeah, all it takes is receptivity, Grady thought.

"Hello, Ben. Glad you could make it," Brian said.

"Me, too." Grady reached inside his paper bag and pulled out a bottle of bourbon. Untwisting its cap, he looked around for a glass, didn't find one, shrugged, and raised the bottle to his lips. He tilted his head back, feeling the year-long tension in his neck begin to dissipate. After the heat of the day, the evening was cool and pleasant. He tilted the bottle to his lips again and swallowed with satisfaction.

Receptivity, he thought. Yeah, that's the secret. All I have to do is be sensitive.

But as he drank and smiled and waited, the miracle that he'd come for didn't happen. He kept looking around, struggling to maintain his calm. Helen and John. Where were they? They're supposed to be here.

They *have* to be!

He swallowed more bourbon. "Hey, Brian?"

"What is it, Ben?"

"My wife and son. Where are they?"

"I'm afraid they can't be here yet," Brian said.

"Why not?" Grady asked.

"There's something you have to do first."

"I don't understand."

"Think about it."

"I don't know what you mean. Help me, Brian."

"Think about the shrine."

And then everything was clear. "Thank you, Brian."

Grady set down the bottle, stood, and left the swimming pool, walking toward the shrine. Inside, candles were lit. He passed the church pew in the sanctuary and reverently studied the photographs above the mantle, the pictures that grief-destroyed parents had hung there, the heart-breaking images of the eight dead children.

Is that all it takes? Grady thought. Is that all I need to do?

He removed his wallet from his trousers, opened it, caressed the photographs of Helen and John that he always carried with him, and removed them from their protective, transparent, plastic sleeves. After kissing them, he set them on the mantle.

Now? he wondered, his heart pounding. *Now?*

But Brian and Betsy don't have their photographs up here. The couples who were killed in the accident, *their* photographs aren't here, either.

Maybe, though, Grady wondered. Maybe if you've been here long enough, it isn't necessary to put up photographs.

The children. They never had the chance to come here. They died before Brian built the shrine.

Heart pounding faster, Grady turned and left the shrine, hurrying back to the swimming pool. There he saw Helen and John waiting for him, and his chest hurt unbearably. Helen was holding out her arms. John was jumping up and down with excitement.

Grady ran.

Reached them.

Embraced them.

And felt his arms go through them just as their arms and bodies went through him.

"No!" he wailed. "I need to touch you!"

Then he realized. He had to give them time. In a little while, he'd be able to hold them. He spun to face them.

"I love you, Ben," Helen said.

Tears streamed down Grady's face.

"Dad, I've missed you," John said.

"And I love both of you, and I've missed you so much that—" Grady's voice broke. He sobbed harder. "It's so good to—"

Grady reached for them again, and this time, as his arms went through them, he felt as if he'd reached through a cloud. The sensation was subtle but unmistakably physical. It was happening. They'd soon be—

Grady's knees felt weak.

"Sweetheart, you'd better sit down," Helen said.

Grady nodded. "Yes. The strain's been . . . I think I could use a rest."

As he walked with his wife and son toward the swimming pool, Brian, Betsy, and the others nodded with approval.

"Dad, the kids in the pool are having so much fun. Can I take a swim?"

"Absolutely. Anything you want, son. Your mother and I will watch."

Grady sat in his chair by the pool. Helen sat close beside him, stroking his arm. The sensation was stronger. Soon. Soon he'd be able to hold her.

Betsy called to him, "Ben, would you like a steak?"

"Not right now, thanks. I'm not hungry. Maybe later."

"Any time. All you have to do is ask."

"I appreciate that, Betsy."

"Maybe another drink would improve your appetite."

"I bet it would." Grady raised the bottle to his lips. Helen stroked his arm, and now her touch was almost solid. John dove into the pool.

"Together," Helen said.

"Yes," Grady said. "At last.

It became the most wonderful evening of his life. In a while, Helen's touch was totally firm. Grady was able to hold her, to hug her, to kiss her. And John.

When the sun disappeared, a full moon lit the darkness, illuminating the festive specters.

There was just one problem. Before Grady had driven to the compound from the mausoleum, he'd made several stops in town. One had been to the liquor store. Another had been to the courthouse, to find out who'd owned the land that Brian had purchased to build the compound. Grady had hoped to be able to question whoever had owned the land and to find out if there was anything unusual about this area, anything—even an old campfire story—that might provide a hint, the start of an explanation for this miracle.

But the former owner had long ago moved away.

Several other stops had been to Brian Roth's former hunting companions. Grady had hoped that one of them might be able to describe what had happened to Brian the day they'd taken him hunting in this area. He'd hoped that they might have an explanation for Brian's sudden determination to buy this land.

But none of them even remembered that afternoon.

Grady's final stop had been to his attorney. Ida Roth's lawyer had already been in touch with him. Ida was determined to contest the will and make sure that Grady didn't inherit the property. Grady was shocked to hear his attorney say that Brian Roth had clearly not been in his right mind if he'd amended his will while contemplating suicide. Brian's own attorney apparently agreed. The consensus was that Grady would lose his fight against Ida. The compound would be denied to him.

So as Grady sat beside his wife and son, watching his eerily moonlit companions near the pool, he kept drinking and brooding and telling himself that he couldn't bear to be separated from his family again.

But what was the alternative?

Grady hugged Helen and John. "You might want to take a walk."

"We'll stay," Helen said. "So you won't be afraid."

"You're sure?"

"Yes. I don't want you to feel alone."

Grady kissed her, drank more bourbon, then unholstered his revolver.

He understood now why Brian and Betsy had made this choice. How lonely they must have felt, seeing their dead children and eventually their dead companions. In their presence but not truly with them.

Grady cocked his revolver. The final speck of his sanity told him, your wife and son aren't real, you know. The others aren't, either. This is all your imagination.

Maybe, Grady thought. Maybe not.

But even if it is my imagination, when Ida gets control of the compound, I'll never have the chance to see Helen and John again. Even if I only imagine them.

It was an agonizing dilemma.

It required more thought.

So with his wife and son beside him, Grady held his revolver in one hand while he drank from his bottle with the other. The alcohol made him sleepy. The specters were beginning to fade. He'd soon have to make a choice, and he wondered what it would be. As the stupor from the bourbon overwhelmed him, which would feel heavier? Would the bottle drop from his hand first? Or would the revolver?